Tempest

Tempest

All-New Tales of Valdemar

Edited by
Mercedes Lackey

DAW BOOKS, INC.

DONALD A. WOLLHEIM, FOUNDER

375 Hudson Street, New York, NY 10014

ELIZABETH R. WOLLHEIM
SHEILA E. GILBERT
PUBLISHERS

www.dawbooks.com

Contents

A Small Quarrel
Stephanie D. Shaver   1

Girl Without the Gifts
Janny Wurts   23

Unimagined Consequences
Elizabeth A. Vaughan   41

Feathers in Flight
Jennifer Brozek   56

Blind Leaps
Ron Collins   75

Haver Hearthstone
Fiona Patton   86

Unraveling the Truth
Dayle A. Dermatis   105

Sparrow's Gift
Michele Lang   119

Harmless as Serpents
Rosemary Edghill & Rebecca Fox   136

The Apprentice and the Stable Master
Brenda Cooper   157

Unexpected Meeting
  Nancy Asire   174

A Trip of Goats
  Elisabeth Waters   192

The Ones She Couldn't Save
  Louisa Swann   201

One Last Night Manning the Home Station
  Brigid Collins   218

Only Family Matters
  D. Shull   232

Medley
  Jessica Schlenker & Michael Z. Williamson   246

A Tangle of Truths
  Angela Penrose   268

The Unwanted Gift
  Anthea Sharp   286

Dawn of a New Age
  Dylan Birtolo   302

BloodLines
  Phaedra Weldon   314

In Name Only
  Kristin Schwengel   333

Ripples and Cracks
  Larry Dixon and Mercedes Lackey   354

A Small Quarrel
Stephanie Shaver

The rain had finally let up in western Valdemar.

Highjorune should have been leagues behind Herald Wil, and his prisoner—the traitorous Bard Ferrin—safely delivered to the Heralds and Master Bard (still) waiting at Forst Reach.

Instead, he sipped shamile tea by a dying fire in the Crown of Lineas Inn while flipping through the worn pages of a book with names like Taylore, Emile, Carris, and Fent in it. Master Bards, all suspected of the same treason Ferrin had committed: conspiracy against the throne. Malfeasant use of their Gifts.

Not in that list: "Madra," the name Ferrin had given for the agent of "Lord Dark," a mysterious figure who had encouraged his efforts to start an insurrection in Highjorune. Wil had no idea who either one was, though he highly doubted Lord Dark had been born with that name.

Wil hauled himself out of the comfiest chair in the Crown. Ystell, the new owner, wanted to rename it something more patriotic and less nostalgic. The Queen's Crown or the Hanged Bard, though the latter seemed a bit too grim for Wil.

He pulled on his boots to traverse the muddy grounds to the privy. Bard Amelie, who had assisted in the arrest of Ferrin, had left that morning as soon as the rain stopped, even though some roads were still impassable. She'd gladly gamble if it got her out of Highjorune. He didn't blame her one bit. He'd have gone with her—

But . . .

He couldn't, because he had someone else to consider. Someone who couldn't be out in driving rain and flooding roads, seeing as she'd yet to turn five years old.

Wil rode Circuit under very special circumstances: with his daughter, Ivy. The Companions had even volunteered one of their own to be her nanny.

Being cooped up indoors for a week while they'd waited out the storms had been hardest on her. One could only spin a top or a tale so many times. The need for freedom in littles that age simply ran too deep.

Relieved and ready for bed, Wil tromped back through the empty kitchen, leaving his boots by the door. Tomorrow. Tomorrow they could leave. But tonight they enjoyed a warm bed, and the Companions a stable.

:*Ahem. I am* not *in a stable. I am in the stockade courtyard outside the jail, watching four Guards drink from a wineskin and offering me not so much as a mushy apple.*:

Wil chuckled as he climbed the stairs. :*You'll trade off with Aubryn in a couple of candlemarks, and then you'll get your comfy stall. Just be glad the rain's let up.*:

The Companion sighed.

:*I'll bring you apples next time we meet,*: Wil added.

:*My Chosen makes it all worth it.*:

:*Delivering Ferrin to the Queen will make it all worth it.*: Wil opened the door to the bedroom, being quiet so as not to wake Ivy.

But.

He paused, head cocked, listening.

He did not see the telltale lump on the bed nor hear gentle breathing. Panic sprung up, and he flung the door wide.

The light spilling in from the hallway revealed an empty bed. Ivy was missing.

His first thought: *She went to the privy.* But she couldn't have. He'd just been there.

His second: *She's been abducted.*

A sweep of the room—*mostly*—dissuaded that notion. No signs of struggle, and no one intent on stealing someone's child bothered to take her boots and cape along.

Unless it was someone she trusted . . . He shook off that thought for the moment. A lantern was also missing. Far more likely that . . .

She left on her own?

He took the stairs two at a time, yanking his boots back on and grabbing a lantern before running out the kitchen door.

Vehs sensed his alarm. :*What's wrong?*:

Wil sent a blur of thoughts and images as he swept the inn grounds.

:*Maybe she's with Aubryn?*: his Companion said.

He darted into the stables, to where the second Companion in his entourage dozed in her stall. Her head lifted sleepily as he approached, but she came fully awake when he asked, "Is Ivy here?"

:*No.*:

A stream of curses began to pour out of his mouth. Aubryn emerged and stood shoulder-to-shoulder with him.

:*I'm on my way,*: Vehs said.

Wil felt the burst of a new, different unease. :*No—*:

:*Ferrin's asleep, and the Guards know not to approach him without one of us present. Also, I'm halfway to the Crown already.*:

They checked alleys and yards, Aubryn scouting the road ahead. Wil looked for footprints on the muddy road, but the day's foot traffic had obliterated any chance of a clear trail. He listened, but aside from dripping eaves and the odd barking dog, the village slept.

Their sweep took them near the old Lineas palace. Aubryn cantered ahead into the three-walled courtyard and returned moments later with nothing.

Wil's hands trembled, but a calm, rational part of him kept thinking. She'd vanished, but where? Why? And how far could she have gotten?

:*Nothing on the south side of town,*: Vehs said. :*Where are you?*:

:*The old castle,*: Aubryn said.

"*Ivy!*" Wil bellowed, though it seemed pointless. Like many small children, Ivy simply didn't respond to her name most times.

:*I could try a Mindcall, but it would probably wake up anyone the least bit sensitive in town,*: Aubryn said.

:*What about that song Amelie sings?*: Vehs asked, appearing down the road and racing toward them.

:*Uh. What?*: Wil said.

:*The one Ivy likes to finish, about Maiden's Hope flowers. She can't resist. "Pure white blooms—"*:

Wil gathered a deep breath and warbled:

> *"Pure white blooms, perfume of hope!*
> *I pray that you don't get eaten by—"*

A distant voice piped out, "The goats!"

Wil sprinted toward it, down a small road off the Palace to an old stone building. He saw the little lantern first, then the figure beside it, crouched in the mud.

"Ivy!" he yelled, the Companions thundering behind him. She looked up, startled, then grinned.

"Dada!" she said, holding out a hand. "I got snails!"

Wil stared at her, torn between furious screaming and relieved sobbing.

Ivy kept grinning as she got to her feet, oblivious to her muddy clothes and the chaos she'd caused.

"I got snails," she repeated, stuffing them into a jar.

"Sleep in the loft?" Ivy said as they arrived back at the stable.

"That's what I said," he said. "Get up there. Take off your clothes. I'll go fetch fresh ones."

Vehs had gone back to his guard duty and Aubryn to her stall. Ivy looked dubiously at the loft ladder, then scrambled up it.

Wil leaned his forehead against a wooden post. He felt hollowed out. Parenting was hard.

"Ivy, you can't do what you did tonight," he said, straightening and speaking into the darkness. "It's dangerous."

She peeked over the edge of the loft's wooden platform. "Why?"

"Because dada's a Herald, and there are dangerous people who want to hurt you."

"Why?" Her shirt sailed out of the loft. He caught it midair.

"Because you're my daughter."

"That's dumb."

"I know."

"I'd bite them."

He rubbed his forehead. "I'm sure you would."

"Hard." Her pants dropped from above, and he saw her peek out again and chomp at the air comically.

"Ivy . . ." He sighed, then smiled. "Where did you put the snails?"

She held up the jar.

"Hand it down."

"Dad-d-d-a-a-a—"

"Please."

She acquiesced, pouting.

:*Keep an eye on her,*: he thought to Aubryn, leaving the jar on one of the stable's tack shelves before collecting the soiled garments.

:*That's why I'm here.*:

He dug up fresh clothes from the saddlebags, left the dirty ones by the laundress' door, and had just arrived back at the stable when he felt Vehs's alarm.

:*What's wrong?*:

:*I don't know,*: the Companion said. :*All four of the guards are asleep, and the gaol door is open. I can't fit in there. I'm going to find someone who can.*:

Wil cursed and sprinted to the ladder, throwing the clothes up to his daughter. "Aubryn, watch her," he said. "Vehs needs me."

Ivy leaned out. "Dada? Can I come?"

"*No.*" She cringed at the severity of his tone. Feeling guilty, he climbed the ladder halfway and kissed her cheek. "Stay here. *Do not* leave unless Aubryn says to. Okay?"

"Okay," she whispered.

Then he jumped down and ran out.

The narrow cell had served as a slaughter chute. One small quarrel had forever silenced Ferrin's testimony.

Wil stood in the entry, taking in the scene of blood and

gore. He'd gotten past the point of wanting to flip the nearest table and had slipped into a quiet mix of anger and sickness.

:*This is my fault,*: Vehs said.

Wil walked back out into the courtyard without replying. The four sleeping Guards were all being roused by another, mixed expressions of confusion and shock on their faces. Wil scanned the area. Four stools for them to sit on. A few skins of the wine Vehs had observed. One sword on the flagstones. So one had drawn his weapon before—what?

:*Watch out for me,*: Wil said.

:*Always.*:

Wil leaned against a wall and pressed his hands into the stones.

As a Herald Trainee, Wil and his teachers had thought him a Foreseer; he had Visions, and a gut instinct that bordered on prescient. But a few years ago, his Gift had taken an odd turn—it started showing him the *past* in addition to the future. It worked with objects, places—sometimes people, too.

Now he skimmed the surface of the courtyard's last few candlemarks. And Saw—

—*Vehs and the Guards, Vehs departing through the sally port, and, not long after, a knock at the gate. Two of the Guards went to answer. A brief conversation, and then they unbarred and opened the gate.*

A woman strode through, dressed in a black—no, just a very, very dark green—cloak with a deep hood. She had her hands on the arms of the Guards, who escorted her, meek as lambs. The other two stood in alarm and confusion; one began to draw his sword. She slid forward like a snake, darting between them, and her hands caressed their faces. Both Guards crumpled to the ground.

She stood a moment, slightly bent. Wil could hear her panting slightly. Then she straightened and faced the first two, still standing obediently nearby.

"Where are the keys?" she asked.

One unhooked a ring of keys from his belt and handed it to her. She brushed her hands on their cheeks, and they collapsed.

For a few moments, Wil saw her more clearly. Sweat sheened her face, and she breathed hard. She smiled.

—*I know her,* Wil realized with a shock.—

Her visit inside the gaol only took a few minutes. She emerged again and left. Half a candlemark later, Vehs returned.—

Wil released the moments, reorienting back into the now.

"Are you all right, Herald?"

Wil looked up at the Guard, the one who'd been waking the others, digging to remember her name. Sergeant Bergen. She'd been the first Guard Vehs had found. She had a stern, square face, close-cropped graying hair, and the lean frame of a career military woman.

"We're looking for a woman, about so high." He held his hand up to his shoulder. "Dark green cloak, curly golden hair, pale skin."

The Guard's eyes lit up. "We'll start looking."

"Be careful," he said. "I don't know how . . . but she seems to have some sort of . . ."

He hesitated. He didn't want to say "magic." Magic didn't happen in Valdemar . . . *Or that's what we all said before Hardorn summoned demons and Herald-Captain Kerowyn came along* . . .

Still. This could be a Gift. But the idea that one of the Gifted would carry this out . . . "Some sort of . . . sway," he said at last. "Maybe a drug or toxin. Just . . . be careful."

Bergen looked confused by this, but she saluted and went off to assemble a search detail.

Wil took a lantern and walked back into the gaol. He strode down the hallway and past the other empty cells. Two of Ferrin's accomplices had been here until a couple nights ago—Wil had been able to determine they knew relatively little, and he passed sentence for the Guards to carry out. Probably a good thing, too. He had no doubt that if they'd still been here, they would have received the same treatment as Ferrin.

Back in the dead Bard's cell, Wil held a handkerchief to his mouth. Then he set the lantern in the doorway and stepped into the cell. Doing his best not to touch the blood, he sat on Ferrin's cot.

:*Okay, Vehs. One more time.*:

:*I'm here.*:

He took a lungful of fetid air and flung himself back across the candlemarks. The smell of blood vanished, and in his mind the cell appeared again, the same room with a completely different setting—

—Ferrin tossed and turned on his cot, sleep clearly eluding him.

This didn't go on for long. There came the heavy iron chunk of the hallway's bolt sliding back and the rattle of keys.

Ferrin sat up at the first sound and had stumbled to his feet by the second. He stood frozen in the patch of moonlight streaming in through the cell's lone, high window. Before the door opened, he'd set his face in a practiced half-sneer.—

—Expecting me, *Wil thought.*—

—But a Herald wasn't who stepped inside. The sneer melted briefly into wide-eyed shock, then settled into a fixed smile.

"Hello, Ferrin," she said.

"M-Madra!" The frozen smile stretched wide, and a lilt crept into his voice that Wil recognized as the Bard trying to exercise his Gift on her. "Get me out of here!"

Her smile curved higher as her hand moved within the depths of her cloak. "Oh . . . definitely not."

Something gleaming peeked out from the folds of the cloak. Machinery whirred, and a bolt burst through Ferrin's chest with alarming force for what must have been a small weapon. Viscera and blood splattered. The Bard grunted, surprise and alarm on his face as he stumbled backward.

"Lord Dark sends regards," Madra said, shaking her cloak back into place before walking away. Limited by his current position, Wil could only watch her go.

Ferrin collapsed forward, gurgling.—

Wil bore witness a little longer, then released the moments back to the past.

He sat there in the gloom, turning over this new information. Madra.

She hadn't been Madra when he'd last seen her. But names could change.

That smile . . .

Wil didn't get up immediately. He sipped from his flask and let his nerves settle before hauling himself off the cot and back out to where Vehs waited.

He leaned his forehead against his Companion's neck.

:*You need to rest,*: Vehs said.

:*No.*: Wil pulled himself into the saddle. :*We need to look for Madra.*:

Wil draped against Vehs's neck, utterly spent.

They'd spent two candlemarks searching for Madra, and he'd finally yielded to exhaustion after nearly falling out of the saddle. The Guards would keep hunting—not that he had any confidence they would find her. She was probably half-way to Zoe by now. Or Forst Reach. Or Qorthes. They wouldn't find her. Not like this.

That face. That voice. I know it.

The smell of Ferrin's slaughter and his murderer's identity conjured an old memory. So long ago, before Lelia died and before Ivy lived. On a blood-soaked battlefield near the Hardorn border, though not amongst the dead and wounded. Lelia lying on a cot in an airy tent as a Healer finished looking her over. Wil had paced, powerless to help.

This hadn't been the first time they'd seen what Ancar's Mages could weave. That had been the first war. This, the second, had had its own horrors. Hardorn had withdrawn two days ago, but that didn't mean an end to the work. Not for the army and certainly not for the Healers and Heralds. Even Bards had their jobs, circulating amongst the convalescing and soothing them with their music.

Lelia had been doing just that when she'd collapsed. No one had needed to tell him. He'd just known. Sometimes his Gift could be useful all on its own.

"Exhaustion," the Healer said, not hiding her annoyance. "She shouldn't be doing what she's doing anyway."

Wil frowned. "Why not?"

She tucked a lock of raival-gold hair behind her ear. "Honestly, it's not my place to tell you. *I* shouldn't even be here, dealing with—" She gestured at Lelia. "—*this*. People are dying every second I talk to you."

"Should I grovel, Your Highness, or will you tell me what's wrong?"

Her eyes narrowed, and she opened her mouth to respond, but Lelia beat her to it.

"Don't need . . . a Healer," she said, her eyes sliding half open. "Thank you . . . Androa. Tell Grier thanks . . . too."

The Healer looked down on her. "I take it you know."

"Yes." Lelia's eyes flicked over to Wil. Then she smiled, very slightly, and told him.

Of course, it had been so very like Lelia to announce her pregnancy on a battlefield. But the memory now had another significance, because that surly Healer—the one who'd wanted to rub into his face how *grateful* he should be that she'd deigned to attend to Lelia—looked an awful lot like Madra.

He'd known her as Androa Baireschild, the sister of Healer Grier and *Herald* Kemoc Baireschild.

:*You're sure?*: Vehs asked.

:*No. We'll need more. But maybe we can salvage something out of this mess. Like—how'd she get here so fast? How'd she even know?*:

:*Has she been here the whole time?*:

:*Maybe.*:

:*By the way—we're here.*:

Wil hadn't even noticed his Companion's arrival at the stable. Bad. Sloppy. How could he protect himself—much less Ivy—if he wasn't even aware of his own surroundings?

He dismounted and wearily slipped the girth on Vehs' saddle. He wanted to sleep, but he stank of sweat and carnage, and the last thing he wanted to do was subject his daughter to that. He trudged to his room for fresh clothes, then to the bathhouse to rinse off.

:*I stopped her trying to get out again,*: Aubryn said.

Wil paused in the doorway of the bathhouse, drooping. :*I should remove the ladder.*:

:*That would only encourage her to jump down. Escape is what children do.*:

Wil sighed and stepped into the bathhouse, running the pump to fill a bucket with cold well water. The Companion had a point.

:*You should give her more to do,*: she said.

Wil stripped naked and scooped cold water on his head and shoulders. It did little to wake him.

:*She's a little girl with an active imagination and energy to spare,*: Aubryn continued. :*She's going to cause trouble from time to time. Children want to explore. And you do no favors protecting her from that, or by trying to shelter her from every nameable harm.*:

:*What do you suggest? Advanced grappling techniques?*:

:*Simple escapes and some basic self-defense wouldn't be a bad start.*:

:*That's crazy. She's four!*:

:*She's also riding Circuit with her father. You're deluding yourself if you think you and I and Vehs can protect her from everything. I know all about you, Herald. You're scared of losing her. As you lost Lelia and your sister—*:

:*Okay, we're done,*: he said. :*Bad enough I have one Companion lodged in my skull—*:

:*Hey!*: Vehs protested.

:*No offense. But I need my own thoughts for a little while.*:

He could all but hear Aubryn's snort coming from the stables, but her thoughts receded.

Back at the loft, Wil flopped over the lip of the platform and onto his back, staring into the darkness as he wiggled off his boots.

Ivy crawled over and wrapped her arms around him. "Dada," she said solemnly.

"Ivy. You need to go to sleep."

"My snails. They're cold, Dada."

"Your snails are fine."

"No-o-o. I need to put a blanket on them."

Wil kissed her forehead. "Your snails are sleeping. So should you."

"Not tired," she said, but Wil rubbed her back, and her

breathing grew deep and even. Only then did he let out a long, exasperated sigh that perfectly summed up his day. Night. He didn't even know what time it was anymore.

Wil forced himself to relax, to release the tight muscles in his shoulders. His thoughts blurred, sliding into the borderland between consciousness and sleep, where the absurd seemed perfectly rational.

He wandered through mist and shadow, stars appearing and disappearing overhead. At one point, Lelia appeared and put her arm around his waist. Their stroll seemed no different from any other they'd taken together in Companion's Field.

A woman in midnight blue crossed their path, her black hair in small braids. Amber beads dangled from the ends, clicking softly. Her blue eyes regarded him with a mix of caution and curiosity. Lelia slid away, and the two women wandered off together, speaking so low he couldn't make out the words.

In the curious way of the borderlands, Wil then found himself back in Ferrin's cell, lit clear as day. Ferrin was there, but also someone else—lurking at the edges of his vision, never quite fully manifesting. Wil saw a white-toothed grin and remembered another murderer with a crossbow from years ago.

Ferrin sat on his cot, the bolt still sticking out from his chest.

He touched the protrusion, then looked at Wil and said, "Such a small—"

"Quarrel!" Wil gasped, sitting up, heart racing. Ivy stirred beside him but didn't wake. A brief Mindtouch on Vehs revealed the Companion also slept.

He launched himself down the ladder. Aubryn turned to watch him.

"Do you ever sleep?" he asked as he pulled on his boots. She snorted.

"I need to do something," he said. "Won't take a candlemark. Let Vehs sleep. He needs it."

:*And you don't?*:

Wil shook his head. "Can't now."

He jogged out of the stable, heading back to the stockade.

*   *   *

Wil walked out of the gaol and sat down against a wall, contemplating his gruesome prize.

Sergeant Bergen approached, a bucket and a handful of rags swinging from her fist; she dropped them at his feet. "Find what you need, Herald?"

Wil held up the quarrel, turning it between his blood-streaked thumb and forefinger. It both fascinated and terrified him. Hollow, light, but extremely hard, with a flanged tip. It hadn't distorted at all, despite splintering Ferrin's sternum.

The device she used fit inside her cloak. So small. So destructive. Very worrying.

"You ever seen anything like this, Sergeant?" he asked.

Bergen squinted at the bolt. "Not in my Queen's army. Tedrel, maybe?"

"Let's find out." Wil closed his hand over the bolt, shifted into a cross-legged position, and stepped through time's door.

Fragments of vision jerked him roughly between past and present. He saw himself holding the quarrel, Madra's hands lifting it from a leather pouch—and he sensed *something* more, some weight of memory attached to the bolt. He pushed for it, strained, tried to claw past Madra's hands—but—

No good. He came back to now and dropped the quarrel into the water, rubbing until the blood came off. He raised it into the light just flooding over the horizon. There—a series of characters stamped into the shaft. A craftsman's seal.

"Not Tedrel," he said, washing his own hands off, the cool water steadying and grounding him. "These look like Shin'a'in symbols." He slipped the quarrel into a pouch and hung it around his neck.

"You look a bit pale," Bergen said.

"It's the Whites."

She raised a brow. "You ain't wearing Whites."

He looked down at his blood-spattered beige garments. "Hunh."

He slid up the wall to stand, using it for support until he got to his feet. Taking a couple of deep breaths, he started forward.

To his surprise, Bergen took his elbow. "Come on."

Together, they walked slowly back through the streets. At

some point he cleared his throat and said, "I don't really need an escort."

"We lost Ferrin on my watch," she said. "I won't lose you, too."

"It wasn't your fault, Sergeant. Ferrin should have been on his way to Forst Reach days ago. Bad weather and bad luck are the only things that kept that from happening."

"I wasn't trained to assume things would always go according to plan."

"Really, it was my fault for letting Vehs leave."

"You're assuming this miscreant didn't have plans for him, too."

Wil felt a shiver go down his spine. "Companions are hard to kill."

"There you go assuming." She glanced at him. "You have a daughter."

"That I do."

"You love her?"

"More than you could ever know."

"Well, there ain't enough of that in the world. So if it's all right with you, I'm your escort this morning, Herald."

Wil nodded. "Thank you."

"Though, being a Herald, I know it's only a matter of time before you decide to throw yourself on a bonfire to save a twig."

He smirked. "I like to think I'd throw a bucket of water on it first."

"Well, maybe that's because you have your child riding Circuit at your side."

They rounded the curve in the road that revealed the Crown. Bergen shuffled to a stop and let go of his arm.

"Take care, Herald," she said.

"You too, Sergeant."

"You don't report to me. Call me Bergen."

"Well then, I'm Wil."

She afforded a smile. "Wil."

Wil limped the last few steps alone. When he got within stone's throw of the stable, he heard, :*I thought Bards were more your style.*:

Wil started a bit. :*Aren't you sleeping?*:

:*I was,*: Vehs said. :*Then someone decided to take a rough ride through history.*:

:*Hunh. And you didn't come get me?*:

A mental yawn. :*Walking builds character.*:

:*I once again require a change of clothes.*:

:*And get some sleep.*:

:*Maybe . . .*:

:*We can watch the wee one. Sleep.*:

Wil passed through the kitchen, waving to Ystell, who waved back over a half-finished pie. He swiped some cheese and bread before heading back to his room, devouring it as he undressed.

:*We'll be leaving soon,*: he told Vehs.

:*You know where we're headed next?*:

:*No.*: He touched the last thing on him, the pouch holding the quarrel. He had no intention of taking it off. :*But I'll make this tell us.*:

Rest and buckets of willowbark tea worked wonders.

Wil spread out a map of Valdemar on the table. He sat and drummed his fingers as his eyes ran over it, one corner weighed down by the pouch with the quarrel inside. His eyes flicked to it, then back to the map. Shin'a'in. He couldn't read it, but he remembered the distinctive alphabet from his language classes, so different from the scripts of Valdemar and its neighboring countries.

He swept his fingers along the southwestern border of Valdemar. If he took the quarrel on face value, that it had come from the Dhorisha Plains or that direction, then one of the southern routes would have to be its mode of entry into the kingdom.

The Baireschild estates are in the south . . .

Kemoc had been in line for the throne once. Then Elspeth had been Chosen. How much had that upset the Baireschild family?

Wouldn't be the first time someone close to a potential heir has committed treason to get what they wanted.

Wil focused again on the quarrel. :*So. How'd this get into Valdemar?*:

:*A gryphon flew it in?*: Vehs said.

:*If we want to start conjuring imaginary gryphon couriers, might as well ask if there's a tunnel under the country or magic doors between Katashin'a'in and the Forest of Sorrows.*: He scratched his cheek. :*Though it might help explain how Madra found the time to get to Highjorune and arrange an assassination . . .*:

:*Assuming she wasn't already here.*:

:*There is that.*:

He drew out the quarrel and curled his fingers around it. Such a small, lightly regarded item would be hard to read, and every day that passed, it got a little harder.

Wish I had access to the palace workroom, he thought wistfully.

:*Oh. Hm.*:

:*Hm?*:

:*Well. I mean. It's a long shot, but . . . something similar might be back at Lineas Castle.*:

Wil pushed away from the table. :*Let's go.*:

:*Chosen, maybe you should rest up a little more?*:

:*We are failing Valdemar.*: Wil's lips flattened. :*I don't intend to let Madra get away.*:

Vehs sighed. :*I'll meet you at the door.*:

Centuries ago, something had happened at Lineas Castle to nearly destroy it. A quake, a Mage battle, a bit of both. And for reasons likely tied to local pride and nostalgia, and despite Herald Tashir annexing the country to Randal, someone had decided to partially restore the palace. Parts remained crumbled—it added to the romanticism—but enough had been restored that ghost walks were a regular occurrence, taking curious visitors to see where Herald-Mage Vanyel had fought and won one of his greatest battles. Look closely, the guides might say, you can still see the bloodstains and the ghosts of his enemies.

Wil didn't need a guide's embellishments to feel the palace's history closing around him as he wandered the creaky hallways. Dust covered everything. Light came in through the windows, but he'd brought a lantern in case he wound up down below in the cellars.

He trekked through the remains of the Great Hall for the third time and stopped to take a drink of water.

:*I have no idea what I'm looking for.*:

:*Just stay on the ground floor. You'll find it.*:

:*No, I won't. This is futile.*:

:*Focus, Chosen.*:

:*On what?*: Impatience aggravated his irritation as he walked down a corridor off the Great Hall. :*There's nothing*—:

A closet door caught his eye, an innocuous entry into what should have been an old linen or storage closet. A thicker-than-normal layer of dust covered the handle.

Why bother to restore that? he thought, turning the handle, perhaps the first person to do so in centuries.

His lantern light revealed a tiny round room inside, pale floors, ceilings, and walls, all of a completely different construction from the rest of the castle. The moment he stepped inside, he felt the same peculiar muffling as in the mysterious "workroom" in the Palace. He actually gasped a little.

:*You were saying?*:

:*I owe you* so *many apples.*:

:*Get me the extra-mushy ones.*:

A basalt column rose up in the center of the room. Wil eased himself onto a seat, and touched it lightly. Warm. Just like the one in the Palace.

He kept one hand on the column and wrapped his other around the quarrel, and reached—

—*Past a vision of himself, twirling the quarrel in the sunlight*—

Past Madra, loading the quarrel into what looked like a thin metal tube, the device clicking *as the bolt settled in*—

To a room. A tent, actually. Huge. An iron stove crouched in the center, glowing with heat. A large pipe connected to it, exhausting out through a hole in the canvas. A tall man with black braids and a leather apron used tongs to pull a

*steaming bit of metal out of water and toss it onto a pile of
its siblings. He barked something at a scrawny girl, who began to work a bellows, melting metal for slag.*

*And in one corner stood Madra, her hood down for once,
the glowing forge-light revealing her proud face and the
smiling curve of her lips.*

*Time lurched forward again, to an in-between moment. To
a cave, and Ferrin and Madra, and another unloading crates
from a wagon.*

Madra, speaking, "Lord Dark will be pleased."

And—

*And then all of that dissolved, and for a moment he saw
something—like the heart of a small sun, pulsing beneath his
feet. The floor and walls had vanished, and he didn't understand what this had to do with the quarrel, but it called to
him, invited him to reach down into it—*

:NO!:

Vehs yanked him back from whatever he'd been about to
do, grounded him flat-footed back in the room. Waves of dizziness washed over him.

:*I*—: he thought, and blacked out.

He woke to someone gently pushing him, and Ivy's voice.
"Dada, wake up."

He sat up, blinking against a massive reaction headache
thundering through his brain and narrowing his vision down
to a small tunnel. The lantern provided thin illumination. Ivy
looked on worriedly.

And then: *Ivy?*

:*Aubryn sent her,*: Vehs said, in the gentlest mind-voice
possible. Even so, it lanced through his mind like a stiletto.
:*Come, Chosen. We're waiting.*:

Ivy handed him a flask. A sniff identified the contents as a
weak willowbark tea mixed with plenty of honey. He'd ask
where she got it later. He drank it all quickly, then gathered the
lantern and took his daughter's hand. She half-led him out,
back through the main entrance. The fresh air helped, but the
stabbing light of the sun stirred up nausea and more pain. Vehs
already knelt to help him on, much as Aubryn did for Ivy.

The moment they arrived at the Crown's stables, Wil slid off Vehs and stumbled over to an empty bucket to throw up tea and undigested bread and cheese. His head thundered louder, but he gripped on to the sides of the bucket and lurched to his feet, determined to stay in the here and now.

:*Go rest.*:

:*No,*: Wil said, thinking back to the visions in the castle. To the moment in the cave with Madra, Ferrin, and . . . one other.

He could feel Vehs's alarm. Wil turned to meet his Companion's eyes.

"Help me," he said.

The Companion didn't hesitate. He knelt, and Wil took a few unsteady steps toward him, then paused and addressed Aubryn.

"Don't let any of the Guards near her," he said. "Understand?"

His daughter watched all this with puzzlement on her face, then ran over to him and handed him a jar.

"My snails will protect you," she said, perfectly serious.

How did she get these down? he thought, confused.

:*Children,*: said Aubryn, :*find a way.*:

He took them and kissed Ivy's cheek.

"I'm sure they will," he said.

Sergeant Bergen walked into the jailer's office and took a seat at her desk. Whistling to herself, she opened a ledger containing the schedule for the watch and began planning the next week.

"Have to admire your commitment to the role," a voice said.

She looked up, startled. She hadn't noticed the Herald leaning against one wall in a shadowy corner of the office. She couldn't see his face, but she could sense his mood. Not good.

"Excuse me?" she said. "What do you mean, Wil?"

"I don't know, Carris. What *do* I mean?"

She feigned confusion, casually moving one hand under the desk. "Who's Carris?"

"Oh, just a Bard removed by her Circle for abuse of her Gift. Not to mention a knack for false-face and imperson-ation. She won a disproportionate number of very large bets while impersonating a Guard."

Only from people who otherwise wouldn't miss the money, she thought, heart hammering in her chest. Outwardly, she maintained her perplexed aura, cocking her head. "And . . . you think *I'm* this person?"

As she said it, she reached into the leather holster strapped under the desk, and closed her hand around—

Not what she expected. Something slimy that crunched as she closed her fist on it. She pulled out a hand dripping with goo and snail shells.

"I have good reason to believe so, yes," the Herald said, holding up one of Madra's small, silver crossbows. "I re-moved *this* before you came in. Replaced it with a present from my daughter."

"That's . . . disgusting."

"So's impersonating a Guard. What happened to the orig-inal Bergen?"

She shook the handful of dead snails off onto the floor and wiped the rest on the table, sighing. "Ask Madra. She does the dirty deeds. I just forged the transfer paperwork." She spread her hands. "Now what?"

"Now?" He folded his arms. "I think it's fair to say if you had wanted to kill me, you would have done it last night. Or any of a number of times I was vulnerable in front of you."

She shrugged. "Wasn't keen on making Ivy an orphan."

"You also had every opportunity to kill Ferrin."

"I didn't hate him enough to want his blood on my hands."

"Fair enough. So how long have you 'been' Bergen?"

"As long as Ferrin needed watching."

"That long, eh?"

She laughed a little. "Ferrin did his job. If you hadn't come along, I daresay he would have succeeded. He had a talent for inspiration that made up for the recklessness."

"As you have a talent for infiltration."

"And caution. I know when I'm on the losing side." Carris put her chin in her hand. "She's just going to kill me, too."

"You mean Androa Baireschild, right?"

Carris's brows lifted. "Havens, Herald, you've figured out quite a bit, haven't you?"

"It's funny. People think that murdering a problem makes it go away. But all it does in Valdemar is get a Herald involved. And they always underestimate us."

Carris laughed, a little bitterly. "Really? Because you did so well with Ferrin."

"Yes, but this is different." He pointed to her. "I'm not giving her an opportunity this time. We're leaving. Now."

Carris sat on the bed box in the Waystation and held up her chained hands. "Is this really necessary?"

"Yes." Wil moved aside as Aubryn stepped into the Waystation to stand beside Carris.

"Lady Bright," the Bard said with a moan. "I'm not going to sleep tonight."

"I pity you." He patted Aubryn's withers. "Thank you."

She snorted.

The ground outside the Waystation felt springy under his feet, a gift of the recent rainfall. The sunlight glowed rich amber, the color that came just before dusk, when things felt a bit magical. His Companion stood in the shade of a tall oak, nibbling at a pile of mushy apples. Ivy waited for her father with a staff—newly liberated from the stockade—that reached the height of her shoulder.

Wil had somehow found his second—or possibly third—wind. Catching Carris had helped. Buckling himself into his saddle and nodding off as they rode away from Highjorune had also helped.

He studied Ivy, retrieving his own staff from where it leaned against the wooden siding of the Waystation.

:*Vehs, is this right?*: he thought. :*Teaching her this?*:

:*To quote Aubryn: Children want to do things,*: Vehs said. :*Teach her to protect herself, you'll have less to worry about.*:

"All right," Wil said. "First lesson. Hold it like this."

He held the staff horizontal and straight out, hands evenly placed.

She mimicked it perfectly, watching with focused intent.

They kept going until the light faded, and they collected snails after dinner. They slept on bedrolls spread out on the floor.

He dreamed Lelia watched over them from the Waystation hearth, singing of flowers and goats as they slept.

Girl Without The Gifts
Janny Wurts

Folk in the forest village of Ropewynd claim that nothing beyond the spun yarn and stout rope sold to traders and fishermen ever mattered to the outside world, far less involved the greater affairs of the Queen's Heralds in Valdemar. Yet their eldest granddams say different. Perhaps their tale holds the truth.

On the morn they recall, the quiet seemed ordinary. Kaysa sat in the flood of spring sunlight, her sightless gaze flickered in shadow by the whirring spokes of a spinning wheel. Her foot pumped the treadle, while newly made three-ply yarn hissed through her fingers. The rattle from the lazy kate by her ankle told her the bobbins were almost empty. Fourteen years of age and pleased with herself, she expected to finish before the weaver's loft became stifling. Spinning made cozy work in the cold. But the limestone cavern, where her father and brothers wound rope, was her favorite place in the summer.

Better, her mother's scuffed tread climbed the stairs. Help would speed the task of tidying up.

"Kaysa!" Mam's cry of dismay shattered her contentment. "By the Lady Trine, girl! That's not the cream thread! Why didn't you wait? Sella or I should have lent oversight before you got started!"

Kaysa bit her lip, shamed. She had not managed alone but had collared her younger brother in the predawn gloom. Sorting in haste by her candle, he must have mistaken the color.

Mam would be worse than annoyed if she knew. Open flame was a risk in the weaving loft. Kaysa braked the wheel, resigned. Her desire for an early start was to blame.

"Oh, my dear!" Mam's patience, as ever, forgave her mistakes. "Things will come right, child. I'll dye a new lot of plum thread for tomorrow, and we'll thread the loom for Mistress Sarine's cloth later. The Katashin'a'in surely will fancy that shade of bright yellow with burgundy. Your skein can be sold to the traveling traders without waste."

But the comforting words scarcely masked the frustration. Kaysa's acute hearing caught her mam's quiet sigh. A daughter born blind, no matter how determined or resourceful, would always burden the family. The loft's stores were low. Drought had dried the retting ponds early, before what might become a poor harvest. Flax fiber was scarce, so mistakes were all the worse, possibly leading to a shortfall.

Kaysa did her best to make amends, rethreading the loom for the change. But morning was spent by the time she had swept the cut threads from the floor. "Is there anything else?"

"The men's lunch," said her mother. "You'll take the basket along to the cavern?"

"Of course." Kaysa snatched up her stick. Three clicks through her teeth with no echo told her the slat door was propped open. She tapped her way through, rushed down the loft stairs, and turned for the pantry. Her mother's silent disappointment followed her through the baked heat of the dirt street.

Her remote village within Pelagiris Forest was small. Kaysa knew every familiar smell and sound, likely all she might ever know in the proscribed course of her life. The path to the caverns marked the limit of her independence. She crossed two alleys, turned left past the chattering laundresses. Splashing through the puddled suds, she passed the cobbler's, to the tap of Enid's hammer studding a boot sole with tacks. The faint absence of echoes told her no wagons were parked in the lane. She crossed, chasing the smell of cooling bread from the bakery, aware of the cooler air where the packed earth became rutted grass, and the glassblower's shop gave way to the cottager's crofts, and the sty for Cobi Merrin's pigs.

A path turned into the forest beyond, cool shade lively with birdsong. There, Kaysa's oldest brother, Nayce, had staked out a string line to guide her. He had ever been the staunch advocate behind her yearning for freedom. The string calmed her parents' concern, though she had known every step of the way since childhood. Kaysa passed the massive oak where the trail turned, ahead of the slope toward the creek. Upstream lay the entrance to the moist cave, where the ropewalk wound the twine and the rigging rope sold to the fishermen at Lake Evendim.

A cloud snuffed the sun's warmth. A roaring gust rattled the boughs overhead and buffeted Kaysa sideways. Torn leaves and sticks pelted down. The wet scent of storm charged the air, scant warning before the sky opened. Hard wind and sheeting rain battered Kaysa. She dropped to her knees in a vain effort to shelter the lunch basket from the ferocious onslaught.

Tree limbs cracked and fell. The *whoosh* as uprooted trunks toppled and slammed into the ground struck so near made Kaysa tremble in terror. Huddled, soaked to the skin, she clung to her stick. The sharp clicks she used to avoid objects were useless in the downpour. Helpless, she could do naught but wait while the deluge rampaged around her.

The squall whipped through and died with unnatural speed. Kaysa uncurled, shaken, and swiped sodden hair off her face. The lunch for the men was ruined.

"They'll be hungry and plenty annoyed," she grumbled, uneasy at the thin sound of her voice in the wake of the weather's ferocity. Spoiled food was the least of her woes amid the slick footing of the puddled path. She turned in a circle, unable to locate the twine guide for security. Instead, her tracking stick swished through a wrack of drenched foliage. A downed tree branch crossed her way forward, the litter of splintered wood too dense to shove through.

"Blast!" she exclaimed, annoyed by the prospect of rescue.

After the disastrous mishap with the yarn, the loss of self-reliance made Kaysa grind her teeth in frustration. Sighted folk took for granted their ability to surmount their unforeseen predicaments.

Her granddam's advice, given when three-year old Kaysa had hurt herself while playing, came back to her now: *"If you don't risk the knocks in life for yourself, the choices of others will limit your days. Safety will tame every dream that you have, until you destroy your free spirit."*

Either wait to be saved, or go ahead and handle the setback herself. The sun's steamy warmth made waiting unbearable. Kaysa claimed independence, left the wet food, and struck out for the cavern. Lacking the guide string, she relied on her stick, flicking the greenery on either side and mapping her course across the pooled ruts carved across the trail.

Careful progress brought her to the slope toward the brook, where slicked moss and downed sticks challenged her footing. She inched forward, her balance betrayed when a loosened rock overturned. Kaysa skidded and fell. Her long, downhill slide crashed into a wrack of debris. More fallen trees, trunks twisted to splinters, blocked her straight course to the creek. Kaysa stood, banged up and shaken. Off the path, she was in trouble over her head. The slope oriented her sense of direction. She could hear the swollen roar of the creek. Descent should be possible, if she took care, with the way to the caverns directly upstream. The uphill course offered greater uncertainty, the washed out path too easy to miss.

Jaw set, determined, Kaysa gripped her stick. She followed the downed trunk by touch and discovered the deadfall had torn down additional trees as it toppled. The root balls had rolled on the steep terrain, carving up clinging mud and wedged into a jam. The impasse blocked Kaysa's progress, deflecting her downstream into the ravine. Far removed from the path, scraped and muddy and hot, she perched on an overturned boulder.

"I am not lost!" Scared, but not panicked, she knew by the steady splash of swirled water the stream was close. Cooler air meant the sun had dropped behind the crest. The dense tangle of branches was thinning. She mustered her courage. Left no better choice, she continued downward, step by cautious step.

Despite every care, she slipped again. She tumbled downhill into more gnarled limbs, then lay skinned and gashed and knocked breathless. A day gone bad, with the afternoon passing. The basket abandoned in the path would cause worry, enough to send searchers to find her. That embarrassment had not happened since she was ten and had lost her way home from the market.

"In trouble, neck deep." Kaysa flushed to imagine Da's scolding for her latest stupid misjudgment. Alone in the stillness, nursing a bruised shin, she heard the groan of another large creature in pain. An animal caught in the branches thrashed once and subsided to labored breathing.

Kaysa forgot her predicament. The foliage to her right shuddered again, as the trapped creature struggled in balked effort to free itself, then stilled again with a snort.

"Someone's horse?" Kaysa disentangled herself, grasped her stick and stood erect with a chill of foreboding. "You're a very long way from the road!" Too far for a traveler's mount to have bolted and come to grief in a natural storm. The worst of the damage, in fact, seemed to center upon the downed animal.

The rider seemed nowhere in evidence, no good sign. She could not search by herself. But if she could free the horse and bring help, some good would come of her own disaster.

Kaysa proceeded cautiously from branch to twig, guided by sound until her questing hand encountered a lathered coat. The horse jerked at her touch, startled, if not too badly injured.

"Easy, fellow." But all was not well. The animal was down. The distressed rasp of its breath and the tang of fresh blood overwhelmed her awareness.

"Let's sort you out." Kaysa stroked the animal's heaving flank. The beast lay on its side, still bridled and saddled. The leather felt gouged, either by violence or from scraping through obstacles in riderless panic. Kaysa knelt over the prostrate animal. She eased the girth buckle, then gently explored up the neck through the tangled mane. Sticks were tangled through the hair, clotted from bleeding scrapes. The reins were stripped to loose threads, snagged in the fallen branches and pinned when the tree toppled over.

"You're lucky, fella," Kaysa soothed, concerned to find no sign of the fallen rider.

The horse lifted its neck when she untangled the straps. "Whoa, fella!"

Kaysa had no more chance to check for broken bones. The distraught animal gathered its legs and arose. It shook, to a jangle of stirrups, then stood, uneasily trembling.

Perhaps dazed, it stayed still while Kaysa recovered her stick and shoved to her feet. A whuff of hot breath told her where to reach for the trailing reins. "Let's see if you're fit."

The animal steadied under her gentle hands. Other than mud and more sticky contusions, she found nothing worse than one inflamed pastern. Lame, but not crippled, the horse laid its battered head on her shoulder.

"Can you walk?" Kaysa tugged the reins, tried a tentative step. The horse seemed able enough to go forward. "Help me get back to the village, and I'll take you to our Healer."

She turned the game creature uphill, one hand gripped to the bossed breast strap in hope that its sighted guidance might steer her from further mishap.

Dewfall and the thick, forest silence meant dusk was falling. The loss of the sunlight left Kaysa no means to determine direction when the ground leveled out. Since the horse shouldered onward without hesitation, she chose to trust its purposeful guidance. Then she caught the wafted scent of torch smoke, followed by mixed voices, arguing. Kaysa halted the horse the moment before the anxious party encountered her.

"I wasn't lost!" she called over their noise.

"Lost?" The village laundress' gruff exclamation filtered through the trees, sharpened by worried relief. While the clamor quieted, over crackling brush as massed footsteps headed in Kaysa's direction, she ranted, "Where were you? Sulking? Your mama was sick with anxiety when you failed to return. The men are not home from the ropewalk yet. Did you ever deliver their meal?"

"The storm—" Kaysa began, then faltered as she realized the forest around her was dry. The freak squall had not afflicted the village. No one here realized the workers' route home would have had to bypass the downed trees. If they had encountered her abandoned basket, quite likely they had stayed in the forest to find her.

"What storm?" snapped the laundress, stomping to an exasperated stop. "Fool girl! Hasn't rained a drop all day long! Kaysa, where were you? Save us, you're covered in mud! And dear, what a mess you've made of your clothing!"

Someone behind must have carried a torch. Kaysa sensed the scolding's momentum take pause, as the people crowding the laundress' heels caught first sight of the creature behind her.

"An unnatural squall raged through the forest," she explained firmly. "Broken trees blocked the path. Some terrible misfortune overcame a lone traveler, who lost this poor horse." The injured animal's need lent Kaysa a confidence beyond her years. "Has anyone heard of a stranded stranger?"

"Horse?" The laundress' exclamation seemed shaken. "Child, that's no common traveler's nag! That's a Herald's Companion!"

Kaysa swallowed, aghast. Disability had tripped her, again. Denied sight, she could not determine the Companion's color or recognize the embellished tack without its distinctive bells. "A search will need to be raised for the Chosen, who may be unconscious or hurt." She lifted her stick to clear the way forward. "Will you please let us through to visit the Healer?"

The onlookers moved away with a rustle, and flame light must have revealed the Companion's smeared coat. Clay mud and bloody scrapes changed their stark surprise to concerned exclamations.

The Companion's arrival upended routine. While Kaysa delivered her charge to the Healer, the council gathered in earnest discussion. The rope workers were informed and sent looking for the Herald where the freak storm had broken the trees.

"There's vicious magic abroad," insisted the boy who hauled the water for Rowsen's infusions.

His teen brother, arrived with a handcart of wood for the

fire to heat the kettle, said more. "Sorcery, no doubt, or some other evil come from Rethwellan."

"Nonsense, don't exaggerate," Rowsen scoffed, and to Kaysa, "Sit down! We'll put the Companion in the shed, where I'll hang a lantern for adequate light."

"I'll take him," Kaysa insisted. Ordinary weather had not ripped through the wood. Mere mishap did not waylay a Queen's Herald.

The Companion shivered, crowding her as though reluctant to part with her company. "I can help with the saddle. I'll rub him down and steady his head while you tend him."

"Very well! You've earned your place, I'll warrant, since without you, the Companion would have been lost." Rowsen strode ahead, brusque. "Your bruises can be treated afterward."

Kaysa followed the healer's scuffed steps, aware by changed sound as he entered the shed. She helped strip the marred tack while the lad forked down fresh straw bedding. "Bilt?" Rowsen called. "Fetch hay and a pail from the dairy barn. When you get back, I'll know which herbs and salves I need from the stillroom."

Kaysa braided a straw wisp to groom the Companion's caked coat. "I don't think the Herald met with an accident."

"Don't tempt ill fortune," Rowsen exclaimed, muffled as he bent to examine the Companion's stocked foreleg. "But, perhaps. The saddle is bloodstained. Chance did not strip the bells off that bridle."

More, the Companion still periodically shivered. Whether from fear or the shock of his injury, Kaysa lacked wisdom to tell.

Soon Bilt scurried in with the pail and the hay, voice raised by excitement. "People are saying Kaysa's to be a Herald! Think maybe the Companion has chosen her?"

Kaysa caught her breath. No. Surely not. No special quality was required to save a helpless animal snagged by a deadfall. The magnificent creature had not been at liberty to select which person stumbled into him to grant help.

"Companions Mindspeak with their Chosen," Rowsen corrected, still bent to his work. "If Kaysa had been recognized, she would never have mistaken him for a traveler's hack."

"You knew where you were going, though," Kaysa whispered against the Companion's taut neck. She had no extraordinary ability, no sense of a bond between kindred spirits. The creature's dispirited manner suggested only the distress of bereavement. If the Herald survived, surely the Companion would have returned for his Chosen the moment he was released.

Rowsen interrupted her thought. "The Companion must be returned to the capital. Heralds are the Queen's business, and the wise at Haven must sort out his plight."

"I should go," Kaysa blurted. Her balked desire to have a purpose and experience the world beyond the village clamored against her sound sense.

"Perhaps." Rowsen dismissed her longing and stood up, drying his hands. "That decision's unlikely to happen tonight. I've your hurts to mend when I'm finished here, and the Companion is unfit to travel before his sore leg recovers."

The searchers who combed the forest found no trace of the Herald in the storm's wreckage. Evil was abroad, everyone agreed. The storm that had struck had been nothing natural. Kaysa sweated over her chores. She spun yarn and helped thread the loom in the loft. Every spare moment, she slipped away to be with the Companion. She lingered in the darkened shed through the evenings, while the council debated who should be sent to the Queen.

"No. Kaysa, you can't!" Her da banged down the worn pulley he was mending, exasperated by her passion to go along. "The open road is no place for a blind girl! Summer's labor is critical, anyway. The village can't spare another able body to lead you through every step of a difficult journey."

Pleading changed nothing. Her appeal to Mam only earned her more scolding. Kaysa escaped, near to tears. She twisted fresh straw into a wisp, and in darkness where no one would see her misery, stroked the Companion's satin coat. His attention seemed distant, his stilled pose aloof. Then he scrubbed his healing scabs against her shoulder.

"You're getting better." His sore leg no longer needed a bandage. His limp was improved. Though he shuddered often

with residual trauma, Kaysa recognized his restlessness to be
away.

"You know where you're going," she sympathized. "You
don't like waiting for a delegation." Only one person needed
to visit the Queen to report where the Companion was found.
Kaysa alone could describe the fell weather that had overtaken his Herald.

She was the sole witness. Anyone who spoke in her place
must repeat her account secondhand. Who else could answer
questions directly, with no vital memory of the details? "I
should go," Kaysa grumbled, "no matter the difficulty."

Clearly, the duty to the realm was hers, if her burdensome
blindness had not clouded perception.

*If you don't risk the knocks in life for yourself, the
choices of others will limit your days. Safety will tame every
dream that you have, until you destroy your free spirit.*

"Granddam was right." Alone in the dark with the Companion's whuffed breath on her neck, Kaysa understood she
must seize her moment. Or else grow to adulthood confined,
forever beholden to others.

Kaysa packed in the night, then carried her sacks of clothes
and provisions on soundless feet to the shed. She needed no
torch. She tacked the Companion by touch and tied her goods
to the leathers. The village still slept when she set foot in the
stirrup and climbed into the Herald's scarred saddle.

"You know where to go," she told the Companion, then
knotted the slackened reins on his neck, and left his head free
to fare onward. A soft snort, the sharp surge of a forward
stride, and her journey to Haven began. Not down the rutted
lane through the village, but by way of the forest, where pur-
suit was least likely to follow.

Perhaps to evade some unseen threat, Kaysa thought with
a hollow chill. She was on her own, committed to the Companion's charge. Gone beyond sight of friendly oversight,
under the shadow of an unknown danger.

During two days' ride through the wood, the pair encountered no one. Kaysa ate in the saddle and slept in catnaps,

tense with the thrill of being out on her own and convinced the Companion's direction held purpose.

When her food stores ran low, their track wended through a village, remote and small as her own. The folk flocked to her when they sighted the Companion. Kindly strangers replenished her foodstuffs. Kaysa was offered a bed for the night and stabling for her mount.

She declined politely. "We are bound for Haven as fast as travel can take us."

Nobody commented on her blindness. No one seemed concerned that she was not a Herald or questioned her right to fare abroad on her own. She stated her thanks for the grain and provender and left the settlement behind.

The Companion bore her through the forest again, pressing the pace with scant rest. Aware his mission was urgent, Kaysa trusted his guidance. She slept in the open, washed in the streams, and sheltered under an oiled wool blanket during the summer showers.

The Companion never strayed when she loosed him to browse. He was always waiting for saddle and bridle in the cool hush before dawn.

Five days farther on, with supplies short again, the Companion guided her into another outlying village. The moment his hooves clopped on the packed lane, Kaysa recognized a larger settlement. The doubled clang of two smith's hammers rang from a sizable forge, undershot by the creaking bass rumble of a turning mill wheel. A hawker sold pies to passersby, and the wafted smell of cooking meat suggested an inn, beyond the rumble of someone rolling spent barrels out of a wine cellar.

Kaysa let the Companion take her into a busier street, stone paving overshadowed by buildings and puddled with runoff, where women chattered by a public well. A wagon ground past, noisy with crated chickens and chased by a barking dog.

The Companion seemed unfazed by the commotion.

"We'll need to find grain and water," Kaysa murmured, stroking his neck. The smell of a nearby stable suggested an inn large enough for a carriage yard. The Companion went that way without her bidding, through the cool of a quiet back alley.

The echoes of each hoof beat diminished just before they emerged into the open. The heat of full sunlight flamed on Kaysa's face, and the white Companion drew instant attention.

A child shouted. Someone leading a cart team took pause to a jingle of harness. Footsteps approached, a heavy-set person puffing in flustered haste.

"Welcome to Beckley!" gushed a fruity, male voice. "I'm the town mayor. So pleased you've arrived. The journey was difficult, yes? You and your Companion look famished."

"Thank you. My name is Kaysa, and—"

"Of course, of course!" The pompous official nattered nonstop, "Your arrival's expected. Come along. Welcome! We'll address your needs." An impatient clap brought a scurrying groom. "See that the Companion is comfortably stabled."

Worn from the saddle, Kaysa dismounted. While experienced hands took the reins, she reached to untie her guide stick and blanket roll.

"No need, don't trouble yourself," the official insisted, clasping her shoulder and hustling her along.

"But," Kaysa protested, "I can't—"

"No matter, your blindness presents no problem at all." Her corpulent escort towed her away, benignly insistent. "The boy will bring your things straightaway. Delighted for the honor! Here's the inn stairs." A puffed pause for breath, then, "Maisell!" he bawled. A clatter ensued past the open door, perhaps a dropped mop by the sudden splash of slopped water. "Our girl in the taproom will show you to your quarters."

When Maisell arrived to the rasp of damp hands being hastily dried on a towel, the mayor instructed, "Kaysa requires a wash and a meal. Lend your help while she refreshes herself. I'll send word when the council assembles."

Kaysa found herself whisked away to Maisell's kindly stream of chatter, eagerly asking after the Companion without giving pause for reply. Then, "Here's your room. There's a basin and pitcher in the left corner, and a stool by the bed. Make yourself comfortable. I'll have the bath tub arranged in a trice."

Maisell spun, shouting back downstairs for soap and towels, while Kaysa traced her fingers along the wall to find her way through the room. Tired and hungry, she let the barrage of Beckley's hospitality defer her questions and answers for later.

She never meant to fall asleep when, replete from her meal, she reclined on the inn's feather mattress. Roused by Maisell shaking her, she sat up confused by the unfamiliar surroundings.

"The council's assembled," Maisell announced brightly. "Feels like we've waited forever to resolve this unhappy business."

"What business?" Kaysa stood up, alarmed. She had come so far on her own! How could she escape being sent home if word of her escapade had overtaken her?

"Ah! You weren't already told?" Maisell's tone did not suggest an admonishment as she hastened her charge downstairs and across the carriage yard. "We've a dispute between two rock-headed neighbors needing a settlement."

Kaysa tripped between steps. Did these folk assume she was a Herald sent by the Queen? "I can't—" she confessed in flustered contrition.

"Oh, I'm sorry!" Maisell's airy apology trampled over her uncertainty. "I know you can't see. Forgive me, I ought to have been minding your feet!"

The close echo told Kaysa they neared a large building. The buzzed murmur of people gathered inside drifted through the opened windows. Maisell guided her firmly through the wide door, where the mayor's resonant voice announced her by name, then clasped her hand and ushered her to a seat.

"We'll start immediately. Soonest begun, soonest finished, eh?" Fatuously pleased, he chuckled at the platitude. "Queen's business won't wait. Let's not let our little problem delay you any longer than necessary."

Kaysa's cheeks heated with awkward embarrassment.

Uncertain how to correct the mistake, she scrambled to find an honest evasion from humiliation. "I'm bound straight for Haven on an urgent matter. Let me sit for the hearing and bear the account to a higher authority."

"As your business requires." The mayor cleared his throat. "Though a scrap over strayed cattle scarcely seems to warrant the Queen's attention." The floorboards squeaked under his weight as he moved to begin.

Kaysa folded her hands in the pretense of confidence. She was an excellent listener, more than able to recall detail. In good faith, she might witness this case with intent to deliver a clear report for a lawful resolution.

Firmed by that resolve, she sweated through the formalities as the village council was called into session. The contentious parties were brought forward, with lots drawn to determine which would speak first. Swished cloth and the creak of wooden chairs quieted as hesitant footsteps stopped before Kaysa's seat.

"Mistress Velle, if you please," stated the woman come forward to present her case. The quavering voice was an elder's, too timid to deliver an echo. Kaysa sat attentively straight as her testimony unfolded.

"I have a large meadow, but only one cow," the plaintiff began. "My land borders a brook and provides quality grazing, even in drought. I tether my cow at midsummer and hire a man to cut hay. There's always enough to last the winter over. Sometimes there's extra to sell. My neighbor pens a bull in the next field, where the grass is less succulent. The brute breaks through often and gobbles our fodder. I am not wealthy. My husband is bedridden. Without lush forage, the cow's yearly calf does not fatten for market. We lose the best price at sale and also the coin for our surplus hay." The woman drew a slow breath, her pause suggestive of a shy person, sweet as a wren, and not wont to exaggerate. "I've asked that my neighbor pay for the lost crop and compensate for an underweight calf sent to market."

"Thank you," said Kaysa. "Is that all?"

"Yes, if you please." But the trace of iron behind the courtesy suggested Mistress Velle planned to dig in her heels.

Kaysa had listened to many a quarrel between her older brothers. Their voices always revealed more than words, sometimes with a finer nuance that sighted folk could overlook. Eager to be done, she gestured to prompt the other side of the account.

A thumped tread approached her chair and stopped to a belligerent stamp of impatience. The second plaintiff declared herself, bossy with injury. "Mistress Sten, if you please. My loose bull is scarcely at fault for the hay because Mistress Velle's cow has claimed the benefit for years. Her calves always sell for a tidy profit. Yet she pays nothing for my bull's service. A fair settlement owes me compensation all the more, since this spring the cow has birthed twins. That's why Velle's pasture is overgrazed. She'll gain by two calves, a bit underweight, while I claim the stud fees for her animals should be paid in full. Why dispute? My prime bull makes his issue the more desirable."

Kaysa paused. "Is yours the only available bull?"

"In fact, no," Beckley's mayor qualified. "Master Gamon's bull stands for half the fee. That's what Mistress Velle has offered to pay. She prefers to service her cow at low cost, since she breeds her to maintains a milch cow and not for quality herdstock. If you please, that's the impasse we cannot resolve. These charges are argued, year after year. Both parties refuse to be reconciled."

Kaysa winced for his suppressed shame, that two farmers' petty feuding should require intervention by a Queen's Herald.

The bold thought occurred to her that perhaps the problem might not need Haven's oversight, after all. Kaysa stood, resolved to suggest an amicable settlement. For truly, the deadlock over the cattle was not at the root of the matter.

"The difficulty here is not due to lost hay, or fair dispensation of stud fees, but the fact the fence between the two fields is not stout enough to keep the livestock separate."

"But the fence belongs to Mistress Velle! That's not my problem," Mistress Sten said in acrid defense.

Kaysa inclined her head toward the retiring neighbor. "Your fence, Mistress Velle, is in poor shape?"

The silence stretched, until the answer emerged, quavered by reluctance. "My husband's been ill. He cannot make repairs. More hired help and new boards are too dear, while Mistress Sten fattens her bull on my grass, his prime condition maintained at our expense!"

"Oh?" Mistress Sten blustered in objection, "Don't claim the calves you've sold haven't fetched a steep price, lent the bloodstock advantage of my prize bull!"

Kaysa held up a hand. "Might I put forward a compromise that resolves both complaints, hereafter?" When the antagonists quieted, she resumed. "When the weaned calves are sold, use the profit from one to rebuild a strong fence. The price of the second will be divided between you. No one gains this year. The loss of the hay and the balance of the bull's fee are to be forgiven, on both sides. But hereafter, Mistress Sten's bull will stay where it belongs, kept at her own expense. Mistress Velle regains the benefit of her pasture and the choice to manage her cow as she pleases."

When Mistress Sten stirred to take umbrage, and the whisked flounce of skirts suggested Mistress Velle also stiffened for further complaint, the mayor broke in, "I suggest both of you settle on these terms. If the Herald dispatches your problem to Haven, you might face additional fines for recalcitrance. The outcome imposed by the court might be worse, and I won't tolerate further acrimony at everyone else's expense!"

It was the solution, fair enough to stop argument. While the clerk pattered forward to draw up the documents, Kaysa begged gracious leave to continue her journey.

Mounted inside the hour, she left Beckley with replenished provisions. The Companion beneath her seemed driven by fresh urgency. He snorted and shivered, pace quickened, although the breeze harbored no scent of turned weather. Kaysa knotted her fingers in his silken mane, nervous and unable to see whether unnatural clouds gathered. Whatever ill fate had befallen the Herald, his body had not been recovered. Doubt unsettled her for the first time. She feared her impulsive choice might have foolishly thrust her into harm's way. If she failed to reach Haven, all would be lost. Not least, her folly placed one of Valdemar's valiant Companions at risk.

"Run," she whispered into his ear. "Stay safe at all costs and keep going, even if I tumble off!"

The Companion surged forward, head raised, his manner alert.

Shortly, Kaysa heard approaching hoof beats, sweetly mingled with bells. Several voices, pitched with concern, drifted nearer.

Then the travelers sighted her. "Look!" The shout held shocked recognition. "That's Lark!"

Within moments, Kaysa found herself surrounded, gusted by the excited snorts of several inquisitive Companions. A woman called through the commotion, "Who are you? Where's Tarron? What's befallen Lark's Herald?"

"I don't know." Kaysa clung to the trembling Companion, and described the freak storm, Lark's mishap, and the bloodstains on his empty saddle. "Our village sent searchers. No one found your Herald. I was returning the Companion to Haven to seek the Queen's aid."

A tense pause, filled with the stamp of uneasy hooves and the creak of shifted leather. The huddled stillness of the Companions suggested communication between them, but Kaysa lacked the sensitivity to share.

"I can't understand what Lark saw," the female Herald declared shortly, sounding uncertain and worried. "His mind is a tangle of darkness and pain, as though Tarron fell to madness."

Kaysa waited, too polite to ask questions.

Then the young man sighed. "Tarron's been overdue," he explained. "Rumors describe some uncanny disturbances, perhaps caused by dark magic. We're sent to inquire. If Lark's memory is damaged, he can't be healed here. This grim news must reach Haven forthwith. We'll have to split up if we're to settle the outstanding matter at Beckley."

Kaysa flushed. "A difference over cattle? The two parties have been reconciled." Self-conscious but certain she had done right, she outlined the terms of her impromptu settlement.

"Nicely done! You've arbitrated as well as any Herald," the young woman exclaimed, surprised. "I'm Lara and to my right, Arif and Jess. We ride for Haven immediately. Word of Tarron's fate must reach the capitol."

Kaysa swallowed, distressed. "He died?"

A pause, before Jess amended with difficulty, "Perhaps worse, he's held captive. Lark would never have left his side, else. We need your testimony, if you're willing. Can you ride along with us, despite the fact you're not Chosen?"

A thrill coursed through Kaysa. "My sightlessness won't be a burden?"

The Herald never hesitated. "Certainly not. Lark's taken you this far. Your courage and strength accepted his lead, no matter the danger."

"I must go myself. No one else can speak for me." Kaysa patted Lark's neck, warmed inside. Because she had dared to strike off the limitations imposed by her well-meaning family, all of the world was open to her. Possibilities existed, as never before. The Goddess alone knew how a Companion selected their Chosen. Once Kaysa reached Haven, who was to say the rare privilege might not fall to her?

Unimagined Consequences
Elizabeth A. Vaughan

Dear Lord Ashkevron,

I write in the hopes that you may be willing to open trade with my lands. I wish to secure a breeding stock of chirras *from you. My predecessor in title had some* chirras *that adapted well to the southern climes and produced a wool in their undercoat as fine as I have ever seen. I am hoping to do the same.*

Honesty requires that I be truthful and say that my supply of coin is limited. However, I can offer wool, both raw and spun, and fine embroidery if that suits your need. Please let me know what your terms would be, as I am anxious to establish a herd.

I am also given to understand that you may have some men who have served in the Tedrel wars, and who now are of uncertain future. My lands suffered greatly in the loss of our menfolk, and if there are any wishing to journey here and make a new life for themselves, they would be truly welcome, if they are of a mind to work hard. Sandbriar, for all my affection for it, is not for the soft, or faint of heart.

Sincerely,
Lady Cera of Sandbriar

The hut was as Alena remembered it, in the deepest part of the woods, a cold burn pit in front of it. It was colder now that winter was upon them. Taking a deep breath, she rapped on the doorframe with a mittened hand. She could feel Gareth's glare on her back from where he stood with their horses. But she didn't want to scare the man within.

Her lady needed Ager's skill with *chirras*, and Alena was determined to secure it for her.

She tightened her heavy woolen cloak around her and knocked again. This time the door trembled and swung open on its own.

"Hello?" Alena called out, peering into the darkness. She wrinkled her nose at the smell of old drink, sweat, and other noisome things. Breathing through her mouth, she stepped inside. "Hello?"

Something stirred in the shadows beyond. A low fire burned in the hearth, not enough to warm a man, much less a room.

Alena cleared her throat. "You may not recall meeting me," she said. "You were drunk at the time. I am Alena, handmaiden to the Lady Cera of Sandbriar." She spoke into the darkness, where she could hear breathing. "We were here—"

"It was she I frightened," an unsteady voice whispered. "That was weeks ago. I—" There was a slight movement in the dark. "I remember. Did I hurt her?"

There was regret in his tone, but Alena wasn't there to forgive. "In fairness, no," Alena scowled in the voice's direction. "Truth be told, it was another that hurt her. But you . . . you scared her. Brought it all back." Alena lifted her chin and didn't take the accusation out of her voice. "Almost worse than hitting her, to my way of thinking."

"Didn't mean . . . I would never . . ." the man's voice—*Ager's voice,* Alena reminded herself—faded off.

"Come out where I can see you," she demanded.

Ager moved into the light, kicking a bottle as he shuffled forward. His hair and beard were wild and unkempt, his body thinner than Alena remembered. Torn, stained clothes and filthy hands. Not so frightening as she remembered, somehow. Pitiful, truth be told. Still, she was glad of Gareth outside.

She crossed her arms over her chest. "My lady is writing to the north, to a Lord there. Lord Ask . . . Asker–"

"Lord Ashkevron?" Ager's hands trembled. He folded his arms and tucked them into his armpits when he saw her staring.

"Yes," Alena said. "She has asked to trade for *chirras* . . . and—" She clamped her mouth tight on her next words. Ager didn't need to know that her Lady had offered places to any men willing to work. No need to remind him of the war's losses. He'd had his own. No need to remind him of that.

"*Chirras*," came a whisper.

Alena took a deep breath. "My lady has a fine cellar." She raised her chin. "I'm here to say that if you will come when the animals do, if you will aid my lady, and stay sober in the doing, then I will get you as many bottles as you can drink, aye, and make sure you don't choke on your own spew in the process."

Ager blinked at her. "What?"

"She'd be horrified that I made this offer, but still I make it to you. You can drink yourself stupid, as little as I care, so long as you sober up when she has need of you," Alena said, trying to keep the exasperation from her voice. What didn't he understand? "You help my Lady, give her advice so as to see to them, and I'll see to your lodgings in the manor and your drink and see you cared for and buried decent when all is said and done." Alena gave him a careful look. "And make sure you eat enough to keep body and soul together."

"Haven't had a drop since she left here," came another whisper. "She was so afraid . . ."

Alena looked around, and raised an eyebrow of doubt.

Ager finally managed to look her in the eye. "The head-man of the village berated me most of the rest of that day. Never raised my hand to a woman before. Wouldn't raise my hand to a woman, never. Broke every bottle that day. Haven't had a drop since."

She looked at him, suspicious. He'd not be the first to make such a claim. "Still smells foul in here."

"Been sick," Ager said, his arms growing tight. "Not an easy thing, going off the drink so fast."

"Right mess you are," she agreed. "You just . . . stopped? All of a sudden?"

"Yes," Ager spoke as if the words pained him. "Been thinking, too, on all the things the drink blurred. All the pain." He took a long, shuddering breath. "Not an easy thing."

"No," Alena said. "Not easy to let yourself hurt. But pain just lies inside you like rotten meat. Gotta come out, one way or another."

"That too," he said dryly.

They stood together in shared silence for a moment, then Alena broke it. "Think on my offer," she said. "It still stands. Drunk or sober."

"Even clean my spew?" Ager straightened, a glint of humor in his eyes.

"There's a lot I would do for my Lady," Alena said simply. She turned to go, and paused at the door. "Gareth and I, we brought some food for the road. Bread, cheese, a bit of dried meat. I'll leave it with you. Eat something. And bathe before you come to the manor."

"As you command, lady."

Alena gave that the sniff of disdain it deserved. "And my offer?"

"I will think on it," came the reply.

Well enough, she thought as she left. *Well enough.*

Lady Cera of Sandbriar caught herself about to squirm in her chair like a child.

"My lady, I know you have strong feelings about the matter," Athelnor, her steward and friend, looked as uncomfortable as she felt. "But sooner rather than later, suitors for your hand will appear. You must be prepared for them."

"A year and a day of mourning." Cera straightened in her chair. "That is the traditional—"

"Yes," Athelnor said quietly. "You cling to that phrase as if the day will never come."

"Well, since we are not yet to the Mid-Winter Festival, it is not yet a concern." Cera shifted again. "What do you think of the draft of my letter to Lord Ashkevron?" Hoping the change of subject wasn't too obvious.

Thankfully, Athelnor let her have her way. With a resigned look, he started searching through the papers on his desk.

Cera wiggled her stockinged toes a bit closer to the fireplace. Athelnor's office was snug, and the shelves of books and records surrounding them gave it a cozy air.

She settled back in the chair, enjoying the warmth. Winter held Sandbriar firmly in its grip, a different kind of winter than she was used to. The cold was thinner, sharper somehow, the snow like hard diamonds instead of the flat, wet flakes she'd known in Rethwellan.

The manor house was kept warm, due in large part to the number of people they'd crammed within its walls. The elderly, women, and children, and if it had not been enough, Cera would have brought the herds into the Great Hall.

Marga and Athelnor had declared it unnecessary, and, in truth, the animals were probably happier in the fields and barns. Still, Cera smiled to herself. It had raised a joyous chaos when she'd put forward the idea in the Grand Hall one night, more from mischief than necessity. She chuckled at the memory of the horrified faces around her, until they had realized she'd been joking with them.

But her pleasure in the memory faded quickly enough. Oh, they'd get by with the food they had, but come spring it would be the hard time, when supplies ran low and the first crops hadn't yet come in. The women of Sandbriar were knowledgeable in the ways of making meals stretch and none would die, but they'd all be a bit leaner come spring.

Still, she worried for her people and her lands. She didn't want to burden Athelnor any more than he already was.

The steward leaned forward in his chair, catching her attention, her draft in his hand. "It seems a bit . . . needy, my lady. A bit too eager. It places us in a bad position to bargain, or so it seems to me."

Cera sighed. "Athelnor, we *are* in a bad position to bargain."

"True," the elder man gave her a pained look. "But need we reveal it so blatantly?"

A snort came from Gareth, sitting on the floor near the fire, sharpening a dagger. He and Alena had been out the last few days, checking farms and households for any in need or distress. But Athelnor insisted that his grandson learn more of the operations of his office, and Cera had agreed. Gareth was not so enthusiastic about wasting a fine winter morning, but he had bent to his grandfather's will.

"You should try your hand at drafting, Gareth." Athelnor held out the parchment. "Would do you good to practice your skills."

Gareth's face held such a look of horror that Cera burst out in a laugh. Before Athelnor could insist or Gareth protest any further, there was a knock at the door. One of her youngest shepherds stood there, cap in hand. "Beggin' your pardon."

"Come in, Jorin." Cera turned in her chair. "Warm yourself by the fire."

"Thanks, my lady, but there's a problem down in the barns. The others went to fetch old Meroth, but I thought you'd want to know."

"The cold does bad things to his old bones," Cera scolded. "His dogs aren't that much better off. What's so wrong that you would pull them from his warm hut?"

"We were bringing in the herd, to check them over like ya said, and—" The lad turned red in the cheeks. "Well, one of the rams is trying to mount everything in sight, and the ewes keep giving him puzzled looks, being as they're all bred and none's in season. But he won't stop trying. Makin' a ruckus, he is."

"Pizzle rot," Cera and Athelnor both said at the same time. The lad's blush got deeper. "Beg pardon?"

"Nothing surer." Cera stood, slipping her feet back into her boots. At last, something she could do that didn't involve worrying over what might be. "Let me get my cloak and grab some ointment for the poor thing and we'll see to him."

"Pizzle rot?" The lad repeated. "What's pizzle rot?"

"Just what you think it is, my lad," Athelnor said.

"Hold him tight now," Cera said, trimming knife in hand. "I have to shave the matted hairs around—"

She was interrupted by the ram, baaing and meh-ing at the

top of its lungs. It had taken four of the lads to corner him and wrestle him into position.

"Or I'll come do it for ya!" Old Meroth shouted. The old shepherd, grizzled and gray, sat on a stool by the closed barn door, with his three elderly sheep dogs at his feet. Even with his right arm lifeless and the side of his face sagging, he had opinions. "Time was I could've wrestled that ram all by myself, aye, and seen to him with the other hand."

His dogs all looked as though they agreed.

Jorin, struggling to keep the ram's head still, muttered something that Cera chose to ignore.

"Phew—what is that reek?" The shepherds around her turned their heads away, grimacing.

Cera reached in through the wool and took the scabbed and oozing mess firmly in hand, careful to aim it away from herself.

The ram screeched then, sounding almost human. The men all winced in sympathy.

"I know, I know," Cera crooned. "I know it hurts and it's sore, but I've got to shave you clear, lad. And that smell is going to get worse when we loosen and peel off those nasty scabs."

The men all grimaced.

Cera set about it, carefully working the blade close to the skin. "We'll need a wet cloth to try to loosen them first. It's the least we can do for the poor lad."

"I'd say," one of them muttered.

"Just look," Cera said, displaying the tender bits.

More winces all around. The ram sagged in exhaustion and gave a weary bleat.

"We'll clean you up," she crooned as she worked the knife through the thick, filthy hairs. "And then some ointment for the next few days, and you'll be as good as ever."

The barn door opened, and a slim man walked in, Gareth right behind. "Excuse me, Lady Ceraratha?"

"Get that door closed," Meroth snapped. "That ram gets running free, we'll not catch him before the damn thing rots off."

The door closed. The young man cleared his throat politely.

"Lady Ceraratha, I am Ellison, Lord Cition's youngest son. Perhaps you have heard of me? My father sent me to offer our respects and to enliven your Mid-Winter Festival."

Cera didn't look up from her task. "I'm a bit busy at the moment."

Gareth's voice was a growl. "He insisted, Lady Cera."

The ram found renewed energy and kicked out, struggling, making its displeasure known loudly. Cera pulled her knife back, letting the lads get a better grip.

"Gonna have to pen him after this," Meroth called out. "Unless you lads fancy chasing him around the fields, trying to anoint his nethers?"

The lads all denied a desire to do so as they wrestled the ram back into submission. Cera kept her grip gentle but firm as she waited to begin again.

"Lady Cera?"

This time Cera looked over her shoulder to see a fine young lad standing there, dressed in clean, stylish woolens and leather gloves, looking cold and miserable and out of place. He wore a fashionable hat with an elegant feather that couldn't be the least bit warm.

Ellison doffed his hat as he caught her eye, and bowed. "I know that there was no formal invitation, lady, but my father felt now was a good time to express our good will toward you and your holdings. I—"

"Thank you," Cera cut him off with a rising sense of frustration. "But, as you can see," she gestured with the knife. "I am slightly busy at the moment."

Ellison frowned. "Surely another could do this job? There's no need for the Lady of Sandbriar to perform such a task." He took another step closer, nose wrinkling at the stench.

Cera was having none of that. "These are my herds and my ram, and I will have the tending of—"

Which was when, to her horror, the ram let loose with a torrent of foul-smelling 'frustration' all over young Ellison.

Who promptly fell to his knees and vomited.

They all stood in deep, terrible silence for a long moment, the ram, the shepherds, and Cera, watching the poor lad.

Cera cleared her throat. "Perhaps Gareth could see you to the manor," she said calmly, proud that there wasn't a hint of laughter in her voice. "I'll be along as soon as we've finished here."

Gareth got the lad's elbow and helped him to his feet. He guided him carefully around the mess, and headed toward the door.

"What . . . what was that?" Cera heard Ellison ask.

"Pizzle rot," Gareth said.

With the ram seen to and penned for future treatments, Cera had returned to the manor to wash and change. Marga had assured her that Ellison had been welcomed with a bath in his room and his clothes taken for cleaning. "Not quite sure how we get that stench out, but we'll try our best." The older woman shook her head. "A nice polite boy, don't you think?"

Cera hated to disappoint, but best stop that thought in its tracks. "Marga, I am still in mourning for my late Lord Sinmonkelrath."

"Yes, Lady," Marge said. "I do know. A year and a day." The older woman looked her straight in the eye. "You're the Lady of Sandbriar, and a good Lady to your land and your people. But part of that stewardship is the passing down of your titles and seeing to your people. And that requires an heir."

Cera flushed, but did not look away. "A year and a day, before I can consider that," she clung to the thought.

"A year and a day," Marga confirmed, but didn't hesitate to continue. "But that day is coming, Lady." She dropped her gaze then, and added softly. "And they're not all like your late, cruel Lord." She nodded down the hall before Cera could respond. "The young man is with Athelnor, in his office."

Cera nodded, and brushed past, holding her head high. What Marga said was true enough, but she'd had her fill of charming younger sons. If this one had in mind to come courting without so much as a by-your-leave, well, then he had another think coming.

She opened the door to find both men talking, and they

rose as she swept in and took her usual chair. "Athelnor," she nodded to him. "Ellison," she said, and instantly regretted the chill in her tone.

Ellison, however, didn't seem at all bothered by it. "My lady, I should apologize."

That caught Cera by surprise.

The young man continued with a courtly bow. "I fear that, in my eagerness, I barged in without thought as to what impact it might have on your task."

"I think it had more impact on you than on the ram," Cera said, gesturing for both men to be seated.

"True enough," Ellison's face was rueful. "My poor hat may never be the same." To her surprise he flashed her a grin, lighting up his whole face. "Pizzle rot. Who knew?"

His laugh was open and free, and Cera relaxed enough to smile. Ellison's nature seemed kind enough. He certainly didn't seem someone to be feared.

"Lord Cirion sent his son with an escort," Athelnor said. "Guards and three wagons, stuffed with hams, sides of beef, wheels of cheese, and dried fruits and vegetables. A handsome gift," with a questioning tone in his voice.

Cera wasn't about to ignore the obvious. "A handsome courting gift, indeed." She frowned at Ellison. "I must tell you that I am still—"

"No," he interrupted. "It's not a courting gift. Well, it is," he amended with a shrug. "But it's from my father."

Cera glanced at Athelnor to see that he shared her confusion.

"My father did send me to court you," Ellison explained. " 'Get in early' " he said, deepening his voice and waving his hands in the air. " 'Stay until after the Mid-Winter festivities. Dance with her, talk with her, woo her.' " Ellison was turning a bit pink. "That was my father's thought. But that is not why I've come."

"It's not?" Cera blinked.

"No," Ellison said. "This is." He reached down by his side and brought up a leather bound book of loose pages, and opened it to show them. "See this?"

There, pressed between blank pages was an old, old handkerchief of fine cloth. Embroidered on its corner were two bright red birds perched on evergreen needles. As fine a work as Cera had ever seen.

"It's lovely," she breathed.

"It was my great-grandmum's," Ellison said. "And she bought it from Sandbriar."

"From here?" Cera asked.

Ellison nodded. "She said that it was as fine a work as she had seen, and she envied its detail. She was ancient when I was born, and older still when she first taught me weaving."

"Weaving?" Cera asked. "Cloth?"

"Tapestries," Ellison replied. "Huge hangings for the walls of stately halls. I'd steal time from my 'lording' lessons to have her teach me her ways. Her all hunched over her loom, weaving fine and complicated pictures into cloth. Da didn't argue so long as her work lined his walls. And his purse."

"Tapestries," Cera breathed, thinking of the ones she'd seen along the halls of the Palace in Haven. They'd been lovely, and thick enough to block the worst of drafts. She'd marveled at their quality.

"Let me show you," Ellison pulled his chair closer to hers. "See these drawings? These are some of her works."

Cera breathed her delight. The picture was of a hunt, with gaily-dressed men and women mounted on proud horses, hawks on their wrists and hounds at their feet.

"And these are mine," Ellison added, thrusting more drawings into her hands.

These were of landscapes, a wide vista of lovely mountains, streams, and waterfalls.

"These would be enormous," Cera said.

"These were designed for Great Halls." Ellison's excitement showed through him. "They take up to a half-year, depending on the complexity."

"Your great-grandmother taught you this?" Cera ran her fingers lightly over the picture.

Ellison nodded. "Yes."

"What have you woven?" she asked.

"Nothing." Ellison's face tightened. "When she passed

away, leaving her last work still unfinished on the loom, my father had it dismantled. He didn't believe I had the skill and saw no reason for me to continue it."

Cera nodded, sharing his obvious pain and understanding the frustration behind those words.

Athelnor coughed, drawing their attention. "If you are not here to court our lady, why have you come?"

"To prove to myself that I can do this," Ellison said quietly. "Based on this." He gestured to the handkerchief. "And from what we'd heard, I'd hoped that the Lady Ceraratha . . . Lady Cera might understand. Not that you aren't pretty, Lady," he paused, flustered. "But I—"

"You want to be free," Cera said, the knot in her chest loosening. "But we've no looms that would take—"

"Father only dismantled great-grandmum's loom, he didn't destroy it." Ellison gave her that grin. "The loom is in the first wagon, under the hams."

Cera let herself grin back. "And her unfinished panels?"

"Well wrapped, under the cheeses," the young man replied.

The Mid-Winter Festival was a bright, warm day in the cold, dark winter.

No bards had wandered south this year, and so her people had taken it on themselves to provide the entertainment. And what they lacked in talent, they more than made up for with joy.

Children put on skits, sang songs, and recited poetry. Adults sang for the crowd, too, and there was a constant swirl of music for dancing. Wine, ale, and beer flowed, and the cooks had readied a fabulous feast, supplemented by the gifts of Lord Cirion.

Cera had not seen much of young Ellison since his escort had departed and the wagons had been unloaded. There'd been enough foodstuffs to share with her villages and farmsteads, and Athelnor had seen to a fair distribution, brightening everyone's holiday.

Ellison had been in a dither when it came to the loom, unloading it and setting it up in one of the attics. Once it had been set up, he'd started working immediately, and soon he had to be reminded to eat and sleep. He'd hopes of finishing his great-grandmum's tapestry by next fall.

She'd inquired a few times as to his progress, and he alternated between almost manic joy and utter despair over it. Still, she'd caught a glimpse of the work he'd done. It looked wonderful, despite Ellison's protests to the contrary.

Cera thought it best to just pat him on the shoulder and leave him to it.

She smiled at the newest chorus before her seat at the high table, the tiniest of babes, singing of the coming spring. Later, after the feast was done and the little ones had been sent to their beds, things would take a bawdier turn. She'd heard a whisper that as an entertainment, Meroth and the other shepherds were planning to recreate the pizzle rot treatment. Apparently, Ellison had even offered to recreate his role.

She looked forward to that.

But even better was what she'd received this morning. She tucked it in her bodice and smiled every time the paper crinkled as she moved. Just a short note, written in a rough hand, from Lord Ashkevron. No fancy flowery language, but it still made her heart sing:

> *'Chirras breed like rabbits up here. I'll send a herd, and you're welcome to them. My Lady likes your kerchiefs. Send more.'*

The Great Hall was filled with light and joy and laughter this night. Cera sighed in contentment. There was no telling what the future may hold, but no worth in the worrying either. Tonight, she'd celebrate. Tomorrow, she'd write to her father, tell him of all that had happened.

"My Lady." Athelnor stood before her table.

"My Steward." Cera smiled, but hesitated. He looked so serious.

"There is one that would lay a petition before you, My Lady."

Cera set her cup down. She'd been told of this tradition,

but she'd not expected any to have a need. "Have the petitioner come forward."

From the back of the hall, a man started walking toward her. Clean-shaven, in plain shepherds' clothing. An older man, lean, with a look of having been ill recently. His stride was unsteady, and there was a hint of desperation in his eyes. He stopped a good distance from her, as if unwilling to come any closer.

There was a stir in the hall, and the music fell silent. Whispers began, but Cera couldn't make out the words. Whoever this man was, she didn't recognize him.

To Cera's further surprise, Alena stepped forward, standing behind the man's shoulder, as if supporting whatever plea he was about to make.

The man stood silent, his eyes downcast.

"What would you ask of me?" Cera asked.

"Forgiveness," came the rough answer.

Like a bolt of lightning, Cera felt her entire body flinch at that sound of his voice. Her ears roared, and all she could see—

Sinmon's face, distorted with rage. "Stupid cow," he roared and raised his hand to strike—

Harsh words, violent blows, and the pain of rejection for no fault of her own . . .

The man before her cleared his throat, and her vision cleared.

"Forgiveness, Lady Cera," he continued. "I am Ager, who—"

"The man in the charcoaler's hut," she finished, sitting there, numb, fear washing over her. She had the urge to run, to hide, but . . .

Cera looked out then, seeing again the warmth of the room and the support of her friends and her people. And reminded herself again, for the thousandth time, for the ten thousandth time—

. . . no fault of her own . . .

Once again, Ager's words pulled her back.

"Aye," and his regret was thick in his voice. "I've come to aid, lady, if you will have me. Aid with the *chirras* if they come. Aid with the sheep flocks and goat herds until then. I once had a right hand at the trade."

No. She shook with reaction, clasping her hands under the table to ease their tremor. No, she couldn't—how could she? To see him every day, to have to work with—

Trine above, no.

And yet, even with that thought, even with her physical reaction, she forced herself to stop. To think.

He is not *Sinmon.*

Her choice, she reminded herself, not an easy choice, that was certain. But she would face it time and time again, and each time she would choose.

Choose to push past her fear. Her doubt. Her shame.

"Our first meeting." Cera swallowed to moisten her throat. "It was not a good one."

Ager nodded, then straightened. "I must apologize. My actions that day were unforgivable." He looked up. "And I have given up the drink ever since."

Alena moved her head, her hard nod catching Cera's eye. Vouching for him. And Alena was not one to trust easily.

Cera's fear ebbed. She'd nothing to fear from this man. And in truth, if she sought forgiveness for her own non-existent faults, she should also offer it to others.

"No," she said slowly. "Not unforgivable. In truth, I should not have confronted you so, when you were suffering."

She drew a calming breath. "Be welcome in my service, Ager. Your labors will be most welcome. Athelnor will see to you, I am sure. For now, join us in the revels."

Ager bowed, and at Alena's quiet word, he took a seat amidst the tables.

Cera sat for a moment, feeling contentment return, warm and quiet, sweeping through her. She stood and lifted her glass to the crowd. "My people," she called out.

Glasses were raised all around.

"To the future," Cera said. "To our hopes, our dreams, and the labor of our hands. May we all prosper in Sandbriar."

All joined in the cheering.

Feathers in Flight
Jennifer Brozek

:Jump on my back!: Hadara all but yelled the mental command as she and Kitha fled from the Pelagiris-changed creature chasing them.

:Are you mad? I'm too heavy!: Kitha's smooth mental response belied her ragged pants as she sprinted next to Hadara. She glanced over her shoulder to look at the horse-sized, two-headed wolf monster, a twin to the one that had most recently hunted her and thrown her into the wings of her new gryphon companion.

:You're not. You're still thinking you're human. You're no heavier than a small hertasi. *Get on my back. Now!:*

Kitha obeyed the gryphon's demand and leaped for Hadara's back. She landed with a soft *flump* behind the modified pack the gryphon wore and grabbed two handfuls of feathers with all that she had.

:Claws. You have claws now.:

Relaxing her stranglehold on the feathers, Kitha shimmied up between Hadara's wings, half on the pack, half on the gryphon's back, and gazed ahead. The edge of the Dhorisha Plains, in the form of a high cliff, came into view.

She glanced behind. The wolf creature was gaining on them. Too fast for her to pull arrows and have any chance of hitting it.

With the monster behind and the cliff ahead, she wasn't sure how they were going to escape.

:Look ahead. I need to see.: Panic tingled Hadara's mental voice.

Kitha snapped around and gazed ahead, trying to keep her eyes trained where she thought Hadara wanted to see. The edge of the cliff approached at full speed, and Kitha suddenly understood Hadara's plan. *:No . . . no . . . No!:*

:Yes! Keep your eyes open.: There was pure determination behind her mental words.

:You're blind!:

:Not when I'm with you and I can fly. It's the only way.:

Kitha fought to keep her panic at bay—and to keep from looking back at the snarling monster closing in behind them. She hunkered close to the gryphon's body, craning her head up to keep the edge of the cliff in sight. *:This is foolish!:*

:It'll work. Trust me.:

Then there was no more time or land. Kitha's mental shriek was matched by her vocal one as the two of them launched into the air. Though, instead of sounding like the human she'd been born as, she sounded like a terrified hawk. Kitha moaned at the height and closed her eyes.

:Eyes open. Eyes open!: Hadara bobbled as she flapped her wings hard. Though they were flying, it was in a distinct downward trajectory.

Kitha forced her eyes open and looked ahead. She could see farther than she ever had before. On the ground, she hadn't had the opportunity to use the eye on the hawk side of her face. As distant images snapped into view, showing her the beauty of the plains below, her panic receded a small bit. *:So high . . . .:*

:Not high enough.: Hadara spread her wings out, putting them into a slow glide. *:Too much weight.:*

:I told you!:

Hadara clacked her beak. *:Not you, silly. The food the Vale insisted we take with us. I only know you're there because you've got a death grip on my feathers.:*

Kitha tried to make her hands open but couldn't do it. *:Sorry.:* There was no comfortable way for her to ride the gryphon's back with the supply pack there.

:Don't worry. Just start looking for a safe landing spot. Mostly flat, not a lot of rocks or foliage.: Hadara craned her

head in automatic memory of flying, even though she couldn't see through her own eyes.

:It's the plains. Mostly tall grass and flat.: Kitha matched Hadara's movements. The more time the two of them spent together, the more in sync they were when Hadara shared Kitha's vision . . . and when she did not.

:There. To the right side of that mound of rocks.:

Kitha focused on the area Hadara wanted and watched it. The grass over that patch of ground was short, giving the gryphon a good view of what the landing area actually looked like. She couldn't help glancing around at the plains though. She'd never seen them like this before. Might never see something like this again.

Hadara chuckled, a low trilling sound. *:Still happy you insisted that we don't have an escort?:*

:Yes. No courier, changed or not, worth the title needs an escort through the plains. And you don't count. You wanted out of the Vale as much as I did.:

Hadara ignored that second part. *:Are you talking the plains being changed, or you?:*

Kitha shrugged. *:Yes. I may be a Change-Child now without the ability to speak, but I still have my training and my wits. I'm still capable.:* Capable was the word both she and Hadara shared as sacred. Kitha gazed at the approaching landing spot. *:And even more capable with you.:*

Hadara sent a touch of affection through their link at the compliment. It had been a long time since someone had told her that she was an asset. As kind as her people were in the k'Leysha Vale, all of them treated her like an invalid at best . . . or something that could be catching at worst.

She pushed that aside and focused on the landing site. It had been months since she'd flown, and Hadara didn't want to admit she was nervous at the heavy landing.

:Too late,: Kitha said. *:I can feel it. It's the animal side of me.:*

This time, Hadara clacked her beak in annoyance. Sharing a mind with someone as closely as she did with Kitha was new to both of them, and sometimes thoughts leaked. *:Didn't want you to be afraid.:*

Kitha pushed her fear aside and focused her will into the task at hand—landing safely. :*Just tell me what you need me to do.*:

:*Watch the ground and don't close your eyes.*:

:*I can do that.*:

The closer they got to the earth, the faster the land seemed to go by. Kitha felt the minute wing shifts Hadara made to slow them as they approached the mostly smooth landing spot. It made her wish she could fly on her own. It also made her stomach lurch as she realized—

:*Too fast, Hadara, too fast!*:

:*I know. I know!*: The gryphon squawked as Kitha shut her eyes. "Open! Eyesss open!"

Kitha opened her eyes with a will and braced for impact as the ground rushed at them.

They bounced as Hadara hit the ground and half-launched herself back into the air. A man's height above the ground, she flapped her wings in a frantic attempt to keep them from hitting the earth beak first. They hovered for a long moment, then descended with gentle bump to the ground.

Kitha let herself fall from Hadara's back and hit the dirt with a louder *thump*. :*By the Star-Eyed, I can't decide if I liked that and want to do it again, or if I'd rather be nailed to the ground.*: She gave a long whistle as an exclamation point from where she sat.

"Now that you have fflown, you'rrre going to want to do it again." Hadara turned to gaze blind eyes at her. "No matterrrr how much you love the grrrroound rrrright now."

Nodding with an affirmative whistle, Kitha popped to her feet. :*Do you want to keep using my eyes while on the plains?*:

Hadara considered this. Much to her surprise, the answer was not an immediate "Yes." :*I think, perhaps, it would be good for me to get used to the sounds and smells of the plains without my sight. You will not always be there.*: She withdrew from Kitha's mind and settled back into the darkness. For once, it wasn't as lonely as it had once been.

Kitha acknowledged her friend's need for independence. :*I will need to learn the silent language as well.*:

"Yessss. Not everrryone has Animal Mindsssspeech."

:*Yes. That's going to be interesting to explain. Those with Mindspeech aren't going to understand why we can't communicate.*: She gave a soft *chrrr* of annoyance. She missed the ability to speak aloud.

Recognizing the discontent, Hadara headed it off the only way she could. "Ssssooo . . . which way is hhhhome?"

Kitha looked around. :*I need to climb that mound there. You'll be all right?*:

:*I am capable of fending for myself for a time.*: Knowing that she meant well, Hadara kept her mental voice bland.

Giving an apologetic chirp, Kitha sent, :*Sorry. I'm still learning. I'll be back soon.*: She scampered away on light feet.

Sighing, Hadara forgave the Shin'a'in Change-Child. They were so much alike that they complemented each other well, but they were also different enough to still make incorrect assumptions about their abilities and comfort levels. These things would work themselves out in time.

She listened to Kitha moving through the long grass. She could pick out her companion without difficulty. Hadara turned to listen to the other sounds around her. The wind, the grass moving, small rodents, the buzzing of insects. Nothing out of the ordinary. At least as far as she knew. She settled in to absorb her surroundings.

Something that sounded like a step caught her attention. Hadara turned toward it, scenting the air and listening as hard as she could. The sound didn't happen again, and if it was there, it was downwind. She opened her mind. If someone was there, they were Mindshielded.

Still, her hackles rose. Hadara felt as though she was being watched. She almost called out to Kitha to look for her, but she stomped that thought as soon as it rose. She wasn't a gryphling in need of reassurance. She was a full-grown gryphon who could, and would, defend herself.

Hadara half-mantled her wings as she stepped toward where she thought the sound had come from. There was a scent, faint. A strange one. But she could not tell if it was man or beast. She would keep on guard.

*　　*　　*

:The land has changed so much. But many of the signs are there—new and old.: Kitha removed her pack and Hadara's.

The gryphon stretched, luxuriating in the lack of extra weight on her back and the removal of the discomforting cinching belts. "You can find the Tale'sssedrrrin?"

:Yes, I can. It'll be a few days walk. Less if we had mounts.: She paused, then probed with a delicate thought. *:You are fine here, on the plains?:*

Hadara flapped her wings. *:Yes. I think so. Why do you ask?:* She was careful to keep her emotions smooth.

Kitha gave a shrug in the form of a whistle. *:New place. Strange sounds and scents. The plains are different than home.:*

"Sstrange sssscents. Yesss." She debated, then gave a mental shrug. *:There was a point where I heard something. Thought I was being watched. A scent I couldn't place as man or beast.:*

Kitha was silent for a long few heartbeats. *:Maybe. There could be scouts out here. If there are, I didn't see them, and I know what to look for. With the Dhorisha Plains so different after the Mage Storms, I wouldn't be surprised that there are. Shin'a'in have the best scouts around.:*

:I think the Vale scouts would take offense at that.:

:Good thing they aren't here.:

They both laughed at the thought. Hadara sobered first. "How will yourrr sscoutsss rrreporrt the ssstrangenesssss of ussss?"

The question made Kitha sober as well, and she shook her head. *:I don't know. I hope they recognize my clothing— what's left of it—and the way we keep camp. We will be watched. Then someone will decide what to do before we get too close to the clan.:*

:The most likely scenarios?:

:Attack or conversation. There's not much else we do. Hiding won't be an option, because I will see the signs on where to go.:

"I will hope for convverrrsssation."

:As will I.: Kitha moved to Hadara's side, her mental voice both serious and bereft of emotion. *:When we travel, I*

would prefer you borrow my eyes. I mean no disrespect. You are capable. But the plains are dangerous, and you are new here.:

Hadara laughed, smiling with her beak wide, tongue lolling. *:Of course. I just don't want you thinking you needed to nursemaid me.:*

Kitha gave a whistle of both laughter and surprise. *:Never that.:*

"What arrre they?" Hadara and Kitha bolted for the high rock mound with smooth sides.

Kitha didn't respond. She only had eyes for the promise of safety. She knew she could climb and Hadara could fly up. It could be a rough landing for the gryphon, but worth it. Behind them, Circle-Changed monsters swarmed.

The size of newborn foals, the monsters looked like a cross between *kadessa*, the small rodents that dug holes in the earth, and *pretera* grass cats. Their bodies were sinewy, with heavy back quarters and dexterous front quarters. Their heads were a mixture of rodent and grass cat with too many teeth. Everything about them screamed their wrongness.

As soon as they reached the small butte, Kitha sprang at it, digging her clawed hands in. She looked up as she climbed. *:Fly to the top. Do it now!:* Even as she scrabbled for her next handhold, she continued looking up to let Hadara know when and where to land.

One of the monsters leaped up and caught Kitha's booted ankle in its clawed paws. She gave a hawk scream of pain and held on. The boot protected her somewhat, but one of the claws had pierced the leather.

:I'm coming!: Hadara fluttered down to rake at the creature with her talons, forcing the mutated *pretera* cat to let go.

:I'm fine. I'm fine. Go high.:

:Not until you're out of range.:

Kitha debated the argument for a heartbeat more, then decided it wasn't worth it. She looked up and climbed. Her injured ankle throbbed, but that was all. There was no telltale sting of poison. At least, not yet.

When no more attacks came, Hadara did as she was

asked—flew to the top of the rock and waited. Kitha made it there a couple of minutes later. She collapsed on the uneven rocky surface and panted in exhaustion, muscles trembling.

Down below, the swarm of hungry monsters scrabbled at the rock, looking for an easy way up. With Kitha's eyes closed, Hadara listened first, then reached out to touch their minds. She withdrew with a shock. There was nothing there but hunger and the hunt. These things could not be reasoned with.

:It's like the rodent's need to feed mixed with the cat's need to hunt.:

Kitha sat up and gave an interrogative whistle.

Hadara gestured toward the edge of the rock. *:Them. We can't talk them out of hunting us.:*

:Does that ever work?:

:Sometimes.:

Kitha considered this, then peered over the edge. *:I count twelve . . . thirteen. Maybe if I kill a couple, they'll eat them and leave us alone.:*

:Might work.:

As Kitha unslung her bow and prepped her arrows, she gazed around the plains. She wasn't paying attention, but Hadara was. "Ssstop. Go back."

Kitha looked at Hadara. *:What?:*

:Look to the north, down by the bushes.: Kitha looked where Hadara instructed, following the gryphon's lead. *:Down, down, left, left . . . there. Those bushes . . . I swear I saw a human shape there.:*

:A scout?: Focusing in on the bushes, Kitha stared, examining what she could see against the bright afternoon sky.

"Maybe . . . All brrrrown."

Kitha knew it could be anything. If it was a scout, they were under no obligation to help. Just watch and report. She shrugged. They would help themselves before asking for help. Starting with the creatures below. She aimed and shot true.

The rodent-cat screamed its pain, worse than the sound of accidentally stepping on a cat's paw. That scream was cut short as the rest of them leaped upon it, tearing it to pieces and eating even as it died.

Kitha swallowed hard. These creatures needed to be reported to the clan and killed in case they weren't sterile from the magic taint.

She followed that up with four more arrows. The same result each time. As soon as one was mortally wounded, the rest dispatched and ate their former packmate. Kitha knew it was going to be a long afternoon.

While stuck on top of the small butte, they ate, lightening their packs. Hadara took the time to rest while Kitha took in the plains around them. Nothing was trying to kill them up here. Hadara kept half a mental eye open and thought about her companion, and she smiled inwardly at how confident the girl was despite their circumstances. It never occurred to the half Shin'a'in courier that they would not make it.

Kitha, unaware of the scrutiny, took advantage of the light and the height to look for courier and clan signs to tell her which way to go. She kept coming back to the set of bushes Hadara pointed out. There was something down there.

Kitha glanced at the gryphon, admiring her beautiful plumage. *:When we get down, we'll go see what's over at those bushes. Good spotting.:*

Hadara, who had settled into a half-doze with her wings out and her beak open to keep from overheating in the sun, woke up again. She blinked sleepy eyes. "What of ourrr otherrrr companionsss?"

She looked over the edge of the butte again. Five dead and eaten. Eight still up and moving. They leaped for the rock with chatters of frustration when they saw her watching them. Kitha wondered if she would have to kill all the magic-changed creatures to get them to leave, but as the sun began to set, the pack turned as one and ran off, away from the direction they were traveling.

:Afraid of the coming dark, or another predator?: Kitha looked around, heart beating faster. She could not help but *chrrr* her sudden spike of fear.

"I do not know," Hadara admitted. "I do not sssssmell morrrre prrredatorrrsss."

The two of them took a long look around the horizon line,

but there was nothing to see. Once Kitha was satisfied, she shrugged. *:Time to get down.:*

:We should glide. We'll cover a lot of distance. Make it to those bushes in minutes instead of hours.:

Kitha could feel the ache in Hadara's words, the desire to fly again. She nodded. *:I'm game, but what about the weight of our packs?:*

:They're lighter now, and I'm more used to the weight.: Hadara leaned forward. *:Please?:*

Nodding, Kitha gave a low trill that served as a chuckle. *:Only because we need to get there before the last of the daylight fades.:*

This time, when Kitha clambered onto Hadara's back, she did so with care. Instead of grabbing handfuls of feathers, she gripped the pack's straps and settled in. Hadara kept her head down so Kitha could see where they were going. She set up on one side of the butte top, then, with only anticipation as a warning, took off running. Kitha kept her eyes open this time and cried out in pleasure as they took off into the air.

The ground rushed by them, but Kitha's hawk eye kept the view clear. She risked a glance around for predators but saw none. She focused forward on their target, the clear spot next to the scrub bushes. As they closed in, she felt Hadara shift and slow down. The two of them landed with a gentle bump.

:Getting better at this.: Kitha stroked Hadara's neck feathers before sliding off of the gryphon's back.

:Getting back into the swing of it. I was a good flyer.:

Kitha chirped her approval, then examined the area around her. Now that she was on top of it, it was clear that it had once been a small campsite for a Shin'a'in scout. One used as a marked point for several from the small scratch marks in one of the rocks. *:You did see someone. They've been watching us.:*

"Why not help?" Hadara cocked her head at Kitha. "We werrre in ttrrrroubble."

She shrugged and gave a low whistle. *:That isn't our way. We watch. We see what you can and cannot do. We report. I still may have some of my Tale'sedrin markings on, but I don't look like I once did. They don't know who we are.:*

"You hhhhave a point." The gryphon ruffled.

"You two are a very strange pair, indeed. One blind, but not. One mute, but not."

The voice came from behind them. As they whipped around, they both saw a tall, lean man in nothing but dark brown. He stood there in serene stillness, his weapons sheathed.

:Kal'enedral. Sword Sworn.: Kitha put herself between the stranger and Hadara. *:Speak for me?:*

:Of course.:

While she stood and gestured, Hadara spoke. "Grrrreeting, Kal'enedrrral. I am Kitha shena Tale'ssssedrrrin. My companion is Hhhadarrra of k'Leyssssha Vale. I wasss caught in the Mage Ssstormsss . . . and changed. I don't know the sssilent language yet. But Hhhhadarrrra can speak for me."

"I am Verik shena Liha'irden. I was told to look for a strange pair traveling across the plains. I did not help because you both handled your problems on your own." He looked up at Hadara. "How do you see?"

Hadara raised her beak, fluffing up her crest feathers at the implied challenge as she turned milky white eyes in his direction. "Kitha allowsss me the ussse of herrr eyesss when I need it."

Verik nodded as if that answered everything. "I will lead you to the Tale'sedrin camp. It will take a day or two . . ." He stopped, silently regarding the two of them as Kitha gave a sharp whistle of negation and shook her head.

"We arrre capable. We will find it oursssselvesss." Hadara keep their words simple, despite their mutual explosion of anger.

Verik gazed at Kitha, giving Hadara the impression he was staring at her breastbone. "That is exactly why I need to be with you, Change-Child. I believe you to be Tale'sedrin. Others may not be so accepting."

Hadara felt Kitha's mental wince of pain and sadness at the man's deliberate use of the word *Change-Child*. Kitha hesitated, then gave Verik a low whistle of acceptance and turned away, hiding her emotions from the stranger, but not from Hadara. The gryphon shifted forward, trying to give her friend comfort through closeness.

* * *

:This is going to be harder than I thought.: Kitha's mental voice was filled with suppressed anguish as she watched her clan come to greet the Sword Sworn and his companions. A gryphon on the plains was not unusual in these recent days after the Mage Storms, but the Change-Child was— especially in the company of the Kal'enedral.

Children Kitha had teased and played with less than a year ago now looked at her with suspicious or fearful eyes. She refused to raise her hood, though. This was what she was now. Either they would accept her, or they would not. It looked to be not, and this was a stab to the heart.

:Hush that kind of thought. You're only looking to see the bad. There are those who are curious, that don't turn away. Look and see. Acknowledge them. Stop walking like you're going to an execution.:

Those same children Kitha use to tower over now looked her in the eye. Everything was familiar but wrong. It was so much bigger than it should be. It made her realize that Verik was not tall. It was she who was small. She hadn't realized it in the Vale because she'd been so disoriented. Now that she was home, her new perspective was a forceful reminder that she was different. Inside and out.

:It's you they're looking at.: Kitha's response was one of deflection. They both knew it, but she still pulled her shoulders back and raised her chin, then took a calming breath.

Hadara raised her head and shook her feathers. *:Well, I am magnificent.:*

Kitha smiled as much as her mutated face would allow. She was glad to have Hadara at her back—figuratively and literally. Then she saw her mentor, Jerda, and her stomach plummeted. The iron-haired Shin'a'in courier elder was as still as stone. She could not read a single thought or emotion on the older woman's face.

Verik stopped before Jerda and spoke in a low tone that did not carry. Kitha looked around. None of the other elders were nearby. That was unusual. When strangers came, or Kal'enedral, for that matter, at least one was nearby to watch.

:They knew we were coming.: Hadara drank in the images

and sounds around her. *:I don't think they know what to do
with you . . . us.:*

Kitha gave a sad, soft chirp. *:You're right. At least I'll be
allowed to report in one last time.:*

Verik and Jerda turned to the pair of them. Kitha stepped
forward with Hadara behind.

"Zzzhhha'hhhai'allav'aaah—" Hadara started to give the
Shin'a'in greeting, then stopped as Jerda swept Kitha into a
huge hug, holding her as if she were a lost child now found.
Suddenly blind as Kitha sobbed in hiccups and chirps on
Jerda's shoulder, Hadara withdrew from Kitha's mind to give
her the privacy of grief with her mentor.

As she listened to Jerda's soothing murmurs and the whispers of the crowd around them, Hadara felt Verik by her side.
"This might take some time. The two will communicate with
each other. Let me take you someplace more comfortable.
The children are curious."

For a moment, Hadara felt a pang of jealousy and fear. It
would be the first time she was away from Kitha since they'd
met. Hadara stomped that into the ground. Kitha was just a
mind call away. She nodded. "Lead on, Ssssword Ssworn.
The childrrreen arrre welcome."

A short time later, Hadara was proving to the children of
the Tale'sedrin clan that blind did not mean deaf or slow as
she played a modified game of tag with them. It was Verik
and her against at least a dozen of the younger children,
while the older kids, awkward in that stage of being interested in such games but no longer feeling they should play,
called out encouragement and laughter.

:To your left.: Kitha mentally called as she returned with
Jerda at her side.

Hadara let herself be tagged by the small girl on her left and
collapsed. "Capturrrred! I hhhave been capturrred." She presented the girl with one of her looser feathers. "Fairrrr won."

The girl grabbed it with mumbled thanks and ran off to
show her friends.

"Children, I'm sure all of you have something to do. I
need to talk with Hadara and Kitha now." Jerda's tone was

one of command. With a chorus of good-byes, the children slipped away before work was found for them.

Kitha offered Hadara the mental link to her eyes. Hadara almost didn't accept it. She didn't want it to be a crutch. But, the closeness of the link was too much to deny. The world appeared in her mind once more.

"*Zha'hai'allav'a*, Hadara of k'Leysha Vale. Thank you for escorting Kitha home. We need to talk."

Hadara, now looking at the older Shin'a'in woman, nodded. "Yesss. We ssshould." While Kitha seemed that much more relaxed, Hadara knew that when anyone said, "We need to talk," it was never a good sign.

Jerda led them into a large tent that had the marks of being recently cleared out. Clean hay and grasses were piled in one part next to a cot. *:Where we'll be staying?:* she asked.

:Yes. For a short time.:

:Then what?: As Hadara settled in, she noticed that Verik had joined them as a silent observer. He sat on the far side of the tent with paper and drawing inks. It was a curious thing, but she kept her curiosity to herself.

As if reading both of their minds, Jerda answered the question as she took a seat. "The question now, is what to do with you two, Kitha, Change-Child or not, you are a full courier of the Tale'sedrin clan. You returned with Quenten's message and have proven yourself. Hadara, you are not of the Tale'sedrin clan, but it is clear you and Kitha have bonded. Perhaps Lifebonded even. The shamans don't know or aren't speaking. Neither is the Star-Eyed or her sworn ones."

Jerda continued to speak as Kitha and Hadara both felt a jolt of surprise. *:Lifebonded?:* Kitha sent. *:Is that possible?:*

Hadara shook her head. *:I don't know. I know . . . I'm happy with you.:*

:And I, you. I mean . . . not in a romantic way. Just . . . :

: . . . content,: they both finished, then shared a moment of affection.

"—back to Quenten of Bolthaven." Jerda stopped speaking, and an awkward silence descended. After several long moments, she asked, "What do you two think?"

"Ah . . ." Hadara began, "Apologiessss. Wassss sssur-prissed at what you sssaid."

Kitha wrote with swift strokes on her own paper. Hadara didn't need to read it. The words were clear in her head as she wrote.

We didn't hear anything after the word 'Lifebonded.'

"Hmph. I thought you already knew. Bonded, certainly. No one knows just how much." The mirth in Jerda's voice was clear. "I said we have another message and would like the two of you to return to Quenten of Bolthaven. As both of you have been affected by magic, he might be able to help you."

Kitha wrote again, and Hadara was content to allow her to take the lead.

I need to let my family in Jkatha know what has hap-pened to me. Why I probably will never return. While those of the Vale accept me as I am, and the clan understands what's happened, I don't think those of the more civilized society will. We don't know.

"They will if I'm with you," Hadara said as Kitha showed Jerda the paper. "Grrryphonsss arrre ssspecccial."

Jerda nodded. "Of course. We'll send a courier to them. Your family will be informed. Don't give up yet. Quenten might be able to help."

As a ripple of tangled emotions cascaded through their link, Hadara answered for both of them. "We will deliverrr the messssage. Then we will sssseee." Neither of them wanted to say more until they'd talked about everything. There was a lot to say that could not be said in front of others.

Sensing they wanted to be alone, Jerda stood. "I will let the elders know." She gave Kitha an affection touch on the shoulder and left the tent.

Verik stood and moved to Kitha's side. "You should in-clude this in your letter. It is good to let them know what you look like now, in case you change your mind and wish to visit them one day."

Kitha, and Hadara with Kitha's eyes, looked at the drawing Verik made. It was of Kitha as she was now: part-human and part-bird. Her head was covered in the mottled feathers of a young red-tailed hawk from brow to neck. The left side of her face from cheekbone to brow had the feathered face and golden eye of a bird. Her right half was of a lovely young woman. Her nose and mouth was a blend of beak and lip. From her strong chin down to her neck was human, but feathers could be seen disappearing into her shirt.

Kitha whistled in surprise.

"You hhhave made me beautiful," Hadara translated.

"I draw what I see."

Hadara covered for Kitha's sudden embarrassment. "You forrrrgot to drrrraw the magnificccccent me. I'm herrrr companion, afterrrr all."

Verik gave a light smile. "So right. I will do so before the letter is sent off. For now, I have other duties." He left the tent while Kitha continued studying the picture.

:Am I beautiful?: she demanded. *:You saw the way the children ran and stared.:*

:You were a stranger then. You are not a stranger now. You are a curiosity now. Like me.: Hadara considered her words. *:You are beautiful to me. I think from side to side, each part of you is beautiful. Taken as a whole, however, it may be too jarring for some.:*

Kitha thought about that for a long time as she gazed at each part of the drawing. Then she folded it with care and put it with her belongings. She did not say anything else and kept her thoughts to herself.

Hadara pulled back from Kitha's sight, giving her privacy once more. And giving herself the privacy of her own roiling thoughts. She waited as Kitha moved through the tent, puttering.

Thoughts whirled about in Kitha's mind. *Lifebonded? Another trip to Bolthaven? What do I want now?*

When she couldn't stand it any longer she asked, *:Do you want to be fixed?:*

:Am I broken?: Hadara kept her mental voice as neutral as possible.

:You're blind. It was magically done.:
:Yes.:
:I don't consider you broken. You saved us. Twice.: Kitha gave a small caw of frustration. *:I'm part hawk. It was magically done. Am I broken? Should I be 'fixed'?:*

Hadara thought about the problem they faced. There was more to it than just the concept of infirmed, disabled, or deformed. *:You're asking, if Quenten can fix either of our magical maladies, will we still be able to talk like*this? Or if Quenten can fix only one of us, will we lose the bond we've created? Correct?:* The gryphon felt Kitha's wordless guilt, and cut it off. *:None of that now! If your malady can be fixed and give you a more normal human life, then you should do it! I am blind, but not incapable.:*

Kitha gave a small hawk shriek. *:But I feel* whole *with you. I don't want to lose that.:*

It was the difference in their age speaking now, Hadara understood Kitha's fear. She soothed the young woman with soft *chrrrs. :I feel the same. If we are Lifebonded, that will not change, no matter what Quenten or any shaman does. If we are not Lifebonded, we will not lose the experience or memory of this closeness.:*

:He probably can't do anything anyway.: Kitha couldn't tell if she hoped this to be true or not.

"Maybe. Maybe not. But, forrr the sssake of trrrrying, we musssst," Hadara said, then continued mentally, *:Otherwise, we might become so interesting that we'll gain the attention of a* kyree. *Then where would we be?:*

Kitha laughed her bird laughter. *:I don't know. Stuck with a talkative* kyree? *All right. We'll deliver the message and then we'll see.:*

Hadara joined her laughter, but she kept her thoughts to herself. People of all species could be as cruel as they could be generous. Only time and experience would tell if they needed to find a way to cure Kitha of her magical affliction—or make her appear more human than she was now.

Two days later, with backpacks reprovisioned, letters written, and Kitha reintroduced to her Tale'sedrin kin, it was proving harder to leave than was to arrive. Verik put Hadara's pack on her as Kitha, surrounded by the clan's children, demanded to hear their names spoken in "the hawk language" before she left.

"I fear you will need to drag her away from her adoring cousins." Verik cinched the modified backpack until it was firm. "They are enamored."

Hadara tilted her head and listened to the children's shrieks of delight and laughter at their own poor mimicry of Kitha's "hawk names" for them. "I've hhhearrrd they hhhave alwaysss been ssso." She shifted, adjusting the weight of the pack. "Time to go." She followed this up with a mindcall to Kitha. :*I am ready.*:

:*Coming.*: Hadara heard Kitha's soft whistle of negation to the children, followed by a chorus of disappointed groans.

Verik walked out of the tent with Hadara at his side. They'd come to an accord over the last two days that he walked on her left, with his shoulder grazing her feathers. He'd led her around the camp until she became familiar with it. With that, she did not need to borrow Kitha's eyes. It was something she would practice with Kitha—out of sight of the Shin'a'in.

Hadara accepted Kitha's mental touch as the young woman reached her side and sight bloomed once more before her. The children in their colorful clothing milled about. Some of the adults of the camp came to see them off. Jerda was at the head of this group.

The four of them walked together, Jerda and Kitha in front, Verik and Hadara behind, toward the edge of the camp. A small parade of the children and curious followed.

"Verik will deliver the letter to your family and stay long enough in Jkatha to answer their questions." Jerda gazed ahead, not looking at Kitha as she spoke. "I don't know if Quenten can help you or Hadara. If he can, all the better. If he cannot, you both know where home is."

Kitha whistle her thanks, manipulating her voice into the rhythm for the Shin'a'in language.

"Thank you," Hadara repeated for Kitha and for herself. She also touched Verik's shoulder in thanks and good-bye. The Sword Sworn put his hand on her neck in wordless reciprocation.

Kitha opened her arms for a hug and received it.

Hadara saw the tears in the older woman's eyes before darkness descended again. *:We will be fine.:* She sent to Jerda, *:We will care for each other.:*

:I know.: The old courier steeled herself. Vision returned. "Go swiftly, and come back to us."

:Let's go before someone embarrasses themselves. Like me.: Kitha's Animal Mindspeech was full of joy.

Hadara ruffled her feathers. "We will returrrn." She straightened, then, using her borrowed sight, she bowed her head to the Tale'sedrin clan and walked out of the camp with her chin high and Kitha at her side. The children cheered their good-byes.

The two walked side-by-side in the general direction of north without looking back.

:When we are out of sight of the clan, I want to try something.:

Kitha gave her an interrogative whistle.

:Look at my back, at the pack. It's been modified to allow you to ride.: Hadara kept walking in a straight line, even as the image in her head shifted to look at her back.

:You want to fly more?:

:I am a gryphon. We won't be able to fly far at one time. But think, a courier pair who can fly as well as walk and find their way. If you need a small thing couriered instead of magic sent . . . :

:And people will, in this age of magic's drought.:

Hadara lolled her mouth open in a smile. *:They can call on us.:* She paused. *:We can do this whether or not you have been cured of your maladies. I am a strong Mindspeaker, too.:*

Kitha's unconscious anxiety dissipated. *:But what of you?:*

:I am capable without my sight, though I enjoy the use of yours. The darkness isn't that dark with you at my side.:

Kitha stopped and hugged Hadara tight. *:Thank you.:*

:Thank you.*:* Hadara nuzzled Kitha's head feathers. *:Come now, Quenten of Bolthaven and the world awaits!:*

Kitha nodded, and the two of them set off toward Rethwellan and their future.

Blind Leaps
Ron Collins

Startled, Nwah snapped out of a daydream.

Her fur tingled. A delicious knot of pressure seeped from her body as if she breathed it out in a single, long exhale. It was late in the afternoon. The sound of water sliding over rock came low to her ears. The smell of the forest was delicate fronds of fir trees over the coarse aroma of river wort. A spider spun her web overhead, silently, but with ancient movements that made Nwah feel something deep inside her.

She felt embarrassed, though she couldn't say why.

:*What's wrong?*: Kade asked as he ambled up the creek bed, his net dripping water. His pants were wet to the calves.

:*You've been fishing again,*: she replied. He had been doing that a lot.

:*We need to eat.*:

Nwah whined as if to agree. She stood, shook debris from her coat, then sat back down. She didn't mind fish, but there were better things to do with her time, and she could get a rabbit pretty much whenever she wanted.

Kade sat beside her and ran his hand over her shoulder. They had been together for nearly six years now. He was growing, nearly a man. He was tall and thin. His dark hair fell over his eyes. The contact of his fingers on her shoulder felt unusually bothersome.

:*You were moaning a moment ago,*: he said. :*Are you all right?*:

:*I'm fine.*:

Kade nodded as if to say he believed her.

But, of course, she wasn't.

The source of her discomfort—a strong musk: purely *kyree*, firm, powerful, and gloriously male—was impossible for her to miss, even from all the way across the open hollow. She had known others of her species. She had been birthed in a den with several siblings and grew up in her mother's pack. She understood life in the pack. But this was different. This thing that was happening to her was a physical need that hurt as good as it felt, like licking at a healing wound.

Three separate odors came to her. Three males.

Their guttural barking was audible to her *kyree* senses, even if Kade couldn't pick them up. It was more a chattering stutter than anything else, a sound that reminded her of her brothers bickering in the den, but harsher and more interesting.

Kade stared silently out over the creek as he drew his knees to his chest and wrapped his arms around them. Nwah knew him well enough to see he had something he wanted to say.

:*Are* you *all right?*: Nwah asked.

:*I . . . I want to leave the forest,*: Kade replied.

:*Why?*:

:*I don't know,*: Kade said. :*It's just . . . there's got to be something more to life than the Pelagiris*:

:*These woods give us food and water and shelter from the storms. What more is there?*:

The current floated a leaf downstream.

:*The trees and plants,*: Nwah said, :*they increase your healing, too, right? You learn from them.*:

:*They did. At least they used to. But if I have to work with another fern, I think I'm going to throw up.*:

Nwah chuffed her amusement.

He pushed hair from his forehead and turned to her. :*My Pa used to tell me stories when I was a kid. They were about Mages and Heralds, and great fights over things that mattered. I remember one story about two Healers—*:

:*Tamsin and Cinnabar, right?*:

:*Yes,*: he said, sitting back with a grimace that said he realized he'd told the story too many times. :*They changed the world.*:

:*All Healers change the world.*:
:*Some more than others.*:

Nwah waited. The rut of the males was firm now, equal in strength to the intensity of Kade's anguish.

The idea of leaving this place made her unhappy.

:*The Pelagiris is our home,*: she said. :*We can't leave.*:
:*We can always come back if we don't like it.*:
:*I don't think it works that way.*:
:*It will be all right,*: he said.

She stood up, and the pull of the males grew even stronger. It was as if they had tapped a line of power and cast an invisible force that leaked from the trees and welled up from the ground. It made her body shiver in a beautifully horrible way. She was going insane, she thought. Being out of control like this made her uncomfortable in ways she couldn't describe. A wave of shame crossed her mind, but she couldn't say why.

She wanted to talk to Kade about it, but that felt wrong. To tell him about this felt too personal. It would be like rolling onto her back and exposing everything she knew to him. And he was her link-mate. How would he react to the idea that she so strongly desired something beyond him?

On the other hand, the energy it took to hide her desires from their link had been draining.

Now he wanted to cut her ties to their home.

:*No,*: she said as she backed off. :*I don't like it. I won't go.*: Nwah leaped into the creek bed and ran upstream.

Kade let her go.

:*All right,*: he said as she raced up the creek bed, running hard, feeling the ground flow under her paws. :*We'll stay here if that's what you want,*: he said as blood pumped through her body and the scents of water and rock and the distant tone of musk made her shiver. :*I'll stay here with you,*: he said as she raced around the bend.

For some reason, that just made her more angry.

Like he was better than her.

Like he was a martyr or some kind of a hero, and she was just selfish.

She left the creek bed and ran uphill through the thickest part of the wood.

She liked to run.

She liked dashing through the woods, racing free and letting the moist air dry her eyes as her muscles stretched and her breath came in great gulps. They had been in this part of the woods for long enough that she understood everything about the land. She raced up the hill of hard dirt, bounding past where a slab of granite jutted into the air. A dead tree, struck by lightning in a recent storm, would be just past this swell. She gave a blind leap and came down on it. A deft pirouette later, she twisted in midair to land on an open ledge and charged up a nearly sheer cliff that left her at the top of the ridge that looked down over the valley.

It was high ground, her favorite place.

To the north, tree-clotted hills rolled under the late-afternoon sun. To the south, open glades scattered themselves amid copses of fir and birch. Two pair-mated hawks soared over the creek that cut through the valley below, watching for a meal and diving to the ground in a dance that was as familiar as life itself. Afternoon was drawing to evening, and the forest was preparing for the change. Deer stood beside the creek, drinking. A bobcat stalked quail at the edge of a clearing.

This was her home. It was what she knew.

But Kade's words rang in her ears now, and she couldn't ignore the grassy plains stretching out beyond the edge of the woods and over the darkening horizon to places where civilizations loomed.

She remembered earlier days, before Kade, when she had been paired with the warrior named Rayn. Nwah had been so young then, so naïve. Rayn had promised to take her to a distant place called Oris, where she had been born. Nwah remembered being excited by the idea. But then Rayn had died accompanying a childhood friend to Katashin'a'in, a place Nwah knew nothing about except that it was in the grasslands, far away, and that it was arrived at by traveling a path open to the ambushes of Hawkbrothers and many other such dangers.

Rayn and her friend perished, and Nwah had nearly joined them.

Only Kade's healing touch had saved her.

Rayn had been bold, daring, and good with a sword.

Kade was calmer, a simple boy with a heart that was kind and caring. He had always valued simple things. He had always been interested in safety above all.

What had gotten into him?

Why would Kade want to leave the Pelagiris?

Why would he throw this life away like that?

A grumble came from behind her, and a wall of musk hit her like a branch strike.

She heard their footpads as she turned to them.

It was the males: all three she had sensed earlier and another, a neutral with black streaks running in its pelt. They stood in a clearing in front of a thin line of elm they had arrived from, panting as she was, licking their chops and grinning in their *kyree* way. They had come around the valley as she ran. Any other direction, and she would have smelled them earlier. Only now that they were upwind did she get the full aroma of their maleness. It almost knocked her over.

The elder was clearly a leader. The others, both younger boys and the neutral, were probably no older than Nwah. One of the younger males took a step forward. The other gave a yipping howl that echoed through the valley.

Nwah barred her teeth and growled from deep in her throat.

:*Stay back,*: the elder warned the youngers.

:*But she's in season,*: the boy whined. :*You can smell her from three hills away.*:

:*Yes, she is. But we are not ruffians.*:

The elder stepped closer and stood between Nwah and the boys, forefeet planted and his chest thrust forward so that the lighter fur below his jawline caught the breeze. He was strong despite his age. His eyes were deep. He carried a scar across his jawline that reminded her of her own broken past.

:*I am Patock,*: he said to her. :*Which of us will you choose?*:

Nwah backed to the ledge. She could leap down if need be, though it was a long drop, and she would need a perfect landing or risk breaking a bone.

:I don't understand,: she replied.

He appraised her, and his eyes widened. *:You are young,:* he said. *:This is the first time you've come to season, isn't it?:*

Nwah glanced back down the cliff.

:What is your name, young one?: Patock said.

:Nwah,: she replied.

:You will select which of us you wish to pair with.:

:I am paired with Kade.:

:That is the linking,: the elder said in a way that made her feel uncomfortably good. *:I am talking about something completely different.:*

His demeanor grew darker as he waited.

Or maybe not.

She was confused. She wanted to run, but Patock stood there with power radiating from his mere presence. He was so strong and so real that she thought she might drown in desire. She felt pressure. The need to present for him froze something inside. She wanted. She needed. But she didn't understand what was happening, and it scared her.

The clumsy sound of someone crashing through the woods came from below.

"Nwah!"

It was Kade, speaking aloud and running toward her. His big, clumsy feet ripped through grasses and wildweeds. He held a dagger before him and hacked at branches that got in his way.

He is coming to save me, she thought. He had heard the howling.

:Stop!: she called.

But it was too late. One of the younger males gave a wild hunting yowl and took two bounding steps before flinging himself off the cliff toward Kade.

Nwah leaped, too, twisting, landing deftly and jumping to a flat rock, then across a fallen moss-covered limb to land on the path just as the male gathered himself into a final coil to launch himself at Kade.

Kade raised his dagger, eyes suddenly wide with fear.

She yowled and leaped onto the back of the younger male, knocking him off balance as they flew through the air and fell to the peat-covered forest floor. Nwah rolled to her feet, low-ered herself to the ground, and gave a ferocious growl as she faced the male.

The *kyree* collected himself, then posed despite his defeat.

:*Come back, Maral,*: the elder male called out. :*Come back before I agree to have Tellol punish you.*:

The attacker showed Nwah his teeth. Then, despite raising the hair on the scruff of his neck, he backed off and returned to the pathway, where he stood behind the elder.

Patock stayed where he was, waiting calmly until Maral returned.

:*Choose,*: he said to her once the youth was back in place.

Nwah stared at the elder, then back at Kade.

:*No. I will not pair with anyone.*:

She turned to Kade. :*Come,*: she said as she slowly turned away.

Kade walked beside her.

As they slipped through birch and evergreens, Nwah glanced over her shoulder and saw the profiles of the three males staring down from the cliff.

:*This is our way, young one,*: the elder said. :*It is who you are.*:

Nwah dropped her gaze and continued down the hill.

As they walked out of sight, Maral gave a barking howl.

:*I'm sorry,*: Kade said when they arrived back at the cave they were using as their home. :*I thought you were being attacked.*:

The sky was darker, now. The air was thick and the breeze had quieted.

:*It wasn't an attack.*:

:*Looked like it to me.*:

:*It wasn't.*:

:*How do you know?*:

Nwah considered the question.

It was true that she had felt intimidated, but she under-stood what it meant to be attacked, and looking back on it, she knew the males had not moved against her in that way. Patock had a sense of nobility about him, and the boys had not actually gotten out of line toward her. Yes, they were forward, but even Maral had been controlled. She could also not deny that her body shuddered with the memory of being so close to males of her kind.

She wasn't certain what the confrontation had exactly been, but it most definitely wasn't an attack.

:*I just know,*: she finally said.

Kade waited to see if she was going to say more.

When she was silent, he turned and went to start the fire he would use to cook today's catch.

Nwah was surprised to find his silence hurt.

She had wanted him to ask for more.

He clearly knew she was shielding something, but wasn't going to press the issue. At the same time, she was certain he'd been hiding his own desires from her for some time, too. He was not the type to come to the decision to leave the woods on the flip of a tail.

How could he be linked with her and not want to talk about this?

She considered opening her senses to him right then and there, just dumping them out for all to see, hitting him with the entire situation at once. But Kade *was* her link-mate, he deserved more from her, especially after he had come crashing to her rescue, as clumsy as the effort had been. She loved Kade, in her way. That was true. Their link would always be the most important thing in her life.

But Patock's parting words clung to her.

Nwah was proud of being a *kyree*.

She liked being able to run and to feel the forest as deeply as she could. She liked thinking of her mother. The memory of wrapping herself into a warm pile with her siblings as pups would always make her happy. She liked the way her coat warmed in the sunlight. She liked the way the elder male had appeared above her, silhouetted in the evening glow, strong and beautiful.

And she was young.

These sensations she was feeling, all of them, were who she was.

Everything was so confusing.

Nothing about her life seemed fair.

She watched Kade pick up wood and make sure the ring of stone that would keep the embers from traveling was properly placed. It struck her then that she might be looking at things the wrong way. *Sometimes life is about sacrificing for someone else,* she thought. *But other times it's about letting yourself be who you truly are.*

If that was right, the key was knowing when to give and when to take.

Then again, if it was done correctly, perhaps it's all giving.

Life was hard in this way.

Confusing.

She *wanted* him to know who she was. But just as much, she wanted Kade to trust her enough to show her who *he* was.

He struck the kindling, and a flame was born.

:*Kade,*: she said.

:*Yes?*:

:*Where would we go?*:

:*What do you mean?*:

:*You want to leave the woods. Where would you like to go?*:

:*It's all right,*: he said. :*I know you don't want to.*:

She felt the truth under his tone, though.

:*I know there are colleges,*: she said. :*But I thought maybe we could go to Oris first. That's where Rayn lived. I would like to see that place, if you don't mind too much.*:

:*Are you serious?*: Kade said.

:*Yes,*: Nwah replied. :*I think we should go.*:

He smiled. :*I would love to see where Rayn was from.*:

The heat of his heart made her happier than she could say.

Nwah stood, then walked to the lip of the cave to breathe the air around her. The scent of burning kindling filled her, but underneath that she sensed soil and damp wood from near the creek. The sound of leaves rustled in the wind, and a branch creaked. Birds called in the distance. Over it all, the rising wall of maleness that had been calling to her for days rode as strong as the rumble of thunder across a cloudless sky.

Her body responded to it, but this time she felt a sense of power that hadn't been there before.

:*Where are you going?*: Kade said.

:*Back to the* kyree,: she said. :*There's something I want to do.*:

:*Something you want to do?*:

:*Yes,*: she said.

:*What?*:

Nwah hesitated for just a moment, recognizing, despite herself, the sense of taking a blind leap into the dark forest. Then she opened her thoughts carefully. She peeled back the essence of what she had been feeling and gently laid herself bare before him for perhaps the first time in her life, letting him see everything about her decision.

He blinked once, blushed, and then smiled in a silly, adolescent kind of way. Then the smile turned to a simple grin, and something clicked into place somewhere in Nwah's heart that she never knew existed. His need to see new things, to travel and learn, was strong. If he didn't do them he would shrivel—slowly, yes, but one by one the things that made him Kade—the passions and the desires she knew and loved—would dry up and die.

She felt the image of him standing in the creek with his net.

Then she turned to the cave opening, and peered out into the valley.

She was no different. If she didn't live her own life as well as theirs, she would be no better off than Kade cloistering himself in the woods.

:*Have a good time,*: he said. :*I'll save some fish for you.*:

:*That would be great,*: she replied. :*We'll leave in the morning.*:

She left the cave and padded down a path that was growing toward nighttime. Her eyesight was fine, though, and she understood the lay of the land here well enough she could trace the path blindfolded. Not that she needed directions with the trail of musk in the air that was strong enough to raise the hair along her neck.

Her whiskers extended, and her body responded to the call in ways she was already beginning to enjoy.

She would choose Maral, she thought—the one who had charged to her defense, the one with the lean flanks who had flung himself into the open air at the onrushing human without regard for himself.

Yes, she thought, her heart pounding in her chest.

She would choose Maral.

The young one may be foolish now, but if a litter came from this pairing, she wanted her pups to be brave.

Haver Hearthstone
Fiona Patton

The dawn air was electric with unshed rain, the dark clouds piling up on the eastern horizon heralding a potentially violent storm to come. As Hektor Dann and his older brother, Aiden, of the Haven City Watch stepped from their tenement house onto the smooth cobblestones of Iron Street, he glanced up with a speculative expression. Autumn storms were commonplace in Valdemar's capital and usually welcome. They swept the summer heat and stink away, leaving everything clean and shining and everyone calm and eager for cooler weather, but only if the storms broke quickly. If they lingered on the plains or, worse, if they passed by the city all together, then . . . well, their granther, himself a twenty-five year veteran in the Watch, had summed it up years ago.

"Days like this gets everyone antsy wi' fights an' squabbles breakin' out all across the city 'tween regular, honest folk. Everyone looks to us to sort it, an' there's nuthin' harder than sortin' regular, honest folk. They all think they're right an' the other's wrong, they won't see sense an' you can't make 'em, not even with a few hours in jail. Give me a nice, simple lurcher or lifter any day. At least they don't go callin' on yer own Ma to get 'em out."

Hector could see his point. The regular, honest folk of Iron Street had a sullen, resentful look in their eyes, as if they were already piling up grievances. But, he smiled to himself, the Watch had just the thing to put everything right today. Their youngest brother, Padreic, had been to the Iron Market first thing that morning, and had come back bursting with news.

Haver was back in town.

As the two men headed down the long, ten blocks to the Iron Street Watchhouse, he couldn't help but grin as the first test of their news presented itself in the form of local ribbon-weaver, Holly Poll, seated on the front steps of her tenement house, her day's work laid out beside her and her customary scowl set firmly in place.

"Good mornin', Missus Poll," Hektor said with a broad smile.

"What's good about it?" she snapped. "I been after your worthless lot to do somethin' about them back there for three days now, an' no one's come near. I want 'em seen to, you hear me?"

"Who seen to?"

"'Who seen to,' he asks? Who do you think, you addle-pated half-wit? Them two what lives in the flat behind mine. They been at it for three days now; day an' night, night an' day, like a couple of randy alley cats, window wide open an' no curtains to speak of, right in my plain sight. I tol' your useless younger brothers, *Constables* Jakon and Raik, to get 'em sorted two nights ago, an' again last night. Yesterday I tol' just-as-useless him beside you—don't you roll your eyes at me, *Corporal Aiden Dann*—an' now I'm tellin' you, *Sergeant.* That's four useless Dann boys told in three days. Who do I have to go to, your mother? Don't think I won't! I used to watch Gemmee in her cradle for her own Ma when she went to take her Egan's supper to 'im at the Watchhouse years ago . . ."

Hektor let the diatribe flow past him as he tried to think who she might be upset with. The two in the flat behind hers . . . "You mean Deem an' Kiera?" he asked when she finally paused for breath.

"Who'd you think I mean, her gran an' granther?"

"Well, Deem's jus' back from five months on the river. Kiera's bound to be happy to see him. They'll settle down after a day or two. They always do."

"It's *been* a day or two. It's been three. Happy's one thing, causin' a disturbance is somethin' else. You get it sorted, Hektor Dann, or I will. I know what's what around here."

"I'll send a constable 'round to ask 'em to close their window as soon as I get to the watchhouse, all right?" Hektor glanced down at her basket with an innocent look. "New ribbons?"

Her expression softened at once. "They are that. Haver's back in town," she declared, as if passing on a state secret. "'E got in late last night, an' a course the gate guard let 'im in as 'e should 'ave, knowin' Haver as 'e does. My Jez had a dram with him up to the Cooper's Arms. Brought me home some lovely colors, all the way from the Sweet Grass Valley, with a little bottle of scented hand salve thrown in for good measure. An' 'e picked up a bottle of hair tonic fer 'imself. Haver says it works wonders—takes years off a man. My Jez had a fine head of hair in his younger days. Lookin' forward to runnin' my fingers through it like I used to. Show them two back there what real lovemakin' looks like."

Hector and Aiden made their escape before any more details were forthcoming, but if Jez Poll had spent the night at home instead of in a watchhouse cell, Haver really did have magical powers.

They carried on their way until the next test, local iron merchant, Benj Granstil, stuck his head out the door of his shop and motioned them over with an imperious wave. Hektor and Aiden shared a conspiratorial smile as they crossed the street.

Most of the businesses along Iron Street were as expected: small metalmongers selling anything from used hand tools to cutlery and nails from narrow shops with narrow closes between them leading to small workshops at the back used for limited repair work.

Benj owned one of the larger establishments on the corner of Iron Street and Saddlers Row, with two display windows flanking a stout wooden door banded with iron strapping and a large, complete workshop and forge in the back. Consequently, he felt himself to be in a somewhat higher social class than his neighbors, with typical results: The local youths liked to hang about across the street from his shop, pretending to look menacing and generally annoying him on purpose.

Today was no different. Two Bardic students lounged against the wall of a local wireworker's shop, gitterns at their backs and equal expressions of crafted disinterest on their faces.

"Master Granstil," Hektor said formally—Benj had never been one for what he called frivolous familiarity.

"See those young miscreants off at once, Sergeant Dann," the merchant ordered without bothering to return his greeting. "They're driving away business."

Of the belief that Benj was managing that all on his own, Hektor tried a conciliatory smile. "They're jus' waitin' on Peggi an' Sally," he said. "You know they always walk 'em up to lessons this time of day."

"Miss Peggi and Miss Sally have already gone past with their new beaus," Benj retorted. "Apparently they've had some kind of falling out. And I'm not surprised," he added. "They're always causing some embarrassing commotion or another. Last week it was at the Hart an' Star, the week before that it was at the King's Arms. Musicians, my Aunt Fanny, noisemakers and mischiefmongers is all they are. I wouldn't be surprised if they were both in the employ of some petty criminal or another, paid to keep a look-out here."

"Oh, come on, Benj," Aiden said, unable to keep the impatience from his tone. "You've known Ken since he were a little. He's yer own cousin Marla's boy. You made 'im 'is first whistle."

"Tell you what," Hektor added before Benj could formulate a retort to this impertinent remark. "Why don't we ask 'im to hie up to the market an' fetch yer parcels down from Haver for you? Didn't you tell us last spring you'd ordered up a new shawl for Missus Granstil all the way from Langenfield? 'E'll have it unpacked by now, I expect. She wouldn't have to wait for it 'til after shop hours that way. How 'bout that?"

Benj eyed him with suspicion, but he unbent enough to nod stiffly. "Very well. I have some ointments I have to pick up myself later; I'll not entrust him with the money for those, Marla's boy notwithstanding," he added, glaring at Aiden.

"But if Haver trusts him enough to give him the shawl, he can bring it around back. I've already paid for that."

He stomped back into his shop and would have slammed the door if it hadn't been made so well that it only swished shut behind him with the sound of well-oiled hinges. Hektor and Aiden shook their heads, then crossed the street to where the two youths were already bristling with innocent indignation.

"We're not doin' anythin' illegal, Hek," the older one said at once.

"I know, Ken, but how's about you do us a favor an' go do it somewheres else?"

"What's in it for us, eh?"

"I'll put in a good word for you with Jakon and Raik tonight." Hector cocked his head to one side. "'S it true about Peggi an' Sally? I don't need the particulars," he continued as both youths deflated, "but look, Haver's back in town, yeah? An' he's usually got a whole whack of gittern strings an' tunin' forks an' the like. Why don't you get on up to the market an' buy Peggi an' Sally a few musical trinkets or a bottle of scent an' then apologize to 'em for what ever you said or didn't say."

The youths brightened. "That'd work, yeah," Ken agreed. "Peggi always needs new strings."

"Right, an' while yer at it, bring Benj's parcel back for 'im, will you? Mind, it's for Ruby," Hektor added sternly as Ken's expression took a mischievous turn, "so don't dally. The sooner he gets it given it to her, the sooner we'll have peace back on the street."

"That was easy," Aiden noted as the two youths hurried off.

"It was," Hektor agreed. "Thanks to Haver, I think it's gonna be a good day."

"You are optimistic, but I think I might just agree with you."

The mood at the watchhouse, however, was somber. Night Sergeant Jons gave Hektor a warning look from under his bushy eyebrows.

"The Captain has a visitor in from foreign parts," he said,

jerking his head toward their commander's closed door. "Neither of 'em seemed particularly happy this mornin'."

"Visitor?"

Jons shrugged. "'Bout his age. Military bearing. We weren't introduced. Stop bouncin' about like you've got to pee, Runner." Sergeant Jons turned a jaundiced eye on Padreic, who'd come up behind them, almost vibrating with excitement. When the boy made some effort to stand still, Jons nodded. "That's better. Now then, is there some piece of information you'd like to add to our discussion?"

"'E's a cap'n from the Lower Devin garrison," Padreic blurted out at once. "Name's Willan Elbert. Old friend of our Cap'n Torell from way back. He's stayin' with 'im for a fortnight or two, on account of him just been retired an' his wife dyin' last year, 'E might be stayin' here permanent. They took a tour of the street first thing and came in wi' faces like thunder. Somethin' about the market."

"There's been no official report on a problem at the market. Still . . ." Jons and Hektor exchanged a look. Padreic's fountain of knowledge and gossip was already legendary. No one quite knew where or how he got his information, but he was unfailingly accurate.

"Best get up there an' scout around, Paddy," Hektor said.

His younger brother took off like a shot.

"Anything else pressin'?"

Sergeant Jons nodded. "Holly Poll."

"Right. Kiel?" Hektor turned to Corporal Kiel Wright. "Take Rane up to Deem an' Keira's place, will you, an' ask 'em politely to maybe go an' see Haver an' buy some new curtains?"

His old partner grinned but jerked his head at a young constable hovering nearby.

"No Jez in the cells this morning," Jons continued, as the two men headed out. "In fact, there's no one in the cells at all, you have a full complement of hale and hearty watchmen all going about their appointed business without having to be told to, an' all's well with the world, it seems."

"The magic of Haver," Aiden noted.

"Apparently." Jons handed the nightly reports and rosters

over to Hektor. "Oh, and you're to report to the Captains the minute you get in."

"There's a man who has set up shop in the Iron Market, claiming to be a purveyor of fine and exotic wares from foreign lands."

Hektor blinked in confusion as he tried to sort out the strange captain's words. "Purveyor . . . ?"

"A peddler, Sergeant," Captain Torell supplied.

"Oh. You mean Haver, sir?"

"Haver?"

"Haver Hearthstone. 'E's a travelin' merchant. Sells quoifs an' inks an' the like. Fair Master Smith Linton always keeps a spot at the market open for 'im. 'E's been comin' 'ere for years."

"He's a cheapjack and a confidence trickster," Captain Elbert interrupted in indignation. "And Haver Hearthstone is hardly his name. We are well versed in his ways in Lower Devin, where he claims to be Desmon Hearthstead. In Briarley Crossing, he's known as Brian Hearthease. Up and down the river, it's the same, a different community, a different appellation."

"Most folks are happy to see 'im," Hektor tried. "'E brings news an' hard to find goods from beyond the walls."

"News which is, no doubt, twisted to suit himself," Captain Elbert countered. "And goods of uncertain origin carrying fraudulent, not to mention highly disrespectful, claims of quality and effectiveness."

"Sir?"

"He's selling a hair tonic," Captain Torell explained. "Which apparently contains genuine Companion feces as it's main ingredient."

"Sir?"

"Dung, Sergeant."

"Dung?" In Hektor's tiny office across the hall from the Captain's, Aiden gaped at his younger brother. "Companion dung?"

"'Parently."

"An' that's helps hair grow, how?"

"I have no idea. Ask Haver."

"Well, how would 'e even collect it?"

Hektor raised his hands before turning a glare on Padreic, who was leaning against the door with the perfect elan of a twelve-year-old. "An' why didn't you tell me the foreign Cap'n was as bald as an onion?" he demanded.

Padreic's eyes widened. "How was I s'posed to know it were important? You figure 'e tried some of Haver's tonic, an' it didn't work?"

"That's what I'm thinkin'."

Aiden scratched at the growth of beard along one side of his jaw. "So . . ." he ventured after a moment. "Disrespect aside, which ain't technically illegal, would it be fraud or theft?"

"How can it be theft? Is dung even somethin' you can steal?"

"Rae Witawer might say it was, if someone had the contract on cleanin' up Companion's Field, say."

"But it coulda come from any road in Valdemar," Padreic pointed out. "Heralds an' Companions travel all over the countryside, an' so does Haver. Maybe he does have a contract. Then it wouldn't be theft, would it?"

"Fraud then, if it doesn't work. But maybe 'e used it wrong?"

"Either way, the Cap'n's charged me with runnin' 'im off or arrestin' 'im," Hektor said.

Aiden shook his head. "You can't. It'll cause a riot. Everyone loves Haver."

"I know."

"Well . . ." His older brother stretched, then headed for the door with an evil smile. "That's why you have the stripes on your shoulder. Good luck, Hek."

"Oh, no, you don't. You're comin' with me, *Corporal.* If there's gonna be a riot, I'm gonna need your help."

"My dearest Sergeant Dann, so good to see you again! A father to be, so I'm told! And you, Corporal, number three on the way as well? Your mother must be so proud. I'm sure I have a few packets of herbal tea made up for nausea here somewhere, and maybe a baby's rattle or two? Just let me look. A special price—not for the Watch of course, I know you don't hold with that, just as your father didn't—but I'd be allowed to set a special price for a denizen of Iron Street, wouldn't I?"

Haver dug into the pack at his feet while, across the Iron Market, the gathered smiths and their customers glared at the two watchmen in silent warning. As Aiden had said, everyone liked Haver.

The merchant was a tall, well-muscled man in his early forties, with thick, curly brown hair just going gray at the temples, an easy smile, and twinkling green eyes that lit up whenever he spoke. He was well dressed in a light leather apron over good, serviceable clothing that spoke of prosperity without ostentation. He had a sleek, well-fed donkey tethered beside a small closed cart, and the wares he chose to show off were clean and well made, laid out on a long table. On upended crates to either side were several jars and bottles with colorful labels, including the bottles of hair tonic that had caused Captain Elbert such umbrage. Haver saw their eyes turn that way.

"Fantastic stuff, if I do say so myself," he said with a beaming smile. "Works wonders. But you won't need it for years to come, either one of you. If you ever do. Egan and Thomar both had fine, thick heads of hair, as did Gemma's Da, Preston, as I recall. Ah, here we are."

He set two small, wooden rattles on the table before busying himself with measuring out several kinds of dried leaves into a muslin bag.

"Your Padreic was by first thing this morning, as you no doubt know, and filled me in on all the news." Haver winked at the boy hovering behind them, and Padreic grinned back at him. "Your Kasiath apprenticed to the Watchhouse Bird Master, that's wonderful. I know Thomar was very proud of her." He straightened. "I was so sorry to hear of his passing. He was a good friend to all. Ah, that reminds me." He turned and rummaged through his pack again. "He was making payments on a very special item. Now where is it? Ah-ha!"

He turned to reveal a tiny, derthenwood bird in the palm of his hand. He set it down on the table and beamed as Hektor and Aiden bent over it.

The bird was mounted on a perch set into a small, inlaid, wooden box. As Haver turned a tiny key at the back, they watched in awe as music began pouring from its depths. The bird raised itself up and opened its wings in time to the music. Passersby stopped to listen and, by the time the music had stopped, it had cast such a spell of peace and calm about the market that Hektor had to shake himself as if waking up from a dream.

Haver smiled wistfully. "He was going to present this to her when she was accepted by the Bird Master, but he never got the chance, so I'll leave that up to you." He laid the bird into a box filled with straw and set it beside the rattles. "Let me know how she likes it, will you? The man who made it has passed away now, too, but his son's taken up the trade and is almost as fine a craftsman as his father was."

At that moment, staring down at the tea for his wife, the bird for his sister, and the toy for his unborn child, Hektor decided that no foreign captain was going to run Haver Hearthstone out of town, and glancing at Aiden, he saw that his older brother had come to the same conclusion.

"So, obviously you're both on duty," Haver continued, gesturing at their light blue and gray uniforms. "How can I help the Watch today?"

Hektor took a deep breath. "S'about your hair tonic . . ."

"So if you could maybe tell us what's in it, an' where you get it from . . ."

Haver had listened politely while Hektor had laid out the problem, but now he gave him an apologetic smile. "Well, as I'm sure you know, Sergeant, a craftsman never reveals his secrets." Behind him, Linton nodded in somber agreement. "But I can see how Captain Elbert has put you in a delicate position, so I'll just come along to the watchhouse with you, and this whole misunderstanding will be cleared up in no time." He untied his apron and set it carefully to one side before Hektor could respond to this potentially volatile suggestion. "Oh, would it be all right if Padreic looked after my stall for a bit? Not that I think anyone would steal from me, but a young watchman's presence would do wonders to keep everything running smoothly?"

With Paddy preening like one of Kassie's pigeons, all Hektor could do was nod weakly.

The walk from the Iron Market caused as much of a stir as Hektor feared it would and, by the time they reached the watchhouse, with Haver calling out greetings and offering advice on everything from stomach complaints to how to remove pitch from a tunic, they'd collected a fairly large group of increasingly irate followers.

"'E's not been arrested," Aiden snapped at a pair of smiths who'd planted themselves in front of them. "Which is more than you'll be if you don't get out of our way. Now."

The men moved grudgingly aside, but they kept a dark-eyed stare on the two officers as they ushered Haver inside.

"Cap'ns ain't here," Kiel said before they'd made it ten feet into the watchhouse. "Cap'n Torell got called up to the High Court for some duty or another an' took 'is friend with 'im. Left you a message, though. 'E said *I trust you to resolve this matter swiftly and professionally, Sergeant.*"

Hektor frowned. "What's that s'posed to mean?"

"Get it sorted before I get back, I imagine. An' soon, before them outside decide to become them inside."

"You wanna use the Cap'n's office?" Aiden asked.

Hektor considered it for a moment. "Better not. My office, maybe?"

"There's no room. You've a year's worth of reports strewn all over the place."

"If I might make a suggestion," Haver offered. "Padreic tells me that the cells are empty at the moment, and I understand from Jez Poll that they're quite comfortable; nice and cool. Why don't we adjourn down there until the Captains return?"

"Or you could just tell us what's in your hair tonic an' where you get it from, an' be back at the Iron market before noon," Hektor answered, trying with little success to shake the spell of Haver's all too reasonable tone of voice.

The merchant waggled an admonishing finger at him. "Now, now, Sergeant, as I explained to you earlier, a craftsman never reveals his secrets."

"You're gonna lose trade," Aiden pointed out.

"I'll be fine. If the crowd outside grows too raucous, just bring them in to me. I can see to their needs just as easily there as at the Iron Market. More easily, in fact, because I think it's going to rain this afternoon. If you wouldn't mind sending for Padreic and one or two of his fellow runners to fetch my things, everyone will stay completely civilized, I'm sure. And Toby, of course. I shouldn't want to impose his care on Master Linton for too long. Do you think there might be room in the watchhouse stable for him, Sergeant? He's not a very big donkey, after all."

"Um . . . sure, there's room."

"Thank you, that's very kind."

Haver swept down the stairs like a king heading for a throne room, and Kiel and Aiden shared a look.

"Did 'e just agree to turn the Iron Street Watchhouse into the Iron Street Market?" Kiel asked.

"Seems like 'e did." Aiden turned an unimpressed expression on his younger brother. "That your idea of getting it sorted?"

Hektor bridled. "For now. I'll ask 'im again later. Maybe 'e be more willin' if 'e does lose some trade."

"Sure. Maybe."

Hektor waited until after Nessa, the watchhouse cook, had taken Haver his noon meal, then headed downstairs to find the merchant standing by the open door of the center cell, his wares laid out on the bunk behind him, and a steady stream of customers coming and going. Holly Poll was examining what looked like a bottle of fellis oil in the lantern light, and she spat a rather unflattering invective at him as he approached.

Haver clucked his tongue.

"Now, now, Mistress Poll," he admonished gently, "you mustn't blame the sergeant. He's just doing his job as ordered. Come, have a look at these gloves now, all the way from Errol's Grove. They're as soft as can be, and they work wonders for sore fingers at the end of a long day. You use that hand salve Jez bought you first, then pop them on before bed. They've a special watchhouse price, too. This week only." He winked at Hektor.

"Oh, by the way, Sergeant," he continued. "I've taken the liberty of putting some liniment aside for Sergeant Jons when he comes on duty. Padreic has it up on the main hall desk for him. Works wonders for the joints. We can settle up later. Oh, and Master Smith Linton is coming by for a little packet of hicanth flower seeds for his youngest. I thought it best if he collected them upstairs. You know what his temper's like when he sees these cells; he's still upset that his cousin, Bryce, got the contract for their repairs. Fifteen years ago it was, but the street doesn't ever forget such things, does it?

"Have the captains returned?"

Hektor shook his head. "I just came down to see if maybe you changed your mind about tellin' me about your hair tonic."

"I'm afraid I haven't. I hate to cause you any trouble, but there it is." Haver turned as a young man maneuvered himself between them. "Yes Mister Crendal, I have your eye wash right here. And the flea-wort powder for your mother, of course."

With a sigh, Hektor headed back upstairs.

There was more than a bottle of liniment and a packet of hicanth seeds on the main hall desk when he got there. Several dozen parcels, jars, and bottles, all clearly labeled, sat waiting to be collected while Paddy hovered importantly nearby, handing them out and collecting money as people came and went. Like Haver, he seemed to know everyone's needs before they mentioned them, and he handled their questions and concerns like a professional merchant.

"Is anyone here on actual watch business?" Hektor asked as he pushed himself to the front of the line. "And where's Corporal Thacker? 'E's supposed to be on desk duty today."

Paddy looked uncomfortable for a moment, then shrugged. "'E's in the privy," he explained. "'E's been bunged up for the last two days, so Haver gave 'im a posset an' . . ."

"An' 'e's not bunged up any more."

"'E should be back soon though. Haver says it works wonders."

"But . . ."

"Sarge?"

Hektor turned to see one of the local coopers standing behind him.

"Yes, Mister Beecher?"

"Will you move like? Yer in me way."

Hektor stepped obligingly to one side.

"Packet of pencils an' a block of amba resin for me today, Paddy." As the boy handed his goods over, Mister Beecher glanced at the parcels on the desk. "Do ye know if that poultice 'e promised me is in there?"

"Weren't ready when 'e went through Restinn t'other day," the boy explained in an apologetic tone. "But 'e says Camer Pond's gonna bring it with 'im when 'e brings 'is sheep to market next week. Meanwhile, 'e says's to try this compress 'ere. Works almost as good. That all right?"

"I s'pose." The man handed him a coin, and collected his parcels. "Sarge," he said with an amicable nod before heading out the door.

Hektor just shook his head.

This time he waited until just before shift change to return downstairs. The crowds had gone, and most of the lanterns had been doused. As he headed for the cells, he heard the quiet murmur of two voices and found Haver and his own sister, Kasiath, sitting together on the bunk, their heads bent over a small messenger pigeon. For a moment the scene reminded him so much of the many hours she and their granther had spent together seeing to their birds that he paused, watching as Haver very gently manipulated the creature's leg, then took a fine cloth, dipped it in a jar of something clear, and rubbed it very carefully into the joint.

"There now, little Peachwing'll be as right as rain in a few moments, you'll see. This salve works wonders."

Hektor came forward and, as one, they glanced up.

"Oh, hello, Sergeant," Haver said with a smile. "We were

just finishing up, did you need me or the young Watch House Birder?"

"You."

Kasiath stood. "I'll go then. She does look better. Thank you, Haver." She gave her brother a warning look before leaving them alone.

"I know what you're going to say, Sergeant, and I'm sorry," Haver said at once. "The best I can do is tell you that I obtain the ingredients for my tonic from a most reputable source, and if it's used as directed, it works wonders. One always has a few disgruntled customers; it's the nature of the trade, but once they voice their concerns, they always get over it. I'm sure Captain Elbert will be fine as soon as I get a chance to speak with him. Now, you'd best get home or your supper will get cold."

"But—"

"Good night, Sergeant."

Two days passed. The growing storm had still not broken over the city, the captains had still not returned from the High Court, and Haver had still not divulged the ingredients of his tonic, although the story of the foreign captain's ire was causing it to sell in increasing numbers.

"Maybe we could get someone to figure out the ingredients for us," Hektor said, holding a bottle up to the light from his office window.

"Who?" Aiden asked.

"I dunno, an alchemist or an artificer? Maybe Daedrus knows someone."

"I don't think they do that sort of thing, but Daedrus does know the Cap'n. Maybe he can talk to 'im an' get 'im to leave Haver alone."

"S'worth a try, 'cause I can't think of anything else to do. I'll send Paddy up to see 'im now."

Their youngest brother returned before shift change. "'Daedrus says not to worry, it's all in hand," he puffed.

"'E's gonna talk to the Cap'n?"

"Uh, not exactly. 'E says to leave it to Haver; 'e knows what to do, an' we should all go on home to supper."

"*Haver* knows what to do?"

"Yup."

Hektor gave him an exasperated look, then threw his hands up. "Well, all right, then. I guess we all go home to supper."

The next morning dawned overcast and cold. Haver was standing before the watchhouse, fussing with Toby's harness, his cart packed and ready, when Hektor arrived.

"Ah, good morning, Sergeant," the merchant called out with a smile.

"S'all sorted, then?" Hektor asked.

"All sorted."

"You headin' back to the market?"

Haver shook his head. "Oh, no, all my business here is completed, thanks to your brother, Padreic. He'd make a fine traveling merchant. You let me know if he ever tires of the family business and wants a change. I'd take him on as an apprentice in a snap."

"I'll tell 'im. But you could stay a little longer."

"That's very kind of you, but I'm due in Snake Bends tomorrow, and I need to beat the storm. Oh, and I almost forgot . . ." Haver dug into his pocket and emerged with a small bottle of hair tonic.

"Would you pass this on to Daedrus for me with my compliments? I didn't like to say last night, but I noticed he was getting a bit thin on top. It works wonders, you know."

Hektor accepted it. "Is it really made from . . . ?" He paused as Haver held one finger up with a smile. "I know, a craftsman never reveals his secrets."

"You're learning, Sergeant. Now, you be sure to give the captains my regards," Haver added as he finished tightening a strap across Toby's withers.

"Both of 'em?"

"Of course, both of them. Life's all about making connections, Sergeant, building bridges from one person to another.

But then, you know all about that. You and your brothers know the name and situation of every person in Iron Street, just as your father and your granther did before you. You care about them and their families, and they know it. That's what builds a community. Captain Elbert's part of your community now. And I'm sure that once my morning-after cure has had a chance to take effect, he'll feel much better about things. There now, all ready and just in time, as I think I just felt a drop of rain. I must make haste. See you in the spring, Sergeant."

Haver headed off, calling out good-byes and accepting orders for next season from passersby, Toby clopping obediently along beside him.

Hektor watched him go for a few moments, then headed into the watchhouse, which seemed somehow disappointingly quiet now.

"Did you get 'im drunk?"

Sitting in Daedrus' overcrowded kitchen later that day, Hektor eyed the retired artificer with what he hoped was a stern frown as the old man puttered about making a pot of tea.

Daedrus waved a distracted hand at him. "Hm? What? Have you seen the kettle? Oh, there it is, behind the clock." He turned. "Dear me, Sergeant, you're soaking wet. Would you like something stronger than tea?"

"No, thank you, I'd like you to answer my question. Did you get Captain Elbert drunk?"

Daedrus passed him two delicately wrought teacups, the sugar bowl, a spoon, a small pitcher of milk, and a book on navigation before answering. "Of course I didn't. Captain Torrell and I simply took him to dinner at The White Lily with several of my friends from the Healers' Collegium. We ate, we talked, we remembered those who had passed out of our lives too soon, and we polished off several bottles of very fine wine. As a result, his head was a bit worse for wear this morning, not to mention his stomach, so I imposed upon one of our company to make him up a posset. Have a biscuit, Sergeant. They're fresh today."

Hektor accepted the plate with a resigned expression. "One of your company?" he pressed.

"Oh, yes, as I said, we went to dinner with several of my friends from the Healers' Collegium: my niece, Adele, Lord Markus Indram—you remember him from the first time we met when I'd suffered that minor brow injury—and a few of his colleagues including his brother, Halvar Indram, whom I believe you know as Haver Hearthstone." Daedrus chuckled at Hektor's stunned expression.

"Haver is . . . ?"

"One of the finest Botanical Healers in Valdemar and a powerful Empath. Didn't you know that?"

"No, I thought he was just a traveling merchant."

"He's that, too."

"But how? If he's a nobleman . . . ?"

"Yes, well, Markus always said he was eccentric. He hates to stay in one place. Apparently his gift is better suited to the open road. As I understand it, Empathy can be very draining if it's surrounded by too many people for too long. At any rate, he made Willan up a posset, and they had a nice, long chat. It's all sorted out now. Halvar's good at that."

"Yes, he is."

"And now that Willan has made some acquaintances here," Daedrus continued, "he'll settle in just fine. I'm sure he'll be pleased to see Halvar again when he drops by this spring. I know I will. I've ordered some particularly strong twine and twelve bottles of blue ink from him." Daedrus set the book down on top of the biscuit tin, before turning to Hektor with a smile. "It's all about making connections, Sergeant."

"Building bridges between people?"

"Exactly. Now, as for this . . ." Daedrus lifted the bottle of hair tonic with a haughty air. "Give it to someone who requires it, please. Thinning on top indeed, the nerve of the man."

The rain lasted for two days, after which the weather turned warm and sunny. As Hektor and Aiden headed for the watch-house, they passed the Polls sitting on the steps of their tenement house together. Jez gave them a cheerful wave, and even Holly unbent long enough to nod at them as they passed.

Hektor glanced at Aiden. "Did his hair seem thicker to you?" he asked.

Aiden nodded. "Haver's tonic works wonders, apparently."

"Apparently. Do you s'pose it really is made with . . ."

Aiden shot his brother a look of amused disbelief. "Of course it's not, fool. Bill an' Sue March, the herbalists in Fivepenny Street, 'ave been makin' it for 'im for years."

Hektor rocked to a halt. "When'd you learn that?" he demanded.

Aiden snickered at him. "Yesterday. Paddy tol' me."

"How'd he know?"

"Ask him."

Hektor made to speak, then just laughed. "No point. A craftsman never reveals his secrets."

"What?"

"Nothin'." He looked up the street to where Ken and Peggi were walking, arm and arm, past Benj's shop. "You figure Haver's magic's gonna last until 'e gets back in the spring?" he asked.

Aiden snorted. "Nope."

"You figure it'll last the week?"

"Maybe. Why?"

"Thought if things stayed quiet, I might get you to help me finish up those reports."

"Definitely not then."

"I could order you to help me."

"You could try, and you could die, little brother."

"That's Sergeant little brother to you, Corporal."

"You mean that's do-your-own-paperwork-Sergeant little brother to me, don't you?"

"Jerk."

"Whiner."

As the two brothers bounded up the watchhouse steps, a small messenger pigeon took to the air above them, wheeled about, then headed off across the city toward the distant plains.

Unraveling the Truth
Dayle A. Dermatis

The Valleyford Town Hall was too hot.

The whitewashed plaster walls seemed to press in on Syrriah, even though the space was wide, with a high, peaked ceiling crossed with dark wooden beams.

Part of the problem was the noise: voices raised, everyone talking, no one listening, each individual certain that if they could just make their argument heard (mainly by being louder), everyone else would listen and capitulate and agree.

Outside, winter was just as stubborn, not yet ready to release its grip and relinquish the world to spring. The ground was still too hard to plant, the temperature still dipping low enough at night to sparkle the ground with frost when the sun rose. But each season, while as intractable as a person with an opinion, eventually gave way to the next. Spring would come soon, and it would be time for planting the fields.

Inside, you'd never know the final grip of winter clenched the land outside. A fire on the broad stone hearth took the edge off, and the thick walls, covered with tapestries, clung to that warmth, but it was the press of bodies—bodies of men and women in heated discussion—that made the room tip to fever-hot.

Or perhaps the conflagration came from within Syrriah herself. She'd felt the sudden flush of internal fire before she'd even stepped inside, and now she felt the perspiration spring out on her brow and knew the flush stained her cheeks.

Yesterday afternoon, when she and her Companion,

Cefylla, had arrived, she'd wondered briefly if she were coming down with the illness that had forced her to leave her Senior Herald, Joral, at their last stop.

"It's just an ague," he'd insisted. "A few days' rest, and I'll catch up to you. You'll be fine. It's a simple property dispute. Study the records, talk to the town elders—they'll remember things that never got written down."

Syrriah now knew her symptoms weren't an illness, but that didn't make them any easier.

And she absolutely couldn't take one more minute of this mayhem.

Putting the strength behind her words, learned from years of shouting at four small children before they got into too much trouble, she bellowed, "Enough!"

The sound boomed through the room, the wave of it startling everyone into silence. Syrriah took advantage of the lull to thread her way through the crowd to the low platform at one end of the room. She was of middling height, and it gave her just enough more to project authority.

That, and the Herald's Whites she wore, which commanded respect.

It didn't even hurt that she was only an intern Herald; she'd been in her midforties when a Companion named Cefylla had come to her manor house and Chosen her. Syrriah hadn't told anyone here that she was the intern; a year into her internship Circuit, she and Joral had shifted to having more of an equal partnership. What little she might still lack in hands-on training, she made up for with her experience as a former lady of a manor.

Diplomacy was one of the skills she'd honed in that position.

Still projecting her voice over the heads of the throng, she said, "I understand you all have things to say, and I promise I will hear from all of you in due course. I ask that everyone maintain your composure and be patient."

She wanted to add impolite, un-Herald-like words, which wasn't like her at all. She felt as though she had simply lost patience with everyone already. She gritted her teeth, pushing down the surge of annoyance that licked within her like flames.

A simple property dispute, Joral had said.
As if property disputes were ever simple.

There were two petitioners, second cousins. However, they weren't trying to claim each other's land—they were petitioning together to claim a third party's land. Pretending to be reasonable, they were even willing to split that land, they said, and to give the third party a parcel of the same size, taken from their current holdings.

Claiming another's land didn't seem reasonable at all to Syrriah, but her opinions had no weight against the facts, and the facts were what she needed to tease out of all the parties.

As an Empath, she could tell they both felt justified in their petition. There was no subterfuge; she could sense little animosity.

Syrriah asked that anyone who had no business bearing directly on the matter at hand to kindly leave, and if she had questions for them, she would request they return or seek them out.

At least half of the people left grumbling. She asked the mayor, a woman about her own age, to interview those left and determine whether they truly did have a stake in the proceedings—or just had an opinion.

The departures meant the main hall cooled some, but to have privacy while conducting the interviews, Syrriah chose to use the mayor's office, which was well-appointed but stuffy and close, thanks to another cheerful fire. At least it was quiet, save for the sizzle and pop of the flames. She cracked the window open and moved her chair in front of it.

The chairs were made of dark wood, with finely turned legs and backs carved in a wheat pattern. Syrriah placed a soft pillow the color of currants on hers. Heraldic training kept her fit, but there were some aches that came from long riding that she never could fully escape.

She reviewed her notes and sipped some tea, oversweet with honey, before asking the first petitioner to join her.

Thus far, she wasn't terribly impressed with either of them. They reminded her of spoiled children arguing over whether they had an equal number of cookies, ignoring the fact that they'd stolen the cookies in the first place.

Both had inherited from Arnath Cormier, their great-uncle. When Arnath, who had no direct heirs, had died, his land had been divided equally between his sister's son and his brother's daughter. However, before he died, he'd given one much smaller farm, which wasn't as fertile or well-situated as the other two, to someone else.

But over the past hundred years or so, the wide river that meandered through this broad valley had changed its course . . . and now the smaller farm was on the banks of the river, its soil enriched and easily watered.

In fact, it now had the longest riverfront of the three properties.

"Great-Uncle Arnath obviously intended for his family to have the prime farmland," insisted Bellia Shase.

She was a handsome woman with fine features, perhaps ten years older than Syrriah. Her jet-black hair was pulled back in a formal bun, exposing wings of white on the sides. Her features and mannerisms struck Syrriah as similar to a hawk's: intelligent, sharp-seeing, missing nothing.

She was accompanied by several of her children, there to see what would become of their inheritance. Her husband, Syrriah was given to understand, was traveling on business.

"Certainly he must have," Syrriah agreed, "for that is what he knew would go to his niece and nephew based on inheritance law. However, when the land was divided between them, normally the law sees those boundaries as fixed. My job is to determine which takes precedence under these circumstances."

She asked if Bellia had any papers—correspondence, notes, a journal—in Arnath's hand that spoke to the deeding of the land. Bellia said she'd look. Anything, Syrriah told her, would be helpful. Even a letter about something else, signed by him, would help authenticate other documents.

Syrriah felt another rush of heat from within, another prickling of sweat on her brow, and she knew her face flushed. She sipped some cooling tea and found a small book with which to fan herself.

Bellia smiled then, in sympathy. "You're in that stage of life, then. I could brew you a tisane, a mixture I found useful during that time."

"Thank you for the offer, but to accept might imply favor," Syrriah said. "I may consult with the local apothecary, if you think she is skilled."

Bellia assured her that the town's apothecary was among the best, implying that of course their town would have one of the best. She smiled as she left, giving Syrriah the impression that Bellia was confident they'd had a bonding moment.

Syrriah heard Bellia and her cousin, Rogett Cran, separately, but Rogett gave an almost identical argument. Not surprising, given that they were banding together in this.

Rogett was of his cousin's age, with a craggy face and shrewd, piercing blue gaze. He reminded Syrriah of a great serpent: seemingly still, but aware of everything around him and always ready to strike if necessary.

He, too, was accompanied by his family: his wife, children, and several grandchildren. They crowded into the office, arranging themselves behind his chair.

He didn't try to placate her, offer her anything. He stated his case emphatically and sat back, secure—perhaps overly sure of himself—that she would agree with him. She suspected that most people did agree with him . . . because it was easier that way.

She had to wait until he'd said his piece, several times in several ways, before she could get a word in edgewise.

When she asked about correspondence from Arnath, his wife produced a sheaf of papers. Syrriah thanked her. The wife nodded once and put her hand on her husband's shoulder. She wanted this as much as he did.

Syrriah asked Rogett, as she had asked Bellia, "And what of Jasson and Marna Ford's great-grandparents, to whom Arnath bequeathed the smaller farm? Do you have any notion of his reasoning there?"

Neither Bellia nor Rogett had an explanation for that.

In contrast to the petitioners, Jasson Ford was thirty if he was a day, having recently inherited the farm from his father, who

had died unexpectedly. This was another reason Bellia and
Rogett had come forward with their claim, Syrriah suspected;
they assumed Jasson would have less spine to stand up to
them than his father would have, being of the next genera-
tion.

Jasson and his family hadn't come to the town hall; he had
sent a message that he would be available whenever Syrriah
wished to speak with him, the time and location at her con-
venience. She chose to meet him at his home on his newly
valuable land.

He had a quiet voice, but one that had strength over the
noise of the yard, with a smile to match: not broad, but gentle
and open. He was small and compact—she wouldn't call him
plain but, rather, pleasant. He moved with precision, and his
hands were strong and capable.

"Welcome," he said when Syrriah and Cefylla arrived. "I
would have happily come to you."

"I wanted to see this coveted piece of land," Syrriah said.
She planned to personally inspect the boundaries of all three
properties, of course. But she also was curious about Jasson's
response to the petition and her arrival. He hadn't come to
the town hall to argue with Bellia and Rogett.

:He shows you even more respect than they,: Cefylla said.
The air still had a cold bite to it, but the sun shone, and the
Companion opted to stay in the yard rather than take shelter
in the stables. *:He trusts you to do what is right, without
bribery or bullying.:*

Trust her Companion to be blunt about Bellia and Rogett's methods of persuasion.

Jasson's family home was large, clearly added to over the
generations, functional and comfortable rather than ostenta-
tious. From the yard, the door opened to the kitchen, a generous, homey space with a sturdy, wide wooden table at its
center, weathered silver-gray from age and use.

As in most large homes, the room was a hive of activity.
A young woman and man chopped root vegetables, garlic
and onions, and herbs, adding them to several pots hanging
on iron rods over the fire. In a comfortable spot next to the
hearth sat an old woman in a rocking chair. White film

covered her eyes, but her gnarled fingers were sure and deft with the peapods she shelled into a wooden bowl on her lap. The family must have had a greenhouse and coaxed some plants to ripen early.

Jasson's wife, Marna, was pregnant with their third child. Her brown hair wisped around her narrow face as she strained a pot of cheese curds. The fire's heat crashed up against the heat inside Syrriah, and she asked for water.

"Goodness, of course," Marna said. The servants who were chopping vegetables glanced at each other, and by unseen communication, the man went to fetch the beverage.

"I'm so sorry," Marna said. "We know we'll have to hire more workers this year, so I've been trying to lay in food."

"I'm the one interrupting," Syrriah said. "Thank you." The cool water helped. A little.

A gaggle of children raced in, all younger than ten, not a few obviously related. Wide-eyed and quivering with eagerness, they skidded to an unruly halt before Syrriah. The designated speaker of the bunch, a tow-headed girl with features mingling both Jasson's and Marna's, took a half-step forward and said, "We wondered—we thought—could we—well, may we pet the pretty white horse?"

In her mind, Syrriah heard Cefylla's snort. *:Pretty white horse, indeed.:*

:Hush, you,: Syrriah sent back. *:It's a compliment.:*

She crouched down to the children's level. "The pretty white horse, she's special. She's a Companion—some of you know what that means. In any case, you must treat her with respect. If you pull on her tail, I'll know. Do you understand? She'll tell me if you do."

Solemn nods all around, with another accompanying mental snort from Cefylla regarding what would happen if they mishandled her tail.

"Hold a moment," Marna said. She grabbed several carrots from the table. "Offer her these—and mind she doesn't mistake your fingers instead." As the children ran out, she added, "And I'll make sure they give some to the actual horses later."

Syrriah went with Jasson through to the main room of the

house, an open, beamed spaced that reminded her of the Town Hall. Right down to the tapestries . . . several, in fact.

At this time of day, the room was expectedly empty, but in the evening, it would be a place to gather, eat, play music, debate. Even so, a fire bloomed on a wide hearth, and above it, more herbs had been hung to dry.

She walked over to inspect the largest tapestry. The work was stunning, precise, a deft use of color dancing through the weft. She had been known for her own weaving skill, long ago (it seemed) in her former life.

"The work here seems familiar," she said. "There's a large tapestry in the Town Hall, and several smaller ones . . ."

"All made by my great-grandmother, Trisha," Jasson said, pride in his voice as he stood beside her. "She was renowned for her skill."

Syrriah cocked her head. "There's one hanging in the Palace, too, isn't there?"

"There is," he said. "A small one. I'm surprised you know."

"Her work is exquisite," Syrriah said. "I recognize her style." Then she frowned. This particular tapestry depicted a walled garden, with two people standing inside, lush greenery around them. Their backs were to the viewer, and they stood close but apart, not touching.

It was the decorative border around the garden that had caught her eye. It should have been a regular, repeated pattern of clusters of diamonds—indeed, initially she'd thought it was. But when she looked closely, she saw that the clusters varied.

Given the intricacy of the weaving, she shouldn't be surprised at a few subtle errors. It just felt unexpected, given the woman's skill.

But no one was perfect, and given the beauty of the tapestry, Syrriah guessed few people noticed the minor flaw.

Returning her thoughts to the matter at hand, she asked Jasson what he thought of Bellia and Rogett's claim on his family's land.

"Unexpected, certainly," he said. "Yet not surprising. I can understand their argument: they are descendants of Arnath, not me. But this is the land my great-grandparents received from Arnath, and it seems to me that should be the end of it. River or no river."

"Do you have the deed?"

He shook his head. "Unfortunately, there was a flood—one of the things that made the river change its course—and we lost a number of things. All we have left from that time are the tapestries."

The loss of any papers didn't mean the cause was lost; everyone she'd spoken to had agreed that Arnath gave that parcel of land to Jasson's great-grandparents, and the town had maps from eighty years ago forward showing the land as theirs. It would have been nice to have something in Arnath's hand, though, especially if it shed any light on his thoughts when he bequeathed the land to them.

They walked back into the kitchen. Syrriah intended to ride the borders of the farmland today and of the other two properties as well; Cefylla said they could beat the sunset.

"I heard you asking about the deed to our land," the old woman by the stove said. She might have been blind, or close to it, but her hearing was obviously keen.

Jasson introduced her as his grandmother, Wyn.

"I was indeed," Syrriah said, crouching next to the rocking chair. "What do you know about the situation?"

"This land t'was a gift from Arnath Cormier himself, to my parents, Trisha and Vane," the woman said. "I was born in this house that year."

Trisha of the tapestries.

"So I've been given to understand," Syrriah said. "Do you know why Arnath gave the land to your parents?"

"Mother would never say." Wyn's hands had stilled; she'd shelled every peapod. Lost in a memory, her gaze rested on a spot past Syrriah's left shoulder. "She said she was sworn never to speak of it. But she said the truth was there, if anyone cared to see it."

Wyn's words echoed in Syrriah's head the next morning as she stood in the Town Hall.

She had a mountain of paperwork to review, and she

wanted to chuck it all into the fire, but that wasn't her normal self talking. Sweat beaded on her brow, and she fanned herself. The apothecary, she promised herself. She'd visit as soon as she could give herself a break.

Instead of working, however—she couldn't face all those papers, not just yet—she stood, pressing her hands to her lower back where a persistent ache had settled, and gazed at the masterwork of a tapestry that took up much of one wall.

It was a depiction of the town, the surrounding land, and the entire region, with a skilled use of colors and lines that left Syrriah breathless. Green fields, red begonias, blue water . . . the valley seemed real, nestled between the protective arms of the hills.

Around those hills, a decorative border . . . Syrriah's eyes widened. A border of clusters of diamonds, but as with the tapestry in Jasson's home, the pattern was erratic—indeed, there didn't seem to be a pattern at all.

No, wait—yes, but it wasn't a regular pattern. She could see some repeating elements, but not in a way she could explain.

She recalled tapestries in Bellia and Rogett's houses, clearly made by the same hand. Had they had erratic borders, too? She called them up in her mind's eye. Possibly . . . she'd have to go back and check.

Mistakes in one tapestry were expected. The same mistake over multiple weavings? Highly unlikely, especially in something rudimentary like a border.

And the more she gazed at this tapestry and recalled the others, the more certain she became that there was some rhyme to the seeming unreason.

She was so lost in contemplation that the sudden voice behind her made her jump.

"I leave you on your own for only a few days, and you're already slacking on the job, Intern Herald?"

"Joral!" Syrriah hugged her Senior Herald.

When they had begun her internship Circuit, Joral had maintained the propriety of the teacher-student relationship, but he'd soon learned Syrriah's worth and abilities. Now his round face split into a smile. He reminded her of her oldest son, Shane, who had just completed his own internship Circuit, even though Joral had a good ten years on Shane. It was their eyes, she'd mused, both the lighter brown ringed with dark and the kindness within.

"You caught me," she admitted. "It's not just that I'm avoiding the paperwork; there's something about this tapestry, and others in the area, that has me baffled."

"Tell me," he said.

She pointed out the irregular border.

"I know nothing about weaving, but I trust your expertise," he said. "It does seem unusual." He clapped her on the back. "Catch me up on the matter at hand, and when we've got that resolved, we can look at this again."

He was right about their priorities, and in the mayor's office, she told him about her interviews with the various parties. He agreed with her working position that the law favored Jasson and Marna—the land itself was what had been bequeathed—but agreed they should review the papers, and possibly interview more people before they reached their final decision.

Syrriah sat by the slightly open window again, although it wasn't enough to tame the flush and perspiration, which further distracted her from her work.

Frustrated, she found her mind wandering back to the tapestries and their unusual borders. Finally she got up and went back out to the hall with paper and pen, and sketched the diamond clusters.

"Syrriah . . ." Joral said.

"Just . . . give me a moment," she said. "It's probably nothing—but the tapestries *were* made by Trisha, Jasson's great-grandmother."

"And Arnath deeded the land to her husband," Joral said. "That's a rather tenuous connection to the problem at hand."

She looked from the paper to him. "We don't know Arnath deeded the land to her husband. He could have deeded it to her. Look." She indicated several symbols. "These are both six clumps, and the second symbol in each is the same. What if it's a substitution cypher, and that symbol is an R? Arnath, Trisha?"

"Which means . . ." Joral pulled his chair closer to hers. "That letter could be an A."

"It could have nothing to do with the problem at hand," Syrriah said, but the flush she now felt was excitement.

"It could, or it could not," Joral said. "Still, we should explore all avenues. You should copy the border from all the tapestries." He grinned. "I'll stay here and continue reviewing the paperwork. Fresh pair of eyes, and all that."

They kept the town hall from becoming crowded again by allowing in only the parties directly related to the property dispute: the Shases, the Crans, and the Fords.

There were still more people than Syrriah would have liked, especially given that she still didn't think much of a fair lot of them.

She'd convinced Joral they could stay an extra day so she could consult with the apothecary. Since they didn't have an urgent next stop, he'd agreed.

That meeting couldn't come fast enough.

Now, she tamped down her annoyance, knowing much of it wasn't directly related to the situation before her, and laid out the facts as she and Joral had determined them. She wished Jasson's grandmother, Wyn, could have been strong enough to make the trip to town. The old woman had planted the seed in her brain, a seed Syrriah hadn't consciously remembered until they'd sussed out the meaning in the tapestries.

Trisha had sworn never to speak of the reason Arnath Cormier had given her the land. But the truth had been there all along, right in front of everyone in the town.

"The borders on the tapestries are a code," she told the assembled people. "One of the questions we've been asking is why Arnath deeded the land to Jasson's great-grandparents. Trisha Ford—that was her married name—answered that question in the code."

"This sounds like a trick," someone muttered. One of Bellia's sons, if Syrriah wasn't mistaken.

"You dare question the word of a Herald, an Arrow of the Queen?" Joral growled.

"No, no." The man took a half-step back. "It's just . . . how do we know that the information in the tapestry speaks the truth?"

"Trisha had no way of knowing this would happen generations later," Syrriah said. "But we're getting ahead of ourselves. Let me tell you what happened."

Arnath and his wife had no children; that fact was never under dispute. Trisha had been an artist under his patronage, and they had fallen in love. The terms of the patronage were, in fact, in the town's history.

The story of their love was in the tapestries.

When Trisha fell pregnant with Arnath's child, he couldn't allow the family name to be besmirched, couldn't allow his wife to suffer such indignity, so Trisha was hastily married off to another man, and Arnath gave them a piece of land. A gift for their child's future and for her silence. It was the best he could do without raising suspicion.

Trisha had kept her word, had never spoken the truth. But she'd poured her heart out into the tapestries.

In the tapestry that hung in Jasson and Marna's hall, depicting two people in a lush, walled garden, she had illustrated her love for Arnath and his love for her. In the tapestry in the town hall, which showed the entire region, she'd woven a description of the lands bequeathed to her—and her child with Arnath. In a small tapestry that hung in Arnath's family home—now occupied by Bellia's branch of the family—Trisha stated she understood why Arnath could never marry her or acknowledge their child.

Syrriah suspected that last tapestry would never again see the light of day.

There were more, all on the same theme: hidden messages of unrequited love between Trisha and Arnath and love for the child they'd made together.

Syrriah and Joral had spoken with several elders of the community, one even older than Jasson's grandmother (who was Arnath's daughter, they now knew). The ancient man remembered Trisha's swift wedding, remembered Jasson's grandmother being born soon enough that people had winked and smiled at how passionate Trisha's wedding night must have been.

"So the deed of land was a gift for his bastard," Rogett said dismissively. "It doesn't change the fact that his heirs—"

Beside him, Bellia made a noise, deep in her throat. A hint of a moan. She was, Syrriah guessed, one step ahead of him.

"The laws of inheritance," Syrriah said, "are clear. The more direct an heir, the greater the claim on the property. Arnath died without a will, and at that time, his closest heirs were his niece and nephew—your parents." She indicated Bellia and Rogett. "That's why the land was divided equally between them."

She glanced down at Jasson, biting back her smile. "Now we know there *was* a direct heir: Trisha's daughter, Wyn. Your grandmother. She rightfully has claim to *all* the land, not just yours. I would guess that she would be fine with you maintaining the property on her behalf."

Bellia had pressed her lips so tightly together, they'd lost all color. Rogett looked as though he would be sick.

Jasson looked stunned.

He cleared his throat. "Well. I . . . that's quite something to take in." He glanced at his wife. "I have no interest in taking away someone's livelihood and home," he said, now leaning forward to acknowledge the two people who'd tried to take away his own home. "I also don't have the manpower to work all three farms."

Bellia and Rogett started to look less panicked, but he continued. "I will ensure that proper and legal paperwork is drawn up to ensure the two families are given tenants' rights for as long as they are willing to maintain the lands," he said. "For a small annual rent."

:He seems like a reasonable sort,: Cefylla noted. *:I suspect he'll be reasonable in the rent he charges.:*

Syrriah bit the inside of her cheek to keep herself from laughing. *:I agree. But he's not above seeing them sweat a little, after all they've put him through.:*

Cefylla snorted. *:Get thee to the apothecary, my dove,:* she said. *:You've done enough sweating for the lot of them.:*

Sparrow's Gift
Michele Lang

Loneliness stalked behind Sparrow like a shadow. At the moment, though, she was too tired to run away from loneliness or anything else. Loneliness could pounce and grab her any time, but truly, she wasn't really alone. She'd never be alone again.

Sparrow stretched along a low divan in her little ground-level *ekele*, a sleeping Tis nestled against her breast. The lumpy old couch, a precious relic hauled to the Vale, reminded her of her home village of Longfall. Dust motes hovered in the air like golden sparks, catching the morning light, and she squinted to watch them dance.

The spring morning was silent, the couch was green-faded-to-gray and saggy, and yet this little hut in the heart of the k'Valdemar Vale was the most comfortable place she'd ever rested. Sparrow inhaled the intoxicating scent of baby neck, sensed his heart beating right above hers, and despite all her worries, she knew this moment, this place, as home.

Tis was four weeks old and still nowhere near sleeping through the night. His arrival had been very hard, in part because his father, Cloud Brother, had been called away on urgent Herald business just before Tis had been born. In his absence, Sparrow had been adopted by an unusually bossy *hertasi* named Rork, who had tended to the linens, the maternal feeding and watering. A Healer from Keisha's temple had seen to the delivery itself.

But otherwise, it was Sparrow and Tis, alone, with Rork

to attend to their material needs. And that was going to have to work for the foreseeable future.

A low rustle rose from outside the *ekele*, a susurration of wings beating against the thick foliage surrounding the clearing, where the hut stood a bit apart from its neighbors. The sound froze the blood in Sparrow's veins. The last time she'd heard such an avian racket, it was from a murder of crows, come to warn her of an elemental danger.

And now they had come again.

Sparrow took one last deep inhale, fortifying herself with Tis's scent. She slid off the couch sideways, still clutching her sleeping baby to her chest. In the last few weeks, Sparrow had perfected the contortions of a new parent desperate to keep her little one asleep.

Step one: slide to the floor, still horizontal, but able to mobilize the hard ground instead of the mushy sofa. Step two: slowly, agonizingly slowly, push up against the upholstered side of the couch to a sitting position, still cradling the sleeping baby to her heart. Breathe, check for continued sleep.

Then the challenge move. Step three: plant feet on the ground and use the (questionable) power of your legs alone to lift both you and baby to stand. Sparrow wobbled on step three, and her thighs screamed silently in protest, but she stuck the landing, and Tis slumbered on. Victory.

Gently, very gently, Sparrow shifted her arms to lift Tis higher onto her shoulder. Then she slid along the polished wood floor in her stockinged feet, in a water-bug glide she had learned kept him sleeping. Sleeping baby was the highest goal.

Well, not the highest. The most important goal, over her own life, was to keep Tis safe. The little paradise of her *ekele* had made his survival a much easier prospect. At least until now.

Now, surrounded by crows still unseen outside, Sparrow felt keenly the strain of her isolation. She remembered the last visitation of crows, a few years before, following her from her northern home village of Longfall all the way to the Vale, portending evil and danger.

The crows themselves were kind. But the news they had brought to Sparrow last time had brought her to her knees.

This time, she didn't know if she had the strength to receive their message—a new mother caring for her baby alone, without her heartmate, the Herald Cloud Brother. And now that she was a mother, she felt the absence of her own parents most keenly.

Her mother had died of mountain fever years ago, and her father, Hari . . . her funny, kind, loving father . . . had died only a few months ago. His death was a gentle one, tended by Healers more skilled and gifted than Sparrow, but she grieved his passing all the same.

The last time she had seen him, Hari had reached for her swelling belly and rested his gnarled, arthritic farmer's fingers against her skin. "Little mother," he whispered, his old nickname for her. "Take care of you, as well as the one within."

It was easy then to nod and agree, if only to ease Hari's passing. But now, his words and her agreement took on the aspect of a sacred oath, one that she had difficulty keeping.

Sparrow slid past her encroaching thoughts and reached the securely fastened door, leading directly outside to the lush, blooming Vale. She leaned off-center, then stretched out her left arm to unlatch the latch and pull the door open. Her heart pounded so hard she worried it would wake Tis, the galloping fear of it.

The door creaked, and Sparrow held her breath and glanced down at him. Tis stirred in her arms, his little face scrunched up, ready to cry. Then he burped, sighed, and settled back to sleep.

Sparrow started breathing again. Better for him to sleep through this next part, if she could manage it. She drew the door open wider, and her fear jolted into shock, then wonder.

The thick vines and shifting emerald canopy of trees reaching far above her head were dotted with crows, thick as currants in her mother's long-ago showbread. They waited for her to appear, swinging easily in the branches even as the greenery swayed under the weight of all of their graceful, coal-black bodies.

The spring sky shone blue, pure azure, behind them, and

Sparrow took a deep breath and focused on the clear sky above them all, vaulting high above whatever trouble had brought the crows to her door once again.

"Hello again," she whispered across the threshold. Sparrow did not have the Gift of Mindspeech, or sending, or the other graces of Hawkbrothers or Heralds. But she did have manners, and she knew better than to fear the messengers instead of their message.

How she wished that her heartmate Cloud Brother were here. She missed his silent strength, his gentleness. And in this moment, she also desperately missed his ability to pass into the clouds, to commune with spirits of the air. With Cloud Brother by her side, she would have been able to speak with the crows, and fly with them as well.

But she and her sweet little Tis were creatures of the earth today. And the creatures of air had come to her, not Cloud Brother. Somehow she would have to receive their message another way.

Hesitantly, she stepped out onto the pathway of black flagstones outside her *ekele*, her stockinged feet soaking up the morning warmth of the dark stones. She looked up at the horde, holding her new baby, and couldn't help smiling.

They were as magical as *dyheli*, as Karsite firecats, as Companions. But they were as common, as ordinary, as Sparrow herself. An ordinary kind of magic—her kind. Her brother and sister crows. Come to see the baby and bring her all the news.

One by one, they hopped down the length of woody vines and branches, fluttered down on black-dusted wings, until they clustered around her, at least fifty crows, bright-eyed and shiny black. They cawed and murmured to each other, but quietly, as if they didn't want to wake the baby either.

The largest crow, the size of a red hawk, alighted on the domed roof of her *ekele*, and Sparrow turned back to face him, only a few paces away from where she stood. Her white shift caught the wind and fluttered like a sail.

He tilted his fine dark head, opened his graphite-black beak in a bird-smile. Sparrow hugged Tis to her a little tighter . . . the crow was magnificent, but still his untamed boldness unnerved her.

Sparrow heard a soft rustling behind her, but she didn't dare take her attention away from the crow. With a mother's honed intuition, she sensed the creature approaching meant none of them any harm, and instead the rustle carried within it a quality of unhurried but definite purpose.

:*Are these winged creatures irritating you, my dear?*:

Sparrow's eyes watered with relief. Rork. He possessed an uncanny ability to appear whenever her hands got too full . . . she would never have made it this far without his help.

"Not at all, my friend," Sparrow said. "I know these visitors have come bearing news, but I can't understand them. By any chance, could you?"

Rork laughed, a low scratchy burble of amusement, and Sparrow's heart leaped in hope. Sparrow had no Mindspeech, but Rork certainly did. Perhaps at least he could receive the message the birds had carried to Sparrow from outside the Vale.

Rork stepped forward into Sparrow's line of vision. Tall for a *hertasi*, iridescent and plump, he was the closest to a grandparent little Tis had. She had only known him for a short time, but Sparrow had already surrendered her worries to him and his no-nonsense, bossy ways.

It had been a long time since Sparrow had had an elder around to boss and spoil her. She embraced Rork's calm mastery of all domestic arts, despite her own cooking and cleaning prowess. And now, she hoped he could decipher the urgent visitation of the crows.

Rork opened his beaky mouth, his dewlap flapping in the breeze, his jewel-like scales catching the morning sunshine. All Sparrow could hear was a low snort through his nostrils, but despite her lack of Gift, she sensed the *hertasi* and the crow were engaged in a deep and intense conversation.

Finally, after a long, wordless interval, Rork closed his mouth and swallowed hard enough for Sparrow to see. His eyelids blinked up twice, from under his bright amber eyes.

:*We are all in danger,*: Rork said, matter-of-fact and no-nonsense, as usual.

But his voice shook in her mind.

Sparrow startled, looking up at the crow on her roof. He

tilted his head and stared deeply into her with one bright, shining eye. At the edges of her thought, Sparrow felt an insistent tug, an urgent calling of need.

But she could not translate that urgency into words. She could not answer that call.

"Thank you," Sparrow said. She could not receive the crows' message, but she appreciated their effort and care all the same. Sparrow had learned better than to regret her lack of Gift, because all gifts came attached to sacrificial burdens. But she hated to be rude, and not being able to speak her friends' language seemed an inadvertent kind of thoughtlessness. She couldn't help her inability to speak, and she knew the crows understood her lack.

The crow reached along his powerful back, and plucked out a long tailfeather. He hopped to the very edge of the sloping domed roof, and gingerly Sparrow reached up a hand, her other arm still cradling the sleeping Tis.

The crow released the feather, and it danced haphazardly through the air, tossed about by the fair breeze. Despite its meandering path to earth, Sparrow managed to catch the feather in her trembling fingers.

It was still warm from the crow's body. She waved it at him, then tucked it behind her ear. "We will try to stay safe," she said, though she was pretty sure the crows could not understand her, any better than Sparrow could receive their message. "Thanks again for the warning."

The crow hopped higher onto the roof of the *ekele*, then beat the air with his powerful wings and ascended into the sky. In a whirling cacophony of calls and black wings, the host of crows rose in a swirling column and coalesced into an inky, winged cloud, one that tightened and flew above the canopy of flowering trees surrounding Sparrow's little corner of the Vale.

With a final echoing call, they flew away. And with their passing, all the nervous tension passed out of Sparrow's body, as if her vitality chased after them on their unknown trajectory.

She staggered back to lean against the doorframe of the *ekele*, and Tis stirred in her arms. Sparrow watched them fly away, and part of her wished she could fly with them, part of a great, unstoppable host.

But most of her was grateful to live on the ground, with her little, homely comforts surrounding her. Raising a newborn was hard work, and impossible from a lofty height.

Now that the crows had gone, the day seemed almost ordinary once again. "What was that?" she asked Rork. "How are we in danger?"

But Rork wasn't able to tell her anything more substantial. His Mindspeech was powerful and clear, but the message from the crows was meant for Sparrow alone, and without Cloud Brother by her side, she could not properly decipher it.

:I could not get the name of the danger, the details. They warned me of the Heartstone. The Heartstone, imagine it! From all I can tell, the Vale is protected, all is well. But you and the baby . . . well. Something big is brewing, like a storm. The crows wanted you to know the danger is serious and is real. Be alert and on your guard.:

A cold shock of recognition shot down Sparrow's spine. Before Cloud Brother and his Companion, Abilard, had departed for Herald business in Haven, he had hinted at trouble here at home, too, and in similar words.

Sparrow had known better than to ask why they had been called away. But Cloud Brother had warned her nevertheless. "The council at Haven is being convened because of a waver in the Heartstone here," he told her. "In a number of the northern Vales Heralds have sensed similar disturbances."

"You mean . . ." Sparrow couldn't bear to complete her thought.

Cloud Brother reassuringly squeezed her fingers, to mitigate the sting of his words. "We suspect a coordinated attack. I have spoken to the elders in charge of attending to the Heartstone here in K'Valdemar, to protect it. All the people who need to know, already know. But until I come back, Sparrow . . . please keep this to yourself. No need to alarm all the people in the Vale."

They spoke no more of it, and once Tis had arrived, her heartmate's words had faded into the background. But now,

Cloud Brother's words returned with the crows' warning, to surround the little haven she had created.

Tis squirmed in her arms, coughed and snurfled. He was going to cry in another few moments, she could tell. Either her fear had traveled down the length of her arms and passed to him through their tension, or he simply was hungry. Or cranky. Or in need of something she would need to figure out now.

It didn't matter, she realized, half-happy, half-weepy. Danger, no danger, Mage-level danger or a dirty diaper. Sparrow was already on guard. The crows were kind, but nothing had changed for her, not really. Mothers were always on alert.

So Sparrow remained ready.

The danger came at midnight, in a form Sparrow could never have anticipated.

Mothers of newborns know the phases of the night intimately. There is dusk, the time of great weepiness and crankiness. There is early night, when the best sleep can happen, one hour of early sleep worth two hours of late.

And then the midnight hour. When newborns get hungry, and lonely, and needy. Tis woke every midnight, nursed, got changed into a fresh new nappy, and went back to sleep like a little star fading into the dawn.

And then Sparrow held him, as she did each night, and watched him sleep, watched the long shadows his lashes sent across his cheek. She held him until her arms ached, and she listened to his soft breathing, and the night was soft and full of stars and magic.

Sparrow paid for the midnight hour at 3 a.m., when Tis got up next, but she didn't care. Midnight was her time, and she wrapped it around her shoulders like a soft velvet mantle.

The Vale was all but silent, with only the faint songs of lute frogs and nocturnal birds of paradise echoing through the trees. The crow's feather stayed tucked behind Sparrow's ear, nestled in her tangled hair, a talisman against evil.

She missed Cloud Brother the most in the midnight silence; she missed the warmth of his sleeping body, the loving shelter of his embracing arms. But in a curious way, she also felt the closest to her missing heartmate in the silence of midnight. She imagined him awake in Haven, missing her too, and their mutual yearning tied them close together.

So when Cloud Brother's spirit appeared at the threshold of the *ekele*, Sparrow was not all that surprised. His sending was sharp and true to life, his silver hair glowing in the moonlight, his eyes sealed shut as always, his long, slender legs encased in brilliantly embroidered trews.

Oh, he was beautiful, her heartmate. And he had come to her not in dreams but in her most vulnerable and openhearted moment, her midnight.

He opened his arms to her, and she wanted more than anything to leap into his embrace. But Tis slept on, and she knew that no matter how real his apparition appeared, Cloud Brother and his Companion Abilard remained bodily in Haven. On emergency business, business that compelled his attention both day and night.

A low prickle rose along the small of Sparrow's back and up between her shoulder blades. If Cloud Brother came to her now . . . in this way, more vividly than ever before . . . something was truly wrong.

Tending to the sick as a girl, and immersed in motherhood now, Sparrow had learned the value of patience as a virtue. Cloud Brother's sending was a great and frightening mystery, but the secret of it would be revealed in its own time. All Sparrow had to do was wait and not make the mistake of jumping to conclusions.

He held his arms out to her. *"You are so beautiful in the moonlight, Sparrow . . ."*

A lump caught in Sparrow's throat. Cloud Brother's words were a caress.

But they were false words.

"Who are you?" she asked, her voice surprisingly steady. "Because I know for a fact you are not my heartmate."

Blinded as a child, Cloud Brother's only vision was the true sight of the sky plane, and Cloud Brother had never looked at her on earth in their lives together as heartmates, had never remarked casually upon her beauty like this.

Cloud Brother's eyes opened, and Sparrow stifled a gasp. His eyes had been sealed by blindness many years ago. This

Cloud Brother was an imposter. And had he visited her in her sleep, Sparrow would have been easily fooled, taking his words as dream truth.

But she was awake, and this invader threatened the mama wolf in her lair at his peril. She wasn't afraid, but incandescently angry at this counterfeit being's violation of her baby's sanctum.

His false eyes were black and shiny, crow's eyes. *"You are my woman,"* he said, his voice rough now. *"You do not question me."*

The artifice had crumbled away just like that. Cloud Brother never spoke of her with possession or casual brutality. He and she walked together in beauty, heartmated for life. Possession had nothing to do with the love that they shared.

Alone, alone. The little mother faced this imposter all alone . . .

The word echoed in her mind painfully, mockingly.

Alone.

What could she do now? She had no Mage gift, no Companion to strengthen or Choose her.

Sparrow swallowed hard and forced herself to relax. Tis needed her to stay sharp. Anger kept her fear at bay, but anger by itself was not enough to repel her attacker.

But the crows had spoken true. This was war.

For such a nasty creature to invade the Vale, some basic facts had to be in play. The Heartstone . . .

Rork's words, and her beloved's, echoed painfully in her mind. The wards gathered around the Vale had failed somehow. Cloud Brother and Abilard had to be so embroiled in Herald business that they could not come to stand with her. Sparrow knew in the marrow of her bones that all of these elements were tied together with her solitary state.

She remembered the Change Adept Emptiness, who had invaded the Vale in a similar manner three years before, when Sparrow had first come to k'Valdemar. This false sending reminded her of him, of Emptiness, but in some ways, this was worse.

Because the sending now had impersonated her beloved Cloud Brother so effectively that the sight had fooled Sparrow at first. Long ago, the physical being of Emptiness had walked among them here in the Vale as a man, with a physical man's limitations.

A sending this vivid, in a place so fundamentally hostile to it? Whatever had manifested this sending had enormous, malevolent power. More than the errant Adept Emptiness had ever been able to summon.

Perhaps the coming of Emptiness had created a gap in the Vale's protection, some weakness for an invader to exploit. The northern reaches were always hungry for easier, more temperate territories to the south. And the Vale was a tropical sanctuary in the midst of a vast, almost impregnable forest.

The Vale was a jewel of inestimable price. And a thief had just appeared, through Sparrow's heart, her yearning, to strike at the home that she loved.

Her heart . . .

The Heartstone. The foundation of all the Vale. Sparrow remembered Cloud Brother's warning, and feared this creature's power was stoked by drawing off energy from the Heartstone itself.

If she was right, then the entire Vale, and all of Valdemar, was in mortal danger. Strange mutations of magic still emanated from the wilder regions of Velgarth, and of course she had been taught as a child of the evil Adepts of old, they who had preserved their spirits and lain in wait, seeking to possess a Mage willing to become their tool.

But Sparrow was the opposite of a great Fire Mage, a terrible vessel of destruction. She was a mama, a human *hertasi* among the northern folk. Sparrow enjoyed the quiet, enormous task of setting the world around her to rights, strengthening the life force of the people she loved.

Maybe this was the locus of her power? And this sending sought to possess the least, not the greatest, in the Vale? Perhaps the least of the Vale denizens would prove the easiest for an evil spirit to master.

Goosebumps pebbled up the length of her forearms. Sparrow took a deep breath. Time to test her theories and see if this ghost was as hungry as she feared.

"Begone. Go back to where you came from," she suggested, a little lamely. If only this situation could be solved that easily!

The sending laughed, a hard, ugly sound.

She steeled herself to press her point. "Really, it will end better for all of us if you just go back home."

"Home? I have no home! I am alone!"

His words, a mockery of her deepest, most secret fears, burned Sparrow's heart like a terrible acid. The Vale was beautiful and lush, the most easy and lovely place she had ever known. But it was not the northern village of Longfall, where she had been born, where her parents had raised her. Her beloved father, Hari, her home village as she had remembered it, both were now out of reach forever. She could never return to her first home again.

However, her sympathies didn't cancel out her determination to protect the Vale, her new, adopted home.

She nestled deeper into the lumpy couch, and the feather tickled her behind her left ear, where she had tucked it away. "Now, now," Sparrow chided him, the way she used to fuss at her older brother before he joined the army and disappeared from her daily life. "Just because you feel alone doesn't mean you are, in fact, homeless."

She spoke both to the dislocated being and to herself.

"You come from somewhere. Everybody does, okay? When a body's in pain, the first impulse is to draw away from a helping hand and try to bite it. I understand. Anybody who ever tended a sick critter knows the same. But you can choose your home, your belonging. And I say that if you choose your home, you will never be alone."

The sending smiled at her, a horrible sight superimposed over the face of her beloved Cloud Brother. *"I choose this place, I choose you for mine."*

Sparrow's heart fluttered in fear. The implications of accepting this being's choice filled her with a deep dread. Could accepting this hostile being prove a pathway to disarming him?

After a moment Sparrow pushed the thought away. She

didn't believe so, not when possession, not communion, was the entity's true goal.

Sparrow cradled Tis to her chest, and her rage melted away. She was never that great at righteous anger anyway.

After a moment, she made up her mind. "I am going to do a dangerous thing, visitor."

The sending did not respond, only crossed his arms and blinked his eyes in a way so unlike Cloud Brother, so impatient and hungry, that it made Sparrow laugh in the midst of her alarm. The illusion was so powerful, and yet it fell apart when Sparrow knew to question it.

She took another deep breath, sighed it out. Her strength lay in her authenticity, not in great shows of magical power. Sparrow was going to wield the power she had.

"This is my little baby, Tis. He has no power, none. See? He has the potential to become a great Herald or Mage, given his family and his home. But right now, he is an acorn. His job is to grow."

"His name is Thistle!"

The entity's words filled Sparrow with a terrible panic. She hadn't shared his full name with anyone, ever. For this sending to know her deepest secrets . . .

Sparrow feared now that the sending had already infiltrated her thoughts and soul. How else could it recreate Cloud Brother so perfectly? Know her deep fears of abandonment? Know the true name of her defenseless little son?

This sending was the shadow of Sparrow herself. The malevolent being had already possessed her!

A low wind rose in the *ekele*, as if the air grew thick with ghosts. The currents shook the crow feather loose from behind Sparrow's ear, and it danced in the air between her and the false sending of Cloud Brother.

She focused on the feather, not the invader. Patience would see her through. Sparrow had tended her mother through her last illness, and an echo of that helplessness and despair now passed through her and away.

It was patience and acceptance of terrible circumstances

that had gotten Sparrow through that time. Nothing had been as hard to bear since then.

But this was getting close. Her baby, her little acorn, was depending on her to protect him from this energy, this primal threat to everything that Sparrow loved.

The wind drew up higher, and Sparrow took refuge in it. With a shock of recognition she saw the faces of the Cloud Walker clan, her clan, twinkling like stars in the wind.

She was not alone. In fact, she had *never* been alone. Her clan, the little *ekele*, her love for Cloud Brother, all of this had surrounded her and protected her in a mantle of love.

She was working hard and guarding an outpost by herself. But at all times, she was enfolded in a tapestry of love, connecting clan, family, and home.

This strange entity, trying to possess and claim this tapestry for its own, did not want to transform into a mere thread connecting to the others. It wanted to take the tapestry for itself, add it to a hoard of other tapestries it had already claimed.

The energy that had appeared in the form of Cloud Brother was lost and disjointed, a parasite seeking a host not a home. Sparrow would have welcomed it in to join the tapestry, become part of the family. But it held itself apart, afraid to subsume itself into something bigger and more enduring.

:Hold steady, Sparrow! The Crows and the Walkers are both here! Don't be afraid.:

Sparrow's heart leaped at the words spoken in her mind, loud and perfectly enunciated. Ah, Rork, wonderful Rork. He had not forgotten her, of course he hadn't. He'd sensed the trouble brewing in her little nest, probably before Sparrow herself had, and had rushed to get help from both her own clan, the Cloudwalkers, and the Crow clan, who had honored her the last time the crows had come to her aid.

No Companion could be more steadfast and brave than that bossy, loving *hertasi*. Rork, her champion.

The wind rose into a storm in the room, rendering Sparrow breathless. The sending opened its mouth to scream, but no sound emerged.

"You are welcome to join us," Sparrow said, her farewell

to the invader. "But you can't be coming here just to claim and to destroy us. We won't let that happen."

Without Cloud Brother here, Sparrow could not rise into the wind to fight alongside their Cloudwalker Clan brothers, scouts and adepts swept into the inner storm. Cloud Brother's Gift granted her the ability to fly into the higher energy planes, but only when she was by his side.

Here and now, tethered to the earth, she did her part without him and his Herald's Gift, holding her baby close and protecting him with her own offering. The gift of love and his mother's arms.

A humble gift, but one profound and powerful as well, a gift that walked in ways a great Change Mage could never understand.

The gift of home.

The wind rose to a shriek, violently shaking the walls, and Sparrow bent her head over Tis's body to shield him from the battle. Awake, he wailed, adding his cries to the mayhem rising up against the invader.

The sending of Cloud Brother melted into a ball of white light, no features or sign of humanity remaining. And as Sparrow watched in growing fear, the ball vibrated, rose—

And hurled itself straight at her face.

The pain of the direct assault burned like fire. Sparrow gratefully released the pain and her consciousness as everything went black.

Had she died, gone to join her father?

Was she blinded now, like her beloved?

These panicky thoughts were the first signs that Sparrow still lived, and once she realized she was thinking again, deep down she knew that whatever had happened, matters would set themselves right again somehow.

With a great effort, she forced her eyelids open. Once she realized Tis was no longer in her arms, she jolted fully awake and struggled to sit up.

"One minute, hold on!" Liros Cloudwalker said, loud enough to burn through the fog in her mind. "Give yourself a chance to return, Sparrow. Your son is fine. All is well."

Sparrow's head pounded, as if the ball of evil energy had drilled a hole through her forehead. "But . . . what happened?" she forced out. She felt queasy and dizzy, amazed she was still alive after the pummeling she had just endured.

"You protected your home," said a voice from the doorway.

Sparrow blinked hard and focused. The swirl of light and sound coalesced into the main room of her little *ekele*, now crowded full of scouts and Mages from the Cloudwalker clan. Cloud Brother's friend Liros cradled Sparrow's head, and Rork ran back and forth from the storeroom in the back of the *ekele*, bringing blankets, and cool fruit nectar, and hats, frantically trying to restore order to his domain.

All of it was wonderful, all of it meant home. But that voice, quiet as it was, commanded her full attention.

Cloud Brother. Returned from Haven, after so long and so much.

"The council at Haven found the source of the trouble. The Mage here . . ." Cloud Brother paused, his voice husky.

Sparrow didn't care any more about the Mage, the threat. Together they had repelled the threat, at least for the time being. And Cloud Brother had come home. She could contend with just about anything, knowing he had returned.

He took a half-dozen steps forward, easily sensing his brother Adepts in the room and sliding around them to reach Sparrow's side. In his arms he held his son, baby-blue eyes wide open and calm in his father's arms, where he belonged.

"His name is Thistle? That was what Rork told me."

Sparrow could hardly speak past the lump in her throat. "You weren't here, my love, and I had to name him something! I call him Tis, but Thistle it is, and I don't mind to tell all the brothers in the clan, either. His name is safe with you all.

"After three days, his name came to me . . . a thistle will cling to you, pierce you, and you can find them everywhere, growing like weeds, right? But a thistle is beautiful, too, a golden tuft that you find everywhere. And any healer knows a thistle is a plant of great virtue, a healer of body and mind, and not rare or expensive, but open to all, growing in every open field."

Cloud Brother gently kissed the baby's jet-black hair. "He's a gift, for sure. And so are you."

"But what I don't understand, my love, is why the Mage was coming after me? And why did the Adept come three years ago? What do I have to do with anything? I am nothing special, no great Herald, no Queen. I hope that I am not some kind of magnet for bad or a weakness in the Vale!"

:Quite the opposite, dear child . . . :

It was not Rork, or even Cloud Brother who spoke now into her mind, but Abilard, Cloud Brother's Companion, speaking from afar, and as always, his words sent waves of warmth and peace through her body, along with their meaning.

:It is because you are no Mage that you attract the powerful. Often the powerful crave a safe place, a haven. Thank the Powers for your Gift, Sparrow! Without it, without home, where would any of us be?

:Your Gift is home.:

Harmless As Serpents
Rosemary Edghill & Rebecca Fox

From the moment his hooves first touched the grass in the Companions' paddock, Kenisant knew he was special. He was perfectly formed and beautiful, even more so than most Companions, and gifted (as he knew without a single flicker of doubt) with the sort of insight and sensitivity not vouchsafed to the common run of Companions. Clearly he was meant for great things.

So it was really no surprise at all that he had quickly grown bored with his young playmates in the herd. They were lesser creatures, and—goaded by what was almost certainly jealousy and envy—they never tired of tossing taunts at him: *Vain. Stuck up. Arrogant. Selfish.* He knew their words meant nothing, and really, such behavior was unbecoming to Companions.

It was just as well they left him to his solitary meditations; gods knew he preferred his own company to theirs. They were silly and boring and ill-mannered, and their rambunctious games were nothing more than a waste of time.

After a few weeks of wandering alone through the tall grass, gazing up at the sky and thinking, Kenisant came to understand something that had puzzled him for a long time. How could he, the most splendid and amazing Companion to have been foaled in generations, truly have been foaled at all?

And that was when he realized the truth that had been so cleverly hidden from him. He must be *Grove-Born*. It was the only explanation that made sense. His mother had only pretended to be his mother in order to conceal that fact from the others, lest their spite and envy be too much for his sensitive and generous spirit to bear up under.

Clearly that explained *everything*.

He decided not to embarrass his mother by letting her know he had seen through her well-intentioned charade. Someday, when he was grown and had found his perfect Chosen, he could gently let her know that her subterfuge had been both useless and unnecessary. He could even (now) pity his year-mates, who sensed the truth without knowing what they sensed. How ashamed and humble they would be once his true glory was revealed! He vowed to himself that when that day came, he would be generous and forgiving of their youthful blindness.

But when he magnanimously rejoined the ranks of his year-mates, willing to graciously overlook all their deficiencies, they drove him off with nips and taunts.

Go find your Chosen, Kenisant! That's probably the only one who will put up with you!

Of course, everyone knew you couldn't go on Search until you were all grown up. But now that Kenisant had so much time to think, he simply couldn't help wondering and dreaming about his Chosen. Surely that person would be the most perfect human to be found in all of Velgarth! Perhaps of royal blood—or maybe a great general who commanded armies!

He could see the future so clearly.

He would be on Search, of course (the youngest Companion ever to leave Haven; that much went without saying!), and he would meet his Chosen purely by accident, as he, Kenisant the Beautiful, selflessly and nobly saved a passing stranger from mortal peril. Perhaps he'd even battle a demon from Karse . . .

And his Chosen would gaze into his eyes and bow down to him, kneeling at his feet, saying, "Thank you, oh, glorious blessed one, who has appeared to me, who is unworthy!"

Naturally he would forgive his new Chosen everything, and return with him or her to Haven, where everyone in the Collegium, Heralds and Companions alike, would gaze in

astonished wonder at both Companion and Chosen and see
Kenisant's true glory at last . . .

But dreams of his glorious future could not comfort him for
long. And noble solitude, once it went on long enough, turned
out not to be nearly as much fun as the Bards' songs implied.

It was then that Kenisant had an absolutely brilliant idea
(which was only to be expected, since he was, after all, *him).*
Why wait another two years, or three, to be judged old
enough to go on Search? Why not leave now, at once? If he
was Grove-Born (and he was, of course), did the usual rules
even apply to him? In a few days—weeks at most—he could
return with his Chosen, and everyone who had been mean to
him would be stricken with guilt at what they'd done.

It was a *wonderful* plan.

Kenisant's plan seemed a lot less wonderful six weeks later,
as he galloped desperately toward a stand of trees, hoping
they would shelter him from the onrushing storm. Bad
enough to be pelted with wind-lashed rain and covered from
head to tail in cold mud, but this storm was no ordinary
storm. He could sense *Magery* in the roiling purple-green
clouds spilling over the top of the ridge, and that disturbed
him even more than not quite knowing where he was. (He
wasn't *lost,* of course: Kenisant the Beautiful never got lost!)

He knew perfectly well this storm should be impossible.
There were no Mages in Valdemar, and spells cast outside of
Valdemar couldn't cross its border.

But the aura of the storm made his skin prickle all over.
He laid his ears back and lashed his tail uncertainly. Would
the trees shelter him? Could he outrun the storm? Was there
better shelter to be had? He couldn't make up his mind, but
apparently his body did not require his advice: He found
himself bolting away from the ominous cloudbank with every ounce of effort he could muster.

It didn't help.

The light dimmed as if the sun were setting. Behind him,
wind roared and he heard the trees splintering with a sound
like winter ice breaking.

And then he felt nothing at all.

*   *   *

"I could be home in bed," Brother Junchan announced to his horse. His horse (who had listened patiently to the same complaint many times over the past sennights) was as unimpressed as ever.

"It's a nice bed," Junchan went on. "Warm. Dry. *Unmoving.*"

The horse flicked her tail at a fly on her flank.

Junchan sighed deeply. His warm dry bed would have to wait, probably for more sennights than he really cared to think about. He was here—for values of "here" that included "the middle of nowhere"—because had a job to do.

Junchan had been one of Solaris' loyal followers for a very long time. Even if he was far too pragmatic to believe Her Radiance could ever manage to do what she said she would someday do, oh, in his secret heart (the one most of his friends would swear he didn't have) he had *hoped* . . .

And that hope had been rewarded. Solaris was miraculously crowned Son of the Sun by Vkandis Himself, and she survived an inevitable "unfortunate accident" almost immediately afterward. While the populace of Karse preferred to think of Solaris's survival as a miracle, Junchan knew it was really because of the many long years her secret followers had spent preparing for just that moment.

Many of Solaris' circle had thought that once she gained the Sun Throne and survived long enough to prove that attempting to remove her would be a futile exercise, their labor would be at an end. But Junchan was a cynic (or as he preferred to say, a realist) by nature: he knew the *real* work was only just beginning. Radiance Solaris was still surrounded by the disarray of a priesthood turned corrupt and greedy, and the wreckage of the nation those priests had plundered for years. Even before her throne was secure, Solaris had turned to the task of rooting out those spoiled priests and undoing the damage they had caused. Of course (as Junchan could have told them), dealing with the false clerics only led to yet another problem: there were now gaping vacancies in the priesthood of Vkandis, and far fewer priests than there was work to do.

Theoretically, there were bodies to fill those holes. During Radiance Lastern's long reign, many of those most loyal to Vkandis Sunlord's teachings had fled Karse for other lands, most of them in fear of their lives. They would almost certainly be eager to return to Karse and serve under a true Son of the Sun.

Assuming Solaris could find them.

And so Her Radiance had set Brother Junchan to his task.

His current quarry was a middle-aged, thoroughly undistinguished priest named Ponious, who had served a tiny village called Stervewold until a Voice entered the Morningray Mountains intending to make a name for himself by rooting out heresy in Stervewold and the surrounding villages. Whether it existed or not.

The villagers, having been warned by Father Ponious, fled. Father Ponious, not being a complete lackwit, also fled. The villagers returned when Voice Typerus gave up and left.

Father Ponious (wisely) did not.

Brother Junchan was supposed to find him, tell him that there was a new Son of the Sun, convince him to return, and escort him to Sunhaven.

At least, aided by a large bag of gold and a good horse, Junchan made better time following Father Ponious' long-cold trail than the good father had blazing it.

Kenisant awoke from a very odd dream. He'd dreamed he was standing all by himself in a small boat that was drifting down the Terilee River while the land unspooled backward on both sides. When he awoke, it took him several minutes to realize he wasn't still dreaming, and several more to parse what he was seeing.

This was not the Terilee River. And he was not standing in a boat. He was lying on his side on a sledge, watching the world go by at knee height. There was something bulky wrapped around his right foreleg, and he had the sense of something . . . sticky . . . covering most of his body beneath the thin blanket draped over him. He thrashed, trying to get himself upright, and then discovered he was not merely *lying* on a sledge, he was *tied* to it!

There was forest and grass all around him (as far as he could see), but the sledge itself was being drawn along over a road covered in glistening white sand. Whatever was pulling the thing, it was silent and scentless. He couldn't imagine what it might be, and he thrashed again, trying futilely to reach the ropes with his teeth.

"Now, now, poor white horsey, you stay right where you are. Nothing bad is going to happen to you."

The speaker was walking on the wrong side of the sledge for him to be able to see her. His head wouldn't turn that far, and when he tried, he became suddenly aware that everything ached. All he could tell was that whoever was with him was female, young, and spoke with a strange accent Kenisant had never heard before.

:I am not a "horsey"!: he snapped indignantly. He had a sudden moment of stark terror: was *this* his Chosen? No, that simply was too horrible to contemplate. He would never be able to live down the indignity!

The woman giggled. "Prysane says you say you aren't a horsey! Of course you are, silly! And a talking horsey—that's even better!"

She walked around to the other side of the sledge, and now he could see her. She looked perfectly normal, except for the fact she had a very large snake with pale silver and gold scales resting on her shoulders and coiled around her throat.

:I am a Companion of Valdemar!: Kenisant said. *:Release me at once, or—:*

He actually couldn't think of an "or."

The snake raised its head and flicked the woman's ear lazily with its tongue.

"Poor white talking horsey," the woman said, sounding now as if she were trying to keep from laughing. "You wouldn't like it if I did, you know. But I'm going to make you all better again. And clean, too!"

She reached over to stroke his neck. The snake around her neck regarded him with flat bright eyes.

He could almost swear the thing was *laughing* at him.

*　　　*　　　*

It was another three candlemarks before they reached their destination. During that time, Kenisant had learned a number of really useless bits of information.

The girl's name was Indibar. Prysane was her snake—a moon-serpent, she said. Prysane could hear Mindspeech and apparently could relay it to his mistress, but he was selective about what information he passed on, and Indibar couldn't hear Kenisant directly. As he'd suspected, this wasn't Valdemar, but Indibar hadn't named the location, and Prysane had ignored all Kenisant's questions.

He couldn't convince anyone to untie him, and he couldn't break the ropes.

This was turning out to be the worst Search *ever.*

"Almost there!" Indibar said to him. She sounded cheerful. (She *always* sounded cheerful. It was really depressing.) He vowed that the moment she released him, he would run as fast as he could back to Haven. Not because he was scared (of course not!) but because he carried vital news: There was a snake-wielding *crazy woman* somewhere near their borders.

Queen Selenay would probably insist on presenting him with a medal *personally.*

This pleasant daydream occupied his mind until the sledge came to a stop. They were in a clearing in the middle of a vast forest. Just ahead, he could see a long low building that put him vaguely in mind of a pile of twigs crossed with a haystack. It seemed to be half house and half barn; there was an open doorway, a window with its shutters folded back, and, a little farther along the front, a set of wide tall doors that bore a faint resemblance to the stable doors back in Haven.

As he lay there, wondering what the madwoman would do next, a cat walked through the open doorway to greet them. It was bandaged around the middle and most of its fur had been singed off, but it looked cheerful enough. A raven with a splinted wing announced itself with a loud "caw" as it hopped up from somewhere inside the house to perch in the window, and a wolf with three legs and a bandaged stump where the fourth had been struggled to his feet from where he'd been napping in the shadows.

"See, horsey?" Indibar said. "You'll have plenty of company here until you get better!"

Was she a Healer? Or a mad wizard?

She knelt beside the sledge, beginning to undo the ropes that held him in place. "Now you stay right there once you're untied, talking horsey. You're hurt, you know, and I wasn't really able to treat you where I found you. So I'll have to do it here, and you'll have to help."

Kenisant snorted derisively. Did she really expect him to believe this nonsense? He might have a few bumps and bruises, yes, but Kenisant the Beautiful did not permit such trifling things to impede him. The moment he was free, he lunged to his feet.

But he was suddenly terribly off balance, and the wrapped leg buckled beneath him in a sickening fashion. The blanket had fallen free when he moved, and now he could feel the sting from the burns on his skin.

His vision went white with pain, and he fell to his knees.

:*What did you do to me?:* he demanded, trying not to sound as frightened as he suddenly felt.

"I *told* you to stay still," Indibar said, sounding irritated for the first time.

Worst Search *ever.*

The next two hours passed in a haze of pain and indignity, but at the end of it, Kenisant had been installed in one of the stable boxes attached to Indibar's home. A sling passing under his belly was attached to a turnbuckle in the ceiling. It had two purposes: one, to keep him from falling (or escaping, he couldn't help but think), and the other, to take part of his weight.

Whatever had happened during or after the Mage Storm had left him scratched, burned, and (nearly the worst!) with a broken leg. As if that weren't enough, his beautiful flowing silver tail was *gone!* It had all been burned away or torn loose until only the dock and a few singed and straggling hairs remained.

He looked *ridiculous.*

Of course Indibar told him she could fix him up good as new—but what if she wasn't telling the truth? *(How could she be?* a small part of his mind asked. *She blindfolded you before she took the bandages off. You haven't even seen your foreleg. What if nothing heals? What if you end up like that wolf you saw?)*

It was too terrible a possibility to contemplate. Of course, Companions died (bravely and gloriously) in battle. But that was different! What if he could never walk again—or run? What if he was going to look ridiculous for the rest of his life? His glorious future would be ended before it began! And no one would ever know what had happened to him. He wasn't even in Valdemar!

He wished, very hard, that his mother were here.

Father Ponius was wet and cold and hungry. By now, there were holes in the soles of his boots, and he had absolutely no idea where he was. But that was all right. There were two things he did know, and they were both good things: One, he was not in Karse. Two, the Fury Typuris had summoned to punish him hadn't caught up to him yet.

It was true that Ponius had never actually seen the Fury that followed him, but he knew it was dogging his footsteps just as surely he knew Vkandis was great and good and that water was wet. Typuris was a red-robe. Typuris didn't like him. Red-robes had the power to summon Vkandis' Furies. Q.E.D.

As it was common knowledge that Valdemar was protected by a boundary no demon could cross (other than the White Demons of Valdemar, of course; apparently they were a special case), he had first hoped for sanctuary there. But the thousands of invisible eyes that watched him night and day had soon disabused him of that notion. He'd crossed the border again as quickly as he could and continued eastward, never stopping in any town or village for longer than a day. If he were to tarry, the Fury might catch up to him, and Father Ponius was a kind and gentle man who did not wish others to suffer for his crimes.

It was no crime, he told himself stubbornly. *Vkandis is kind and merciful and reserves to Himself the power to sit in judgment! Nor does He delegate this power to wealthy Voices who presume to speak for Him!*

No matter how completely he believed that, his skin crawled a little each time he gave vent to such thoughts. The Voices might be presumptuous, but their power was as real as their interpretation of the Writ and the Rule was narrow.

He only hoped that someday the Fury would get tired of chasing him.

Kenisant soon realized he was a prisoner of war, and he made up his mind to conduct himself accordingly. He stopped using Mindspeech entirely, since the only one who could hear him was Prysane, who either couldn't or wouldn't respond and who always seemed to be laughing at him anyway.

Unfortunately, that didn't actually mean Indibar stopped talking to *him.* She chattered constantly. When she wasn't talking to him (and calling him *"Horsey"!*) she was singing under her breath. (He was wholly indignant at how soothing he found it.) In the mornings she brought him food and water and medicine (he tried to resist taking it but never quite succeeded). She checked the burns on his flanks and ribs and ran her hands over the splinted and bandaged leg, checking (as she insisted on telling him) for fever. Not for the first time, he almost found himself wishing the mad Healer really *was* his Chosen. At least he'd have someone to talk to then. He'd never been alone before, or in a strange place. If—*when*, he told himself firmly—he made it back to Haven, he swore he'd never complain that it was boring again.

Kenisant the Beautiful is brave and fearless and needs no one! he told himself. And for the first time, the words rang hollow.

"I hate demons," Junchan remarked to his horse. "I don't care if you call them Vkandis' Furies, or Dark Servants, or my Aunt Jaeline—they're demons, and they're trouble."

His horse snorted and pranced anxiously, as unhappy about the faint lingering smell of ozone and what might be the remains of clawed footprints scorched into the forest floor as Junchan himself. "Yeah," he said, stroking his horse's neck soothingly. "Me too."

Though Junchan was only a Lay Brother of Vkandis—and thus possessed exactly as much Magery as his frequently invoked and possibly mythical aunt—he knew a great deal *about* Magery. Quite enough to read the signs and know that Typuris had set a demon on Father Ponious' trail. If he'd had a low opinion of the Voices to begin with (and he had), he had an even lower opinion of (now ex-) Voice Typuris. It was hard enough to control a demon within Karse's boundaries (so he'd been told). It was, apparently, nearly impossible to do so if one had sent it on an open-ended wild goose chase with no deadline.

And while Solaris had banished all demons from Karse at the same time she'd swept the Priesthood clean of its demon-summoners, her power extended only as far as Karse's borders. Which meant, unfortunately, that the demon who was clearly still following Father Ponious had not conveniently evaporated. If only Junchan could be so lucky!

Junchan had absolutely no notion of what he'd do when he caught up to it. He only hoped Her Radiance had prepared for this eventuality as she'd prepared for so many others.

And he prayed earnestly to Vkandis that the demon wouldn't catch up to the wayward Father Ponious before Junchan did.

"I hate demons," he repeated unhappily. His mount sighed gustily in agreement.

"Good morning, horsey! I've brought you a present!" Indibar said as she walked into his stall. It was the start of Kenisant's second sennight of captivity, and in addition to the now-familiar pails and the large canvas bag of medicines, she had what looked like a long bundle of rag strips slung over one shoulder (and over Prysane, too; he hoped the serpent found it annoying). Even before beginning her now-familiar routine, she walked around behind him. He startled in confusion when he felt her tying something to what remained of his tail, but she just kept on tying.

"There!" she said in satisfaction. "It took me a while to make this, and then I had to wait for the burns to heal enough. But this will help until your tail grows back."

He swished his tail experimentally, trying to look behind himself and *see*. Out of the corner of his eye he caught sight of the ends of the bundle of rag strips softly thumping against his flank.

She'd turned him into a *mop*.

He couldn't even manage to summon up the appropriate level of indignation.

But after the morning routine was complete, there was another surprise in store for Kenisant—this time a welcome one.

She loosened the rope until Kenisant was supporting his entire weight on his three good legs, then reached around to unhook the sling and pulled it free. "There you go, horsey!" Indibar said. "Just stay off the left fore. In a day or so I'll take a look at it to see how it's healing." She took a handful of his mane and stared into one eye. "Do *not* go running off," she said firmly. "If you break it again before it heals . . . well, that would be bad."

:Is that what happened to the wolf?: he asked before he could stop himself.

Indibar cocked her head, obviously listening to Prysane relay his words. She frowned.

"No," she said quietly, in a different tone than any he'd heard her use before. "His leg was caught in a trap. He chewed it off to free himself. All I could do for him after that was keep infection from setting in." She took a deep breath, and resumed her expression of determined cheerfulness. "Now go and have fun, nice white horsey—it's a nice sunny day!"

Kenisant limped cautiously out of the stall and toward the open doorway. It was indeed (just as Indibar had said) a nice sunny day. But even the ignominy of his false tail couldn't keep him from brooding over what she'd said.

With his new freedom, he cautiously explored his surroundings. Indibar's house was set at the edge of a pocket meadow surrounded by tall pines. Beyond the trees, the horizon was edged by imposing mountains, their upper terraces still white with snow. A stream ran behind the house, its water icy and pure. Clearly its source was somewhere in the mountains. He felt very proud of himself for deducing that, but the feeling of accomplishment quickly faded. It was something anyone would know. It wasn't *special.*

He'd always prided himself on knowing things no one else did, on having a superior intellect and limitless powers of deduction. But if that were true, he would be able to understand what was happening now. He'd know who and what Indibar and Prysane were. He'd know how to get *home.*

He didn't know any of those things.

He didn't even have the faintest inkling of where he was. This place didn't look like anywhere he'd ever heard of, and he thought he knew at least *something* about all the lands that surrounded Valdemar.

He couldn't even ask Indibar to take him back to the place she'd found him—or rather, he could, but he suspected it wouldn't do him any good. The Mage Storm he'd failed to outrun had clearly flung him a great distance from where he'd been, which was already outside Valdemar's borders. Was anyone looking for him? Did his mother miss him? Or were they all just glad he was gone?

(He thought he might know the answer and tried to pretend he didn't.)

But at least he could look around and see what was here. He turned away from the stream and began exploring again. He discovered there was a simple mews holding hawks and owls, a kennel-like shelter for wolves and dogs and even foxes, and hutches for rabbits and squirrels. All showed signs of carefully tended injuries, and for the first time, he wondered just what Indibar *did* out here all by herself. Cared for injured animals, yes—but surely she did more than that? Where did the hay and grain he'd devoured so thoughtlessly come from? The meat for the others? The bandages and medicine?

He'd never wondered about things like that before.

There were even some horses here (those lowly creatures he and the other Companions only distantly resembled). A blind gelding, his muzzle going gray with age, whose constant companion was a small brindled goat. An ancient sway-backed gray mare, who stepped cautiously, as if her feet hurt her. A skittish bay stallion whose neck was covered with rope scars and whose loins and haunches were criss-crossed with layer after layer of barely healed scars. That made Kenisant shudder a little. Lowly though horses might be, *no* creature deserved to be treated the way the stallion clearly had been. There was a hay-filled manger beneath a simple shelter, and they (as every other bird and beast he'd seen here) were clearly free to leave at any time.

But there was no one here he could talk to.

By now, familiar lands had long since given way to country Father Ponious didn't recognize even from stories. The countryside he walked through was heavily forested, and every breath he took was sharp with the scent of pines. The air was full of unfamiliar birdsong. Imposing mountains, their snowy tops lost in the clouds, dominated the horizon. He thought they might be the Icewall Mountains, but he hadn't exactly packed a map when he fled from Typuris' Fury. Ponious wished he could pause long enough to appreciate the landscape, but he knew he didn't dare stop moving. The Fury was gaining on him. He could feel it.

The only mercy was that this place—wherever it was— seemed to be as sparsely populated as the rocky highlands of Karse. He'd seen a handful of tiny farmsteads, with houses and outbuildings that looked as if they'd been woven of grass and wood like enormous baskets, but that was all. For that, he breathed a quiet prayer of thanksgiving to Vkandis.

Three days later, Indibar removed the splint and bandages from Kenisant's leg. When he cautiously set his hoof to the ground, cramped and long-disused muscles protested, and he shook his head in dismay.

Indibar patted him on the neck. "You need to exercise it gently to get its strength back. And nothing faster than a walk. Not for a while. But soon enough you'll be sound enough to run."

:Please thank the Lady Indibar for me,: Kenisant said to Prysane. It hardly mattered that he'd be able to run—he had no idea where to run *to*.

Indibar patted his neck. "Cheer up, white horsey! We'll figure out what to do when the time comes."

He had no answer for that, even if Prysane were willing to pass one on. What if he had to spend the rest of his life here? Once, he would have conjured up appealing daydreams of Kenisant the Beautiful imprisoned, enslaved, suffering all torments with a meekness of spirit and a shining nobility so great that all who looked upon him would realize what he truly was—a Companion of Valdemar!—and weep with shame over their part in his mistreatment.

But at some point over the last few sennights, that fantasy had lost its power to soothe him.

Day followed day, and soon Kenisant had been with Indibar for nearly a full moonturn. As the moon had waxed toward the full, her human visitors had increased, coming by twos and threes to her rambling house. Some brought injured beasts, both wild and tame, for tending. Others brought gifts of food. No matter what they brought or why they came, each stayed for only a few candlemarks, then went on their way, with Kenisant none the wiser about what they were doing. Some of the injured animals stayed after they were healed. Some left, vanishing back into the forest. Some departed in company with one of the human visitors. And no matter what else Indibar babbled on about (the woman seemed to take silence as a personal affront), she did not tell him anything he wanted to know.

He should go. His leg was sound now—he'd even done an experimental gallop or two. His tail was starting to grow back. In another few moonturns, there would be no sign remaining of his injuries. He knew that he should at least *try* to find his way home. At least in Valdemar, they'd know what he was. And perhaps—if he ran into a Herald and Companion riding Circuit—he could ask the way back to Haven.

But he was oddly reluctant to leave.

*   *   *

By now Kenisant knew the morning routine well. It rarely varied. Indibar made her rounds, tending injuries and feeding her guests. After that would come her own household chores, and once they were done, she would come back to spend time with those who were under her care.

But today, she'd barely gone back inside her house before emerging again, wearing a long, gray hooded cloak and carrying a walking staff. She'd cinched a wide belt over her tunic, and it was heavy with filled pouches. Prysane was (as always) coiled around her neck, but this time the snake looked far less sanguine and relaxed than usual.

:Where is she going?: Kenisant demanded. It almost seemed that Indibar didn't know that herself: she stood in the center of the clearing for a long moment, turning slowly in place as if she were listening for something. *:What's going on?:*

Prysane didn't answer, and a moment later, Indibar strode swiftly away.

Kenisant followed.

"Go back," Indibar said, stopping to face him. Her expression was grave, and her voice held an edge of something that could almost be fear. "Go back and wait for me."

Kenisant shook his head in frustration. She couldn't Hear him, and Prysane (obviously) wasn't talking. His only argument was physical: he stepped past her and stopped, looking back.

"There's nothing you can do!" Indibar said sharply. "This isn't Valdemar, and I'm no Herald. Go home!"

He stared at her in astonishment. She knew who he was. She knew *what* he was. Had she known all along? It made no sense. And if she did, then *why . . . ?*

She strode past him, ignoring his stunned expression.

He wasn't going to learn anything standing here.

He followed her.

His luck had finally run out.

Father Ponious knew he wasn't supposed to believe in luck, in chance, in fortune, in anything but Vkandis' providence and loving and all-knowing guidance. And he *did* believe.

Nevertheless, his luck had run out.

Ever since the moon had begun to dwindle toward dark, each day had brought a new and growing sense of unease. He had hoped and prayed that Typuris, or the Fury, or both would lose interest in chasing one small and insignificant village priest.

Apparently they hadn't.

He'd kept going, knowing it was hopeless, but hoping to reach some wholly uninhabited place. Somewhere with no tiny farmsteads with their basket-woven barns and houses. Somewhere with no roads or fields or orchards. Somewhere he would be the only victim of the Dark Servant. The thought that it might still *exist* after it had slain him was intolerable. With its task complete, it must vanish. Mustn't it?

At last, exhausted and as far as he could get from any road or trail before his strength gave out, Ponious dropped to his knees in the midst of the forest and bowed his head in prayer.

There was nothing else he could do.

Indibar hurried, straight as an arrow, along a trail only she (so it seemed) could see. She'd given up trying to send Kenisant away, as if the need for haste trumped anything else. All Kenisant could think of was that there must be some forest creature who needed her, and if that was true, he could certainly help—by carrying it back to her home, if nothing else. Small enough repayment for all she had done for him.

"Ah," she said sadly, as they stopped.

Over her shoulder, Kenisant could see the small clearing beneath the great trees where a man in tattered black robes knelt, hands clasped and head bowed. At the sound of her voice the man looked up, and then sprang to his feet. He stared at Indibar (at *him?*) in horror. (As much horror as Kenisant stared back with, but . . . no. This man was not his Chosen.)

"Go away!" he shouted. "Flee, for the love of Vkandis! I am pursued by demons!"

"Vykaendys would not permit such," Indibar said firmly. "Not here." Though she gave the name an odd pronunciation, it was perfectly clear to Kenisant who she meant—and apparently also to the man who faced them.

That, at least, would account for the horrified look the little man had given him.

It didn't seem to help. "Go!" the man pleaded. "You and the White Demon with you! Pray that the creature who follows me seeks only my life!"

"I promise you—" Indibar began.

It doesn't matter.

The realization was enough to rock Kenisant where he stood. It didn't matter which of them was right, or even if both of them were. This was what he had been born for. Not for glory and fame. *This.* To serve, to protect, wherever he was called to do so. And at last he could admit the truth to himself: He hadn't "gone on Search." He'd *run away*, because nobody in Haven would play with him, and now he'd never have the chance to be fitted with a Companion's harness and go to seek out the one who would help him serve Valdemar. It was his duty and his destiny, and he'd thrown both away out of vanity and pride.

But right now that didn't matter. He could still do his duty, even if no one ever knew what he had done.

He stepped around Indibar, stepped past the black-robed man, and stood among the trees facing in the direction from which the man had come.

:Go,: he said to Prysane. *:Tell them to go. I've got this.:*

He stood, unmoving, not looking back, until he heard both of them leave. Then he hung his head, grateful there was no one here to see his fear. He could do nothing against the power of a demon save fight with hooves and teeth. And he would surely die.

But at least he would buy the others time.

Junchan gave up and led his mare after the trail vanished into the trees; he couldn't find the signs he needed to track from his saddle, and if he overshot them, he'd have to spend marks circling his own trail until he found them again—assuming his horse hadn't simply trampled them until they were unrecognizable.

He had only the vaguest notion of where he was— somewhere west of Hardorn, maybe. He didn't recognize this forest, and while he assumed the towering mountains on the horizon were the Icewall Mountains, he'd only heard about them in stories. The sun-disk he wore was his only guide. For all he knew, Father Ponious' destination was the Icewall Mountains themselves—or what lay beyond them, if anything did.

He tried not to think about what else was following his wayward priest's trail, or about the fact that the closer he got to Father Ponious, the closer he got to *it*.

Junchan knew perfectly well that Solaris didn't want blindly devoted followers who would set aside their own judgment and rush headlong into mortal danger just because she commanded it. He knew as well as any that she was mortal, and human. That she did not, and never would, speak in Vkandis' name—Vkandis spoke *through* her when He chose. It was Vkandis who was omnipotent and infallible, not His mortal avatar. It was entirely possible that Solaris hadn't known about the demon sent after Father Ponious—or if she had, thought it had ended along with the long reign of the black-robed Priest-Mages.

And so, Junchan wasn't galloping blindly into danger armored with the conviction that Her Radiance knew everything and would not let him come to harm. He was going to take a good solid look at the danger and use his best judgment. It would be a damned shame if he'd spent this much time chasing Father Ponious to the far ends of Velgarth only to see the man die at the hands—or claws—of a demon.

But so far, all Junchan had seen was an oddly shaped scorch mark on the forest floor. It was straight as an arrow-shot and only a thumb-width wide. A faint hint of ozone hung in the air, and the forest-litter beneath it was charred, but there'd been no fire.

He walked on, and soon he saw a swan-white glimmer through the trees. When he reached it, he realized it was neither swan nor horse. It was a White Demon of Valdemar—which, by one of Solaris' first decrees, had become the slightly misguided but noble-minded allies of Karse.

Junchan tried not to get too hung up on politics.

"I don't suppose you can talk?" he asked with resignation.

The Companion fidgeted at him, shaking its head in a meaningful way. Not a grown stallion, Junchan realized. A yearling at best, too young to ride. (Not that he'd ever consider getting on the back of a White Demon anyway.)

"Well, that's a shame," Junchan said. "My name is Junchan. I serve Her Radiance Solaris, Son of the Sun. I don't suppose you've seen a priest around here anywhere? Little man, about so high, bald on top? Probably looks a little threadbare, by now. Being chased by a demon? Not you, of course," Junchan added hastily. "An actual demon, something one of the Voices whistled up. No? Well, I'll just have to keep looking, then. You're welcome to come along, of course. But I've got to tell you, you're a long way from home. Border's over that way," Junchan said, gesturing theatrically. "I think we might be in Iftel. But who knows?"

Kenisant followed the stranger—Junchan—and his horse, thinking that perhaps the wondertales and songs he loved might not be accurate after all. No Bard had ever declaimed a tale of unnecessary heroism or of a death-defying battle that . . . just didn't happen. If they had, who would listen?

All he'd seen while he stood waiting to meet the demon was a brief flash, like a flicker of lightning, and then, maybe half a candlemark later, this rough man came walking out of the trees, leading a concerned-looking bay mare.

Life doesn't care whether you pay attention or not, he thought, and felt very wise. *Life just* is.

And so he followed Junchan back to Indibar's home, and waited to see what would happen next.

"I won't say you didn't have good reason to hotfoot it out of Karse," Junchan was saying. He and Father Ponious and Indibar were all sitting at her kitchen table drinking tea, and Kenisant had stuck his head in through the window, listening shamelessly. Neither Indibar nor Prysane seemed to mind, and the priest and the lay brother were studiously ignoring him. "But I will say, you won't even recognize the place now that Radiance Solaris is in charge. She's making a lot of changes. That's why she sent me to find you."

"But what about the demon?" Father Ponious asked. "You can't mean to say that I was *imagining* it all these moon-turns?"

"I saw as many traces of it as you did," Junchan answered, sounding confused. "And then it just . . . stopped."

"I don't think any demon would choose to come to a fane of Kalanel Moonqueen," Indibar said, sounding amused. "But I think it is even more likely that Vykaendys's Shield stopped it. And rather permanently, unless I miss my guess. But of course, any devout follower of Vykaendys may enter His lands at will."

"'Vykaendys' . . ." Father Ponious said in astonishment. "Surely you don't mean to say *Vkandis* is worshipped here in Iftel?"

"Vykaendys and Kalanel both," Indibar said readily. "What is the sun without the moon to show its glory? Or the moon without the sun to make it bright?"

"Fine!" Junchan said. "But it hardly explains what *he's* doing here," he said, jerking a thumb in Kenisant's direction. "He belongs in Valdemar, with all the rest of them."

"And you will take him there on your way back to Karse," Indibar said. "As for how he got here, well, I think he must have lost his way for a while. But he has found it now. Haven't you, nice white horsey?"

She beamed at him. And Kenisant, if it had been within his power, would have blushed.

The Apprentice and the Stable Master

Brenda Cooper

The door to the room Marala shared with her mother swung open and banged against the wall. "Come quickly," the servant boy, Linal, hissed to her. She knew him by sight and name, but they were not friends; he worked and slept in the main house. He spoke fast, his voice tight with stress. "The new lord fell from his horse."

"What happened?" Marala's mother, Kris, put down her knitting.

"I think the horse threw him. I didn't see it, but I heard it—he screamed like a five-year-old. The stable-master demands that you come as fast as you can."

"We're coming." Kris took a green tunic from a hook by the door and belted it over her olive-drab dress. She glanced at Marala, her green eyes clouded with worry. "I may need help. You're ready to assist."

Marala nodded. Ever since she started showing some of her mom's talents as a Healer, she'd been practicing on the myriad small ills and injuries that occurred commonly in the servant's lives. She'd never been allowed to help anyone except the servants, and a little flutter of excitement filled her.

"Come here." Kris pulled a light green kerchief from a shelf and leaned over Marala, the silky material fluttering in her palm. She fastened it around Marala's neck with a small pin in the shape of a circle. "I've been saving this for you."

Marala touched the scarf, which was a finer silk than most

things the servants were allowed to own in the keep. "Thank you."

Kris smiled back and turned toward the door. "Are you ready?"

Marala used her fingers to fluff her thick red hair. "Yes."

"Hurry up!" Linal hissed. "The Lord Daving demands you now, and Norsk looks ready to kill something."

"We're almost ready," Kris replied calmly. A shadow seemed to pass across her face as she looked down at Marala, who was now just a head shorter than her mom. A smile replaced the shadow quickly, and she whispered, "Do only what I ask you."

"Of course."

"And don't question Lord Daving."

Marala merely nodded, worried at the nerves that would make her mother remind her of something everyone knew. How many nights had she sat huddled in the rafters of the barn outside the ring where the servants were beaten for the slightest offense? She had never been beaten, and she never wanted to be; she couldn't imagine arguing. Hopefully she wouldn't need to. The new lord was young, just returned from a foster after the death of his father in a hunting accident on a neighbor's land. Marala had never met him, but she'd heard no good of him, not even from when they were both small. But surely he was too young to cause much trouble?

Kris grabbed her basket of herbs and simples and handed it to Marala. She nodded to the visibly relieved Linal. "Go on."

He led them out to the central yard of the Keep. Stone walls and stone buildings surrounded a vast yard, which had been cut up with short walls to make fields for grazing, for drilling at arms, and for growing food.

They hurried. Kris's long brown hair swung below her waist in a braid fastened with a healer's green band. Marala clutched the herb basket to her breast. The flutter of fear that beat at her insides surprised her. She knew Kris was good. Lord or not, this was merely a fall from a horse. A sprain or break, and surely within her mother's skills.

Norsk stood on top of a low wall, arms folded, his long black beard resting on his somewhat ample belly, watching them approach. When they got close, he bellowed, "What took you so long?"

Linal started to speak, but her mother cut the boy off and said, "Go home. You did your work." She looked at Norsk and spoke carefully, but with power, as if taming a fractious dog. "We came as quickly as possible. Please show me the patient?"

Anger still tightened the man's face, but he said, "This way," and led them into a barn where a thin man sat with both hands hugging his left leg to him. His right leg extended out, the ankle looking like a great, big ball with red blood bruising already starting on the outside. The slightest ghost of a brown beard had started on his chin, the individual hairs so thin she could barely see them. His face was tight with pain. "Fix me," he demanded.

Kris knelt, looking the injury over without touching it. "You fell from a horse?" she asked.

"What do you care?" the young lord snarled.

Marala winced, but Kris showed no outward reaction. "It will be easier to help you if you tell me what happened."

He stared at Kris, challenging. "The horse fell. I jumped free, and there was a stupid rock in the way, and I landed on it, and it tilted so my foot went wrong."

Kris smiled her calming Healer's smile. "Did it make a cracking sound?"

"No."

"That's good."

Lord Daving seemed to be calming a little, which eased Marala's worry a little. "What compress shall I make?" she asked.

"What would you choose?" Kris asked in return.

"Cat's Claw and Broam Root?"

Kris smiled. "That will do." She glanced at the boy. "How bad is the pain, Lord Daving?"

"I can manage it." Daving clenched his jaw tight.

Marala's hands plunged into the basket, knowing which pouches to reach for from memory. She spread out a square of white cloth and poured the herbs into it, and then crushed it between her palms to release the scents and oils.

Kris knelt over the ankle and leaned down to peer closely.

"*Now*," Lord Daving demanded, "I have to dance tonight. I'm announcing my engagement, and I will need to dance with my betrothed."

Marala had not heard that news, and it seemed early. He had just returned a few days ago and was surely still in mourning for his father. Not that it was her business.

"I'm a Healer," Kris said. "Not a Mage. Even after I'm done with this, you'll need rest. If your young lady is kind, she'll understand."

Marala added water and pressed the compress between her hands again.

"My foster family's Healer could handle this in five minutes. And he'd make me good enough to dance."

Kris raised an eyebrow. "Is he here?"

"Just hurry!" the boy growled.

Marala muttered softly into the cloth, "Help and heal, do the patient well." She held the finished compress out to her mom, pleased that her hands didn't shake.

Kris took the herb-infused cloth and set it gently over the boy's ankle. He winced but said nothing. She curled her hands around the swelling and the cloth and closed her eyes, her face falling into her calm Healer's trance. For a few moments, nothing happened. Birds twittered above them.

"Ouch!"

Kris grimaced, but kept her hands in place.

The boy jerked his leg back. "That hurts."

"Of course it hurts. Give me the leg."

He glanced up at the man, who said, "Let her work." Both men looked angry, which made no sense at all. Kris was doing her best, and whether or not she could heal him enough to dance, she *could* make him better.

Marala whispered to Lord Daving. "It's easier if you give her room and time. Would you like a stick to bite on?"

He seemed to notice her for the first time, and he smiled. She didn't like the smile much, and she leaned back a little away from him. He reached for her arm and pulled her toward him. "You're wearing green. You heal me."

Kris hissed and sat up, abandoning her attempt to help for the moment. "She is not yet fully trained."

"I want to see what she can do," he replied, his voice cold. Kris spoke louder, "She is not ready."

Marala wanted to protest, but the look on her mom's face stilled her tongue. Did her mom know something she didn't?

Daving snatched his leg back and kept Marala near him, his dirty fingernails digging into her.

Norsk looked down at them and grimaced. "Let the girl try."

Even though Kris' voice was calm, a muscle in her jaw jumped and fluttered. "I have far more experience."

"You'll do what I say." Daving's voice sounded shrill and spoiled.

His fingers dug into Marala's arm. She glanced at her mom, and at the man and back to the boy. She should be able to do this. Her mom had reminded her not to argue with the lord before they left, but here *she* was, arguing.

The look on Daving's face made Marala afraid for her mom. She spoke, doing her best to imitate her mother's manner with Norsk earlier. "I will try."

Daving let go of her.

Kris scooted away, finding a place where she could watch all three of them. Her face was an emotionless mask, but Marala sensed anger and regret. There was no time to think about that now.

She gestured, and Daving extended his leg again, in front of her and between her knees. The compress had fallen off. She used a deep, shuddering breath to calm her racing heart and to quiet her fears, and then rubbed her hands together to generate heat and closed her eyes, whispering, *"Give me strength, give me heat, give me healing."* Her hands fell to either side of the injury. Even before she touched it, she felt the hot anger of the wound. Keeping her eyes closed, Marala moved her hands in to cup the swollen ankle, meeting its heat with heat of her own.

At that moment, it was her and the ankle and nothing else. Not her mom, not the angry Stablemaster, not even the boy. She felt the swelling but left it, went past it, searching for the damaged ligaments. The sprain was high, and the tear almost complete. If he twisted it standing up or took a wrong step, he might finish the job he'd started and require a surgeon's hand. She or her mom could strengthen something that had been harmed, stitch together a slight tear, and clean infections, but they could not create new tendons or magically pull a snapped tendon to where it needed to be. She had to do this right, and she had never healed a worse sprain. Especially not a Lord's sprain.

Marala lost her composure, taking in shuddering breaths and shaking.

She paused for a deep breath, feeling the ground under her knees and her curled feet. She called to its warmth and power, to its strength. The ground held them all up, the ground fed the trees and the grasses, which in turn fed the rabbits and vegetables and chickens, the ground was clean and powerful. With the briefest and lightest demand, she tugged some of the ground's energy into her, feeling it gather in her solar plexus like the tendril of a pea vine. With her next breath, she stabilized it and cut it free. It writhed in her stomach, hot and hungry to be used.

Her mom put a hand on her back. Support perhaps, or warning. Either way, Marala barely felt it. She focused, imagined, and blew out a long steady breath, sending the energy down her arms and through her palms into the damaged tendon. She felt it find its target and encouraged it to knit the ripped edges of the ligament together.

The boy screamed and pulled his ankle back.

Shocked, Marala's eyes flew open and met the anger in Daving's eyes. "It was working," she said.

The lord stared up at the Stablemaster. "No. No, it didn't work. It shouldn't hurt."

"Of course it hurt!" Marala cried out in protest. "It was working."

Her mother's hand tightened on her tunic.

"Beat them," Daving said. "And send to the neighbors for a real Healer."

No! Anger practically forced her to stand up. "I would like to see you stand up. I bet you can." She had helped him. She knew it. She had felt it. The energy had not come back into her; it had finished its job with him. She spoke as softly as possible, a soothing speech. "Healing well makes fast changes in tissue. That can hurt greatly, my Lord."

His eyes narrowed.

She held out her hand.

He stared hard at her, his eyes nothing but challenge.

She didn't care. She kept her hand out, kept watching him, daring him to let her help him stand. Time dragged.

If he didn't take her hand, they would be beaten. She forced two words through her thinned mouth. "I'm sorry."

He reached for her hand and she grasped his, which was hot and a little slimy. He grimaced but then set his foot down gingerly and shifted so he was putting at least some weight on it. He stared down, lifted it and set it down, lifted it and set it down. He took a tentative step. "It's still huge."

"Of course it is," Kris said. "The swelling will go down with time."

"I cannot go to my engagement like this," he said. He looked over at the Stablemaster. "Lock up the woman. Bring the girl to me afterward. She did the most for me. She can work on it more before dinner."

Kris stepped between Daving and Marala. "She knows nothing of Court. She cannot go."

She might as well have not spoken at all; Daving was still staring at Norsk. "Bring me the girl after my bath." He took a few experimental steps.

Daving put weight on it. It held. Even though he showed a light limp, he'd surely be able to walk normally in a day or two. He turned and very casually said, "Beat the woman."

"No!" Marala cried out.

Daving smiled. Again, it was the smile that turned up the hair on the back of Marala's neck.

"You cannot beat her for trying to help you!"

It was Daving's turn to remain calm. "I can beat whoever I want. It is not for failing. It is for keeping you from me."

His voice and looks chilled Marala so hard and fast that

she shivered. It chilled her even more that every step he took away from them seemed stronger. She had healed him, but at what cost?

Kris grabbed her and pulled her to her, hissing in her ear, "Run away."

"And leave you?"

"He will harm you! I can't take that."

"I won't leave you."

Her mom got time to hiss, "You must—" before she stopped and stared at Norsk, who was walking up behind them.

"Stop whispering." He grabbed Kris and stared hard at Marala. "Go get your mother some clean clothes. She will need them."

Marala raced back to the servant's quarters and grabbed a fresh shift and underwear, adding a pair of old pants and a pair of her own socks, since the laundry hadn't been done. Norsk would take her mother to a wide yard where the horses were walked to cool down and servants who broke rules were beaten before they were sent home.

Marala heard the whine of the whip before she entered the yard. Norsk's face was still and determined as he raised his hand up and snapped the leather whip backward. Her mom stood in the center of the yard on a stained cloth, blood running down her back.

The whip fell. Kris jerked, but did not fall or cry out. Her green tunic had been removed and hung on the fence.

Marala stopped just inside the gate.

Norsk coiled the whip. Without looking at Marala, he said, "My apologies for the interruption to your day. The young Lord will undoubtedly call for you. I'd suggest you take your mother home, salve her wounds without expending your healing energy, and prepare yourself." He almost sounded kind, although surely Marala was hearing him wrong.

She went to Kris's side and took her hand. Tears hung in the corner of Kris's eyes, but none had fallen. "I'm proud of you," Marala whispered.

The Stablemaster touched her shoulder. "Go now." She glanced at him and saw what might be regret, or worse, pity on his face.

Kris hissed through clenched teeth. "Get my tunic and come." With that, she started home, her back stiff and bloody and her head up. Marala had to run to catch up with her. When she did, Kris turned to her and said, "You cannot go to Lord Daving. You must leave."

"I can't leave you."

"You must."

"I won't."

Kris stopped in the middle of the path and said, "He is healed, but he still wants you. He will do you harm. That was the way of his father, and that will be the way of him."

"What are you hiding from me?" Marala asked.

Kris shook her head. "Trust me and do as I say."

That was all she was going to get. Kris was stubborn enough she'd stand here bleeding until she won, even it meant she bled to death. Marala sighed. "Let's get you to bed." She still clutched the clothes to her, realizing that Norsk had sent her off so she didn't see the beating. "Norsk didn't want to beat you, did he?"

"No."

"Why not? I've seen him beat people before."

"He takes pleasure when he beats thieves. He may be high on the ladder, but Norsk is still a hired hand, and more one of us than one of them. No one wants to beat a Healer who has helped them. He'll help keep me safe even if you run."

Marala lifted her hands from the wounds on her mothers' back. They were now pink strips against Kris's skin. "Lie still, Mom. Rest."

"Pack," Kris murmured.

"I will." First, she needed energy. Healing always made her feel starved and exhausted.

She found the kitchen in an uproar as it prepared for the evening's guests. The rich smells of baking bread and cooking potatoes filled the air, all of it laced by the scent of vegetable stew in a huge pot that was just beginning to bubble. The head cook labored over a whole killed pig, all of her focus on something she seemed to be trying to tie to one of the feet.

"How many are coming tonight?" Marala asked her friend Kathlyn, amazed at the frenetic energy in the kitchen.

"I heard twenty. Yesterday, we were told five. The young lord is crazy."

Marala pursed her lips.

"There's food." Kathlyn pointed at the usual cupboard. "There'll be plenty after this feast, so take what you want."

Marala hesitated at the open cupboard. She was truly starved. Day-old muffins and bread and slightly bruised peaches filled one shelf, and below that, the miracle of a half-eaten wheel of cheese that had been cut into thick slices. She filled the small sack she'd brought and went back to their room.

Her mother had fallen asleep.

While she ate, Marala watched her mom sleep.

The food revived her. She rose and set two pieces of bread, two peaches, and a hunk of cheese on the bedside table for her mom. What if she left and found someplace they could both live? She'd heard that Healers were valuable more than once, and the Stablemaster had reminded her of it again tonight. If they were valuable, then surely they could find a kinder Lord to take them in?

It had to be possible to sneak out. Three other servants had, and she had never seen two of them again. They must have gotten away. One had not—a young woman had come back and been put in chains for three months, and now she worked in the big house alongside Linal and kept her head down. Her face had been scarred by the beating she'd gotten when they caught her, but Marala still thought she was pretty.

The odds seemed good.

Maybe she could sneak out during the feast.

In a candlemark, she was clean, dressed in homespun blue pants and the whitest shirt she owned. A small pack under her bed held the rest of the food, two flasks of water, and clean smallclothes. She had added pouches of herbs to the top to mask the real purpose of the pack.

She folded the green kerchief carefully into her pocket.

With nothing to do but wait, she worried about her mother until the door slammed open and Linal stood there a second time. He had been washed up and dressed in fancy clothes, and this time he spoke formally to her. "Lord Daving requests your presence."

She hesitated for a moment, but then grabbed her pack. "This has some supplies I may need. Will there be a place to put it?"

He shouldered the pack and said, "I can put it with the guests' purses and cloaks. No one will know any different, and then you'll know where to ask for it."

"Thanks." Her mom was still sound asleep on her stomach, but had kicked the covers off her feet. "Give me a moment?"

He looked perturbed that she asked. "Be quick."

"I will." She covered her mom's feet back up and kissed her cheek. "I'm ready."

Their shadows were long in front of them as they walked to the main building, which looked like a small castle, complete with turrets and a tall walkway around the edges. She had only been inside a few times; she was grateful to have a guide. Linal led her to a room on the second floor that looked like a servant's room adjoining a suite of rooms. "Who lives here?" she asks.

"No one. Daving has not taken a personal servant yet. I think . . ." he blushed, and didn't finish his thought.

"Thank you." Her voice shook.

"I'll put your pack away." He left her. She looked out of the window. It would be a sharp fall onto the top of a wooden fence. What had happened to her?

Surely she was safe enough on a feast day. If she could get through the next hour or two, maybe she could slip out through the front doors.

Daving came in, hobbling ever-so-slightly, and handed her a green tunic like her mother's. "Put this on. You'll attend me, and watch out for me, and that will be the excuse for me not dancing."

"I can't wear that. I haven't earned it."

His face tightened. "You have. You healed me today."

At least he was admitting it. "My mother started and would have finished."

He glared at her. "I'll beat her again if you don't do as I say. Besides, there's no fancy Collegium here. Who would tell you to wear green, anyway?"

"My mother."

"Surely she would, to save herself from another beating."

Marala flinched. It wasn't true, but the look on his face suggested he didn't want an argument. "Very well, my lord."

"That's better. I'll send someone in to help you get dressed. Then I will want you to work on my foot one more time before we go out there."

"Yes, my lord." What else could she possibly say? She put the tunic on as soon as he left. There was a mirror, and while she looked as good in the color as her mother, with the same contrasting red hair and matching green eyes, it looked wrong on her. She pulled out the kerchief and put it over her hair, which simply made her look plain.

An older woman bustled into through the door holding a floor-length pale green dress and a pair of brown shoes that were fair more delicate than anything Marala had ever owned. "I'm Beatrice," she said. "Take that off, all of it."

Marala blinked at her, lost.

"You can't attend the Lord in pants. Not at an event like tonight."

Marala obeyed, just like she always obeyed. Each time she said yes to anyone, she felt farther away from her plans to escape. What would they do to her mother if she escaped and got caught?

Beatrice pulled the dress over her head and started murmuring softly. "I know your mother, and I overheard the young Lord. I'm very sorry you are in this position."

Marala looked at the dress in the mirror. She'd never worn anything so fine, or so heavy and useless. She looked like a grown woman in it, which she liked and hated all at once. "Do you know why?" she whispered.

Beatrice's voice was an even softer whisper. "He was a cruel boy. I had hoped the foster would fix that in him." A little louder, she said, "Now put on the tunic."

The colors contrasted nicely, dark green over seafoam. Beatrice made up Marala's face and tightened the laces on her dress. She stood back to admire her work. "You're a real beauty. Be careful."

Daving came back in and dismissed Beatrice.

He took his boot off, sat on the bed, and extended his leg across it. "You may attend me."

She sat on the edge of the bed, thoughts whirling in her head. She didn't like or trust Daving, but her mother . . . there was no way to access the earth from here, not that she knew. How would she reach it through two stories of unfriendly keep? The servant's quarters were all dirt floors. She rubbed her hands together and blew a prayer into them. The normal semitrance state she fell into refused to wrap itself around her.

"Hurry up," he said.

She bit at her lip, rubbing her hands again and closing her eyes. She pretended Kris was sitting on the other side of the bed, watching over her. It helped, a little. She opened her eyes enough to see where to place her hands, trying to keep the illusion that everything was okay. Her hands touched his ankle. She felt the warmth of the remaining swelling and nothing else. She thought of cool things, of ice and streams and water and even snowfall.

Daving groaned, the overly familiar tone of his voice shocking her out of the light level of trance she had achieved. "I hope that helps," she said.

"I do feel better." He reached for his boot, slid it on, and began lacing it.

"What do you expect me to do at the feast?"

"Nothing, unless I ask you to. There is a table in the back for help. Sit there. Watch me in case I want you."

The large central room was full of people. Marala felt awkward and out of place, even more so because of the ill-deserved green tunic he had forced on her. She managed stilted conversation with the two other people at her table—a new falconer and a traveling singer who was not Bardic trained, but sounded as though she might be good at music. At least her voice was quite musical. Both had roles in the evening, and thus were kept in the room, but also here in back, behind the head table.

It was hard to see around the table to the other guests, although from time to time she spotted women dressed in fine gowns or men in full leather dress outfits.

There was no opportunity to get up and leave, and every time she thought of it, she trembled. She ate bread and simple things, ignoring the richer dishes on her plate, certain they would make her ill.

A striking pair of women drew her attention as they came to the dais and spoke to Lord Daving. One wore full Bardic Reds. Not that she'd seen them before, but they fit the picture she'd drawn in her head after hearing about travelers from Haven. She thrilled at a small hope the Bard would sing. The other woman wore perfect Healer's Greens made from fine materials with bone buttons. Marala wished she could hear the conversation. After a few moments they left, although a line had grown behind them, and others approached Daving one by one. Still, Marala couldn't get the Healer from her mind, surely she was a real Healer from the Collegium.

Two candlemarks passed. Many of the diners drank too much, and the talk turned to boasts and loud, if mild, disagreements about the best ways to hunt boar. Kitchen servants began bringing slices of thick brown cake covered in sugar out for the last course.

One of the men at the far side of the head table stood up and took a wrong step, falling from the short dais and hitting his head on the edge of a small rock hearth. The sound was so awful that she heard it from her seat.

She started toward the fallen man, her stomach in knots.

Daving turned around and said, "Come here!" to her, noticed she was on the way, and stood up himself, bellowing, "Make way for my Healer!"

She nearly froze in fear as he called her that. Still, she knelt by the man. Her hands shook but nonetheless set her cheek beside his mouth. His breath was faint, and what remained of it was stuttering, indicating that he must be near death. She looked up at Daving. "There may be nothing I can do for him."

"You must," he said, his voice edged in a command and actual concern. This was someone important to him.

She set her hands under his head, near the place where he had hit the rock, lifting it, and sliding her small fingers along the edges of the indentation. It felt spongy. Wrong. She tried not to feel ill at the crowd and the demands and certain knowledge that her patient was close to death.

How had it come to this in just one day?

She closed her eyes, swaying, reaching down for the power of the ground she sat on. At least that was here. Clean straw lay over it, but if she reached her fingers through she could feel dirt. She began the small sayings they helped her focus. "Earth help me heal. Earth help me open—"

"Here," a woman's voice sounded from behind her. "Here, let me help."

Marala glanced behind her. The Healer. She swayed, and then smiled. "All right."

The woman sat at Marala's back, her long legs stretched out on either side of her, and her hands cupping Marala's hands. She smelled of the sweet dessert, and felt like strength. An eerie calm fell across Marala, and the noise and staring faces faded.

"Now," the woman whispered. "I feel you grounding. Let's do it together. We'll both be stronger that way."

"Okay."

The woman spoke her through her way. "Take a deep breath."

She did.

"Let it out."

She did.

Instructions came steadily, at a speed Marala could keep up with. "Now feel the beating heart of the earth come through you." Pause. "Now ask it to help you heal this man." Pause.

The earth seemed to answer her request. She had never thought to ask.

"Ask it to give you strength to heal and to pass through you, ask it to strengthen his heart and his breath and his lungs." Another pause, longer. "Good. Feel that? Breathe in deeper, take power deep in you, as I take it deep in me." Pause. "Let it out slowly and feel it travel down your arm and into your fingers and into the bone they are close to. Feed the warmth slowly, slowly, so it doesn't hurt."

"Oh!"

"Be quiet, feel."

Marala swallowed and focused. To her amazement, she *could* feel the bones knitting together and strengthening. "That's amazing," she whispered.

"Now we need to stop the swelling in his brain."

"We can do that?"

Another set of instructions, another connecting to the ground, another pull of energy. She could never have done so much on her own. The man coughed one, twice, and pushed up, cursing.

The woman behind her laughed, a low laugh of relief and triumph.

Marala joined her, unable to believe they had saved the man. She turned to get a good look at her benefactor.

"Thank you!" Marala exclaimed. "You're a real Healer."

The woman smiled. "I am. I'm Dionne. And you, too, are a real Healer."

"Oh, no! I could never have done that."

"You'll be able to when we're finished with you."

"What do you mean?"

"Would you like to study at the Collegium?"

Oh. My. "I've never been anywhere," Marala said. "My mother!"

"She can come with us. We've known about her. We managed to get an invitation to this celebration so we could check up on her. I couldn't see her anywhere, and we were afraid something bad had happened."

"It did!" Marala exclaimed. Before she could explain, the harsh sound of Daving calling her name snapped her attention away from daydreams and hope. She was still in the main room of the Keep, and her lord stood opposite her. He held a hand out to Marala.

She hesitated.

He kept the hand out.

She swallowed, afraid to disobey him, but remembering her mother.

The Bard came over. The two women could be twins—or no, Marala amended, they *had* to be twins. If they wore the same clothing, she wouldn't be able to tell them apart. This woman had more authority though, or a different kind. Maybe because she was a Bard? Or because she was from Haven?

People from the capital city weren't always talked of well here, but all the songs said they were heroes. Dionne had just taught her so much, in just moments, and she couldn't wait to show her mother. If they had known how to be so slow and careful, it might not have hurt to help Daving.

The Healer held her hand out.

Marala bit her lip. She had never been anywhere else, but she didn't want to be here any more. Still, she knew a little of bargaining. "Do you promise to take my mother?"

"Of course. And I have already sent for a proper Seneschal to keep track of Daving here until he is of age."

Daving's face had gone bright red. "I am to be married soon. Surely that means I am man enough to run this keep!"

"With any luck, you will be in about five years. I'm Bard Rhiannon, and you are lucky we are not arresting you."

"For what?"

"Beating a Healer."

Her mom. How did they know about her mom's beating? She glanced around the room, and spotted the Stablemaster standing against the far wall, watching the conversation carefully. He did not choose to meet her eyes, but that was understandable. And this would not be the place to thank him. But she would do it before she left.

She looked back at Dionne again. "You can really take us away from here?"

The other Healer nodded. "I can, and I will."

"You'll take us somewhere safe, where we can eat and where we have something useful to do?"

"Yes."

Marala took Dionne's hand. It was rougher than she expected, and stronger. "I've never been outside the walls before."

"And you will never have to be inside them again."

Unexpected Meeting
Nancy Asire

"My Lord . . . my Lord! I ask that you reconsider!"

Levron, sworn assistant to Perran, traveling judge out of Sunhame, representative of the will of Vkandis Sunlord, glanced sidelong at his master. Seated off to one side, he was still close enough to notice the change in the judge's features. He had seldom seen Perran's face as frozen in an expression of repressed anger as today.

The man who stood facing the judge's seat bore a look strikingly similar. A current of unease filled the large room where the trial had finished and judgment had been rendered.

"Reconsider what?" Perran asked, his voice cold as a winter's blast. "You've heard all the evidence against you. Witness after witness has spoken. You have no defense to offer. What should I reconsider?"

"The restitution," the man answered, his voice equally cold. "What you're leveling against me and my family will come close to ruining us."

"You should have considered the outcome of your acts before you committed them," Perran said. "If you'd had any consideration for your family, you wouldn't have lied and, yes, stolen from your partner."

"I didn't lie!" the man ground out. "Not one word of it!"

Perran leaned forward, his arms crossed before him on the table he sat behind. "So you say. Your partner tells us otherwise. This was not one instance. You took a total of one hundred gold soleri over months from your partner. He gave you those soleri to purchase gems for the jewelry business the two of you owned. Those gems were to have been secured in your shop. Now, there are no gems and the soleri are nowhere to be found. Five witnesses have testified that you have spent a lot on yourself and your residence, sending some aid to your extended family in Rethwellan. And here we are. You have no answer as to what happened to the money, no answer as to where the gems are that you were sent to purchase." Perran gestured to another well-dressed man who sat quietly in the front row of spectators. "Your partner has nothing to show for his trust in you."

"I told you repeatedly that I was robbed on the way. I have no idea where the gems are! None! How can I be held responsible for an attack by brigands?"

Perran slapped one hand on the table. "This wasn't the tale you told when questioned by your partner. You told him the gems were stolen from the room in the inn you stayed at on the way back here, not that you were set upon by highwaymen. Which is it? How many times is your story going to change?"

Levron watched carefully as an expression of anger settled on the man's face, hardened his eyes, and thinned his mouth. This fellow could be trouble. It was rare to see a judgment argued after Perran had given it. Representative of the judiciary of Karse, his word was taken to be final and binding.

"My Lord," the man said, his voice dropping to a near whisper. "I ask again . . . please reconsider your judgment."

"Enough!" Perran rapped. "I'll waste no more time with this. I am the voice of the Son of the Sun *and* Vkandis Sunlord. You have given false testimony, have lied before me as representative of the justice of Karse. This is not only earthly justice, but a mark against you when you eventually stand before Vkandis after your death. For your theft of one hundred gold soleri, Kanton, you will repay your partner the exact sum you took from him to purchase gems for your partnership. Hear me! My judgment is final!"

A murmur ran through the crowd that had gathered for the trial. The defendant's partner smiled a smile Levron took to

be relief. The defendant drew himself up in a posture of outrage.

"I have nothing to repay!" he said, his voice rising. "I
don't know where the gems are! I don't know where the
money is! I'll have to sell a great deal of everything I have to
amass that amount!"

Perran stood, the gold collar of his office glittering in the
sunlight that streamed through one of the windows in the
large room. He gestured toward the defendant.

"We're done here," he said, his voice again dripping in
ice. "You may leave now and begin to figure out *how* you will
repay Danti, your partner. That's not Danti's problem, nor is
it mine. By the authority granted me by the Son of the Sun,
whose rule emanates from Vkandis Sunlord, I have spoken."
He waved a hand toward the doorway at the rear of the room.
"If you don't leave, I'll have you escorted out."

Levron sensed the two guards standing behind Perran take
a step forward. He couldn't remember the last time they had
been called upon to bring order to a trial. A rare occurrence,
indeed. Fully armed, their presence was usually enough to
quell any disturbance that arose.

Kanton, the disgraced jeweler, glared at Perran, then turned
his apparent anger toward Danti. He spun on his heel and
stalked toward the door, his exit eliciting another, but louder,
murmur from the people in the room. Levron supposed the
threat of Perran's two guards had been enough to force Kanton
to leave, though his departure reeked of defiance.

With the trial over, the late afternoon opened up as welcome
free time. Perran and Levron had retreated to the rooms allotted them at the best inn in town. Levron could see that the
entire trial had been a drain on Perran. So many lies, so many
witnesses speaking against Kanton. How the disgraced jeweler thought he could win this case was beyond Levron. He
had served Perran long enough to be able to read those who
came to be judged, and there was something about Kanton that
raised his suspicions as to the veracity of the jeweler's story.

"That was a hard trial," Perran said, leaning back in his
chair. "Sometimes they are. And this one was one of the worst."

"I could tell." Levron paused, packing away Perran's black robes and making certain the gold chain of office was secured in their baggage. They would be staying the night and then leaving for the next trial to be held several days' ride away. In the meantime, there was little to do save rest for tomorrow's journey. "Do you think Kanton will be able to repay Danti?"

Perran snorted. "If what the witnesses swore to, he has spent a considerable amount on himself recently. I suppose he can sell a good deal of what he's accumulated."

"He said it will probably ruin him, that he might have to sell his house."

"That's what happens when you betray those who placed faith in you." Perran took a sip of wine from the glass on the table beside his chair.

Levron laughed. "If people were honest in dealing with each other, you'd have nothing to do."

"Oh, I'm sure the Son of the Sun would find something for me."

A furious knock came at the door to their room. Levron glanced at Perran and opened the door.

"My Lord!" It was one of the Perran's guards. "We have trouble!"

Perran stood, his wine forgotten. "What has happened?"

Timar, the senior guard, gestured behind. "Danti has been attacked. Struck down at the entrance to his shop."

Levron looked from the Perran to the guard. "By whom?"

"The word's out that Kanton was responsible."

"Damn!" Perran began to pace. "Have the authorities been notified?"

"They're trying to find Kanton now." Timar squared his shoulders. "If I might suggest, Lord, please keep to your rooms. At this stage, I wouldn't be surprised if Kanton tried to take out his anger on you."

"That's insane!" Levron said. "No one attacks a judge! The judges are the voice of the Son of the Sun and Vkandis!"

"I understand," Timar replied. "But I would still feel better if you don't take any chances until Kanton is found."

Perran rubbed the bridge of his nose. "So it can get worse.

Now, if the witnesses are telling the truth, Kanton has gone from a thief to an attacker. Have you spoken to any of the authorities in town?"

"I just came from there," Timar said. "Fortunately, Danti wasn't badly injured, but he knows who did this to him and he's not surprised."

"It makes no sense. Why would Kanton do something so stupid?" Perran shook his head. "He's well known here in town. Did he honestly think he could get away with it?"

Levron looked back and forth between Perran and Timar. "What do you want me to do?"

"Nothing, right now," Perran said. "I'll stay in our rooms at your suggestion, Timar. You and Farrid keep watch. Your room is next to ours."

Farrid, the second of Perran's guards, hovered behind Timar and nodded. "We'll be there. Call if you need us."

Levron shut the door and drew a deep breath. "If you're not to leave our rooms, I'll go see if we can have our meals sent up here instead of going to the common room below."

"Not a bad idea. You know," Perran said, "if you see any of the authorities, you might mention that Kanton said he has family in Rethwellan. We're close enough that if he's running, he might try to cross the border, thinking he's free of judgment from Karse."

"I'll tell them. But I suppose they already know. From what we've found out, Kanton has lived here for a number of years. I would imagine he's told people about his life and family."

"You're probably right." Perran sat down again and reached for his wineglass. "See what you can do about our meals. And, Levron, be careful. If Kanton has any idea of coming after me, he might go after you as well."

"Me? I'm no one important. I'm just your assistant."

"Yes, but you sat close enough to me at trial, and Kanton might recognize you."

"Truth. I'll be wary."

Levron left the common room after giving instructions for meals to be sent to Perran's rooms and to the room given to the two guards. The afternoon was far advanced, the sun nearly touching the horizon. With nothing to do, Levron decided to take a short walk. Time spent seated at the trial had given him the need for exercise. He began wandering aimlessly, but had gone no more than several buildings away when he was approached by one of the town's authorities.

"You're the judge's assistant?"

"I am."

"We're advising everyone to be careful this evening. We still haven't found Kanton, so we don't want anyone to get caught up in an incident."

"Wise words," Levron said. "I'll be careful."

The man nodded and headed off, scanning his surroundings, looking for anything that could lead to Kanton's capture.

Though he had promised he would be careful, Kanton might, as Perran had observed, recognize him as the judge's assistant. Levron shook his head and stopped in front of a business that was beginning to end the day's commerce. It was of no great importance to continue his leisurely walk around town.

While Perran was handsome to a fault, Levron had always been one to disappear in a crowd. Perhaps the judge was correct. Kanton might have noticed where Levron sat during the trial. This time, his forgettable face could be marked.

So much for aimless wandering. With both Perran's guards keeping close watch over the judge's rooms, Levron decided he would stop by the inn's stables to see that their horses were being well cared for and given extra mash and grain for tomorrow's journey. All his duties to Perran completed, it gave him something to do before the evening meal.

The doors to the stable were opened wide. The smell of hay and horses wafted toward him as Levron approached. A ginger cat jumped up on a mounting block by the stable entrance, stared at him for a moment, briefly washed its face with one paw, and then jumped down again.

"Boy?" Levron called, looking around for the stable hand. He had no need to go into the structure if the lad was there. A simple request for additional feed for the horses Perran, the two guards, and he rode was hardly out of place. He rubbed the end of his nose and waited.

"Boy?" he called again. No answer came from inside the stable. Frowning, Levron decided to check on the horses himself. The light was beginning to fade, and he didn't want to blunder around in unfamiliar surroundings. Best get on with it.

He stepped into the gloaming, remembering where their horses were stalled toward the back of the stable. Halfway there, he nearly tripped over something in his path. As his eyes adjusted to the lack of light, he froze, one foot lifted in front of the other.

It was the stable hand. Levron had come close to walking onto the boy's feet. For an instant, nothing made any sense. Why would the boy be stretched out in the stable?

Levron swallowed heavily and glanced around. He saw nothing in the shadows; the horses seemed to be unperturbed. He drew a deep breath and knelt beside the stable hand. He could see just enough to tell the boy was breathing.

And now was the time to leave. He had no idea what could have happened, but whatever had transpired, the authorities needed to be notified. Levron stood, turned toward the opened doors, and froze.

The point of a knife rested against his neck, the cold steel no colder than the ice that stole through his veins.

"Make one noise and you're dead," a voice whispered in his ear. "Now, slowly, turn away from me and make no sudden moves."

Levron complied, recognizing he stood on the edge of possible death. He closed his eyes and silently offered up a prayer to Vkandis for protection. Though he couldn't see much in the growing darkness, after long hours at trial he could recognize who was speaking to him.

It was Kanton's hand that held the knife, Kanton, who was sought by the town's authorities and who now held Levron captive.

Perran glanced out the window and frowned. Dusk was giving way to night, and Levron hadn't returned yet. He opened the door and called out, alerting his guards.

Timar answered at once, looking up and down the hall-way, his hand close to his scabbarded sword.

"Have you seen or heard from Levron?" Perran asked.

"No, Lord. And we haven't left our room. We're waiting for our evening meal."

Perran nodded. "As am I. He should have returned by now. I don't know where he could have gone."

Timar's eyes narrowed. "Do you think—"

"I don't know what to think. Leave Ferrid here and see if anyone has seen him in the common room."

"At once, Lord."

Perran watched Timar head toward the stairs the lead down to the common room and frowned again. He and Lev-ron had ridden together to trial after trial for years, and this was not normal behavior on his assistant's part.

Levron held motionless, feeling the tip of the knife on his neck. He closed his eyes and thought, but there was nothing he could do at the moment. He had never been one to fight and had no particular skills in that area. He thought out every move he might make, but none of them brought him any closer to release.

"Why are you doing this?" he asked, attempting to keep his voice level. "You're in enough trouble as it is."

"Keep quiet! And don't try anything. As you said, I'm in enough trouble. One slip of my knife won't make much dif-ference now."

"Don't you understand? The whole town's looking for you. Where do you think you can go without being seen?"

"I don't have to answer you. You're part of the judgment that doomed me. Shut your mouth!"

Levron shut his mouth. Kanton shifted the knife blade so it rose to below Levron's ear. Any move he might make could result in most certain death.

A slight rustle came from the direction of the stable hand. By now, he might be returning to consciousness. Kanton ob-viously heard the same thing.

"Now I'm going to walk very slowly toward the doors," Kanton said. "You're going to walk in front of me. My knife will never leave your neck. As fast as you think you can run, I'll be faster. Move!"

"Where the hells do you think you're going to go?"

"Shut up!"

Levron walked slowly toward where the boy lay, the knife never leaving his neck. What would Kanton do next? Surely, he wouldn't compound his troubles by murder.

They paused by the stable hand and then, with no warning, Kanton kicked the boy in the head, once again rendering him unconscious.

The light had nearly fled from outside and the stable plunged into near darkness.

"Someone is going to notice the doors are open," Levron observed. "They'll come looking."

"You think I haven't thought of this?" Kanton grated.

"I'm not sure *what* you thought. This isn't the best place to be cornered."

"You're a smart one, aren't you? Got an answer for everything. Well, think on this!"

Shock, pain, a blow to his head, and Levron fell toward the stable floor before he blacked out.

"Has anyone found Kanton yet?" Perran asked, stopping his pacing to face Timar.

"No, Lord."

"Do they think he's left town?"

Timar shrugged. "They don't think he had enough time. He attacked Danti in the late afternoon, and no one has seen him since. If he's going to try for Rethwellan, it's close, but not that close. He would need time to fashion an escape."

"Damn!" Perran walked to the window and looked out into the darkness. "And Levron? Has anyone seen him?"

"Not since he went to the common room and instructed that our meals should be brought up here."

Perran looked up to the ceiling, at the shadows playing across it from the lit candles. "Something is terribly wrong here. I want you to work closely with the town's authorities. I have the worst feeling that something has happened to Levron."

"And that Kanton might be responsible?"

"You heard what he did to Danti. If he happened upon Levron, why would he avoid the chance to take revenge on someone he sees connected to me?"

"I'll make contact with the authorities again. Will you be safe with Ferrid here?"

Perran smiled. "You two are the best I've ridden with for years. I'll keep my door locked. On your way to speak with the authorities, find out everything you can as to what they're doing."

"Aye, Lord. I'll keep you informed."

When Levron opened his eyes, he saw only darkness. His head throbbed with pain. The next thing that registered was a gag around his mouth. Now he couldn't call for help if he'd wanted to. His arms were tied behind his back, and he was shoved up against one of the beams supporting the stable's roof.

The stable doors were closed now. To anyone passing, it would appear that the custom was over for the day. The only reason the stable would be reopened was if some late night traveler appeared and sought a place at the inn and a stable for his horse.

Closing his eyes, Levron tried to breathe through his nose. It wasn't the most pleasant way to draw breath, but it was all he had left. Not being able to see anything, his sense of hearing was acute. He could hear Kanton moving around. He was trapped in the stable with no apparent way to leave without being noticed.

The town wasn't a large one and, when he and Perran had arrived yesterday, Levron had noticed that there were few residents out after sunset. Those that were generally assembled in the common room of the inn to have a few drinks and an evening meal. Aside from that, the streets were quiet. Perhaps this was the reason Kanton had not left the stable. Who would see him?

The authorities would. Levron was certain they had not given up trying to find him. After all, he had attacked his partner, and that act was certainly enough to take him into custody.

How did Kanton contemplate making it unnoticed from the stable? Even if he was uncommonly lucky and no one was near, the inn was situated toward the center of town. It would take some doing to make it to the open roads for escape.

Levron stirred against the beam he leaned against and opened his eyes. The glimmer of a candle shone to his right, leaving Kanton's face in stark relief. Something about the man was different. When he had stood before Perran at trial, he was well dressed, but now he had shed his fine jacket and was clad in only a shirt and breeches. No longer the prosperous jeweler, he appeared to be just one more citizen of the town.

Kanton set the candle in a sconce and lit a second. The increased light allowed Levron to see that the stable hand was bound and gagged as well only a few paces away.

By now, Levron was certain Perran would be alarmed at his assistant's absence. No doubt he was in contact with the town's authorities. So now they would not only be searching for Kanton, but for him as well.

Levron leaned his head back against the beam and winced at the pain. If he survived, he would suffer a tremendous headache in the morning. At this stage, he didn't know whether Kanton was desperate enough to kill. It was one thing to attack his partner and another to up his crimes to murder.

Or so Levron hoped.

Perran's evening meal sat untasted on a table at one end of the room. He had no desire to eat, even though his stomach rumbled in hunger. Too much time had passed since he expected Levron to return. A cold feeling warred with the pangs of hunger, elicited by a burden of fear. He had voiced his concerns regarding Kanton's desire for vengeance being acted upon if he had encountered Levron. Now, as time passed, he felt certain that something akin to his worries had taken place.

When a knock sounded on the door, Perran jumped.

"It's me, Lord," came Timar's voice. "I have news."

And not good news, Perran thought as he opened the door. Timar entered, closed the door, and leaned up against it.

"No one has seen Levron, Lord. No one has seen Kanton.

It's pitch black out, and there are numerous places someone could hide."

"Are the authorities still searching?"

"Aye, Lord. But their efforts have come to nothing. I talked with the constable, and he said he isn't giving up. He's a worried man right now. With Kanton on the loose, it reflects badly on him and his men."

"He didn't have any responsibility for Kanton's attack on Danti," Perran said. "Nor on the fact no one has seen the man since. Or Levron, for that matter."

"I know, but he still feels responsible for the whole mess. Also—" Timar made a face, "—it's a black mark on the town. Not only do they have a criminal on the loose, but the assistant to one of the Son of the Sun's judges has gone missing. I'm sure you can understand."

Perran nodded. "If you see him, have the constable come to me. I'll need to reassure him that there won't be any retribution leveled on his town."

"Aye, Lord. Ferrid has never left his post by his door in case you called. As long as you don't go out or open the door to anyone but me, I think you'll be safe."

"I imagine I will." Perran attempted a slight smile. "It's Levron I'm worried about now."

Levron closed his eyes, feeling dizziness along with the pain in his head. A feeling of hopelessness swept through his mind. What could he do? Nothing. He was bound and gagged. Kanton was armed with at least a knife. Even in his wildest speculation, he couldn't see any answer to his captivity.

Kanton was pacing now, up and down in front of the stalls. The horses were beginning to nicker and move restlessly. Levron supposed they had missed their nightly feeding, and were trying to get the attention of the stable hand.

As for the stable hand, he watched Kanton's pacing with wide eyes. Levron was close enough to see a large lump on the side of the boy's head. He felt sure he sported a lump of equal size on the back of his own head.

"You!" Kanton stopped in front of the stable hand. "Stand up."

The boy made an attempt, but fell back against the stall. Kanton cursed, shifted his knife to his left hand and grabbed the boy by the front of his shirt, jerking him to his feet.

"You can't talk, so don't make the attempt. Do you know me?"

The boy nodded.

"Did you hear what happened in the trial?"

Again, the boy nodded.

"Do you want to live?"

The stable hand tried to speak, but all that came out was a garbled noise.

"Then you're going to help me. If you do, you'll live, and this so-called assistant to the judge will live also. Do you understand?"

Once more, the boy nodded, more forcefully this time.

Levron watched the exchange, his eyes narrowed. So. Obviously Kanton had hatched some kind of plan to escape. What it was he couldn't imagine. But events were beginning to move forward, and only time would tell what would occur once Kanton's plan was put into action.

"Lord?"

Perran opened the door and Timar entered the room, glancing behind as he did.

"What have you heard?" Perran demanded.

"Nothing much. However, there are a few strange things to report. One of the constable's men was approached by the stable hand's mother. She said she hadn't seen her son for the evening meal. She admitted that sometimes he would take his meal at a friend's house, but no one there has seen him. She went to the stable, but the doors were locked. This is normal once night falls. Though she called his name, there was no response. But she did notice something odd. There's a big ginger cat that lives in the stable and he was sitting outside, staring at the doors and meowing. That cat generally sleeps inside with the stable hand. He keeps the mice away from the store of grain and mash."

"The cat does," Perran said. "And no one's seen the boy either?"

"No one."

Perran drew a deep breath and let it out slowly. "But everything else seems normal?"

"Aye, Lord. Aside from the absence of the boy and the cat waiting outside the stable, the town's quiet."

"Dammit!" Perran slapped one fist against an open palm. "This has gone on too long! We have to do something!"

"I'm not sure, Lord, what we *can* do that hasn't been tried. The watch isn't giving up hunting for Kanton and Levron."

"And now, with the stable hand, we have a third person missing. This is getting out of hand."

"I agree. The problem is, no one has any idea what to do."

"There has to be an answer to this," Perran said. "Kanton can't have vanished from the face of the earth. Nor has Levron, or the stable hand. We're missing something here."

"The cat and the boy," Timar acknowledged. "There has to be some connection there."

Perran straightened his shoulders. "Bring me the constable. I might have an idea that could help find Kanton."

Levon watched Kenton prod the stable hand toward the back of the stable. The ropes around the boy's arms had been removed and he was rubbing his wrists together.

"Do you have a cart here?"

The boy nodded and tried to say something. Again, all that came out from behind the gag was a muffled sound.

"What are you trying to say?"

The boy made a futile gesture with his head toward the back of the stable, moaning at the pain the gesture caused.

"All right," Kanton said, and lifted the knife in his hand. "I'm going to remove your gag. Don't even try to yell for help because then I *will* have to kill you. Do you understand?"

The stable hand nodded, and Kanton tugged the gag down around the boy's neck. The stable hand gasped for breath, coughed several times, but remained still and silent.

"Now what were you trying to say?" Kanton asked.

"We have a cart was brought in for repair," the boy said, his voice trembling. He glanced toward the back of the stable. "Owner hasn't picked it up yet."

"Good. You and I are going to fetch that cart. Then you're going to fill it with hay. Do you understand?"

"Aye."

Levron watched the two of them walk toward the back of the stable, fading out of the feeble candlelight. Was Kanton planning to make an escape on a slow cart? He bowed his head. Desperation could bring about odd thinking.

The cart rumbled forward, pulled by the stable hand. Kanton's knife still poking the boy's back, the stable hand began filling it with hay.

"Now, find me a horse that can pull this cart," Kanton said, "and hitch it up. I'm going to be right behind you, so don't think you can scream or run."

Levron watched as the stable hand led a small horse from a stall. Gathering tack, he began hitching the horse to the cart. When he was finished, he looked up at Kanton, his eyes still wide as saucers.

"Good lad," Kanton said. "Now, you're going to help me load this judge's assistant into the cart and cover him with hay. Understood?"

Levron was jerked to his feet and all but dragged to the cart. Between Kanton and the stable hand, they hoisted him into the cart and covered him with hay. Now, not only could Levron not breathe easily, the hay covering his face made it even more difficult, and his head ached as if it would split apart. Then, Kanton and the boy tied Levron's feet to the side of the cart, making certain he couldn't jump out and run.

"Good lad." Kanton reached out and yanked the gag back up over the boy's mouth and led him at knifepoint to the tack room. "I'm going to shut you in here and bolt the door. Don't think anyone can hear you pounding to try to get out."

Levron tried the rope that bound his feet, but it was tied securely. So much for that. He was trapped beneath hay in a cart that would be driven by Kanton in an attempt to flee the town.

Kanton approached the cart and Levron willed himself into immobility. Something sharp and pointed jabbed him in his right leg.

"Feel that?" Kanton rasped. "That's a pitchfork and I'll stick in you if you so much as move."

Levron fought a sneeze and sniffed loudly, trying to keep quiet as possible.

Then something brushed against his leg, accompanied by the ring of coin. Money stolen from his partner? Levron couldn't understand how this plan might work, but stranger things had happened in his life. Vkandis grant that once he gained freedom, Kanton would abandon the cart and try for the Rethkellan border.

Perran had never in his illustrious career contemplated what might happen next. Guarded closely by Timar and Ferrid, he stood with the constable and five of the town's authorities in the shadows across the street from the stable. There was hardly any light shed by a few lamps lit a distance away, but the constable's face was drawn with worry.

"Do you think Kanton's in the stable?" the constable asked.

"Where else could he be? You've all but turned the town upside down and not found him. And you haven't found my assistant, or the boy who keeps the stable. And look—" He pointed to the closed stable doors. "—that cat hasn't moved. He's waiting for the stable hand to let him in and feed him."

The constable sighed. "So we wait?"

"Kanton has to make a move shortly. It's late, and he knows nearly everyone has gone home. What better time for him to try to escape? He probably thinks the search for him has ended for the night."

"Damned fool!" the constable growled. "We don't give up that easily."

"Hsst!" Timar gestured toward the stable. "Did you hear that?"

Perran froze. The constable and his men drew their swords. The sound of the stable doors being opened seemed loud in the nighttime silence. Immediately, the ginger cat slipped inside, meowing loudly. For a long moment nothing happened, and then a cart pulled by a small horse emerged. Sitting on the cart's bench was Kanton, one hand on the reins and the other holding a pitchfork. The constable held up one hand, silently ordering his men to hold their ground.

Kanton looked around and urged the horse forward. Perran

hardly dared to breathe, his eyes fastened on the approaching cart. As it drew near, the constable lifted his hand and brought it down in a slicing motion.

Suddenly, he and his men surged forward.

"Stop where you are, Kanton!" the constable roared. "You're surrounded!"

For a long moment, no one moved. Then Kanton lifted the pitchfork and held it above the back of the cart which appeared to be full of hay.

"Stand back!" he yelled. "If you want the judge's assistant to live, don't come close. He's right behind me and I'll fill him full of holes if you come closer!"

"You bastard!" the constable said. "You've sunk to this, Kanton? Theft, assault, and now you threaten murder?"

"Get out of my way! I'm riding out of here, and you're going to stay away from me!"

Perran reached out and grabbed the constable's arm. "Levron's in the cart. Don't be hasty. Let's see how this plays out."

"Damn fool! He's going to try for the Rethwellan border."

"That's what I think. Be careful. I don't want Levron hurt."

The constable nodded, but his eyes narrowed in thought. "I'll do my best, Lord, but I think we can stop him. And keep your assistant from being injured."

A swift signal to a man standing a few paces away sent the fellow slowly around to the back of the cart. Kanton was so intent on the men on either side of the cart in front of him he didn't notice until it was too late.

The constable's man jumped up from the shadows and wrestled the pitchfork from Kanton's hand. The disgraced jeweler backhanded the fellow, whipped the horse forward, and turned the cart sharply to his left, intending to run down anyone in front of him.

Two things happened at once. The left wheel of the cart wobbled and worked its way off its axle, causing the cart to lurch onto its side. Kanton was thrown to the ground and the constable's men surrounded him, holding him down on the street, their swords pointed at him. And at the same moment, the hay fell out of the cart, revealing Levron hanging all but upside down, a bag of something caught between his legs.

Perran ran forward, tossing what was left of the hay off Levron and pulling the gag down. Timar and Ferrid cut the ropes binding him to the side of the cart and lifted the bag.

"Lord!" Timar called, shaking the bag. "I think there's money in here!"

The constable stood to one side, a satisfied look on his face. "Caught the bastard red-handed!" He motioned one of his men into the stable. "See if you can find the stable hand. He's probably locked up somewhere inside."

Perran breathed a sigh of relief. From all outward appearances, Levron appeared unharmed, though he coughed, shut his eyes against the pain he must have been feeling, and passed out.

From his position in the bed, his head propped up by two pillows, Levron opened his eyes. His head hurt abominably, and he knew his legs and body were bruised from the fall from the cart. But apart from that, he judged himself fortunate to still be alive.

His eyes sought Perran who sat in a chair beside the bed. "How did you know Kanton would be in the stable?"

Perran smiled. "There was hardly anywhere else for him to go. The bag between your legs contained quite a bit of the money Kanton had stolen from his partner. As for the gems, that's still a mystery. And here's a bit of news for you. The stable hand was released; thanks to him, events turned in our favor. The cart Kanton tried to escape with had been brought in for repairs. The left wheel was loose on its axle. When the boy gave the cart to Kanton, he knew the wheel would eventually come off."

Levron rubbed at the knot on his head, wincing at the pain. "I supposed it was revenge on the boy's part. He was abused and terrified by Kanton for sure." He closed his eyes, trying to will the headache away. "And thanks to Vkandis, you, the constable and his men, I'm alive."

Perran laughed. "It's a good thing, too. I'd hate to have to train a new assistant."

A Trip of Goats
Elisabeth Waters

:STOP THAT!:

Lena knew the goats could hear her perfectly well, but having Animal Mindspeech didn't mean she could control them—especially when there were evergreens in the offing.

She dragged one goat back down to all fours and away from the high wooden gate it had been leaning on. The wreath, unfortunately, came down with it and promptly disappeared into its mouth. She hip-checked another goat away from the fence—*really, who puts Midwinter decorations in their back alley?*—thankful she was wearing the simple sturdy robe of a Novice of the Temple of Thenoth, Lord of the Beasts, rather than court finery.

"A little help would be nice," she said to her companion as she grabbed another goat by the scruff of the neck.

Sven-August grabbed two of the smaller goats, positioning himself so that he, Lena, and the goats they held were between the ones that were still loose and the surviving evergreens. Lena hoped she could get the situation under control, but then a servant opened the gate behind her, and the goats charged through the opening. It turned out that when a person was holding *two* determined goats, she went where the goats went.

Judging from the conditions in the back courtyard, the household was in the process of taking down the decorations. It was eight days after the Midwinter Festival, and the most recent snowfall had been pushed to the sides of the streets, even in the back alleys of the district where the highborn and

192

the wealthy lived. After all, deliveries still had to be made. Still, the courtyard was wet and slippery, and goats were generally more sure-footed than humans. It quickly became a battle: goats against humans, with the evergreens as the prize—and there were a lot of evergreens.

The door to the house opened, and then quickly closed behind its owner. Lena looked up at him, unhappily aware that her boots were scuffed and dirty, her habit was wet to her knees, and that she and Sven-August looked . . . Well, it was a good thing his mother wasn't there to see him. Lady Efanya would *not* be happy.

The man in front of her was a senior Guildmaster, but at least he didn't look terribly upset. In fact, as he scanned the courtyard, he looked . . . was that amusement?

"Good day to you, Guildmaster Jurgen," Lena said politely. "I hope that you had a joyous Midwinter."

The Guildmaster's mouth twitched. "I did indeed, thank you." He didn't address her by name, which meant he was pretending not to recognize her. Lena was grateful for the feigned oversight, and more than willing to be treated as nothing more than a simple Novice. "And I am willing to share my joy with the beasts of the Temple," he continued, "but I would prefer to do so in a more restrained fashion."

"Well," Lena said. "If each piece of evergreen not currently attached to a goat could be moved out of reach, and sight, and smell if possible . . ."

"Do as she says," the Guildmaster ordered, and the servants began stuffing the evergreens into a small brick building. It took a while, and more evergreens fell to the goats, but eventually the edibles were gone, and Lena was able to get the animals to listen to what she said and actually obey her. Sven-August chivied them back into the alleyway, while Lena apologized to the Guildmaster and his servants. He still looked amused, but then, he hadn't been knocked flat by a goat.

"Tell your Prior I will have the rest of the greenery bundled up and brought to the Temple," he said. "I can be certain that it will be enjoyed there as much as it was here during the festivities."

"Possibly more," Lena muttered.

The Guildmaster looked around the courtyard. "All of you go to the kitchens and get some hot ale, and dry clothing if you need it. I don't want anyone sickening from this." Suddenly the servants looked much less annoyed.

Lena thanked everyone again, and retreated to the alley. The goats had taken down the rest of the wreaths and garlands on the back wall, but she decided not to worry about that now.

"At least we can tell the Prior that we followed his wishes about tiring the goats out," Sven-August said cheerfully as they headed back to the Temple. "I'm just glad that didn't turn into a brawl with the Guildmaster's servants."

Lena wondered how Sven-August defined "brawl." Did it have to include edged weapons to count? At least now the goats were inclined to listen to the goat-walking song she Mindspoke into their heads. Normally that was all they needed to stay with her, but they were *extremely* fond of evergreens. Lena kept a wary eye on them as they headed back to the Temple.

Sven-August sighed. "I'm tired. It feels as if we walked halfway across Haven."

Lena shrugged. "We did, but we're almost home now. I think the goats have more stamina than you do," she added teasingly. Sven-August was the little brother she had never had.

He contemplated the goats, who were now frolicking ahead of them toward the temple gate—and their main food supply. "I think you're right."

The goats entered the temple courtyard, and that was when the screaming started. Lena took off at a dead run, leaving Sven-August to catch up. She could feel the Peace of the God descend on her as she ran through the gate, but it was having no noticeable effect on the richly-dressed couple standing next to the Prior. The woman was screaming, and the man was trying to draw away from the goats, an expression somewhere between disgust and disdain on his face.

There was also a boy, their son, judging from his appearance. Lena guessed he was about fifteen, which would make him slightly younger than she was, and slightly older than Sven-August. His dark hair was untidy—probably because the baby goat he was holding was nibbling at it—but he was kneeling in the courtyard holding the kid in his lap and looking delighted. Fortunately for him, the Prior was strict about keeping the front courtyard clear and dry, so he wasn't kneeling in either mud or slush.

After one quick glance at him, Lena directed her attention to persuading the goats that the dangling trim on his mother's dress was not edible, and that there would be food for them in their barn if they went there instead. :*Tell Maia I said to feed you,*: she told the lead goat. She wished she could tell Maia directly, but even though both of them had Animal Mindspeech, unfortunately it didn't give them Mindspeech with each other.

The kid scrambled off the boy's lap and took off with the other goats. The boy looked after them. "Who's Maia?" he asked, apparently talking to the departing goats.

Lena answered, because she knew the goats weren't going to. "She's one of the Novices. She's lived here for years, and she's very good with animals."

"It's all very well for peasant children to live here," the woman sniffed. Now that the goats were gone, she had calmed down. "But I'm not at all convinced that this is the right place for *our* son."

"What 'peasant children'?" Sven-August said angrily. "Lena's highborn. She'd be living in the Palace if she hadn't persuaded the king to let her live here."

"Sven-August," Lena pointed out, "we're wearing Novice robes, we're wet, and we smell like goats. Nobody looking at us would have any reason to believe we're not as common-born as Maia."

"Anyone who thinks less of Maia because of her birth is an idiot—"

Lena grabbed him by a scrawny wrist. *Good thing he hasn't hit a growth spurt yet.* "Let's go help Maia with the goats," she said dragging him after her.

They were still with the goats when the Prior found them. "I'm sorry," Lena said before he could open his mouth. "We were in the wrong place at the wrong time, weren't we?"

"It wasn't your fault," the Prior assured her. "They arrived much earlier than I expected them."

"Oh." Sven-August looked dismayed. "That's why you wanted the goats tired and out of sight. Are they important?" he added in a small voice.

"All of us are important in the god's sight," the Prior said firmly, "and we don't know yet how this will play out."

"We want the boy, though, don't we?" Lena asked. "We can always use another person with Animal Mindspeech."

The Prior looked at her with interest. "I thought he might have it, but I wasn't sure. Are you?"

Lena nodded. "He asked who Maia was before anyone said her name out loud. I told the goats to have Maia feed them, and the kid scrambled out of his lap, thinking *:Maia! Food!:* just before he asked who Maia was—and then the conversation went rapidly downhill."

"It certainly did," the Prior said with a sigh. "Sven-August, while your defense of Lena and Maia was admirable in its way, you might want to wait a bit before you speak next time." He waited for the young man to nod before continuing. "All right, we are going to try something else. Lena, have you seen much of that family at court?"

Sven-August's gulp was audible. "They're highborn?" he asked.

"I think they're minor nobility." Lena tried to reassure him. "I'm pretty sure I've seen them, but we've never been formally introduced."

The Prior nodded. "Sven-August, why don't you go wash up for supper? You'll be eating with the Brothers, as usual."

He waited until the boy had left before turning to Lena. "I want both you and Maia to dress as if you were dining at court and come to my parlor. You can be formally introduced to Lord and Lady Melander, and we can decide if we would do better to assure them that their son is not crazy, or to let them continue to think that he is."

"Why do they think he's crazy?"

"Because he talks to animals."

"I talk to animals."

"You don't do it openly, where people who don't understand Animal Mindspeech can hear you. Go and get ready, please. Tell Maia that she's your chaperone, and both of you should keep quiet as much as possible and follow my lead—as soon as I decide what that will be."

"Yes, Father." Lena hurried off to find Maia and their good clothes. Maia still had the black dress she'd worn to court when Lena had first met her; she almost never wore it, so it was still in perfectly good shape, and the style was a simple one that didn't become dated. Lena wasn't certain what she had that *she* could wear, but if the Prior wanted her to do this, she'd find something.

With help from Maia, Lena managed to find a dress suitable for dinner at court and totally unsuitable to wear any place in the Temple other than the Prior's rooms. Well, it wouldn't actually be ruined in the chapel, which was where both girls changed normal shoes for "proper" slippers, which were useless for anything except a clean, indoor environment. Fortunately there was a short hallway leading from the chapel to the Prior's office.

The Prior seated them in his parlor as if he were making the setting for a play—which Lena suspected he actually was—with her in a centrally placed comfortable armchair and Maia in a straight chair placed at Lena's right shoulder.

"Father Prior," Lena said, "I didn't get a chance to tell you earlier about our encounter with Guildmaster Jurgen while we were out."

"Do I want to know?" the Prior asked warily.

"The Guildmaster said to tell you that he's sending his remaining evergreens here so that the goats can enjoy them as much as everyone enjoyed them at his house during the Midwinter parties."

"*Remaining* evergreens?" the Prior said. "I don't believe I need any more details, thank you. Now," he continued, "when our guests arrive, do *not* stand up. Remember that you outrank them."

"Lena may," Maia protested, "but I don't."

"They won't pay any attention to you," Lena and the Prior said in unison.

"You're sort of the human equivalent to a guard dog for me," Lena added. "That's basically what a chaperone is."

"I'd be insulted if I didn't know how much you like dogs," Maia shot back.

The Prior sighed. "Don't be insulted by anything that happens, Maia. *We* know enough to value you. They're just ignorant highborn, with very little idea of reality."

"Lady Magdalena," the Prior said with a respectful nod as he escorted his guests into his parlor. "I don't believe that proper introductions were made earlier. May I present Lord and Lady Melander and their son Arvid?"

As Lena inclined her head in acknowledgement, he continued. "Lord and Lady Melander, I don't believe you've met the Lady Magdalena Lindholm." He ignored their shocked gasps.

I was right, Lena thought. *They saw Novice robes and a trip of goats and thought, "she can't possibly be anyone important."*

Conversation during the meal was subdued, and Arvid was as silent as Maia. *Probably thinks anyone who outranks his parents is scary*, Lena thought ruefully. Unfortunately, just as the meal was ending, he spoke, although presumably not to anyone at the table.

"There are lots of mice at our house," he said helpfully.

Lena listened just in time to hear the thanks of a barn owl as it took off into the night. Apparently Arvid had included directions. She looked at her lap and bit her lower lip to keep from laughing.

"Arvid!" Lady Melander was both furious and mortified. "I can't imagine why he says these things," she said to the rest of them. "I assure you that we do *not* have mice!"

Her husband may believe that, Lena thought, *but nobody else at this table does.*

"But the owls are hungry!" Arvid protested. "And—"

"Maia," the Prior interrupted him. "Please take Arvid to the chapel. He can compose himself there."

Maia rose silently to her feet. Arvid, after a glance at his parents' red faces, quickly followed her out of the room.

"Please don't be embarrassed," Lena said into the ensuing silence. "I lived in my parents' house as a child, and there are always mice—at least in the outbuildings—no matter how good your staff is." She decided this was not the time to explain just how small a space a mouse could fit through. "He didn't actually say that there were mice indoors, and an owl would only be interested in the ones outdoors anyway."

"He just—*says* things like that," Lady Melander winced. "And during dinner . . . Prior, I am so—"

"Don't worry about it," the Prior said cheerfully. "Conversations at mealtimes here tend to be much more earthy, especially when we don't have highborn guests."

Lena smiled. "He's young," she pointed out, "and he's a boy. We're used to that here—remember the boy this morning who came in with me and the trip of goats?"

Lord Melander looked puzzled. "Trip of goats?"

The Prior chuckled. "It's a game here: trying to find the most outlandish collective names for animals. We acquired a storytelling of crows with Maia, Lena had a charm of finches when she first came here, and she brought a leash of greyhounds back from one of her annual visits to her late parents' friends, Sven-August came with a bellowing of bullfinches . . ."

"At least I didn't bring home the wake of vultures from my last visit," Lena pointed out, "and the Temple already had the goats." She smiled at Lord Melander. "I think they're called a trip of goats because they tend to crowd you until you trip over at least one of them."

Lady Melander looked consideringly at the Prior. "So you feel confident that you could deal with our son's . . . peculiarities . . . here?"

The Prior smiled benignly. "I assure you, we have coped with worse. Would you like us to foster him here? We have several youngsters his age, so we have regular schooling for them—in fact, they get the same education as the children of the highborn who live at the Palace."

"I don't know," Lord Melander said doubtfully. "He is my heir . . ."

"And he'll still be your heir," Lena reassured him. "I'm

still my parents' heir and the King's ward, and Sven-August is the only child in his family as well. It's nice to have each other for company, and I promise you"—she smiled at him—"that our lessons do include civilized conduct, as well as how to behave at court. It's not at all uncommon for a child to be fostered; that's how we learn about people outside our families. That's very useful for anyone who is going to be spending time at court."

"You can tell people he likes animals or not, as you choose," the Prior said, "and you can say that his being fostered here is an act of charity, a gift of his time and talents to the Temple."

Lady Melander looked as if she would be delighted to leave Arvid there when she went home that night. Lord Melander still looked doubtful.

"We're not prisoners here," Lena pointed out. "You can visit him here, and he can visit you." Lady Melander winced, apparently at the thought of having Arvid visit—*I guess the bit about the mice really bothered her*—but Lord Melander looked as if that was what he needed to make his decision.

"I'll talk to him," he said, "and if he agrees, we'll send him to you in a few days. He can't be more trouble than your trip of goats."

Lena suspected that Lady Melander had done the packing, because Arvid moved into the Temple the next day. He slept most of the time for the first two days he was there. Lena remembered that she had done the same—it was a common reaction for someone coming from a stressful home to a Temple filled with the Peace of the God.

Once he could stay awake, Arvid fit in very well with both the people and the animals. Lena and the goats were his favorites, although Sven-August teased her about being equal to a goat. Lena, of course, was not the kind of person who got upset about being likened to a trip of goats. In fact, as she watched Arvid playing happily with the goats, she thought they had done well to get him. This was clearly where he belonged.

The Ones She Couldn't Save

Louisa Swann

Riann never imagined playing a simpleton would someday come back to bite her in the backside. Then again, she'd never thought the day would come when she'd need someone to actually listen to her.

Not an easy task when everyone in this Vkandis-forsaken village thought she had as much sense as a headless chicken.

Which was precisely what she'd always wanted them to think. If the villagers of Brinlevale, a remote village in the farthest corner of eastern Karse, believed she was simple, that she didn't know much more than a six-year-old child in spite of the fact she was almost fourteen, they would never suspect she had dreams.

The kind of dreams that really happened.

"Ya really are a dolt."

Riann pushed herself into a sitting position, dusted off her hands, and looked around dazedly, struggling to remember how she'd ended up sprawled on her back in the middle of the road.

She'd been on an errand . . . delivering dresses that needed mending to Miz Podahl, the seamstress who also owned the fabric shop. Riann glanced at the butcher shop off to her left, then at the general store on her right.

She'd almost made it to her destination, then. Only a little bit farther, past the foundry and the leather shop—

Images of dead and dying villagers flooded into her mind and her stomach convulsed.

"Where ya bound in a such a hurry, girl?" a deeper voice asked.

"She's too stupid to—"

"Shut yer mouth, boy. She's the one I'm wanting answers from."

Riann swallowed hard and focused on the men towering over her, driving the memories from her mind. It took a moment for her to make out faces against the bright glare of the midmorning sun, and when she finally recognized who they were, the world stopped breathing and so did she.

Mikael, one of the village elders, and the Sunpriest Tondjen.

Handehl, the elder's sixteen-year-old son, stood to one side, hands on his hips, glowering at her.

"Beg pardon," Riann mumbled, lowering her gaze to the ground. She rose to her knees and reached for the packages she'd been carrying, gathering her scattered load into a single pile. Her heart thudded painfully in her chest, and her mouth felt dry as the hard-packed road beneath her. Why, why, why did it have to be the Sunpriest?

"Miz Burdock tole me ta hurry," she said, keeping her gaze fastened on the packages wrapped with paper and twine as she pulled them together, keeping her thoughts focused on what was happening here and now, not on what had made her lose touch with reality long enough to—evidently—run right into the Sunpriest. "Says I always take too long, look at too many things, so I stopped looking at things, that way I'd be faster, that's wha Miz Burdock says . . ." She let the words trail off, hoping the men would chalk the incident up as just another one of her clumsy accidents.

One of the packages had torn, revealing the vibrant indigo cloth inside. She exclaimed in horror, pulling the package to her chest and letting tears rise into her eyes. "Miz Burdock gonna have a fit she find out 'bout this." Riann pressed her eyes closed tight, rocking back and forth, clutching the package tight. "Riann did a bad thing, a bad bad thing."

She heard a sound of disgust, though she couldn't tell whether it was from the elder or the priest, followed by footsteps moving away.

When she finally opened her eyes, she was alone in the middle of the road.

She took a shaky breath, and then another, breathing deep the musky scent of sunbaked earth and the surprisingly sweet flowers growing on the brinle bushes outside the village walls. The hard-packed dirt felt warm and solid beneath her, and all she wanted to do was lie down, warmed and supported by the earth below, warmed and comforted by the sun above.

She listened to the sounds of villagers going about their business. No one called out to her. No one offered to help. They were used to her little accidents. With any luck, this would be chalked up to Riann's clumsiness, as quickly forgotten as the other mishaps that were part of her everyday life.

Riann wouldn't forget. She wasn't sure she'd ever get the Sunpriest's look of disgust out of her mind, no matter how hard she tried. She wanted to forget she'd run into him . . .

She wanted to forget what she'd *seen*. What had consumed her vision so completely that she'd run into the Sunpriest like a blind cow she'd once seen blunder into a bull. The furious bull had knocked the cow to the ground, then proceeded to stomp and gore the poor thing until his fury was spent.

At least the Sunpriest hadn't stomped her. Hadn't gored her either.

Not yet.

Slowly, Riann rose to her feet and held the packages tight in her arms, heedless of the chalky dust smeared across the "cape" she'd created from scraps of brightly colored cloth. She straightened her ankle-length skirt, kept her thoughts focused on the packages and getting to her destination.

Everyone knew Sunpriests could pull thoughts out of someone's mind.

Had Sunpriest Tondjen seen her thoughts? Did he know what had really been on her mind when she'd barreled into him?

She kept her head down, moving in the peculiar shuffle-step she was known for, a movement as much a part of her now as her "village idiot" persona. She finally reached the fabric shop on the corner—

And the world exploded in a sea of sparkles.

Her head spun and her vision blurred, and suddenly she wasn't seeing the rough wooden exterior of the fabric shop, she was seeing the village square. The square buzzed with villagers filled with excitement. There were newcomers in town, a wagon family, the first in Riann's memory, traveling in a brightly colored wagon of painted wood and canvas. Mystified, Riann wove her way through what seemed to be a crowd, listening intently to the bits and pieces of conversation.

She heard the words "—twins—" and "—don't look too good—" and then the vision shifted and she found herself looking down from a height that allowed her to see most of the village square. The villagers still filled the square, only . . . their bodies were crumpled and lifeless . . .

Someone screamed as Riann tried to look away and couldn't. The faces stared up at her, lips slack, skin pale, eyes dull and accusing. Adults and children lay tangled together. The bodies swollen, the skin stretched almost to bursting . . .

Slowly, Riann realized what she was seeing wasn't really happening. Not yet.

But the screams *were* real.

And judging by the pain in her throat, they were coming from her.

"There now, girl, what's gotten inta ya? Hush now. Hush."

The voice grew louder, penetrating the hazy shroud that seemed to be covering everything. Riann blinked hard, struggling to see through the haze, to focus on the voice . . .

Until once again she was looking at the fabric shop. Miz Podahl, the shopkeeper, had an arm around Riann's shoulders. She froze in place, words of warning—*Don't let them in! Send the strangers away!*—poised on her lips, words that would tell the shopkeeper she wasn't who she appeared to be.

Words that would wrap Riann in a deadly blanket of suspicion.

It only took one person to call for the Sunpriest. The priest would know in an instant who she was—*what* she was.

And then she'd burn in the cleansing fires—as so many had burned before her.

Generally, Riann "saw" things just before they happened. She'd known her mother was about to die—had *seen* her death—moments before it actually happened, and as she'd grown, the *knowing* and the visions intensified. She'd discovered that the difference between what she'd come to call a *Happening* and a simple dream, waking or sleeping, was the feeling in her gut. When she sensed a Happening, she got a flash of an image, then an awful gut-wrenching sensation that made her wish she could be sick.

Whatever it was that she'd *seen*, happened—generally— moments later . . .

Riann felt her eyes widen in horror as the realization sank in.

Whatever she'd just seen was almost upon them.

She covered the expression, looking around as if searching for something.

"Are there travelers, then?" she asked, lines of worry creasing her face. Everyone knew Riann didn't like change, and travelers meant change. She peered up at Miz Podahl and clung tighter to the woman's arm.

"No one here but us villagers," Miz Podahl said with a smile. "Though t'would be nice to have some folks visit so's we hear somethin' of what's happening out beyond Brinlevale."

She patted Riann's hand and nodded at her legs. "There now. It looks like you've skinned up yer knee. Come along inside and I'll fix it up fer ya. No need ta go looking fer a healer fer that tiny thing."

Riann kept the grimace from her face. Not that there was a real Healer in the village. Yes, they had a Sunpriest. Every village did. But Sunpriest Tondjen was a grumpy old man, resentful of his post and prone to flashes of irrational anger. If he'd ever had a gift for healing, that gift had disappeared along with his reason.

She let the woman help her up, clinging to the plump shopkeeper's arm, and wondered despairingly how she, a girl who everyone thought had the brains of a worm, could prevent the disaster she'd just seen coming.

"I've got a pretty bit a cloth fer ya, too," Miz Podahl said. "But maybe we should get that cape a yers cleaned up a mite afore ya go addin' any more ta the thing."

Riann glanced down at her cape in dismay. "Oh . . ."

"Just dirt, nothing major far as I kin see." Miz Podahl brushed at the cape, beating it as she would a rug, only not quite as hard, though Riann still took a step back. "There now," she said. "Good as new. Well, maybe not new, but at least as good as twas before ya decided to plow the road with yer noggin."

Riann gave the shopkeeper a beatific smile, feeling her worries ease as she did so. It had always struck her as odd that simply smiling could make her and others feel better, but it always had and it, appeared, always would.

"That's a girl," Miz Podahl said, her smile widening. "There's the smile that always brightens my day. Come on, then." The shopkeeper turned and led the way inside.

A pang of guilt ran through Riann as she followed, though she kept her smile in place. She hadn't come up with the simpleton act by herself. She'd learned from the best—her mother. Her mum had been the real thing, though. Old Man Burdock had found Mum crumpled and pregnant in a half-flooded ditch beside the road. He and his wife had nursed her back to health, caring for her—and for her baby when Riann was born.

Miz Podahl led the way past the counter loaded with new bolts of cloth of every color. Riann didn't even stop to look, the burning in her knees increasing as she limped into the back of the store, keeping her mind off the burning by remembering . . .

Mum had done everything the Burdocks asked of her, from scrubbing floors, cleaning fireplaces, and washing dishes to milking the cow. As long as directions were given clearly and she was given plenty of time to complete her tasks, Mum could do most anything that didn't require figuring or scribing.

She cared deeply for Riann, though the caring was more like that of an older sister to a younger sister than a parent to a child. When Riann had turned seven, the relationship gradually changed, with Riann taking over more of the responsibilities that tended to perplex her mother.

And she had been normal, at least as normal as an adult in a child's body could be.

When Riann was eleven, Mum took sick, and Riann wouldn't leave her side. An herbalist came and went, and Mum got worse.

The Sunpriest came and performed a "healing."

Mum never again opened her eyes.

A day later, the priest's assistants came and took Mum to the village Temple. They returned with her ashes . . .

"Have a seat." Miz Podahl waved at a chair pulled up to the kitchen table. "I'll be back in a minute."

Riann eased herself down into the chair, heart aching.

It wasn't long before she'd come down with the same sickness that had taken her mum. She'd experienced her first vision when her mum died, a vision that still gave her nightmares. During the fever that left her feeling weak as a newborn kitten, Riann experienced her second vision: the baker's four-year-old son falling into the village well.

Riann didn't take the vision seriously and neither did the cleaning woman Miz Burdock had set to watching her. The woman claimed Riann's ravings were fever-born and never said a word about them to anyone.

Even after the boy was found dead in the well after being missing for more than a day.

The woman—Riann couldn't remember her name, and she had long since moved away—had shushed Riann when she'd panicked after the boy's body was found.

"Nothin' ta be gained by saying somethin' now," she had said. "Ya keep yer dreamin' ta yerself, elsewise, ya'll find yer ashes being scattered 'cross the fields, just like yer mum's."

It took some time to figure out the meaning behind the woman's words. And to find out the woman had seeded the ground for what came next, claiming Riann's brain had been taken by the fever. But even in her weakened state, Riann could sense the wisdom of the woman's words. By the time Riann felt like living again, she found herself mimicking her mum, in both words and mannerisms, and had continued to do so ever since . . .

"Here we go now. Put yer leg up here and let me get ta

work." Miz Podahl thumped down in another chair and patted her lap. Riann obediently lifted her leg, sliding her chair
forward until her knee was centered on the old woman's
skirts. The shopkeeper bent her head and started gently
cleaning the knee with a damp rag . . .

Two days after Mum's death, Old Man Burdock was
killed by a runaway cart, and Miz Burdock changed. Though
she hadn't denied Riann a roof over her head, that roof came
in the form of a chicken shed, while meals depended on what
was left over from Miz Burdock's plate.

Many of the villagers had taken pity on her. Petre the
baker left a bag—filled with discarded bread heels and rolls
too dry to sell—at the bakery's back door every night. Lavina
at the butcher shop slipped her pieces of dried sausage and
the overdone ends of roasts when she could. Miz Podahl,
seamstress and shopkeeper, gave Riann leftover pieces of
cloth and showed her how to fashion those pieces into items
of usable clothing, like her cape . . .

Riann stared at the silver-and-gray hair streaking the top
of Miz Podahl's head as the woman finished wiping the grit
from her knee. The shopkeeper waved a hand at her bare
toes.

"Bilcha's got some shoes going unused. His girl's feet've
got so big she's wearing *his* shoes now. I'll see if he'll pass
them along to ya. Yer gettin' too old ta be going 'bout without proper footwear."

Riann wiggled her dust-speckled toes. She didn't mind
not wearing shoes. Her feet were tough enough that she never
really paid much attention to putting anything on them until
the weather turned cold and winter moved in. She looked
from her toes back to Miz Podahl's smiling face, and a lump
threatened to choke her throat closed.

Most of the villagers had been kind to both Riann and her
mum. There was no reason for them all to die because *she*
was afraid of revealing her true self.

But she was *petrified* of the cleansing fires.

Every time she thought about telling Miz Podahl what had
happened—to warn the shopkeeper not to let any strangers

into the village—she felt as though someone had punched her in the stomach, and her vision started to darken.

It took the rest of the day for Riann to figure out what she needed to do. At least the villagers were used to her stumbling about, so there was no need to come up with reasons to explain why she'd forgotten to pick up Miz Burdock's mending at the end of the day, or why she'd walked into the bakery and just stood there, staring at the walls.

Heavy thinking, in any form, was not something Riann was used to doing. Yes, over the years she'd worked out ways to prevent as many of the Happenings as she could, but that was more a case of being in the right place at the right time than actually planning something out.

She'd found out the hard way that she couldn't save everyone.

Riann loved children and was often allowed to tend the younger ones when there was an older woman nearby. When she'd *seen* Lavina's mischievous seven-year-old daughter being stung to death by bees in one of her visions, she'd managed to lure the girl away from the newly found beehive before the girl got it into her head to climb the tree and knock the hive down.

She'd come up with a good plan that time, one that would keep the girl from a deadly stinging and teach Handehl—an arrogant idiot who thought he could do anything he wanted because he was the elder's son—a lesson. It hadn't been hard; after she'd gotten the girl safely back to the village, she'd started talking about the hive at the same time Handehl was nearby. Riann knew the boy loved to listen to other people's conversations, either spreading whatever he'd heard throughout the village before day's end or using the information he'd heard to get something he wanted.

He also loved anything sweet. The thought of his own secret beehive was enough to send Handehl on a wild bee hunt.

Riann would never let that boy lay his hands on anything living if she could help it. So she'd asked Lavina's girl questions that drew out the wrong answers when Handehl was near. He'd searched for that hive for over a week, though Riann wasn't certain he'd really learned anything from the experience.

The visions made being in the right place at the right time fairly easy at first. Then the timing between vision and event faltered, and Riann found herself failing almost as often as she succeeded. Sometimes the event happened so soon after the vision, she didn't have time to prepare. She'd been too late to keep Jona from opening her oven. Jona's burns had been so bad—and the priest's incompetency so great—that the old woman had died in agony less than a day later.

But the visions had never come more than a half-day before the Happening occurred.

Which made this vision even more unusual.

The travelers still hadn't arrived, which almost set Riann's mind at ease. If she hadn't had both visions—first the quick flash of dead and dying villagers that had made her walk right into the Sunpriest, then the more extensive vision that had left her screaming—she might have actually thought she'd been mistaken.

But her gut wouldn't let it go.

Which was how Riann found herself slipping out of the village gates after the SunDescending ceremony. Heart pounding so hard she wondered why no one had heard it and followed her, she hid among the brinle bushes crowded tight against the log walls surrounding the village, the same prickly bushes that gave the village its name, and waited for darkness to fall.

The *clack* of the closing gates made the hair rise on the back of her arms. There was no going back now. No waiting and wondering if it had all been a *real* dream as opposed to a vision.

No matter. She had two things to accomplish before dawn. Three, really, if she included surviving whatever terrors the coming night held. First she had to find the wagon family, and then she had to convince them to turn around. If all went well, she'd be back before dawn and would be able to slip back into the village as easily as she'd slipped out.

There was only one road leading out of Brinlevale—or leading *to* the village, depending on which way you were traveling, so Riann didn't have to take time figuring out which way to go.

Unsure what to expect, but determined to be ready for whatever happened, she'd wrapped her heavy winter cloak into a bundle and tied it with twine, then had done the same with a blanket and her winter boots. She'd tucked the dried bread and sausage she'd found at the bakery and at the butcher shop into the boots so they wouldn't get squished before tying the boots into the bundle. She'd managed to hide both bundles in the bushes during one of her trips to the river for water.

The village well had been sealed closed when Petre's boy drowned. A new well was being dug, but harsh winters had slowed the progress. Meanwhile, the river provided the villagers with plenty of water; they just had to fetch it.

A good part of Riann's days were filled with hauling water. First, for Miz Burdock, then for whoever paid Miz Burdock the best price. Miz Burdock claimed Riann was just earning her keep, but some of the villagers disagreed and slipped Riann a coin here and there when they could do so unobserved.

She had those coins with her now, sewn into the lining of her winter cloak. They clinked softly as she drew the bundles from their hiding place in the brush. Hopefully, she wouldn't need the coins, but their soft music was reassuring, a promise that she was ready, no matter what difficulties lie ahead.

Here and there, trees thrust skyward, their deep shadows looming like black giants alongside the road. Dust from the road teased her nose, and the damp scent of the river seemed stronger in the night air.

The moon would be up soon, a fact she'd been relying on. And the clouds that gathered during the afternoon had drifted off as darkness fell, leaving the night sky sparkling with stars that cast their faint light over the road.

Able to see only the faintest outlines, Riann walked cautiously along the road, feeling trapped by the slowness of her movements. She fought down a giggle—strange that she generally moved this slowly throughout each and every day, and hardly thought twice about it. But now, when no one was watching, when it would actually be dangerous to move fast, she resented being forced to move slow.

It felt odd, really, to walk normally, without the shuffle-step she'd adopted after being sick all those years ago. At first, it felt as though she was walking *wrong*, but after a while, the movement felt so natural she began to worry she'd forget the shuffle-step when she returned to the village—*if* she returned to the village—so she started mixing it up, challenging herself to switch back and forth between the two. Thinking about her steps also kept her from thinking about how alone she was out here, by herself, in the middle of the night, on a deserted road.

When the moon finally rose and she could see the road almost as well as she could during the day, Riann forgot about the shuffle-step and walked as quickly as she could, trying to ignore the occasional squeaks and squawks coming from the bushes and trees.

The night air grew chill, and she unfolded her winter cloak and put it on, then carefully pulled the bread and sausage from her boots and laced them on. She allowed herself a quick bite of food, then wove through the brush toward a small stream, intending to quench her thirst. She could still hear the river, though its roar was muted by distance.

She started as something squeaked in a bush near her left foot. Before she realized what she was doing, Riann had turned around and was headed back to the road. She'd try again . . . later.

Near dawn, Riann found what she'd been looking for. Exhausted by the night of walking, she almost passed it by. The family had pulled the wagon—its wooden sides high and sturdy looking beneath a white canvas roof—completely off the road into a small copse of willow trees, picketing the horses by a burbling stream before settling down for the night.

Something was wrong, though. She could feel it. Like a mess of worms in her belly, only worse—like worms in her belly and spiders in her hair.

The wagon looked exactly like the one in her vision, but it seemed . . . vacant. Abandoned.

It couldn't be abandoned, of course. There had been a family in her vision—hadn't there?

The horses moved restlessly, stomping their feet and snorting softly. Riann froze. Of course the horses knew she was there. Horses had very sensitive noses. They could probably smell her.

Quickly, Riann moved closer, staying as far from the horses as she could. No use spooking the horses and waking up the wagon family. They might think she'd come to rob them, or worse. She listened for sounds from inside—voices, snoring, breathing—anything that would tell her that there were other people around.

With a start, she realized that she *wanted* to find people, needed to find them. The walk she'd made from the village had been the only time in her life that she hadn't been around people. Even when she'd walked down to the river for water, there'd always been villagers around, doing their various chores. Awake or asleep or drunk with too much wine, she knew what people sounded like. What they smelled like.

Riann took a deep breath and almost choked. She knew what death smelled like, too.

Panic bubbled in her throat as she circled the wagon. She bit back a scream as she stumbled over something that blatted . . . then moved.

A goat. Tied to one of the rear wheels. The animal scrambled to its feet, bleating plaintively as she passed, but Riann ignored the goat, focusing her attention on the mounds scattered around a smoldering fire ring a little more than a wagon's length away.

Cautiously, she stepped up to the first mound, got close enough to see the crumpled cloak, the staring eyes.

She'd found them—the wagon family.

All dead.

Quickly, she went from body to body around the fire ring, hoping against hope to find someone alive.

And failing.

Five men of varying ages and three women, one barely

more than a girl. It looked as though they'd gathered together for the evening meal and had been seated on logs or stones, facing the fire.

Whatever had happened to them, happened fast. There was still food on some of the discarded plates.

Riann's breath caught in her throat, and the sausage she'd eaten early in the night soured in her throat. Her vision had been true; she'd just misinterpreted it.

The faces staring at her had been *these* faces, not the villagers. The bodies weren't as numerous as she remembered, and they weren't in the village square, but they were swollen, eyes staring, skin stretched—just as she remembered.

She hadn't had to leave the village after all. Hadn't needed to . . .

A tiny sound caught her attention, bringing her back from the edge of panic.

There was something inside the wagon—someone.

Moving carefully away from the fire ring, Riann once again circled the wagon until she found a door in the rear, complete with steps that looked as though they could be tucked away when they weren't needed. She put a foot on the lowest step and stared at the door as if daring it to open.

What if whoever or whatever had done this to the family had seen her? What if they were waiting inside?

Another tiny sound, almost like a weak cough.

Riann lurched up the last stair, grabbed the door handle, and twisted.

The door swung open on silent hinges, moonlight pouring into the tiny room beyond. She had never been inside a traveling wagon before. It looked like a miniature house, packed together neatly in a space that had to be the size of Miz Burdock's kitchen. There were cupboards everywhere, and a bed along one side.

The bed was empty.

Another tiny cough.

It came from the far end of the room.

It seemed to take forever to get from one end of the wagon to the other. The place smelled of recently cooked lamb and something else she couldn't identify.

Until she found herself looking into a cradle.

The baby lying on its stomach couldn't be more than a few months old. A wave of icy cold washed over Riann as she realized that once again she was too late. The tiny form was as still as the bodies around the fire ring.

"I'm sorry," she whispered, all thoughts of the villagers fleeing from her mind. She hadn't seen *this*, hadn't . . .

"I'm so sorry." Her voice broke and she sagged back against a set of cupboards, tears blurring her vision.

The tiny sound came again.

From the cradle in front of her.

With a soft cry, Riann snatched the baby from the wooden box, turning it over and cradling it in her arms. Her nose wrinkled as she recognized the other "smell" she hadn't been able to identify at first.

The baby's face was bright red, as if he—or she—had been crying. The little mouth worked soundlessly for a moment, then opened wide.

Riann had never been so glad to hear a baby cry.

She quickly went through the wagon, finding clean cloth diapers—and not so clean ones—then rapidly changing the little one. And discovering that he was definitely a she.

"Hush now, baby girl," she cooed. "Hush."

Changing a dirty diaper didn't seem to be enough. The baby wrinkled up its nose and let out another plaintive cry. It hiccupped and the crying faded to a weak squeal. Alarmed, Riann looked around the wagon again, trying to find something to feed the little one.

It took some time, but she finally realized that the noise she kept hearing outside was the goat, not some deadly night creature. She found a clean mug in one of the cupboards, laid the baby gently back in the cradle, and hurried outside.

Riann had never milked a goat, but she'd milked plenty of cows. The poor thing's udder was so swollen she was afraid she would hurt the animal when she tried to milk it, but the goat seemed relieved.

"I'll do more in a minute," she promised as the mug quickly filled. There had to be a bucket around somewhere. She'd find it and then . . .

Riann dismissed the thought from her mind. She ran back inside, found a clean cloth she could tie over the top of the mug, teasing a corner loose so it draped down over the side, then let the baby suck on the end of the cloth as she tilted the mug, slowly letting the goat's milk saturate the cloth.

It wasn't the best way to feed a baby, but it worked.

After the baby had fallen back to sleep, Riann took a deep breath and headed outside.

The two huge horses snorted and shuffled as she drew close, but they didn't shy away, seemingly happy for some human companionship. She let them sniff her hand, stroking each of them in turn. "Too bad ya can't talk," she said in a low voice. "Ya had to've seen somethin' of what's gone on here."

She glanced over her shoulder at the fire ring and shook her head. Not some kind of mortal sickness. From what she remembered, babies were the hardest hit when families got sick, and the baby in the wagon seemed just fine.

Some kind of poison, then?

Riann wasn't a Healer, she wasn't even an herbalist. The best she could do was get back to the village and let everyone know . . .

Her breath stopped in her throat so quickly Riann thought she was choking.

She couldn't go back to the village. She'd have to explain why she'd gone wandering off on her own in the dark. How she'd come across an abandoned wagon. How she'd found a baby without a mother.

She'd have to tell them about the vision.

Riann took a deep breath. She had someone to care for now. Someone who depended on her. She couldn't let that grumpy old priest feed her to the cleansing fires.

Moonlight glinted off a necklace hanging around the throat of one of the women. Riann gritted her teeth, walked over and took the necklace from the woman's throat, trying not to touch the icy skin.

She absently noted that the bodies hadn't been touched by

predators, another sign of poison or mortal sickness, according to Old Man Burdock.

Well, if they'd been sick, she'd know in a day or so.

But the baby is fine.

Riann wrapped the necklace, a finely wrought piece of what looked to be silver with a glowing blue stone in the center, tightly in her fist, forced herself to look at the bodies one by one, then headed back to the wagon, planning to set out the moment the sun broke over the horizon.

She'd heard the stories of the Great Traitor, a Karsite captain who'd been "chosen" by one of the white demon horses the Valdemarans called Companions. The Companion had saved the captain from the cleansing fires. When she'd first started having the dreams, Riann had prayed every day for a white horse to magically appear and carry her away.

No white horses had shown up.

So now, she'd have to go to them.

Yes, Valdemar was a long way away, and yes, they had demons.

But they didn't burn children in Valdemar.

All she had to do was get there. She could live with white demons.

And so could the baby.

One Last Night Manning the Home Station

Brigid Collins

As the last rays of a blazing orange sunset gilded the wheat ripening in the fields, the soft southern breeze carried traces of frog song from the forest and mixed them with the cacophony of the small town engagement celebration Yerra was about to sneak away from.

The warmth of the cloth-wrapped pie she'd hidden in her satchel pressed against her hip, its crushed berry and pastry fluff scent teasing her nose.

With a glance behind her, she tightened her grip on the strap across her shoulder in anticipation. She'd seen a flash of white in the trees earlier this afternoon. Footsteps like bell chimes had confirmed her assumption: A Companion waited out there, by the Herald's Waystation outside of town.

The knowledge sent all kinds of exciting hopes whizzing through Yerra's mind. Maybe the Companion recognized her as the one who'd worked to keep the Waystation from complete neglect over the last few years. Maybe Yerra would never have to endure the quiet sleepiness of her small town and its petty squabbles after tonight.

Maybe the Companion was calling her to serve Valdemar in earnest at last.

But she couldn't turn up at the Waystation to meet the Companion empty-handed. That wouldn't reflect well on the image she'd tried to make of herself.

And so she'd decided to take one of Mother's amazing berry medley pies from the party.

"A waste of good berries, is what it is," Mother had said this morning as Yerra and her sisters worked to prepare the pies. "Why we should even attend the party is beyond me. We've no relation to the bride's family, and a good thing *that* is. And now the Millers will be associated with those thieving Carpenters, such a shame. Marli is as selfish a leech as her parents, stealing a nice boy like Barret from the respectable girls of town. I tell you, he'd have taken Yerra when she comes of age next year if it weren't for that wench."

Yerra shuddered at the memory. She'd always known Mother had such designs for her, but Marli's engagement to Barret had saved her from a boring fate.

Not that anything was wrong with the Miller boy, but from the first and only time she'd seen a Herald up close, Yerra had had grander plans for herself. Unfortunately, while she had stuck on how brave and strong the Herald had been, everyone else in town had focused on how he judged the well near the forest to belong to her family's thieving neighbors, and the following animosity between families had continued without cease to this day. The whole community had labeled Heralds as "outsiders" and "troublemakers" ever since.

Yerra didn't belong with such small-minded people.

Her scan of the party didn't reveal anyone watching her, so she figured she had a clear shot to make her escape. Her satchel thumped against her hip as she started slipping away from the revelry. Maybe she should hold the pie in her hands as she approached the Waystation? That would make a good impression on the Companion.

"Yerra, where are you going?"

Yerra cringed at her brother's voice. She must have missed him, too caught up in deciding how to greet the Companion. She didn't answer his question as he trotted up beside her. Luckily, Rhen could carry a conversation all by himself.

"Mother's aiming to get us all out of here as soon as possible," he said. "She wants us to go make our congratulations to the groom now."

"To the groom?" Yerra asked. She'd already kept the Companion waiting all afternoon. She didn't think she could afford to take the time for the congratulations, but she also realized she didn't have much of a choice at this point.

Chewing on her lip, she allowed her brother to shepherd her back to the party. They wove through the people in the square, skirting the edge of the roped-off dancing ground. The bandstand shook to the rhythm of stomping feet, while fiddles and tin whistles sang the merriest tunes their players had to offer. The town didn't have any trained Bards to speak of, but the farmers drank the music in anyway.

Despite that, Yerra caught the unconcealed hostility when members of different families would meet one another's gazes. Animosity crackled through the air like lightning, and dancers kept to their own sides of the square. Odd, since Marli had an uncanny ability to appear wherever fights broke out, ready to slather her own brand of innocent problem-solving over the bickering parties. Maybe she was too caught up with her bridal preparations to put out emotional fires tonight.

Yerra's mother stood with her arms crossed and a scowl on her face when they reached her. The rest of Yerra's siblings waited there, and Father kept his back to the dancers.

"Everyone is here now?" Mother asked upon their arrival. "Good. We'll give our congratulations as a family, and then we can all get back to more practical uses of our time."

Yerra found herself shuffling along with the rest of her family. Her siblings pressed close together, marching in step as they headed toward the bridal table. Yerra pulled her satchel around to her front and hoped no one noticed the tell-tale warmth and aroma of her hidden offering.

At the bridal table, the Millers and the Carpenters sat smiling at each other and acting as though they were having as good a time as their guests. Barret perched on a stool in the middle, but the seat beside him had no occupant.

Yerra's family approached, and everyone at the table looked at them.

"We've come to make our congratulations to the couple," Mother ground out with the barest civility. Yerra winced.

The bride's mother stood and gave them a pinched expression of forced apology. "Marli is not feeling well and is still composing herself in her room. I hope you'll understand when we ask you to delay your joy for her until she can be here to receive it."

"The girl has kept herself locked away all evening. How long does she expect us to wait? My own girls can't afford to waste the whole night when they have work at home to return to."

Out in the main square, some partygoers were lighting the lamps as the sun finally sank below the horizon. Yerra stifled a sigh. She didn't have time to wait out an argument between her mother and Marli's. The desire to look over at the table of food and see if anyone had noticed the space where her stolen pie once sat tickled at her eyes. The urge to dash straight for the Waystation and the waiting Companion prickled at her heels.

Marli's mother held her stance. "She will join us once she's feeling better. She wouldn't miss her own engagement celebration, you know."

Yerra's sister giggled beside her. "I think she's already been celebrating her engagement. Come down with the child-sickness, I'll bet."

The comment set the other girls tittering with laughter, and Barret's face flushed red, though he said nothing to confirm nor deny the accusation.

Yerra's mother stepped forward. "If the girl can't even turn up to a party in her own honor, my girls won't pay the price. We offer our congratulations to the groom."

She swept into a curtsy that fluttered with angry flourishes, and Yerra's sisters rushed to follow suit. Yerra ducked her head.

Behind the bridal table, every person currently related to Marli leapt to their feet. Their faces twisted in as wide a variety of shock and fury as Yerra had ever seen. Her family's insult to theirs would not go unchallenged.

Yerra winced and squeezed her satchel. The strap squeaked in her sweaty fist.

"How dare you ignore our daughter!" came the outraged cry. More followed, of a less than polite nature.

Yerra's family spat back as good as was sprayed over them, and Yerra hunched her shoulders in an attempt to block their screeches out. Nothing reminded her of how little she cared about these ridiculous fights than when one cropped up like this.

But tonight Yerra felt something from the battle. Anger of her own simmered inside her, frothing against her ribs as the sky grew darker. In her head, she pictured the flash of white she'd seen fading away and heard the soft bell chimes of a Companion's hooves cantering off, sick of waiting.

Yerra sidestepped between two of her sisters. Once the fight got into full swing, she would duck out and finally make her escape.

At the bridal table, the groom's family had joined the fray of insults, leaping to defend their soon-to-be daughter. Barret stood on his stool now, his hands waving above his head as he tried in vain to get the attention of all three families.

"Please," he cried, "Marli wouldn't like any of this. Stop fighting, at least for her engagement!"

Yerra rolled her eyes. At least he was a good complement to Marli, if he agreed with the girl's ideals, but good luck to both of them in getting anyone in this town to agree with one another. For all the townsfolk hated outsiders, they hated each other just as much, if not more. No matter what Marli had ever done to prevent them, the bickering and fighting carried on as usual.

But Barret kept trying, raising his voice until finally he let out a bellow that rivaled the blacksmith's. Every head in the crowd and at the table wrenched around to stare at him.

Yerra slipped away as he spoke, but she forced herself to focus on the continuing debate behind her, made herself listen to the way it thrummed through the crowd and built into a crescendo of pitiful bitterness that chased after her even as the ripening wheat rustled around her in a secluding embrace.

She never wanted to forget the small place she came from when she left for Haven. It would help her keep things in perspective when she dealt with serious Herald business.

Night descended like a thief dropping from the trees, but Yerra had come to the Waystation outside of town many times under the cover of darkness, and she knew the path intimately. She would not stumble over some protruding root or startle at the sound of night creatures going about their business.

Besides, there could be nothing to fear of a forest with a Companion waiting somewhere in it.

The light sweet perfume of a night blossom drifted on the breeze that fluttered the leaves. An owl hooted somewhere above Yerra's head. Dirt still damp from the rain two nights ago softened her footsteps. She shifted her satchel so the strap didn't bite so hard into her shoulder, and the adjustment sent another waft of berry scent floating into the warmth of the night.

Yerra took a deep breath, letting the familiar forest soothe her nerves. The ridiculous rivalry between her family and the Carpenters, not to mention the tensions running throughout the entire community because of that rivalry, had keyed her up so she was about ready to lash out at someone. Though she didn't care one bit about the fighting, she couldn't avoid the effect of all that misguided energy flying around back there. It piled on top of nerves already jangling from the prospect of meeting a Companion to turn her into something of a wrung out mess as she'd made her way through the wheat fields.

Now the enveloping darkness of the forest came into her through all her senses, cooling the heat of her anger, calming the tumult of the frustration dancing within her. In this place she could be herself. Alone on the path to the Herald's Waystation, she could unwind herself from the small-town farm girl into what she knew herself to be in truth: a daughter of Valdemar.

And she was ready to serve her real mother any way she could. She'd been ready from the one and only time she'd seen a Herald and his beautiful Companion. Unfortunately, his ruling in favor of the Carpenters had only fanned the flames of hatred between the two families. Yerra didn't understand the argument. Their property had a stream of clean water running through it, and they had no need of a well.

The Waystation lay a way into the forest, a suitable distance from town, so that any passing Herald would not be a burden on any one family, but close enough to get into town quickly should the need arise. Not that the need ever arose in this town, and even if it did, the Herald would find no welcome awaiting any attempt to provide aid.

To Yerra, the distance made for a pleasant bout of exercise and a chance to clear her head.

Once she passed the old oak up ahead, she would be within sight of the Waystation. She came up beside the tree, her fingers outstretched to brush against the trunk as she always did. She'd been out here so often that the patch of bark had worn smooth under her touch. Every time, she pretended to draw power from it, power that she would return by putting it into the care of the station. She knew her efforts were not in vain whenever she would return to discover the supplies depleted or a piece of the station that needed repair. Heralds used her station as they passed through on their way to other, more receptive towns.

Fallen leaves crunched under her feet as she rounded the trunk, and the Waystation came into view through the branches of the trees ahead. Its simple wood and plaster structure didn't exactly blend into the forest, but the underbrush grew right up against it, and the foliage curled along its walls in a welcoming embrace. A stack of firewood stood under a protective roof on the side nearest Yerra. The pile had shrunk since the last time she'd been here.

Light spilled from the window and open door to lie in flickering patches on the ground. Yerra froze, her fingers still pressed against the old oak.

Someone was using the Waystation right now. A Herald had taken some of the firewood Yerra had cut and now had a fire going.

And if a Herald was here, that meant the Companion she had seen could not be here to choose her.

Disappointment built thick in her throat, and she swallowed several times. She'd been *so sure* tonight would be her last in her hometown. She'd considered herself already halfway down the road to Haven, and having to rein her imagination in and plod back toward home stung like the lash of her father's belt.

Blinking against the burn in her eyes, Yerra drew her hand away from the old oak. She swallowed again. Soft sobs drifted through the trees, and it took Yerra a few breaths to realize the sounds weren't coming from her.

The Herald in her station was crying.

Yerra's heart beat faster. The Herald needed help. Shaking herself, Yerra forced her disappointment to the back of her mind and pulled her thoughts back toward station upkeep. She may not gain a Companion of her own tonight, but she could do something to help a Herald in need. That would have to be enough.

"Hello?" she called. Thank goodness her voice didn't waver around the lump in her throat. "Is everything okay?"

A sharp gasp came from inside, and the sobbing cut off. As Yerra approached the entrance, the heavy wooden door wrenched itself closed. The rock that had held it propped open clattered over the ground, flung away into the bushes.

Yerra stared. Her jaw dangled, and she closed it with a snap. She knew Heralds had strange powers, but she'd never seen anything move on its own like that!

The sobs had resumed, though their choked rattling made it obvious the Herald was trying to stifle them. Yerra padded along the path, angling for the window in the rear. She tried to be quiet, hoping the Herald wouldn't realize she hadn't turned away, but as she drew almost close enough to peer inside, the shutters shook themselves free of their restraints and slammed closed.

Yerra watched the dust drifting down to the curling ivy below the window. Soft rays of moonlight filtered through the canopy to spark off the motes.

She'd caught a flash of white inside the Waystation just before the window closed.

Hot determination swept through her. The Herald must have heard about the reception she could expect from the people in this town and probably thought Yerra had come to spew hatred at her while she was injured or sick. The realization made Yerra's fists curl up, and she stomped back to the front of the station.

"I'm here to help you," she said as she approached the

door. She tugged on the handle, but the door didn't budge. "I'm the one who keeps this place in good condition. I'm not like everyone else in town. Please, I . . ."

She trailed off as she heard the soft whicker of the Companion inside. No response came from the Herald, but the crying had ceased.

Yerra gave another gentle pull on the door. It remained closed, but at least the shaved plank bent a little at her pressure. She made herself relax and let the calm of the forest seep back into her.

"I promise you, I live to serve Valdemar and her Heralds. I won't let the townsfolk know you're here."

Yerra held her breath and strained her ears. Her heartbeat thudded in the silence.

Finally, after a soft scrape of movement, light footsteps approached the door. Yerra let go of the handle. The pie in her satchel bumped against her thigh when she took a step back. At the reminder of her stolen offering, she plunged both hands into it and removed the pie, still wrapped in her handkerchief.

She held it before her with a smile she hoped didn't reveal any of her still-churning disappointment and waited as the door creaked open. Light spilled out, momentarily blinding as Yerra's night vision adjusted.

Marli stood framed in the open doorway. Yerra took in the dirty tracks of tears on the bride-to-be's face and the way her shoulders quivered. The girl gripped the doorframe hard enough her knuckles were as white as the Companion curled on the floor behind her.

The girls stared at one another, both speechless. A snort from the Companion broke their silence.

"Oh, Yerra," Marli said. "What am I going to do?"

The few touches Marli had made to the Waystation—the flickering fire, the neat stack of wood beside the hearth, the bed she'd dragged over for Yerra to sit on—lent the place a homier feel than Yerra had ever been able to achieve.

She plucked at the blanket covering the bed, recognizing it as one she'd taken after her sister discarded it. Marli had straightened it and smoothed the wrinkles of Yerra's inexpert bed dressing before returning to sit on the floor, curled absently against her Companion's side. She'd introduced him as Taren.

Yerra stifled the prickle of jealousy. "I thought you were ill."

"I had to tell my mother something so she wouldn't come looking for me. I couldn't keep this a secret if I went to the celebration."

"The other girls think you are with child," Yerra blurted. Anguish spread across Marli's face anew, and Yerra wished she could un-share the speculation.

"Barret and I have not . . . we are not . . ."

Yerra rushed to cover Marli's stuttering. "It's okay, I understand. Not that Barret himself is objectionable, but I wouldn't want to get married, either."

But fresh tears welled in Marli's eyes, and Yerra knew she'd said the wrong thing again.

"I *do* want to get married. I love Barret more than anything, and I was so looking forward to being his wife, to helping with the mill. I wish I *were* with child. We wanted to wait and have a proper marriage. But now . . ." Marli turned her gaze to the clean-swept stone floor. "I don't want to leave home, Yerra. But what will everyone *say*? My family are the only ones who tolerate Heralds, and everyone else hates them outright."

Beside her, the Companion Taren whuffled at her shoulder, a gentle caress obviously meant to provide comfort.

Yerra forced her fingers to unclench and smoothed the new wrinkles she'd put in the blanket. The effort of meshing her old image of Marli, quiet, homemaking, and obedient, with the idea of her in Herald's Whites, left her trembling. Her own face replaced Marli's in that mental picture all too easily.

How could Taren have chosen Marli?

"I don't know. When I went to fetch water, he was waiting for me beside the well," Marli answered.

Yerra cringed. She hadn't meant to ask her question aloud. But the answer she'd received sent a whole new streak of bitterness through her. That stupid well, the one she'd never cared about before but that had their families so tied up in knots.

If the Herald had declared differently, *Yerra* could have been the one fetching water today.

She drew her gaze to the Companion, knowing the reproachful twist of her own face wouldn't impress him and yet unable to stop herself. He met her with his own deep blue stare. Afraid to blink, as if doing so would break the communication between them, Yerra shivered. She thought if she strained hard enough, she could hear a voice speaking into her head, the way she'd heard some people were able to do.

But she was deceiving herself, and the effort left her with nothing but a pounding headache and a sinking heart. She had no mental ability of her own that would attract a Companion to Choose her. Whereas Marli . . . well, she'd done that trick with the door earlier, and the window shutters. And Marli always seemed to appear whenever conflict arose in town, ready with a soothing smile and a suitable solution for everyone.

As Yerra lowered her gaze to look through the floor, a truth emerged from deep inside her, as though dragged up by Taren's lingering eyes.

Her work in tending the Waystation had never been for the duty to Valdemar she claimed. She'd merely been hoping to place herself in an advantageous spot, a place where she might have a good chance of presenting herself to a Companion. Even earlier this evening, when she realized a Herald waited in the station, she'd hoped to be repaid for her help with a ride to Haven.

Her fingers tightened on the blanket once more, and hot tears splashed onto her lap. To her horror, the bed dipped beside her, and Marli's arms curled around her shoulders. How selfish was she to accept Marli's comfort when the bride-to-be had her own pain to grapple with?

Shuddering and sniffing, Yerra pushed away from Marli's embrace. She tried to do so gently, but had no idea if she succeeded. Her wrist scrubbed across her eyes, and she turned toward Marli.

"Sorry. This isn't about me. What . . . what do you want to do?"

Marli's shoulders sagged. "I want to make this town a happy place again. Like it was when we were little girls. I can see things happening elsewhere, and I keep an eye out for fights springing up. And I want to marry Barret, but I also want to be with Taren, now that he's in my life."

Her eyes flicked to where the Companion remained curled on the floor, and Yerra watched adoration slide onto the bride-to-be's face.

"You have the opportunity to make all of Valdemar a happier place with Taren," Yerra said.

"Yes," Marli said, but her tone was tinged with sadness.

Yerra made herself continue. "If anyone from our little town is an ideal Herald candidate, it's you. You can apply your skills on a grander scale for a more noble cause."

"But I love this place, and this is the cause of my heart." Marli's voice grew wet. "I want to stay."

And Yerra wanted to leave, wanted it more than she wanted her next breath. No amount of wanting would make it possible for her, though.

"It's not about what either of us wants," she said. "It's about what we have to do. You must go to Haven, Marli, to become a Herald. You've been Chosen. Valdemar *needs* you. I don't have any choice but to stay here and be a dutiful daughter."

A final realization hit her, and she gasped at the shock of it. "With you leaving, I'll probably have to marry Barret next year when I come of age."

To her surprise, Marli laughed, though tears threaded through the sound. "Looks like we have drawn each other's desired lots, with no way to trade them."

She reached across the bed and caught Yerra's hands. "The only way we can make this okay is if we can trust each other to fill those roles the way we'd want them filled. You will work to return peace to our town, and I will do what I can to serve Valdemar as a Herald."

Now it was Yerra's turn to laugh. Here sat Marli, the town's problem solver, spouting another ridiculous solution.

"I don't think I ever had Valdemar's best interest at heart. I just wanted to escape."

Marli shook her head. "Look at this Waystation. All the work you've done to keep it up and running, it has not gone unnoticed. Even if no other Herald has been this way in the past two years, I appreciated the stocked shelves and ready firewood when I needed sanctuary tonight. Being in here, I can feel your devotion to the Heralds in every bit of comfort you've brought inside."

Yerra gulped down a fresh wave of tears. From the floor, Taren whickered, his eyes steady on her. From their depths, she drew up the confirmation that he'd sensed her devotion as well.

"I'd thought for a moment that I'd been too wrapped up in my dreams for myself," Yerra said, "but I do want what's best for Valdemar. Of the two of us, you're it."

"And," Marli continued, "if you can provide me with the secure knowledge that our town will be as well-maintained as this Waystation, that you will care for Barret where I cannot, I can gather the strength to see that your hopes for Valdemar are carried out, too."

Yerra did not trust her voice any longer, so she swept Marli into a tight hug. Marli returned it, and after a few chiming footsteps, Taren dropped his nose into their embrace. Both girls laughed, then cried, then laughed again.

"I wish you and I had been brave enough to be friends before this," Marli said as they broke apart to wipe their eyes.

Yerra agreed. "We can be brave now. The engagement celebration is still going. Maybe our families have stopped fighting."

Marli's eyes slid out of focus. "They haven't."

"Then we'll have to go together to make them stop."

"But first, we should take care of that pie you stole for me."

"We can eat it on the way. The fighting's gone on too long already."

The two girls worked together to bank the fire and tidy the Waystation. When all was set right, Yerra followed Taren and Marli outside, closing the door behind her with a firm tug as she always did. She didn't want any forest creatures creeping inside to make a mess of her place.

Marli pulled herself onto Taren's back, the movement natural and smooth. She held a hand out to offer Yerra a ride as well, but Yerra shook her head. They were going to make a statement to their families, and her place was on the ground.

Taren's hooves chimed as the three of them headed back to town through the darkened forest, and though Yerra's emotions tugged at her so she hardly knew one thought from the next, she joined Marli in eating the stolen pastry. Both of them agreed that her mother's berry pie had never tasted so good as when it was sealing a pact of peace for their families, their town, and their country.

Only Family Matters

D. Shull

Serril walked unseeing down the hill, away from the cluster of
buildings that housed the Healers' Collegium, away from the
yelling that—once again—marked whatever fight had started
this time between Ostel and Brone. No doubt it was the same
old song that had been sung for the past three weeks since
Marta had passed away in her sleep: who would be the next
Dean of the Healers' Collegium. No doubt they would find
him eventually, begging him to be the neutral party to mediate
between them. Unless he simply wasn't there to begin with.

Being a neutral party had seemed so reasonable, back when
he was in training to become a Healer. Don't get involved,
don't pick sides, just keep your head down and let things get
resolved by the people in charge. It had worked just fine, thank
you very much, though more often than he'd have liked, he
found himself caught in the middle of a fight *because* he didn't
pick sides. And as he gained seniority, his neutrality itself became a target when other Healers asked him to mediate .

Serril was fairly certain that none of them had ever noticed that his breath got short when they did that. Serril was
very certain that none of them knew about the bile that rose
in his throat, the edges of panic, the sudden sense that everything was finally going to fall apart, the way it had in his
family. Healers were often passionate people; it wasn't their
fault that when they started yelling at each other, he had entirely too clear memories of his childhood hiding place under
his brother's bed.

Serril let the tears fall even as he sped farther away from his home of more than a decade. He hadn't even talked to any of the precious Mindhealers, because it wasn't as though he was actually broken in mind. *It's just scarring from a painful childhood, and everyone has that*, he thought for the thousandth time as he put even more distance between himself and the Collegia. And he was certain that if Brone or Ostel found him, they'd either laugh it off (Brone was astoundingly insensitive for a Gifted Healer) or sigh and say that their present was more important than his past (Ostel's parents had been doting and wealthy; their donations had built a greenhouse and let Ostel learn Healing craft).

Enough! Serril ducked into an alley and ran through the breathing exercises he'd learned from Marta when she mentored him. It hadn't even occurred to either of the two contenders that he might be dealing with the additional grief of losing a friend and a mentor. Neither one had ever trained with Marta, except perhaps in their early classes with several other students at the same time. Marta had been an Empath as well as a Healer, and she had immediately picked Serril out as needing extra attention.

Keep breathing. Exhale all the hurt and sorrow, inhale the untainted air. Marta's words came back so strongly that for a moment, Serril thought she'd come back from the Havens to scold him. He hiccupped, felt the tears slow, and let the cool autumn air flow in through his nose, and out, warmed, from his mouth. Marta had been a mother to him, more of one than either of the parents who'd raised him.

It took him a good while to calm down and set himself in order. He hadn't been wearing his Greens when he'd left— *bolted, let's be honest here*—so to any passersby, he was just another face in the crowd. He thought it might serve him better to hide here in the crowds around the city; after all, if he wasn't a Healer today, nobody would need him, right? With a sigh, Serril acknowledged that the urge to disappear was another leftover from his childhood. Sooner or later, he'd have to go back up to the Collegium and face his colleagues; but if he had his way, it'd be later rather than sooner.

Once he'd made the decision to stay in the city for a while,

Serril found it fairly easy to just blend into the crowds. It was a market day, when the farmers brought fresh-picked fruits and vegetables to the city, and more than once Serril regretted not bringing his money along. The apples in particular were quite fragrant, and more than once his mouth watered at the sight of a roasted ear of corn.

His wandering also brought him to the edge of a cheering and laughing crowd. The throng was large enough that Guards were stationed nearby, but even they appeared to be enjoying themselves. Serril wove and ducked through the crowd to find a good spot to see what was going on, and he found himself in front of one of his favorite vendors. Linn always had good food and was good company, and she grinned at Serril as he leaned against one of the awning poles.

"Not having any of their nonsense today, are you?"

Serril had recovered enough to nod and smile a bit; his voice would probably take a little while longer to be usable.

Linn, who had seen him this distraught before, handed him a flaky pastry in a bowl. "Eat, it'll do you good. And pay attention, this is one of the best traveling shows I've seen. They should cheer you right up." She grinned at another customer and allowed as how her chicken was the best flavored for ten streets in any direction, even those fancy restaurants where you'd have to pay in gold for the privilege of standing in a line.

Serril had tucked into his food, finding the chicken inside to be very tasty, and tried to manage both the bowl and looking over the crowd. A raucous cheer suddenly arose, and the people in the front waved their hands in the air. Then, to his amazed eyes, they circled around the crowd to the back, letting the people behind them move forward to see more clearly. He'd seen it happen, and still he couldn't quite believe it.

Linn said, loud enough to hear, "Like I said, they're one of the best I've seen. Got the whole thing down to an art, so it's clear they've been doing this for a while. You should go up when you're done; they change the audience when they change the act." Serril gaped a moment, then ate more of the delicious pie. *I haven't seen that level of coordination out-*

side of military training. It took him a few moments to finish his meal while watching what he could of the show.

It looked to be several people, performers and musicians, and this particular act seemed to revolve around people hitting each other with inflated sheep's bladders on sticks. Apparently this was incredibly funny for the people in the front, so there must have been dialogue to go with it, but Serril couldn't hear anything over the laughter in front of him. At the last, right before the last sheep's bladder popped, he deposited the empty bowl onto Linn's counter and managed a "Thank you," before the crowd surged forward, taking him with it.

Where the last act had been comedy, this one was fairly dangerous. A young woman juggled knives at first, prompting gasps from the crowd as she started with two, then moved on to three, then four. Serril found himself wincing every time a knife came down point first, and cheering as the young woman caught them with a grin and a relieving lack of blood.

He'd thought it was a solo act, but then someone else came on stage, bowed to the audience, and was strapped to a large plank with a bullseye painted on it; for the literate in the crowd, the word *TARGET* was painted above the bullseye. The target strapped to the board was grinning as though this was the best joke ever heard or seen as the knife juggler became a knife thrower.

The first knife went *thunk* into the board between ribs and underarm, and Serril had a brief moment of panic at the thought of the knife missing. There were several major blood vessels very near that spot, and even he would be hard pressed to Heal a wound like that, given how far he was from the stage. After the next three knives hit the board and not the person, Serril realized that his breathing was quick and shallow. The knife thrower seemed to know what she was doing, but that didn't stop Serril from being anxious about an accident. A number of the crowd in front of him apparently didn't like this particular part of the show; he moved forward so that he could now hear the people on the stage.

"Serves you right, Zanner! You shouldn't be making fun of my age!" The young woman mock snarled as she grabbed another knife from the table next to her.

"But, Jayin! Just because you're sixteen as of right this morning—"

The young woman screeched. "ZANNER, NOBODY IS SUPPOSED TO KNOW THAT!" The musicians began playing a fairly common melody, usually played for autumn birthdays, and at that the young woman yelled, "AND DON'T YOU START, MOTHER! I KNOW WHERE YOU LIVE!" The woman leading the musicians merely grinned and continued playing. The crowd, sensing the mood, started cheering at Jayin, wishing her a happy birthday and throwing coins onto the stage.

Jayin held up a silver piece that had landed at her feet, and yelled, "This doesn't excuse this lowlife of a sibling for telling people it's my birthday!" Zanner continued grinning, and Jayin spun on the erstwhile target with a clearly mock glare. By this point, Serril was not even ten feet from the stage, and he saw the wicked gleam in the young woman's eye. "Why don't we scare your ears a bit, make sure you don't hear anything you're not supposed to anymore!" The first knife flew true and *thunked* into the board on the side facing mostly away from the audience. The second knife flew, and *thunked* solidly into the board on the side toward the audience, clearly missing the young person's ear.

"I give, I give, I'll never listen for things I'm not supposed to know again, like how your favorite stuffed animal is a—"

Jayin screamed for all she was worth, the crowd cheered and threw more money onto the stage, and a man ran to the front and said so everyone could hear, "Thank you so very much for coming to see the Avelard Family Traveling Show! That's our last act of the morning. We'll be back after the midday bell to continue to astound, entertain, and amuse you! We hope to see you again soon!"

A couple of people picked up the board with Zanner still on it and ran off the stage to the accompaniment of fast, silly music. Jayin bowed and immediately took herself off the stage in the opposite direction. Meanwhile, a couple of the musicians went around the stage, gathering the coins people had thrown, looking pleasant and cheerful and waving to the now disappointed crowd as it began to disperse.

Serril narrowed his eyes. Something was very wrong, but he might have been the only person in the audience to notice the trail of blood that led off the stage.

Now Serril cursed his lack of Greens. He had a medallion under his shirt that marked him as a Healer, but he had no idea whether that would be as recognizable. There was nothing for it, however, so he pulled himself up onto the stage even as the performers started yelling at him to get down.

To the nearest one, a young man dressed in autumn colors that suited his hair, he said, "I'm Healer Serril. I was out for a walk this morning, and didn't want to get mobbed, but I saw at least part of what happened. Please, let me help." To punctuate this, he pulled out the metal disc, embossed with the mark of the Healers Collegium, and showed it to the young man. "If it's not serious, then I'll be on my way after a bit of bandaging. If it *is* serious, then at least you'll have someone with the Gift who can mend your friend."

Before the young man could answer, a woman—the very one Jayin had identified as her mother—bustled out. "I suppose you won't go away even if we tell you it's a minor cut, will you?" Her voice was firm, as much as the glance she gave him, and she narrowed brilliant green eyes. "Fine, fine, you might as well come backstage. First time for everything, I suppose. Avelard family secrets and props all exposed to strangers and meddlesome busybodies who just happen to be standing by." She didn't reach out and grab him, she just gave him a look that reminded him of some of the governesses he'd had as a child. Serril bit his lip, but now that he was on stage, he could see that there was more blood than could be accounted for by a minor cut.

"I'll follow, I'll keep my eyes down, and once I'm done, I'll be out of your way."

"I suppose that'll do. I'm Ella, Master of the Music, and the one who herds all the cats of this show. You'll do well to jump when I say, sit when I say, and speak politely while you're here. We're a family and not performers backstage."

"I understand." And Ella strode off, leading Serril through a series of halls that were nothing more than cloth strung on rope until they arrived at an open space enclosed by a small ring of wagons. There, Serril saw that Zanner was still strapped to the board, and Jayin was kneeling next to the injured performer, biting her lip and looking concerned. At least the young woman wasn't prone to panic, even when she'd managed to wound someone by accident. *Maybe it's the performing life*, Serril thought.

"We've got a Healer who just happened to be in the crowd and not in his Greens. Young man, why don't you introduce yourself before you go over to Zanner and see what's what."

Jayin stood up immediately. "Do we *know* he's a Healer? He just jumps up on the stage and you believe him?"

Ella sighed. "He's got the medallion they give to the ones who're Gifted, my heart, so he's not a fraud by any means." She paused and gave her daughter a look. "So, we make sure Zanner's all Healed up before the next performance, and you'll need to practice your throwing a bit more, my heart."

"It wasn't my throwing that was the problem, Zanner moved!"

"I'm right here, you don't need to yell." Zanner sounded a bit stressed but, oddly calmer than Serril would have expected. He shrugged, marking it as another oddity of the performing life.

"Do I have your permission to come over, examine the wound, and, if necessary, Heal you?"

Zanner, still strapped to the board, chuckled weakly. "If I say no, it's not like I can get away, right?"

Serril blinked. "Are you usually this calm in the face of a possibly dangerous wound?"

"Yes, yes I am, and everyone here will tell you it's my wicked sense of humor." Zanner wiggled four fingers a bit in a come hither gesture and said, "Yes, you have my permission. Just don't go poking into anything that's not your business, you understand?" The finger wiggling somehow managed to take in chest and hips.

"Unless I'm bedding you, your gender is none of my business as your Healer; unless the knife went that far off target?" That got him a weak chuckle, and Serril went around to Zanner's other side to find that the knife had cut through part of the cartilage of the ear. Most of it was still attached, but there was enough blood to concern Serril.

"It's a good thing you had a Healer nearby. Reattaching this should be the work of a few moments." Serril looked up to see some very blank expressions, and he blinked. He couldn't tell what they were thinking, even though he hoped they were glad to have him available. Had they never had an accident that required a Healer before? "Ah, yes, some clean water would be good, so I can wash out the wound before I Heal it. Um. Are the knives clean?"

"I boil them in hot water before the show; the last thing I want to do is run the risk of making Zanner sick if the knife doesn't fly true." Even if today were *not* Jayin's sixteenth birthday, she was the very model of a grumpy teenager, crossed arms and all. Serril was already off balance by how the performers were behaving around him, but at least her behavior was more or less normal.

"Okay, that's better than some of my students, so points to you for that." Someone handed him a waterskin, and he rinsed as much of Zanner's blood away from both sides of the ear as he could. Then he set to Healing, and as usual, most of his concentration was taken up by the knitting together of flesh, cartilage, and blood vessel. But he was still aware enough to realize that Zanner's ear had been cut more than once and that it had been Healed more than once as well. And that the people standing around him were quite frankly as disapproving of him Healing one of their own as any Holderkin who'd had to rely on herbs and fermented barley for their healing.

When he finally stood up, the most muscular man he'd ever seen (*could I ask him to pose for some of our students learning musculature?*) escorted him politely but firmly back to the gathering space in front of their stage. A small coin was left in his hand, and before he could say anything else, a makeshift curtain had been dropped in front of the stage, and he was left staring at a mystery.

Which was precisely when Tessa found him. "What in the blazes are you doing away from the Collegium, Serril? You should have heard the shouting between Ostel and Brone this

time, and I am in no way ready to put myself between them. I
have a horror of being the Dean; otherwise I'd step in and tell
them both to back down! We need your cool head, please?"

He followed, certain as anything that there was a mystery
here at the Avelard Family Traveling Show, but just as certain
that there was nothing he could do at the moment.

Serril rushed out of the Collegium just after sunrise, this time
in proper Greens, headed down to where the traveling show
had performed yesterday. He hoped against hope that they
hadn't moved on, even though he remembered their expressions when he'd healed Zanner.

He was bleary from a lack of sleep and crying into his
pillow. Ostel and Brone had indeed been deep into a shouting
match over who would be the next Dean, and he'd spent far
too long calming them down. And then even longer shivering
in his bed, and then under it. After a night like the last one,
Serril reflected, he'd be better off disappearing into the Palace Archives, where nobody could find him. Instead, he was
on what he hoped was not a wild goose chase.

And indeed, the traveling show was still set up as though
for another day's worth of performances, even though it was
too early for a crowd to form. The curtain from yesterday
blocked the stage from view, though Serril suspected there
were plenty of ways to see through the curtain out to the
audience. He paced back and forth in front of the curtain for
a few minutes, trying to maintain some level of politeness
while trying to figure out a way to get someone's, anyone's,
attention. He wouldn't go through the curtain just because he
had suspicions, but all the same he couldn't just wait outside
until someone invited him in. Finally, he bit his lip, planted
himself in front of the stage, and took a comically deep
breath. He was no Bard, but he'd sung enough to know the
kinds of songs that got people's attention, especially the
songs that made them ask you to just *stop* singing.

But before the first note even came out of his mouth, one
of the performers he'd seen yesterday jumped through the
curtain, put a gentle finger across his mouth, and sighed. "No
need to torture us, or sing, or whatever it was you'd planned

on doing. Come on back. Ronnet was fairly certain you'd be back, and nobody would take a bet against him." She gave him a lopsided grin. "I'm Conna. Goodness, have you been up all night worrying at this? Do we need to send for a Healer?" Serril was almost certain she was teasing, but for some reason this hit a particularly sensitive spot, and he felt the tears well up in his eyes.

"Conna, are you making someone cry again?" Zanner called out from the curtain, but when both performers saw Serril, they jumped down, and between the two of them escorted the Healer backstage to the open area where he'd healed Zanner just the day before. It all happened so quickly, including the water in a mug and the camp chair, that Serril didn't quite have time to completely fall apart.

The well-muscled man knelt by Serril, made sure he drank water, and then said, "I'm Ronnet, strongman, accountant, and one of Jayin's fathers. You've met Ella, her mother, and when you're a bit more together, I'll introduce the rest of the family." Serril nodded miserably, drank more water, and pondered how in the world he could salvage anything from the disaster of going to pieces in front of these people.

Another man, this one a warm brown to Ronnet's blond, knelt to Serril's other side. "Hallo. I'm Hallen, Master of the Show, and the other of Jayin's fathers. We've been in Haven a few days, and we've heard some rumors about upset at the Healer's Collegium, what with the previous Dean having passed away a few weeks ago." Hallen hummed a moment. "I'm going to guess you're not one of the candidates, but you're probably stuck in the middle, and it's easier to just not be there when things get unpleasant."

Serril looked up into Hallen's face at that, but there was only a knowing smile and warm brown eyes.

"You'd ask me how I know that, but truthfully it's just a matter of knowing people as well as I do and seeing how you reacted yesterday and today. I have to be able to read an audience to know which parts of the show they'll enjoy. Good Healer, you have the air of a man brought low by events, heart-hurt and weary, and you're also wearing your robes backward."

Serril made to stand up, almost completely mortified now, and Hallen's smile immediately faded. "Gods, man, I was teasing about your robes." He whistled, and Conna, Ella, and Jayin immediately bustled over with a platter of bread and cheeses. "Eat, you've likely not put anything in your stomach since yestereve, or I'm not a father." He paused. "And perhaps you need to unburden yourself to some very discreet people." Serril heard a strangled gasp from somewhere around him, but before he could look around, Ronnet had gently pushed him back into the chair and put a piece of bread in his hand.

Overcome by kindness, Serril bowed his head, wept, ate bread and cheese, and told the assembled performers not just about the politics in the Collegium but about *why* he was reacting so poorly to it. Some part of his mind was yelling, screaming, asking him why he was sharing private things with a group of strangers, a traveling show. Another part of him was grateful to have an audience for once, instead of being the audience.

By the time he'd finished his food and water, he'd shared some of the darker things about his childhood, and he felt at least a little better. The faces around him (when he'd been able to look up) were more than sympathetic, and there had even been a few mutters about finding incompetent parents and hanging them upside down in the rafters of their attic.

"Well." This time it was Ronnet who spoke. "Sure as I know my numbers, that does not sound like any kind of a healthy family. And let me guess. You've not been to a Mindhealer, even though you're up at the Collegium, because other people have had worse childhoods, and it's not that you're broken as much as you're a bit sore from dealing with all of that. Am I too far off?"

Serril just stared at the strongman. Jayin giggled at his expression, and said, "My father Ronnet says it takes a strong man to balance the books and a stronger man to balance people."

Serril looked down at the ground again, even more certain that he'd made a colossal blunder by coming here to find the Healer hiding in the traveling show.

Ella put a hand on Serril's knee and sighed. Serril looked up into green eyes and saw unshed tears there. "We've had more than our fair share of people come to us just as wounded and sore from dealing with their families, which is why we made this family all on our own. We're not Healers or Mind-healers, but we make sure that the people who spend time with us get a healthy family, instead of a hurtful one, so they can see what good families are like. Zanner's family is Hold-erkin, and so couldn't stomach a child who didn't fit their mold. Conna and Hesby and Wenn, they've got their own stories to tell; and Zanner has given me permission to share."

The woman who'd teased Serril at the curtain said, "I'm sorry I managed to jab a thumb into your wound. I'd have teased you a little differently if I'd known. That's one of the things we do for each other here, is figure out where the sore spots are, and figure out ways to either work around them or help make those spots a bit less sore." She smiled, and handed him a piece of cheese. "My mother drank herself senseless, and I was the eldest, so I never had a childhood. Being here? I get to have siblings instead of children."

Serril took the cheese, and nibbled thoughtfully as Hesby talked about parents who disappeared for days on end, and nodded as Wenn described a situation somewhat similar to his own. He could see how they worked and how they helped each other. The one thing he couldn't be fully sure of was which one of them was the Healer; but he knew it would be something of a crime to take that person away from the family.

Finally, he sighed and stood up. "I came here to look for the Healer among you. I'm sure you've already guessed that. Someone is in need of training, because they've got a Gift, but I can't take that person away from this family—as healthy as it is—just to throw them into a situation where we are most definitely *not* a family right now. It just isn't fair in the slightest to whichever of you has the Gift. I'm sure I'd get thrown out and my Greens taken away if I mentioned this to anyone at the Collegium, but I'm also sure that I won't say anything to anyone there.

"All I ask is that you maybe stay in Haven a few more

days, let me teach what I can, and come back to the city as often as you can. Maybe winter here, so that I can sneak away from time to time and teach whoever it is." He sighed again. "I'm fairly sure that I don't have to worry about mis-use of the Gift; my main concern is that you don't hurt your-self in using it. That *is* a danger, if you're not trained. And just in case, I can train you on more than just gross anatomy and the various coughs and colds you're likely to get by trav-eling all over." He smiled slightly. "Thank you for the food and water, thank you for listening, and I'll be on my way now." As he turned toward Ronnet, to ask to be escorted out of their backstage, Jayin stepped up and gave him a very se-rious look.

"What if I came with you voluntarily?" She shook her head as the rest of the family gasped around her, and turned to face them. "We've had some really close calls, both with you all and with me. I've been lucky as anything so far, but that can't last. There's too much I don't know and too much risk that next time I'll nick Zanner's neck and not know how to put my dear sib back together." She turned to Serril and smiled at him. "Plus, it seems like while you're helping me, I could be helping you. After all, you don't really have a family, do you? You could be an Avelard by adoption, the way everyone else here is."

Serril opened his mouth to say something, and instead he started crying again. Within moments, he was enveloped in a hug, everyone in the traveling show huddled around him, murmuring reassurances. Jayin held him from one side, Ron-net from the other, and Serril felt safe for the first time in a very long time.

Jayin laughed as she looked up at him. "Besides, I'm pretty sure we can't convince you to run away and join a traveling show, you know? But if I go with you, you have to make me a promise or two."

Shakily, Serril asked, "What are they?"

"*You* need to get yourself to a Mindhealer. You've gone through so much, even if you haven't told us all of it, and if I'm going to have you as a mentor, you need to be able to handle me and my quirks. That's the first thing. The other thing is that you let us adopt you right now. I'm pretty sure mother and fathers won't object, and that way, when the show comes back to Haven, you can visit your family and have an excuse to not be up at the Collegium."

"You're not even my Trainee and you're already telling me how to run my life," Serril said with a wobbly smile on his face. "You're right about the Mindhealer, of course, which will likely make you insufferable for at least the first month. And if your family will have me—"

From behind him, Hallen said quite clearly, "There's no question here in my mind. Do any of you have any objections?" Before anyone could say anything, he added, "That means serious objections, Zanner, not something silly like he reattached your ear backward, or that we already have a Healer in the family, we don't need two of them." After a moment of silence, everyone laughed, including Serril.

And once the laughter died down, Hallen, Ronnet, and Ella all took Serril's hands, and Ronnet said, "Healer Serril, whatever family you came from, whatever your history, know this: Should you accept our offer, from this day forward, you are an Avelard. We will come if you call, we will feed you if you are hungry, we will hold you while you weep, and we will support you as you do good in the world. All we ask in return is that you do the same for us. Do you accept?"

"With gratitude and joy, I do." Serril's tears rolled down his face, his cheeks hurt from smiling, and as his family cheered and hugged him again, he felt a knot just under his heart loosen. *This is what family is supposed to feel like.*

Medley

Jessica Schlenker &
Michael Z. Williamson

"What'll you have?" the innkeeper asked.

"Blackberry mead and—what's your special of the day?" Jeris' last trip through here had been personal, before his mission with the Shin'a'in. Blurry memories had prompted him to halt early for the night. Halath, his Companion, had agreed, as they were enough ahead of schedule.

"Mutton stew and bread," the man replied.

"That, please."

"Girl'll bring your stew 'round."

He nodded and then meandered to an empty corner table.

Lost in recollections, he started when the food was put down in front of him. He glanced up to meet *her* startled expression.

"Um, hello." He sort of smiled. She was probably married now, her figure softened. She smiled back reflexively, then winced as the owner yelped.

"Excuse me," she muttered, heading in that direction. The tavern owner stood, stiff and angry, scowling at a little girl. Jeris gritted his teeth and didn't interfere. The barmaid—matron now, apparently—stopped beside the girl, obviously interceding for her. The girl nodded glumly, darted behind the counter to gather supplies, and set about cleaning tables.

She kept her head down as she worked, posture sullen and dispirited. Jeris watched her in distant concern.

:Does she look well cared for?: Halath asked.

:Yes,: he replied. *:Just unhappy.:*

:She's young,: his Companion replied. *:No doubt she'd rather be playing than working.:*

However, when the girl looked up and met his eyes, he felt as if he had been slapped. From the earliest he could recall, he'd heard how his sister and he looked like twins. But for the girl's sun-lightened hair, he was looking at *her* twin, twenty years past. *:Lord and Lady,:* he breathed to his Companion. The girl stared back, studying his face.

The barmaid—he couldn't recall her name yet—stopped cautiously by the table. "Is it not to your liking?"

"No, indeed," he replied. "It's all delicious, much as I remember."

She blushed and glanced at the girl. "Finish up quickly, Cara. Grandpa needs help with the dishes."

The girl looked at her mother and back at Jeris, questions obvious in her expression. "But why—"

"Now, Cara."

"Yes, Momma."

"She's a pretty girl," he offered carefully once Cara was out of earshot.

Her mother smiled ruefully. "Are you taking a room tonight?"

"Yes," Jeris replied, even as Halath tartly commented, *:You'd better!:*

She smiled again, less rueful, and left to tend to other patrons. Jeris watched her for a moment before cleaning his bowl and stacking it with the mug. He appeared to have given her more than enough work the last time he'd visited. No sense in giving her more than necessary now.

His room secured, Jeris sought comfort with Halath. It could be coincidence the little girl looked so much like his sister . . . Heralds weren't supposed to have *accidents* like this. Their training on the matter was strict, and female Heralds took appropriate precautions.

"How did this even happen?" he muttered. Assuming his suspicions proved correct.

:Well, when a Herald and a pretty, provincial barmaid get together . . .: Halath snarked at him. His Companion seemed

both amused and irritated at this turn of events. *:You'd not be the first to succumb to fine liquor and excellent company. You liked her conversation even without the mead.:*

"I wish I remembered more." Fragments of memories flashed—a chimelike laugh, notes from a lute, soft skin, rough but gentle hands. Did she still play?

Cara slipped into the stables. "Oh! Excuse me, sir," she said, hiding an apple behind her back. "I do not wish to disturb you. The horses can wait." She looked doubtful about that.

Jeris shook his head, smiling. "Perhaps they can, but my Companion appreciates frequent meals." Halath snorted his opinion of the jibe. "I can assist you, if you'll tell me what you need."

Cara hesitated before nodding. "Thank you, sir. Our stable hand has been ill these last few days, and that dappled gray in the corner is—" She bit her lip. "—feisty. He tries to step on me."

Jeris glanced at the gelding and nodded. "Certainly. And which fine animal is that apple for?"

She blushed. "I brought it for yours, sir. Momma says Companions and Heralds bring good luck and happiness."

:Oh, I LIKE her. Can we keep her?: Halath stuck his head over the stall half-gate and whickered at her.

"He approves," Jeris said with a grin. "I shan't get in the way of him being cosseted."

She smiled shyly, offering the apple up to the Companion. "The hay's over there, sir," she directed. Halath's favorite part of their Shin'a'in adventure had been the children, and he missed being feted by them.

Halath delicately took the apple from her and whickered his pleasure.

She rubbed his nose and under his jaw, then politely excused herself.

Jeris took the narrow stairs up to his room. The planks jutted from the stone wall, held on the outside with timbers and rails. They were barely wide enough for a man with gear.

A figure came around the wall as he reached the first landing, and they bumped.

"Your pardon," he said.

It was she, the neck of her lute jutting over one shoulder. She half-smiled, gesturing down at the main room. "Retiring already? Cara and I will be entertaining the patrons shortly, as we do most nights."

"I was considering it. You still play, then, and sing?"

"Aye," she agreed, "although Cara has more of a voice than I do." She lowered her voice a bit, "Cara's particularly good at keeping rowdier patrons from causing a ruckus. My father appreciates that enough he even pays another helper for the evenings she sings with me."

"Then you didn't go to the Bardic Collegium?" He felt disappointed on her behalf.

"No," she said, looking only a little wistful. "And Cara upset my father's plans for me even more than becoming a Bard would have." Jeris winced, and she shook her head. "She is my luck and my happiness." More loudly, "Come, you should listen to her sing."

"We need to talk," he replied in an undertone.

She replied in kind. "Later, yes. Which room are you in?"

He told her, and she nodded. "Once Cara's settled for the night." She started back down the stairs. He gave her a moment, then followed.

Another truly excellent blackberry mead complemented the music well. *Her* voice was richer with age, more mellow. When Cara joined the song, however, even Jeris felt hard-pressed to not be sucked in completely. Her voice held the hallmarks of childhood, but the talent remained clear. *:She must go to the College,:* Jeris said. *:That much talent, this young? She could be dangerous without training,:*

:Much like our magelings of before,: Halath agreed.

"Another, Soressa!" a burly patron called to the pair. *Soressa.*

"Any preferences?" she asked the crowd. Several called out songs, only some he recognized. She conferred with her daughter, then strummed the lute again.

They performed for over an hour before Soressa rose from her seat. "It is late for us, my friends. Time to get this one to bed." She nodded at Cara. Ignoring the muted protests, Soressa gathered Cara up. The girl looked tired, and Jeris wondered if that was from the hour or the exertion.

:Depends on how her talent works,: Halath mused. *:I don't know much about the Bardic Gift myself. Just that there's only been a few Heralds with it over the years.:*

Sitting on the edge of the bed, Jeris stared at the walls of the quaint, serviceable room as he swirled the remainder of his second stein. He should not begrudge Soressa tending to her daughter, but it *had* been over an hour and a half since she'd taken the girl to their rooms.

Anxiety pushed him to his feet, to pace. A light knock on the door proved to be Soressa, and he let her into the room.

"So," he said.

"So."

"You've been well?" *Stupid question.* "And your daughter?"

"Well enough," she allowed. "Cara is sleeping. Some performances exhaust her more than others."

"She sings well," he said.

"She does, and her singing soothes the crowd." She claimed the only chair. "I didn't initially intend her to perform tonight."

"Why the change of plans?"

She looked away briefly. "I wished her father to see her perform. Being a Herald means he may not return for some time."

He swallowed. "So, she is . . . ?"

"Yours, yes."

"I . . . I'm sorry. I had no idea. It's not . . . it's not something I would have needed to think about with another Herald. You could have sent word to the Collegium. Even if I was away, they would have let me know. Possibly even brought you there."

"I considered it," she said. "But there were other considerations in play, I'm afraid. I'm my father's only remaining family in the area. I felt . . . bound to remain here. Anyway, she upset the plans my father had for me. But I'm afraid he may be renewing those plans, with her in my place."

"What kind of plans?"

"Early marriage, at best. Perhaps even to the man who was my intended eight years ago."

Jeris stiffened. "That's . . ."

"Unacceptable. Yes. He's well-to-do, but I never felt safe or comfortable around him. He's already *my* elder. He's certainly too old for Cara."

"Cara should be at the Bardic Collegium, Soressa. She's got the Gift; that's why she tires from singing the way she does. She needs training," he urged. "You could take her to Haven, yourself. They may even still train *you*."

"The Bardic Gift? Where would that have come from?"

"Certainly not me," he replied. "I can't carry a tune if it's in a bucket with handles."

She laughed at that. "Can you take her with you?" she blurted. "She'll be safer with you on the road than with me, and I can't leave here. Not yet."

"Possibly," he said nervously. "But Herald missions have a tendency to become . . . complicated, at the best of times."

"She cannot stay here," Soressa insisted. "My father will not agree to her leaving, of course. But she must leave, the sooner the better."

:What do you think?: Jeris asked Halath.

:Soressa seems worried enough about the girl's safety to warrant concern. We're supposed to just be part of a formal dinner in a week's time? Nothing strenuous, just one of the Lake District's own Heralds attending?:

:Supposedly. I expect politicking and at least a bit of Heraldly intervention will be called upon.:

:We should be safe enough to take her with us.:

He reluctantly nodded. "Does she have an animal of her own?"

"No, but some are for sale in the village, at the other stables."

:I can carry her, too, if necessary. She's not that large.:

"We'll look in the morning, then."

She sighed, relief obvious. She stood up. "In the morning, then."

"Wait," he said. "I—" He stopped. He knew what he *wanted.*

"I think you're slightly overdressed," she replied.

He stared. That . . . *was* in line with what he wanted. "You don't need to go back to Cara?"

She smiled. "Not immediately." She stepped closer. "That is, if you don't mind? I haven't since you were here last." That was surprising.

"Then I will endeavor to make it worth your while," he said. He bent to kiss her and found her trembling. False bravado but not false desire. She melted into the kiss.

"Do you like her?" Jeris asked Cara as she fumbled with the saddle and gear on the pony. The girl shrugged, but she sat in the saddle well enough. By Shin'a'in standards, the pony would barely rate as an equine, but by the standards of "reasonably healthy, trained, and tempered, albeit expensive," she'd have to do. The girl would travel longer and more comfortably with a girl-sized saddle and animal than on Halath.

"What will Grandfather say?" Cara asked.

"He knows you're leaving with your father to visit your other relatives," Soressa assured her. *Well, he will in an hour or two, at any rate.* "You know how difficult it is for him to wake up in the mornings lately."

Cara nodded.

Intellectually, the knowledge that Jeris was "her father" sat heavy on his mind. Emotionally, he was gauging her against the magelings and other students. By expectations molded by Shin'a'in children, she seemed younger than her eight years. He feared she would be baggage for the mission. She would not add to his image as an aloof, professional extension of the Queen.

"We need to get going," he said. His obligation to her outweighed his misgivings. The girl was his—a result of his actions. *Vigorous actions, much like last night's.* They'd have to adapt. *At least she ought not have a sibling from last night.*

Soressa hugged Cara. "I love you," she said, kissing the girl's nose.

Cara's eyes teared up again. "Do I have to go, Momma?"

"Yes," Soressa said. "You'll be safe. Right now, I don't think you can be so with me."

"What about you?"

"I'll come for you just as soon as I can, my love." Soressa pressed another kiss to her cheek, and Jeris saw Cara trying to stifle a sob. "Be good for your father."

"Okay." The girl's voice was very small.

Jeris mounted the already saddled Halath. Soressa handed him the pony's reins, which he tied to his saddle horn. "Take care of her for me."

"Yes." What else could he say? A moment more to appreciate the beauty of the woman looking up at him, full lips, full figure, committing them to memory. Her eyes showed distress, but her expression was calm.

Jeris felt heartless as he directed Halath and the pony to the road. He gave Cara what privacy he could by pretending to not hear the quiet crying.

:She understands that her mother believes it necessary,: Halath said.

:I still feel terrible.:

:That makes four of us, I think,: his Companion replied.

From Soressa, he knew Cara's experience outside of the inn was minimal. Running the calculations in his head now, it appeared that, between the slower pace and her inexperience, the week allotted for reviewing the situation in person would become three days.

"Are you angry about me?"

The sudden voice and question jarred him from his reverie.

Well, that was blunt. Though not as sullen as he feared it would be.

"I am not," he said. "Surprised, yes. I don't have much experience, though, so please let me know if you need anything. I'll try to make it happen."

"How long until Momma follows?"

"I don't know. As soon as she can."

"Where are we going? Does she know?"

"She does, yes. The Collegium, eventually, but I have a job to complete for the Queen. I also haven't seen my . . . *our* . . . family in some time, and I intend to visit them." He glanced down at her, trying to smile. "They'll be pleased to meet you."

"What is the Collegium like? Momma couldn't tell me."

She sounded fascinated, albeit nervous. The grief of separation would no doubt return, but for the moment, he could entertain her with stories of the Herald Collegium and what he'd heard of the Bardic Collegium. He also told her a bit about Highjorune and what he knew of the troubles there a few years' past.

"We have to go there?" she asked.

"Yes, I have to follow up, but I don't expect any more problems. It may be boring for you, though."

The girl shrugged.

They rode silently for a while, until she said, "I do like the wilderness. I only left town once before."

"This isn't really wilderness," he said. It was a well-traveled road. "But it's not a town, no."

In fact, they were approaching a Waystation. After a stretch and some food, they got back on the road. It was still light, with enough time to make the next inn before it got too dark and she too tired to continue.

The outskirts of Highjorune could be seen ahead. Jeris was proud of the girl. She'd been miserable the second day and most of the third, from muscle ache and homesickness, but she'd complained little. Perversely, the "lack of maturity" in comparison to a Shin'a'in of similar age meant she was less likely to challenge him but required more direction.

She *was* grumpy and sullen intermittently, and he occasionally felt inclined to snap at her. Instead, he encouraged her to ask questions about anything and everything, hoping to distract her and draw her out.

He almost rued that decision. Once emboldened that she'd not be snapped at for asking, the questions didn't. stop. even. for. breaths. For *hours*. When not asking questions, she sang. Soressa had taught her a lot of songs, and she had a knack for making up ditties on the go. That pattern continued through most of the third day, as well. This morning was more musical with fewer questions.

"Is that Highjorune?" she asked.

"Yes."

"It's big."

"Indeed."

As they approached, the dull roar of humanity and the change from freely blowing breezes to stale and stagnant air struck him, as it did every time. He glanced at Cara, who was hunched up as if afraid.

They rode through to the larger inn, near the Palace. For her sake, he would insist on staying there for the duration of the visit. It would be more homelike and hopefully less overwhelming than the Palace. Once there, he secured a room and a meal for both of them. A messenger was sent to the Palace to alert the Herald there of his arrival.

He had clean Whites for official duty. She had her best, if meager, clothing packed as well. Acquiring formalwear for her was unlikely, but he was uncomfortable with either leaving her or bringing her along. The stories of Ancar's treachery ensured most Heralds acquired a distaste for formal dinners, even those Chosen later.

For now, they waited for the Herald temporarily assigned to the Palace. A crowd entered the inn, looked around briefly, and departed. "I've seen that group before," Cara whispered. "They come through our town every few months."

"How do they act?"

"Rudely and very crass, but they have money. They don't fight often. Momma prefers I stay in the back while they're in the dining room."

That was interesting. Were they merchants? Bandits? Something else?

"You should probably avoid singing while they're around, then," Jeris said, still in an undertone. "We don't want them to recognize you."

She looked discomforted. "Not sing?"

"Your voice is distinctive," he explained. "And remember what I told you about the problems here a few years ago."

"But I won't make people do what they don't want to," she protested.

"I know that, and you know that. They do not."

Her expression was somewhere between offended, worried, and distressed at the thought.

*   *   *

They ate dinner in the main room of the inn.

"Herald Jeris?" a woman asked.

He looked up. "Herald Letia. It's been a while."

"Indeed," she said, sitting across from Jeris. "And this is?" She nodded at Cara.

Jeris made the introductions, leaving his relationship to Cara vague. They caught up on the past few years, and Jeris asked about the situation here.

She glanced at Cara and around the room. "Later. I'll eat with you, and we can talk after dinner."

Cara liked to hum or sing quietly during meals while not actively eating. Being unable to obviously bothered her. She perked up when others talked about music, and a patron pulled out a well-worn gittern. Others called out songs for him to play. He invited the audience to sing, and they did. Even Jeris could tell his playing was only mediocre, but Cara seemed riveted to the performance. He nudged her a few times when she started audibly humming. A few songs later, he nodded to Letia and roused Cara from her fixation.

"So, shop talk, I'm afraid," he said when they gained the seclusion of their hired room.

Letia raised an eyebrow and nodded ever so slightly at Cara. Jeris nodded.

"The city remains unsettled, in my opinion. Ferrin did quite the number on the townspeople. When they're not restless about politics, they're terrified that someone who can sing might be out to control them."

Cara shuffled a bit, ready to protest. Jeris spoke to cut her off.

"What's the purpose of this event I am supposed to attend?" He knew his instructions from the Collegium, but it always a good idea to check.

Letia said, "The mayor thought a feast celebrating the improved prosperity over the last two years was in order, now that things are more peaceful. The Lake District had profitable fishing seasons, Lineas better harvests than hoped, and the weather is lovely for early summer. He suggested a couple of Heralds from this area may be of benefit. I was born and raised here, which is why the temporary assignment to the city council," she said. "The Circuit Heralds told me you'd come back, so I sent the suggestion to Haven. I hope you weren't already on assignment."

Jeris laughed. "Only the assignment of writing five years of gleaned Shin'a'in culture, language, and customs into archival copies for the Collegium."

Cara piped up, "Will you show me that when we get to the Collegium? I should like to know."

"If you're still interested, certainly," he replied.

Letia gave him another look. Reluctantly, he relayed his belief Cara might have the Bardic Gift, and certainly a strong musical knack. "Oh," Letia said. She knelt down in front of Cara, to the girl's eye level. "I know it's probably hard for you, but for your safety, you need to not sing where you might be heard, okay? Particularly where people might not be on their best behavior or making their best decisions, like an inn."

Cara nodded slowly. "I like singing. I just want to sing."

"I know, sweetie, but here isn't the place. When I see you in Haven, I'd love to hear you, though," Letia said, standing back up. She looked at Jeris. "Is she to attend the feast or stay here?"

He frowned. "It's likely to be long and boring, isn't it? Not that—" He glanced around the sparse room. "—there's much for her to do here. Cara? What would you like?"

"May I come with you? I'll be good."

"Would that be acceptable to the mayor?" Jeris asked.

Letia smiled. "I'm sure he can find a place for her. But," she said to Cara, "we need to be sure you're properly dressed. Do you have nice clothes with you?"

Cara pulled her best outfit out of her pack. "Will this work?"

Letia gave it a once-over. "Mostly. We'll need to spend a little time on it and you, though, and do a little bit of shopping."

Cara looked hopeful. "Can we, d—sir?" Jeris suspected she nearly said "daddy." He wasn't sure how he felt about that.

"I can afford a few *reasonable* trinkets, if my fellow Herald believes them necessary," he said. "Letia? Can you help her?"

She smiled brightly. "My pleasure! It's late, and we have a few days to get you fitted out properly. What say you two come to the Town Hall in the morning? You can watch the proceedings, and after that, we go shopping."

Jeris nodded. "A sound plan." Cara beamed.

Letia gave directions to the town hall, then left. Cara settled on the bed, while Jeris prepared his bedroll. She broke the silence. "What should I call you?"

A fair question. Jeris took a moment to respond. "For now, either 'Jeris' or 'sir' is probably safest." A quick glance showed her crestfallen expression. "You're traveling with a Herald, Cara. I'm concerned about the group you noted downstairs. They left after they saw me, which seems odd. If they knew *who* you are, well, they might do something . . . dangerous. If nothing else, I promised your mother to keep you safe."

Her voice was small and more childlike than normal. "Okay." The bedclothes rustled as she nestled in.

Jeris felt his heart twist at that word. Was it him? Was it her projecting with her Gift? He didn't know, and Halath couldn't tell him. He tucked her in and sat down on the side of the bed. "I'm not going anywhere without you, okay? I'll be here in the morning when you wake up. At most, I'll be getting us food." Cara nodded, looking only a little reassured. He gave her a small smile. "Sleep well. Wake me up if you need anything."

She nodded. "Okay."

Jeris settled himself to sleep. *:You sleep well, too, my friend,:* he told Halath.

:And you.:

The Council meeting tended toward the dry and boring, as is the wont of such. Jeris felt pleased with Cara's behavior, though. As a preview of a formal dinner, she was quiet and attentive, with a few questions to him when she didn't understand something.

When the meeting adjourned, they met with Letia near the front dais. Letia introduced Jeris and Cara to the mayor, who—at least to Cara—presented as a jovial, courteous person.

He even issued an invitation to Cara directly. "My friend Herald Letia informs me, young miss, you will be quite lonesome and without escort while Herald Jeris attends a feast at my behest. Would you be so kind to attend? You would be our youngest guest at this part of the festivities, but there will be a Bard to sing."

Cara looked surprised. "Thank you, sir. I would enjoy that."

"Excellent!" the mayor replied. "Herald Letia, I regret I have much to attend to at the moment. Would you be so kind as to escort our guests?"

She nodded. "Certainly, if the Council is done for the day."

"I do believe we are."

"Then," Letia said, "let us be on our way."

A warm, clear day meant the streets were crowded with errand-goers and shoppers. Cara gripped Jeris' hand tightly in the crowd but seemed otherwise at ease. Letia directed them to a shop with trinkets, and Jeris lingered by the entrance. Jeris noted that, other than a few voices here and there that nagged or bickered, everyone sounded content. It took several shops and carts to find all the things Letia deemed necessary, including boots and barrettes and ribbons.

While they wandered around the food vendors for lunch, Jeris realized the underlying mood of the chatter had shifted. A few notes of music drifted through, and Cara beelined for the source. None of the force of Cara's singing accompanied the music being played, but a wary tension could be felt from the crowd. Cara stopped at the edge of the semicircle surrounding a man in Bardic Scarlet, playing a lovingly tended gittern.

The Bard played beautifully, as one would expect from a member of the Bardic Circle. Jeris could just barely hear Cara hum along with the song. He gripped her shoulder in a slight warning, and she broke off with a guilty glance up at him. When the song finished, she stepped into the cleared area. "That was lovely," she said.

The Bard smiled, glanced at Jeris, and then over his shoulder. "Ah, Herald Letia! Are they with you?"

The two Heralds engaging with the Bard palpably lessened the tension Jeris felt in the crowd, and those uninterested in the music milled around and past. "Indeed, Ralin. Jeris came from Haven for our feast, and Cara travels with him, to visit family nearer the shores. Jeris, Cara, please be known to Bard Ralin. Like me, he grew up in Highjorune."

"Quite. Although my home has been less warm these last few years," Ralin agreed, almost affably, with just a touch of emphasis on "home." "But perhaps the feast will restore the town's good humor. And you, young Cara? Will you be at the feast? I noticed you singing the words of the ballad just now."

Cara nodded shyly. "I was trying to be quiet."

"You like to sing?" She nodded. "Do you play at all?"

"A little. Momma plays the lute. We only had the one instrument."

"Well, perhaps if you are in town for long, I may show you a few tricks?" Ralin glanced at Jeris, who nodded slightly. Having her interact with a Bard could only be to her benefit, despite the townspeople's discomfort. Perhaps he could advise on her unwitting use of her Gift.

"I can direct you to them later," Letia put in. "But we came through to eat. Would you like to join us, Ralin?"

"It would be my pleasure." He bent to put away his gittern, and Jeris leaned down, ostensibly to help pack Ralin's folding chair. For Jeris' ear, Ralin murmured that it was to his advantage to be seen with the Heralds.

"I thought so also," Jeris replied.

Jeris and Cara selected their meal at the suggestions of Letia and Ralin. Jeris noted how much more at ease the crowd seemed after Ralin put away the instrument. Over a filling, tasty lunch, they agreed Letia would escort Ralin to their inn.

"It's not that I don't know where the inn is," Ralin commented. "It's just that it seems prudent lately."

"The last bit of trouble was a few years ago," Jeris said quietly. "Is it still such a concern?"

"It had faded for the most part, so said the previous Bard. Stories surfaced from travelers about another one, and the town is tense again. Most would prefer to forget the recent wars altogether, and certainly a bed of treason."

The answer discomfited Jeris more than he liked. Why would the stories resurface now?

As discussed, the Heralds and Cara arrived at the feast together, the two Companions walking side by side, in step. Jeris smothered a smug smile at the awed expressions. No matter how many times a pair of preening Companions were seen, the reaction was the same.

The trio dismounted and joined the amorphous blob, nominally the entrance line, leaving the Companions to themselves. A pair of city-liveried people checked names and directed parties to their seats. Despite the numbers, they were quickly seated near the mayor and council.

"My compliments on the organization so far," Jeris offered to the mayor.

The mayor smiled and declaimed any credit. "I am fortunate in the quality of citizenry."

A liveried woman scurried up to whisper in the mayor's ear, and he murmured back. Standing, he gave a short speech, welcoming the guests and introducing the Heralds. The servers started circulating as soon as the mayor seated himself.

Ralin's playing accompanied fine food, acceptable wine, and pleasant conversation for the first half of the feast. Jeris half wished that Soressa were present to observe Cara's youthful enthusiasm and awe.

About an hour in, Ralin took a break, relieved by a string quartet while he rested. He was seated on the other side of Cara, across from Letia. Cara peppered the Bard with questions about what the quartet were doing. Jeris gently reminded her to allow the man to eat as well. Looking chagrined, she obeyed.

Jeris should have suspected the event was going too smoothly. Toward the end of the quartet's third piece, the first sounds of discord started on the far side of the room. He recognized the man who stood up and gesticulated wildly as being the loudest member of the group Cara had pointed out their first night in Highjorune. The volume escalated, and he and Letia traded glances. "I'll go see," she said.

"I will go with you," the mayor put in.

Before they got there, another man had risen, obviously angry. Jeris didn't see who threw the first punch, but it shortly didn't matter. It seemed the crowd Cara warned them about had arrived to this event itching for trouble. Half of the room was in full brawl in seconds. Children and startled women scattered toward the walls.

"Go," Jeris ordered Cara, pointing at the stairs. Getting her out of the melee area was his first responsibility. She went. He ran to help Letia and the Guard separate the brawlers. There were too many. *This isn't working,* he thought as a stray blow grazed his chin. He reached out to Halath, to ask the Companions to intercede with mass if nothing else.

A small, strong voice chimed through the brawl. It was Cara, standing midstair. He recognized the lyrics of a prayer song to Astera, high, clear, calming. Her hand clutched the railing.

A hush spread out from the bottom of the stairs and across the room. Some stopped and turned to see her. Others just untensed and ceased fighting.

In a few moments, they were all listening to her bell-like tones. *She is amazing,* he thought, *so clear and in pitch, despite her age.*

A deeper voice joined hers, Ralin's voice, and Jeris felt the *pull* of the two, as the Bard picked up the harmony on his gittern.

:Get her out of there,: Halath ordered, breaking some of the hold of the music.

He abruptly realized that Ralin was trying to distract the crowd from Cara's display by overpowering it. He shook himself out of the lulling song and dodged through the crowd to Cara's side. "You need to drop out of the song," he urged at a whisper. "We need to get you out of here."

Her eyes widened and her chin dipped in bare acknowledgement. She softened her portion, dropping to silence at the end of a verse. Ralin's voice strengthened further, a pulling, lulling sound which Jeris found he could only barely resist. He gathered Cara, carrying her down the stairs.

Catching Ralin's gaze as the Bard played and sang, Jeris gave him a sharp nod of acknowledgement. The Bard quirked an eyebrow at him without losing a note or beat. Letia moved to Ralin's side, Jeris assumed for the purpose of taking over the attention of the now-lulled gathering, as soon as the song ended.

He carried Cara out to Halath as fast as he could. She started shaking, even as he hoisted her on to his Companion's saddle. He swung on behind her, and Halath cantered for the inn.

Halfway back, she asked, "Am I in trouble? I just—I didn't want anyone to get hurt. It's what Momma's always had me do during a brawl."

"No. You did your best in a not-good situation. But others may not see it that way," Jeris told her. "That's why you have to go to the Bardic Collegium. They can teach you when it's . . . acceptable."

He offered a brief, silent prayer of his own, hoping he hadn't left Letia and Ralin to an unruly crowd alone. *:Drayl says they're safe, for now,:* Halath relayed the message from Letia's Companion.

Cara was still shaking when they arrived at the inn. Jeris left Halath to the stable hand for care with Halath's agreement. Getting her upstairs and into bed was a priority. He could see the reaction headache already setting in.

He got her settled in, prepped a headache draught, and insisted she drink some before she fell asleep completely. It was the best he could do for now.

:That was more people than she's likely ever seen in one place in her life. She must have poured everything she had into it,: he told Halath.

:She kept it from getting bloody,: Halath replied.

Hopefully the Guard and Letia would be able to sort out

the incident and individuals without his assistance. For now, he needed to care for a little girl due to be in a lot of pain, even with a preemptive draught.

Jeris woke up, disoriented. A small, warm body cuddled against his, and he snapped alert before recognizing it was Cara. Color had returned to her face, unlike earlier, when she had been violently sick from the reaction headache. He'd coaxed more medicine into her, and cuddled her to sleep while she whimpered.

He gently disentangled from the clutching girl, who murmured a protest which sounded like "daddy." He gritted his teeth and took care of a few necessities. He tried to nudge her awake to gauge her recovery, but she just murmured something incoherent and didn't rouse. He went downstairs to order strong tea and breakfast. He found himself thinking longingly of the Shin'a'in morning brew as morning fatigue set in.

He was groggy enough that he didn't register the loud voices arguing outside the tavern until he entered the main room, where the innkeeper stood in the doorway.

"No, you may not disturb any guests under this roof," the innkeeper said.

"She's the little brat from Soroll, the one who squirrels all my deals," a man shouted. "Can't have a little fear to make a bargain go well, not while she's around. Can't even have a healthy brawl. She's a witch!"

Other angry voices joined his at that accusation.

Jeris didn't remember going back up to the room to get her. He realized he was shaking her awake. "Cara, you have to get up, you have to get up *now!*" He was about to pick her up to carry her, still asleep, down to Halath when she opened her eyes blearily.

"Am I late for work?" she asked, still groggy.

"No, yes. You have to get up now, there's trouble."

She tried. She really did. She hadn't recovered from the night before, and was clumsy with fatigue. Jeris swept her up and bounded down the back stairs to the stables. Halath whinnied as they burst in. "You've got to go. Halath will take you to Letia."

She was awake now. "Da—Jeris, sir, please!" She looked scared, but she didn't resist being hoisted on Halath's bare back.

"Cara, some of the people recognized you last night. They're angry, and they're likely dangerous. You have to go to Letia, and tell her that. Halath can find her or her Companion, who can take you to her."

He put her hands up to Halath's mane. "Hold on here if it helps you feel safer. Grip with your legs. He'll keep you on his back as long as you try to stay there. Got it?" She nodded, fingers working into the fine hair. He pressed a kiss to the back of her hand. "I'll see you soon." He flung the stable door open, and Halath left at a canter.

Jeris ran around to the front of the tavern from the stable entrance. The angry crowd huddled at the front of the inn. He wasn't in his best Whites, but these would have to do. "What seems to be the problem?" he asked loudly, in full Herald demeanor.

The individuals closest to him turned, and upon realizing a Herald was at hand, looked a bit cowed. Some started edging off to the sides. The loudmouth at the door, however, didn't turn around, still haranguing the innkeeper. Jeris caught the eye of one of the men slinking off. He hadn't been with the group Cara originally recognized. "You there. What's the fuss about?"

"We, ah, were just concerned, sir, about a guest at the inn," the man stammered.

"And why might that be?" Jeris prompted.

"She's a witch!" another spat at him.

"She caused trouble last night!" a third person said.

"Oh?" Jeris replied, arching an eyebrow. "Please elaborate."

Several people threw out wildly different stories of the events. The voices overlapped, but Jeris got the gist. He raised his hands to quiet those nearest him down.

"How many of you were in attendance last night?" Heads shook, and the quiet spread toward the inn. "Most of you weren't, it seems. I was." The crowd quieted further, drawing the attention of those nearest the troublemaker. "In fact, the . . . *gentleman* over there was near where the original altercation started." People started edging out of the way between them.

Once called out, the man seemed ready for a fight, along with a couple of his bullyboys.

Jeris didn't want to fight, not if it could be avoided. He just had to delay. Most of the crowd were spectators, easily stirred up and just as easily deterred. Many expressions showed second thoughts about a riot against the Queen's representative. They might join in, though.

The three had work knives on their belts, but they hadn't drawn them yet. Jeris had not drawn his sword, either. They were gauging him, considering their chances, and in a moment they were going to charge. The lead man would be in front, of course, and the others would flank. Jeris prepared to move and draw against them.

Down the street to his left came shouting and clatter, above the noise of the crowd.

"Clear the street! Make way!" a voice shouted.

The crowd parted again, now broken into three smaller groups, split by the approaching party.

It was a dozen men of the City Guard in leather armor with halberds, clubs, and swords. Letia was behind but catching up fast, astride her Companion, with Ralin seated behind. With them were another dozen levied volunteers with staves and bars. They fell into a skirmish line across the street, behind Jeris.

"What is the meaning of this?" the Guard Captain demanded.

"It appears," Jeris replied, "we have a less than honest merchant who is irritated by his strong-arm tactics being thwarted in more than one town."

The Guard Captain gave the loudmouth a baleful glare. "We were looking for you, as a matter of fact, for the disturbances last night and previous complaints. It'll be best for you to come with us quietly, instead of slipping off again." The man looked to be weighing his options, still leaning toward a fight.

"That girl is a witch!" one of the others said.

"No, she's a Herald's daughter. *My* daughter," Jeris said loudly.

A ripple went through the crowd, and glares began to go in the tough's direction. The changed mood appeared to be enough to convince him to take the easier option. His posture relaxed, and the other two stood down. The Guard collected them, and the crowd dispersed.

"We came as fast as we could," Letia apologized. "Thankfully, as everyone was already *at* the council over last night, it was faster than it might have been."

"You came in time," Jeris shrugged. "Cara?"

"Safe," Ralin answered. "I'll need to have a few more words with her. Some guidance, until you get her to the Collegium."

"I'd be grateful."

"Remember, you've promised to sing for me when we're in Haven," Letia said, helping Cara onto her pony.

Cara smiled, still shy about it. "Yes. But we're going to father's family first, right?"

Jeris nodded, tying her pony's lead to his saddle. "Yes, Haven after that."

"And I'll be able to sing there?"

"Any melody you wish."

A Tangle of Truths
Angela Penrose

The great hall of Lord Brandin's keep was decked all in black and silver—black draperies with silver embroidery, black bunting with silver tassels, black table covers with silver chair cushions. It was the dreariest baby's birthday party Herald Arvil had ever attended. At least the baby, little Lord Branwell, was too young to notice the funereal air, being only one year old that day.

Lord Brandin's long-awaited heir surviving to his first birthday had drawn guests from all over the kingdom, and even a few from outside it. Brandin, the man known rather wryly as the Lord of the Armor Hills, controlled the flow of iron out of the richest veins in those hills and employed some of the best smiths. The fine weapons and stout shields displayed on the walls, as well as the graceful curves of the wrought-iron chairs and the iron banding on the doors, drew many speculative eyes.

Even Arvil had been lured over to examine a sword and dagger set over behind the table where the gifts for the baby lordling were stacked.

"It's gratifying to see that the Queen of Valdemar thinks so highly of her nobles that she sends a personal representative to an infant's party," said a voice just behind Arvil's shoulder.

He hadn't heard anyone come up behind him, but he turned smoothly with a polite smile on his face. The man behind him had a Hardornen accent, and was dressed in simple but well-made trousers and shirt, with a tooled leather jerkin—fine enough not to insult the occasion, while austere enough not to insult the people of his own kingdom, who were still desperately poor.

"Her Majesty is happy for Lord Brandin, of course. His son is a blessing, this late in his life."

"Of course," echoed the Hardornen. "King Tremane appreciates the situation of a man like Lord Brandin."

Arvil wasn't sure how Tremane, who must have more important things to hold his attention than a baby's birthday party in a foreign kingdom, was even aware of the event. But Tremane was said to be a savvy ruler. Likely he was looking ahead to a time when he could import quality arms and armor for his soldiers.

"I'm sure," he said with a neutral smile, then he gave a shallow bow. "Herald Arvil."

The Hardornen bowed in return. "Paskal of Gramersy, lately of Hardorn."

Huh. The name made Arvil think Gramersy was an Imperial like King Tremane, rather than a native Hardornen. Arvil was no linguist, and Hardorn had several dialects; Arvil couldn't swear he'd recognize an Imperial note in the man's speech if there was one. But if Gramersy had come to Hardorn with Tremane, he was more likely a soldier than a courtier. Although under the circumstances, Tremane's soldiers were learning to manage many tasks.

"Good fortune to you and your people," said Arvil. "And may you have a pleasant stay in Valdemar."

"My thanks," said Gramersy. He bowed again and turned to wander off, heading toward a group of men clustered around their host.

Arvil strolled off in the other direction, watching guests mingle and maneuver. He ignored those rude enough to stare at his limping gait, relic of a bad fall when he was a Trainee. Servants slipped around the perimeter of the room, fetching food and drink for those who didn't want to be bothered with walking across the floor for themselves. Guards lurked in corners and niches, their black-and-silver surcoats helping them blend into the decor.

Arvil spotted a group of men he vaguely knew, local lords and landowners, gathered around an ale barrel. He strolled over and exchanged greetings, then pulled a cup of ale and settled in. The men asked for news from Haven, and Arvil obliged them. General talk moved to local matters, mainly having to do with mining and metalwork and the trade that resulted from both.

Finally, one of the men, a Lord Unter, gave an arch look to Lord Oakley standing across from him, and said, "I'm surprised you didn't bring your daughter, to see whether the babes get along."

Lord Oakley raised an eyebrow and shrugged. "Time enough for that when they're old enough to be interested in more than a teat and a rattle."

"You're that sure of yourself, then?" asked a third man, a Lord Stonefell. "If you've settled things with Brandin, why bother with a marriage?"

"Everyone enjoys a wedding, what?" asked Lord Oakley with a smirk. He was a wiry man who wore his burgundy silks as though they itched. Lines around his eyes and mouth, and gray in his hair, spoke of habitual worry, an uneasy life, despite his smirking.

"You'd cut your own boy out, then?" asked Unter. "Throw it all in with Brandin?"

"Who said anything of cutting my own lad out?" demanded Oakley. "I'll dower the girl well enough—that's fair, that's custom. No more than that."

"Is there an announcement planned for later, then?" asked Arvil, trying to catch up on the undercurrents.

"Not yet, not yet," said Oakley, his voice too neutral to be unstudied. "Just talk. Brandin's lad's not even weaned yet, and my lass barely so. Plenty of time to make it official, at least a year or so."

"But you've an understanding?" Unter didn't look happy with the notion. "You've been talking to Brandin behind our backs?"

"Behind whose back?" demanded Oakley. "I've no obligation to announce my business to all the neighborhood, certainly not before it's settled."

"Stabbing your neighbors in the back is best done in secret, true," said Unter, looking as though he'd bitten into a rotten fish.

"By the Crone, I've stabbed nobody!" snapped Oakley, scowling up at the taller Unter, one hand brushing his belt where he likely wore a blade whenever he wasn't accepting hospitality from a fellow noble. "If you've accusations to be made, make 'em to my face!"

Unter moved back without actually taking a step, shifting his weight to give him a tiny but important bit of space. "One hears things," he muttered. He glanced around for support from his fellows, apparently found none; and turned his scowl down to the floor.

"I'll make whatever arrangements I please," said Oakley, his voice still hard, although not quite so loud. "Just as you'll look out for your own affairs, and every other man here will look after his. If I overstep, I'm sure our good Herald here will be most willing to jerk me back into line."

Arvil, startled at being dragged into a local argument, gave a graceful bow and said, "I'm sure that won't be necessary."

Oakley glanced at him with a snort that would probably have been a laugh had the conversation not been so tense. "If you've a complaint, Unter, take it to a Herald. If not, keep your whining to yourself." He nodded to Arvil, then to the others, then turned and stomped away.

Unter glared after him, then drained his ale and walked off in the opposite direction, his stride stiff with swaddled anger.

Lord Stonefell watched them both go, then shrugged and sipped his own ale. Neither he nor any of the other men left commented, so after a few moments of silent drinking, Arvil asked, "Did Lord Unter hope for a betrothal for his own daughter?"

Stonefell huffed out a laugh and shook his head. "Nah, that one's youngest daughter is nearly twenty. Not that that'd stop some, but he and Brandin aren't so friendly that Brandin would give his new little treasure to that sort of marriage, not without some urgent need. Unter's got some gravel down his craw about Brandin pushing the Barrowlan shaft closer to

Unter's lands than he's comfortable with. He's been whining about it for the last year and more, and he's afraid that if Brandin and Oakley make a firm match of it, he'll lose any chance of winning his case."

"Is Brandin encroaching on Unter's lands?" Arvil asked. "Or rather, under . . . ? I'd need to look up mining law, but—"

"Nah, nah, it's just whining. Mining law says you claim anything under land where you've driven a wooden stake with a hammer. Nobody can drive a stake into the crest of the Armors—it's solid rock, aye? Without a stake, a seam belongs to whoever mines it first. Brandin's following the Barrowlan seam from this side of the crest. He's got the money to pay two shifts and the men to work 'em. Unter can't match him, never had a hope of it." Stonefell shrugged. "That's mining. No sense complaining. That way leads to wine, leads to gout, leads to a miserable death, and for what?"

The men laughed and clanked their ale cups together. Arvil clanked his cup too, but he turned to watch Lord Unter, who had indeed ended up with a glass of wine and looked to be draining it already.

Talk among Stonefell and his cronies turned to a friendly argument over the best quenching bath for something-something-steel-something, so Arvil excused himself to refill his cup and then wander the room.

If Stonefell and company primarily traded in finished goods rather than ore, that would explain why they had little sympathy for Lord Unter, who seemed dependent on mining. If he was afraid Lord Brandin was about to shut him out of a rich source of iron, that would certainly give him a reason for resentment, especially if his rival Oakley was about to make a deal and shut him out.

Still, it sounded like nothing more than the usual ups and downs of business.

Servants began setting up trestle tables in the middle of the hall, and the guests shifted nearer to the walls to give them room. Lady Udette, a sturdy young woman with broad hips and a pretty face—clearly the mistress of the place, in a gray silk dress trimmed in black braid—called everyone to supper soon after, and Arvil found himself seated to her right, in a place of respect to the Queen by proxy. On her left sat Lord Oakley, which seemed to confirm that Brandin and his lady wished to pay him particular courtesy. As a future in-law?

Lord Unter sent Oakley a scowl or two from his place near the center of the table, but that wasn't surprising.

Still, Arvil felt that he was missing something. Had Stonefell and his cronies been a bit too casual? Was Unter too obvious? There was a feeling of tension throughout the gathering, as though something were about to happen, something less happy than a baby's birthday, but Arvil couldn't quite grasp what was bothering him.

Maybe Oakley was plotting—once his daughter was betrothed to Brandin's son, if Brandin died, he might think to move into the power vacuum on behalf of his future son-in-law. Lady Udette was very young, despite carrying herself well, with an air of confidence. She would be easy for a smooth, older man with local influence to sweep aside. Or marry himself, if it came to that.

Too many possibilities, not enough information. Arvil picked at his food, his stomach twisting with tense imaginings. *These are the times when I wish Companions were welcome to mingle indoors,* he thought. *Graya would be more than willing to tell me whether I'm imagining murderous enemies where there are only disgruntled rivals.*

Arvil had often wished the Lady had given him Mindspeech, but with Graya in the stable, he'd have had to narrate every word and action for her. Dividing his attention that way wouldn't be worth the extra mind put to the problem.

Lady Udette kept dinner conversation light, moving from local gossip to comments on the performance of a Bard who'd travelled through the area some weeks earlier. Oakley tried to steer the topic to children and weddings, but Lady Udette fended him off with the skill of a champion fencer. If Oakley had hoped to gain advantage through Lord Brandin's wife, he ended the meal disappointed.

After dinner, the servants served rounds of sugar-glazed gingerbread. While the guests enjoyed the sweet—dividing nearly in half between those who dove into the gooey mess with their hands and those who made an attempt at eating neatly with a knife—a matronly nanny entered the hall carrying a baby.

The little boy was clearly Lord Branwell. The little mite had been scrubbed until he glowed and was wrapped in a long gown of ruffled gray with silver vines embroidered in swirling patterns.

At least the infant wasn't dressed all in black. As much as Lord Brandin seemed fond of his house colors, Arvil suspected Lady Udette had put her foot down.

As the guests noticed the babe's entrance, they began knocking on the table with their knuckles—a sensible alternative to clapping when one had one hand full of gingerbread.

Lord Brandin climbed to his feet, his joints visibly paining him, and said in a voice that filled the room, "Friends and neighbors! I present to you my son and heir, Lord Branwell, who is one year old today." He paused for more knocking, then went on, "I thank you for your presence at this joyous occasion and for the generous gifts you've offered."

He nodded to a servant, who, along with a second man, lifted the table covered with presents and moved it over next to Lady Udette.

The nanny stepped closer and held Lord Branwell up so he could watch his mother unwrap gifts. Little Lord Branwell sucked on his fingers, his eyes half-closed, and completely ignored what was going on. Arvil guessed he'd been thoroughly fed just minutes before and might well fall asleep during "his" party.

The gifts were contained in elaborately carved boxes, or wrapped in fine fabric. Lady Udette made a show of carefully opening each, exclaiming over each item and holding it up to show. More table knocking expressed approval for the growing collection of silver cups, silver rattles, intricately knit blankets, and elaborately sewn outfits the baby would surely outgrow in a matter of months, even if they were suitable for a babe crawling about and learning to walk and getting into everything, which they were not.

Arvil supposed that, much like the party itself, the gifts had more significance to the adults present than to the birthday baby.

Lady Udette undid a precisely tied bow holding a swath of silk around something the size of a large melon. The fabric fell away to finally reveal something a baby might actually want to play with. It was a cloth rabbit, with floppy ears and brightly embroidered flowers all over its body. Even Arvil, who had little expertise in such things, could tell that the sewing and embroidery were particularly fine. Lady Udette squeezed it and smiled; it was obviously stuffed with something soft.

While the guests knocked approval, the lady held the colorful bunny up to her son, bouncing it up and down so the ears flopped to and fro. The baby opened his eyes, pulled his fingers out of his mouth and smiled wide, showing four tiny teeth. "Bah!" He waved his hands at the toy.

A shock of dread hit Arvil like a bolt of lightning— Foresight! There was no image, there hardly ever was, just a *knowing,* and he lunged across the table, grabbing at Lady Udette's upper arms, all he could reach in time.

She squawked in shock and lost her balance, then cried out in pain as Arvil slammed her back against the edge of the heavy table. He winced and babbled apologies while wrenching the toy rabbit out of her hands, then scrambled out of his chair and took several steps backward, away from the baby.

Three of the black-and-silver guards were right there, grasping his arms, something pointy pressing hard between his shoulder blades. Another blade and the guard gripping it appeared between him and the lady, shoving him hard. He lost his balance and fell, his bad leg buckling under him. The guards stayed with him, bodies and weapons alike tracking with him as he crashed to the floor. People shouted, the baby cried, Lord Brandin demanded to know what he thought he was doing . . .

Arvil wrapped himself around the toy rabbit, his only thought at the moment to prevent anyone from taking it from him.

The fear dribbled away, slowly, as the babble and shouting in the room increased. He relaxed, just a little, and just as slowly, but kept a tight hold on the bunny.

"Herald Arvil!" Lord Brandin snapped. Arvil felt a hard

nudge on his thigh with what felt like the toe of a boot. "Explain yourself!"

Arvil took a deep breath and uncurled a bit more. The guard whose blade was still poking his back gave it another warning jab, and Arvil rolled away from the man's lord.

"Foresight," he said, then took another breath. His head started to clear and the pounding of his heart slowed. "The rabbit is a danger to the baby. I felt it."

"A danger to the babe?" bellowed Lord Brandin. "How the deuce is a toy rabbit a danger to anyone?"

"Perhaps he would have choked on it? On an ear?" suggested Lady Udette. Her voice was low and distant, and when Arvil looked up in her direction, he saw she'd been hustled over to the other side of the room by four guards.

The baby was gone. Just as well.

"I don't think so," said Arvil. He shifted again but stayed seated, his bad leg out in front of him and the other one folded under it, the half-cross that was the best he could manage on a floor. He studied the toy and tried to think.

In the arms of a nanny and right next to his mama, a baby would hardly be in serious danger of choking. The shock of Foresight had indicated an immediate danger, not a slower danger to come, if, say, the baby went to bed with the bunny and choked in his sleep.

He held the bunny up to his nose and sniffed. There was an odd scent, but then, the threads used to embroider the toy were particularly bright. Dyes that bright—and doubtless fresh since the toy looked new—might well have a sharper scent than duller, more common colors.

Although that might also be a mask for something. Poison, perhaps? Babies put everything in their mouths . . . .

Arvil licked his finger and rubbed it on a patch of bright red embroidery. Maybe it would leave a stain, some kind of clue—?

As soon as his saliva-smeared finger touched the threads, the whole toy shifted, stretching out of shape, changing. The threads and fabric all melted away, leaving the surface of the thing a smooth swirl of colors that engulfed Arvil's hand, as though it were trying to devour his spit and whatever else it was touching.

Arvil shouted in shock while scrambling to his feet, his voice adding to the roar of surprise and anger that filled the room once more. A woman screamed, and then another, more.

Shaking his hand didn't dislodge the thing, which had solidified around his right hand into a rough sphere bigger than his head.

Lady Udette screamed, "Let me go!" and broke away from her guards to dash down the hall through which the nanny had brought the baby, doubtless where the baby'd been taken away again.

Arvil thought about what would have happened if the baby had gotten his *mouth* onto the bunny and wanted to vomit. He could only imagine what the baby's mother felt when she realized what had almost happened.

Lord Brandin snapped, "Guards, Oakley!" and four of the guards seized Lord Oakley just as roughly as they'd seized Arvil a minute earlier. He remembered that Lord Oakley had been announced as the bunny's giver.

But . . . that made no sense.

"I don't know anything about this! My lord, please! What would I gain from hurting the boy?" Oakley looked frantic and terrified in the face of Lord Brandin's fury.

"Take his *head*!" shouted Brandin, his face red and his hands fisted.

Before the guards could do more than twitch, Arvil shouted, "No! Hold!" and lunged forward, jerking away from his own guards, who'd loosened their grasp. "My lord, wait! Think!" Arvil grabbed a free spot on one of Oakley's arms and waved his free hand—the one engulfed by the bright-colored ball—at the guards, fending them off as well as he could.

"Herald, move!"

"No! In the name of the Queen, hold!" Arvil drew himself up, projecting as much gravitas as he could with one hand looking like it was stuck in a jar, aided by his full court Whites. He glared at Lord Brandin, who glared right back.

The hall fell silent during the showdown, until finally Lord Brandin snarled, "Explain yourself! Now!"

"Lord Oakley is right, my lord. He has nothing to gain by harming your son, and everything to lose. Everyone knows he hopes to marry his infant daughter to your infant son some day, yes?"

Lord Brandin scowled, but nodded. "Yes. We have spoken of it."

"Well, then? What does it profit him to kill the babe? He's scuttling his own boat. That makes no sense. Someone else did this and wanted you to blame Lord Oakley."

"Yes!" cried Oakley. "Exactly! Some enemy of mine—of us both—did this!" He scanned the room, his eyes wide with panic, then shouted, "There, Unter! It was him! He's been complaining of the betrothal for weeks! He said that us joining our families was stabbing him in the back! He said it this evening, the Herald heard him!"

Lord Brandin glared at Arvil. "Well?"

"I did hear him say that," Arvil allowed. "But—"

"There, see!" shouted Oakley. "It was him, not me!"

"I did no such thing!" yelled Unter, who was being dragged forward by two more guards. Two more left Arvil to help surround Lord Unter. "Oakley's trying to ruin me! This was his plan all along!"

Arvil took a few paces away from all the shouting and scrubbed at his face with his free hand. "That makes no sense either. Oakley stands to gain too much by marrying his daughter into the family of 'the Lord of the Armor Hills.' Why would he risk sabotaging that plan just to ruin a man who's poorer and less powerful than he is already?"

"You insolent peasant!" squawked Lord Unter, drawing himself up as much as he could while weighed down by angry guards. "How dare you!"

"Shut up, Unter," snarled Lord Brandin. "He's right. You're highborn, but you barely have a pot to piss in or a window to throw it out of. I call you 'Lord' out of courtesy and respect for your forebears. You've no real power, and Oakley's not fool enough to throw away an alliance with me—to make a mortal *enemy* of me—just to spite you." He clamped his jaw shut and scanned the room, searching faces, his forehead tense and his eyes glaring.

Arvil turned to Oakley. "Where did the toy come from?"

"That's it, it must have been her! I had Lotta make it for me! She's the finest embroiderer for three days' ride! She must have magicked it!" He tried to jerk around and face Lord Brandin. "I know nothing of magic, my lord! Who in Valdemar does? I'd have had no idea where to even begin to create such an evil thing as that, nor even how to find someone to make it for me!"

Lord Brandin ignored him and ordered a guard to go to the village and bring Lotta the seamstress to the keep.

While the woman was being fetched, some of the guests made noises about departing, but Lord Brandin forbade it. "No one is leaving until the foul Mage who did this is dead at my feet."

Arvil set his jaw, but said nothing. He'd allow no murder, especially since the magical trap had hurt no one, fortunately.

Scowling at the brightly colored ball attached to his hand, he shook it, to no avail. The thing didn't *hurt,* but he wanted it *off.*

At any rate, for attempting to murder a baby, the culprit might well be executed, but it wouldn't be done by a raging father. Lord Brandin was in no state to listen to dissenting counsel, however, so Arvil decided to keep his peace for a while and hope the man calmed down soon.

Servants passed food and drinks to the nervous crowd, and eventually the guard returned, hauling an elderly woman behind him.

"Lotta the embroiderer, my lord," he said, shoving the woman to her knees before Lord Brandin.

"You made a toy rabbit for this man?" demanded Brandin, jabbing a finger at Oakley.

"Yes, m'lord!" said the woman, nodding her head in quick jerks. "Did the babe not like it? I could make something else? Whatever he'd like, anything!" She sank down, cowering, burying her face in her hands, curled upon the floor and shaking.

"Something else?" Brandin roared. "Do you jest? Another

of *these?*" He grabbed Arvil's arm and waved the colored blob at the woman.

She peeked up from between her hands, looked, knelt up, stared. "My lord? I don't understand. What is that?"

Lord Brandin looked like he was about to explode. Arvil laid a hand on his shoulder and said, "Peace, my lord. Everyone is denying, and we need the truth."

"Yes," said Lord Brandin. "Do your truth magic. Force the truth from them all and we'll see who the villain is."

"I cannot force the truth, my lord," Arvil said, his voice even and calm. "I can reveal lies, however, and that should suffice."

Lord Brandin muttered something, but Arvil ignored him and went to one knee in front of the embroideress.

"Calm, Mistress Lotta. This will not hurt."

She stared at him, her eyes huge and round despite his reassurances. He took a breath, then another, grounding and centering. He imagined a blue-eyed wisp of fog and began the rhyme.

A minute later, a murmur ran through the assembled crowd as the old woman's head glowed blue with magic.

"Have you the Mage Gift?" he asked, getting right to the point.

"No, m'lord," she said.

The blue glow remained.

"Truth," said Arvil. "Do you know who cast a spell upon the toy rabbit you made for Lord Oakley?"

"No, m'lord."

Arvil sighed. That would've been too easy.

"So there is no doubt, Lord Oakley, approach."

Oakley stepped carefully forward, still surrounded by guards. Arvil gestured the guards to move back a few steps, then cast a Truth Spell at Lord Oakley.

"Did you enchant the toy?"

"No."

"Do you know who did?"

"No."

"Lord Unter, approach."

Unter strode forward and stood before Arvil, his arms

crossed, glaring around at the staring crowd while Arvil cast the spell over him. He too answered "no" to both questions.

"There," said Unter. "I am innocent, that proves it. I'll take my leave."

"No, stay," said Arvil. "We're not done yet." He turned back to Lord Oakley and asked, "Who knew you'd commissioned the toy rabbit? Who knew Mistress Lotta would make it for you?"

"I don't know," said Oakley.

Lord Brandin brought his fist down on the table and cursed. Then to Arvil, "Now what? Do we question everyone here?"

The crowd shuffled and murmured, and Arvil felt exhausted just thinking about it. "No, not unless we have no choice. What if—'"

"Wait, m'lord," said Lotta. She cringed back, as though expecting a clout.

"Well, what is it, woman?" Lord Brandin said. "Speak!"

"One of the visitors knew. He came to my house to ask about a gift, to see my work. Nothing pleased him, and he went away again, but he looked about the place for some time while I was sewing."

"Do you know who?" asked Arvil. "Is he in this room?"

"I don't know," said Lotta. She struggled to stand, and Arvil helped her with a hand under her elbow. She wandered the room, squinting at folk, clearly nearsighted.

Some folk shrank back while others leaned forward, clearly eager to be seen and exonerated. She moved through the crowd muttering, "No, no, no . . ."

Finally she stopped—in front of the Hardornen envoy.

Paskal of Gramersy stood glaring at her while she studied his face, and he made no attempt to escape when she pointed at him.

"That one," she said. "That's the visitor who came to my house."

Arvil closed his eyes for a moment; the situation had just complicated itself tenfold. Bad enough that such an evil thing should happen in the middle of a local squabble for power and wealth, but such a horrible crime committed by a representative of King Tremane could break the too-new treaty between Valdemar and Hardorn, pulling a large stone out of the alliance.

Well, then, he thought, *it's my good luck that I won't be the one unpacking that sack of angry cats.*

He ushered Mistress Lotta out of the way, and cast the Truth Spell on Gramersy.

"Did you enchant the toy rabbit?"

"Yes."

"Did you intend to murder the baby?"

"Yes."

"For the Lady's sake, *why*?"

Gramersy stood straighter and looked Arvil right in the eye. "I have served my Lord Tremane for eighteen years," he said. "I have carried out his orders."

The glow around his head remained, bright and blue.

The room exploded in angry shouting, but something was saying, No, no, no . . . in Arvil's mind. Herald Jinnia, who'd trained him as a lad, had always said that grammar was a sticky tangle and that you had to unwind it when using the Truth Spell.

Have served. Have carried out.

Arvil stared hard at Gramersy. "Did King Tremane order you to murder Lord Branwell? Answer yes or no."

"Yes. I always followed his orders."

The blue glow blinked, then returned.

"You lied, just for a moment," said Arvil. He waved to quiet the crowd and gave Lord Brandin a hard stare until he backed off, fury in his eyes. "Answer yes or no, and only yes or no. Do you serve King Tremane this minute?"

Gramersy snarled, "Yes! Damn you!" The blue glow faded, then returned.

Arvil smirked at the Hardornen. "Who do you serve, right this minute?"

Gramersy just glared at him.

"He's a Hardornen!" cried Lord Brandin. "That's enough. Whether his orders came from Tremane, or from some lackey of his, it's all the same!"

Arvil kept his gaze on Gramersy and saw a spark of triumph in his eyes at Brandin's angry declaration.

"No," said Arvil. "Curse him, this is exactly what he wants. Hold . . ."

He took a breath, then another.

No, this wouldn't work.

Before he could think what to do, Gramersy snarled a tangle of words and jerked a hand at Arvil's. Before the guards could grab him again, the weight covering Arvil's hand shifted and began to ooze up his arm.

The Hardornen didn't struggle against the guards; he let them drag him back a step while he laughed.

Arvil stared at the man's open mouth, then lunged at him and swung the magicked blob at his face.

A high-pitched shriek escaped Gramersy's mouth as he jerked his head to one side. Arvil cried, "Let him go!" and the guards jumped away.

Gramersy flailed for a second while the blob spread over his ear, covered the back of his head, and oozed around toward his face. He gestured and shouted a spell just before the blob finished engulfing his head. The thing fell off him, falling to the floor in a pile of rags and thread.

The guards grabbed him once more without waiting for a command.

"Good," said Arvil, who'd just had an idea. "I need help. Bring him. I need my Companion."

He led the way, with Gramersy and half a dozen guards and Lord Brandin and most of the guests all parading after him, out to the stables.

"Graya!" he called as he entered the stableyard. "I need help. I need to lean on you."

She met him out in the yard, and he leaned against her satiny neck. "I need a second stage Truth Spell," he said, his voice low. "Lord Brandin is ready to execute the man who tried to murder his baby, and if he kills him before we have answers, it could restart the war. We *need* to know the truth. Help me?"

Graya whinnied outrage at the news, then huffed grain-sweet breath in his face and nodded.

"Bring him," said Arvil, waving at the prisoner.

The guards hauled Gramersy up in front of Arvil and forced the man to his knees.

Arvil grounded himself deep in the earth, took a long, centering breath, and felt Graya's strength wrap around his own.

Fog.

Blue eyes.

A rhyming spell, over and over and over, then more, more, farther than he'd ever had the strength to go, Graya buoying him up . . .

Done.

"Who ordered you to murder the baby?" he asked.

Gramersy's eyes widened, then he snarled, struggled, before saying, "No one!"

More shouting, denials. It seemed impossible that such a horrible act could have been committed by a stranger who couldn't possibly bear a grudge against people he'd never meet.

"Why did you try to murder the baby?"

Gramersy tried to clamp his mouth shut, but it was useless. "For the Empire! I am loyal to the Emperor, and Tremane is a traitor! Dying at the hands of ignorant westerners who can barely wield magic would be the least he deserved!"

"And disrupting an alliance that might well hold off the Empire is just a bonus, I wager."

"You'll never defeat the Empire!"

Huh. He believed *that,* at least. Well, he was entitled to his opinion.

"Why spread the blame? If you planned to be caught all along?"

Gramersy scowled and said, "Tremane is no fool. If I didn't *try* to hide, you'd have known it was a lie. I made sure the old woman got a good look at me. But you!" He lunged toward Arvil, but the guards jerked him back. "Everyone knows only a handful of Valdemarans have magic! Why in all the hells are you *here,* in this backwater?!"

Arvil said, "I go where my Queen sends me," then turned away.

A fanatic, eager to die for his loyalty. It made a kind of twisted sense.

He turned to Lord Brandin and said, "That's enough for now. I'll take him back to Haven, where he'll be questioned more thoroughly."

"No! He's going to die by *my* hand!"

"No, he's not." Arvil stepped forward, ignoring his uneven gait, and stared Lord Brandin in the eye. "His offense against you is grievous, but this is larger than you or me. If this man has any information that could help us when the Empire comes, then we must have it."

"But—"

"*No.*" Arvil represented the *Queen,* curse it, and no local lord, no matter how wealthy or powerful, was going to disrespect his office. "I've decided, and that's an end to it. You have your son, whole and healthy. Go hold him, thank the Lady he's safe and that all your black finery won't be needed for a funeral this day."

Lord Brandin stepped back in shock, then looked down at his fine black jerkin and trousers and seemed to shrink in on himself.

"I . . . yes. Yes, I will." He straightened up and nodded curtly at the Herald. "You'll take half my guard with you when you go. I'll not have that whoreson escape on the way to Haven."

"I'll welcome their escort," said Arvil with a shallow bow. It was true enough, and it would let Lord Brandin salve his pride.

He watched the lord turn and walk away, ignoring his milling guests, the well-wishers and the eager traders and the envious neighbors, and head back to his keep, to his wife and child.

Arvil hoped he would remember what was truly important, for at least a short time.

The Unwanted Gift
Anthea Sharp

"—And then she put the whole room to sleep," the Bardic Trainee said, her voice breathless with wonder.

The other Trainees at the table listened to her tale, nodding and agreeing as they ate their lunch—a hearty soup with slices of freshly baked wheat bread.

"Mhm." Tereck Strand held back a snort and instead shared a skeptical look with his best friend, Ro. "The whole Collegium fell asleep. Right."

While the story *seemed* impressive, Tereck thought it far more likely that a few people in the audience had succumbed to the heat and utter tedium of listening to the apprentices play for two hours at the Midwinter Recital. In the way of the Bards and Heralds, however, the tale had been exaggerated, the natural effects of a warm room and boredom attributed to mystical powers.

Once he might have scoffed openly, but attending the Collegium for the past few years had taught him a bit of diplomacy. Along with history, mathematics, writing, and swordplay. Everything a lord would need to eventually govern a keep.

A keep and a father, both awaiting his return to assume his duties as heir. It was what he'd been born to do, after all.

He glanced down at his blue robes, the color signifying his status as a noble-born student attending the Collegium strictly for the practical education. Another six weeks and he'd be shed of them and on his way back home, where he wouldn't have to pretend that the wide-eyed Trainees around him possessed special powers.

Although he had to admit that the Heralds, at least, seemed to actually possess Gifts. They strutted about in their white uniforms, showing off their Companions, who frankly made the skin on the back of his neck itch. But the Bards and Healers? Nothing special there.

"If you'd been at the concert, you would've seen what Shandara did," the bardling said, voice indignant.

"No doubt." Tereck spooned up the last of his soup. "But that was months ago, and there's no winding the clock back."

"Speaking of winding," Ro said, bumping his shoulder, "I think we should go fishing this afternoon, since there'll be no classes."

"You always want to go fishing, in some form or another."

His friend grinned back at him. "Yes, but this time I mean for trout, not pretty girls. I saw fish rising upriver yesterday evening."

"I'll meet you at the gates, then."

"But you'll miss the Healers' demonstration," the Trainee said.

"I've no need to stand about watching the townsfolk parade their ills into the Collegium," Tereck said. He had little use for the quarterly event and usually spent the precious free hours in sport of one kind or another.

"We can bring the Healers a fat trout to revive," Ro said, his brown eyes sparking with laughter. He scooped up his dishes and stood. "Meet you soon, Tereck."

"You Blues are all the same." The bardling scooted off the end of the bench and shook her head at Tereck. "You'll be in need of a Healer's Gift one day, you'll see. Then you won't be so quick to dismiss it."

"Maybe so."

Even if there *were* such things as healing powers, which his entire family doubted, back home at Strand Keep they had the herb woman and the bonesetter, and that was all anyone needed.

*   *   *

Sunlight glinted off the Terilee River as Tereck and Ro cast their lines into the water. The late spring afternoon was warm, with just the edge of coolness waiting for evening to come. The rooftops of Haven rose downriver, lazy curls of smoke rising from the tightly packed chimneys.

"Are you sure you saw fish in here?" Tereck asked after a half hour spent in companionable silence.

"Doubter." Ro squinted at him. "That's your problem, you know. No faith."

Tereck shrugged. He didn't need faith, he needed real results. Practical folk, the people of Strand Keep, and he saw no reason to change.

"Look, I'll prove it to you." Ro pulled his line out and stepped closer to the fast-moving river. "I'll cast right here. When I pull out a huge trout, you'll have to admit you were in the wrong."

The edge of the bank was eroded, undercut by the current. How deeply, Tereck couldn't tell, but the water had clearly taken a huge bite out of the underside. A chill crept up his spine as he thought of the dark, hungry river flowing beneath.

"Ro," he said, his muscles tensing, "I don't think—"

The earth gave way, and Ro yelped in surprise. Tereck lunged, his fingers grazing his friend's tunic, but he couldn't stop Ro's plummet down. Half of the bank splashed into the frigid water, taking his friend with it.

"No!" Tereck tossed his pole on the muddy ground and, heart pounding, stared at the rippling water.

Jump in after Ro? No—then there would be two of them drowning, not just one.

Instead he sprinted along the bank, trying to keep up with Ro. Already the current was bearing his friend away. Perhaps someone in the city would see him and fish him out—but with the river swollen with spring runoff, it was a slim to nothing chance.

Ahead, a downed tree stuck out into the river. It was Ro's only hope.

"Grab that snag ahead!" Tereck yelled, hoping Ro had the presence of mind to listen. And that the water hadn't already seeped the strength from his hands.

For a heart-freezing second, nothing happened. It seemed certain the river would sweep Ro away and suck him down to his fate. The thought made bile rise in Tereck's throat.

Then Ro's arms came out of the water and he feebly swam toward the tree. Just as the current carried him past, he managed to take hold of a water-blackened branch. He hung there, arms wrapped around the snag, his face pale as chalk.

Tereck forced himself to run faster, his feet pounding the earth like a hammer. *Hurry!* It was clear Ro's strength wouldn't last for long.

"I'm coming," he called. "Just hold on!"

Water sluiced over Ro's head, and a stab of panic went through Tereck. He leaped into the river beside the dead tree. Stones turned under the leather soles of his boots, and he fought for balance. The river was icy, fed from the melting snow off the peaks. It foamed about him, saturating his clothes and snatching the breath from his lungs.

The water rose up to Tereck's chest. The current slapped him against the tree, pummeled him and grabbed at his legs, but he slogged grimly forward.

Ro's lips were turning blue.

Almost there.

Bracing himself against a stub of broken off branch, Tereck stretched out his arm. The wood dug painfully into his shoulder. "Take my hand."

"I. C-c-c-an't." Ro's teeth chattered so hard the words were barely audible.

Tereck took another step and nearly tumbled into the river himself. Clenching his jaw, he leaned forward, letting the current pin him against the tree. Just as Ro lost his grip, Tereck managed to catch his upper arm.

The other boy's weight almost swung him forward into the depths, but Tereck dug in his feet and hauled Ro toward him. The muscles in his arms burned with effort, and his ears were full of the roar of rushing water. Gasping, he got his arm around Ro's chest and, inch by inch, backed out of the river. His friend lay unmoving, waterlogged and barely conscious.

After an eternity, Tereck stumbled to shore and pulled Ro

up onto the muddy bank. The Terilee hissed and grumbled, as if unhappy they'd escaped its frigid grasp.

Tereck went to his knees, gulping in air, but Ro just lay where Tereck had dragged him, head lolling on the stringy grass. His skin was tinted gray. His chest no longer rose and fell.

Fear stabbing through him, Tereck scrabbled to turn his friend over. He couldn't let Ro drown. Not after managing to pull him out of the river. Not after all the other scrapes they'd survived. With numb fingers, he felt for a pulse in his friend's neck. It was impossible to tell if his hands were too cold, or if Ro was actually . . .

Pressure built in the back of Tereck's skull. His body buzzed, as if it had suddenly become a home for angry wasps, and they wanted out. *Out.*

His vision blurred, and it was almost as if he could see *into* Ro's body. There was a dull orange ball of light in the center of his friend's chest. As he watched, its glow dimmed.

No!

Moving on instinct, Tereck placed his hands flat on Ro's cold chest. He shut his eyes and imagined his palms opening like a door, letting the wasps fly free. Heat swept over his skin, then ice. He shivered, but he kept pushing whatever-it-was into Ro's body.

Ro coughed, and Tereck opened his eyes. With that strange double sight, he saw his friend glowing, as if he'd swallowed the sun.

"Tereck?" Ro asked, his voice a hoarse whisper.

"I'm here. You made it." Tereck slumped forward, exhaustion crashing through him. "We both did."

His thoughts scuttled away from what had just happened.

He'd pulled Ro out of the river, that was all.

Shouts from down the riverbank made him glance up. A group of townspeople headed toward them, carrying blankets. He glimpsed the bright green cloak of a Healer and drew in a long breath of relief. Followed by a quick catch as his lungs tightened. A Healer.

But no one had been there to see what Tereck had done. Nobody would be able to tell. It had been a result of cold and shock, anyway. A hallucination.

Holding that thought close, Tereck put his hand on Ro's shoulder and waited for their rescuers to arrive.

After a quick inspection by the Healer, a deep-voiced man who introduced himself as Master Adrun, Tereck and Ro were bundled up and taken in a wooden cart back to the Collegium. Tereck was so tired, he didn't mind jouncing about in the back with only the blanket for cushioning.

"I'm admitting you to the House of Healing," Master Adrun said as the cart pulled into the courtyard. "We need to make sure you're both well enough to be up and about. Near-drowning is a serious business."

"I wasn't in the river long," Tereck said. "Just long enough to pull Ro out."

The Healer gave him an appraising look, one eyebrow slowly lifting. "I see."

"I feel perfectly fine," Ro said, then spoiled his announcement with a harsh coughing fit.

The cart stopped, and Master Adrun helped them both disembark. Ro practically hopped out, but Tereck felt as stiff and creaky as an old man. He was grateful for the Healer's support as they went into the House of Healing, and even more grateful to sit on the bed in the austere double room Master Adrun guided him to.

Ro perched on the other bed, his dark hair drying in fly-away tufts.

"Now," Master Adrun said, pulling a chair up between the two beds, "tell me what happened, in as much detail as you can remember."

"We were fishing," Ro said. "I went too far out on a bank that was undercut and it collapsed, dumping me in the river."

"I tried to grab him," Tereck said.

"The Terilee runs fast this time of year," the Healer said. He turned his attention back to Ro. "So, you were plunged into the water. Then what?"

"It was cold." Ro shivered and pulled his blanket tighter around his shoulders. "I tried to keep my head up, but it was hard. Then I heard Tereck shouting at me to grab onto a snag."

Tereck nodded. "I ran beside the bank, though I wasn't

sure what I could do. But Ro heard me, and he held on until I could wade in and get him out."

"And was he conscious when you managed to pull him from the river?" Master Adrun asked, watching Tereck intently.

"Mostly, I guess. I don't really remember." He wasn't sure if the Healer believed him, but he could hardly tell the man what had *really* happened.

In truth, he didn't even know himself.

"Hm." Master Adrun turned his gaze to Ro. "What do you recall of it?"

Ro shrugged. "Just that Tereck got me out, and then you came with help."

"I'm very glad you escaped the river," the Healer said. "It's a good thing Tereck was there."

His words held an extra weight that made Tereck squirm inside. Somehow, Master Adrun seemed to suspect something odd had happened at the riverbank, though how he could guess, Tereck had no idea.

"I'd like to keep you both under observation for the rest of the afternoon," the Healer said, rising. "I'll have some strengthening tea brought, and then you both can rest."

Tereck nodded. Weariness pulled at his limbs and eyelids.

"But we can go later this evening?" There was an impatient note in Ro's voice, and Tereck recalled that they'd made plans to go with a group of Blues to an inn that night.

The idea didn't hold much appeal at the moment, but surely, once he slept a bit, he'd be good as new.

Dusk had fallen when Tereck opened his eyes again, gray light filtering through the room's single window. A mug of cold tea sat on the nightstand, and the bed Ro had occupied was empty, the blanket rumpled.

Slowly, he sat up. He still felt weak, and he wanted to sleep for another year. Even more pressing than sleep, though, was the sharp hunger in his belly. He hadn't felt this ravenous since the summer he'd grown three inches.

A light tap came on the door.

"Hello?" Tereck called.

The door swung open to reveal Master Adrun, bearing a tray from the Common Room. Tereck nearly groaned at the smell of stew and a fresh-baked roll.

"Good, you're awake," the Healer said. "How do you feel?"

"I'm starving."

A small, knowing smile crossed Master Adrun's lips. "I thought you might be."

He set the tray on the nightstand, then plucked up Ro's abandoned pillow and slipped it behind Tereck's back.

"I hope you don't mind if I eat," Tereck said, unable to take his eyes from the tray.

"It's why I brought you food." Master Adrun pulled up the chair and settled himself next to Tereck's bed. "Go ahead. And I hope *you* don't mind if I ask some questions in return."

Wary, Tereck glanced at the other man. "I suppose."

His caution couldn't overcome his hunger, though, and he pulled the tray onto his lap.

"You're a lord's son, correct?" Master Adrun asked.

Tereck nodded, his mouth full of buttered roll.

"I take it you came to the Collegium for a lordling's education," the Healer continued. "Do you have a history of anyone in your family having a Gift of any kind?"

Startled, Tereck nearly choked on his bread. He swallowed the bite, then answered. "Uh, no. Not at all. My family doesn't hold with such things."

"Doesn't hold with them?" Master Adrun sounded dryly amused. "We often don't have a choice in such matters."

"I wouldn't know about that." Tereck picked up his cup of water and took a hasty swallow, unable to meet the Healer's eyes.

"Where, exactly, is your father's domain?"

"In the east," Tereck said. "Strand Keep lies a bit off the East Trade Road."

"Near the Hardorn border? That might explain it." Master Adrun leaned forward. "Tereck, I want you to be completely honest with me. Have you ever felt something inside yourself, perhaps an odd or uncomfortable sensation, especially around someone who's hurt?"

"Never," Tereck answered, holding the Healer's gaze. Mentally, he added *before today*. "Are you implying I have the Healer's Gift? I assure you, I don't."

He couldn't, no matter *what* had happened by the river.

His life was already mapped out. In less than two months he'd finish his schooling and return to Strand Keep, ready to take his place beside his father. As the eldest son, becoming Lord Strand was all he'd ever wanted out of life.

Certainly he didn't want some kind of mystical healing power—even if he believed in such things. Which he didn't.

"Hm." Master Adrun leaned back and folded his arms. "I find it somewhat odd that, despite the fact your friend nearly drowned, *you* are the one still abed while he is out carousing. Healing carries a cost, young man."

"I don't care what you think." Anger sparked in Tereck's belly. "I have a future mapped out, and it doesn't include any of this Gift nonsense."

The last words were an echo of his father's opinion whenever a Bard or Healer visited Strand Keep. They never stayed long, despite his mother's attempts at hospitality.

Healer Adrun gave him a disappointed look—as if being a Healer were somehow better than being a Lord. "I can see there's no talking to you about it," he said. "At any rate, I'd like you to spend the night. You can leave in the morning, once I look you over."

"What about Ro?"

"Oh, he's in fine health. When you're discharged, I'm sure he'll be happy to see you."

"That hardly seems fair." Tereck scowled at the abandoned bed.

Master Adrun gave him an undecipherable look. "I think it quite fair, given the circumstances. Now, finish up your dinner and get some rest."

Despite his dismay that Ro was free to go and he was not, Tereck had to admit, deep down, that food and sleep sounded more appealing than going out. Not that he'd say as much to the Healer.

"Fine," he said. "But you'd better release me in the morning. I have classes to attend." *And a Collegium to graduate from as quickly as possible.*

The next day, a Healer Trainee brought him breakfast, which Tereck wolfed down.

"Could you bring me another cinnamon bun?" he asked. Might as well use his sickbed status to good effect.

"I'll try," the lad said. "Might need one for myself, too, as is." With a wink, he took the tray and whisked out of the room.

A few moments later, a tap came at the half-open door.

"Yes?" Tereck said.

To his surprise it was not Ro or Master Adrun who entered, but a young woman with light brown hair, dressed all in scarlet. A Bard.

As if he needed another person with so-called powers meddling in his life. The Healer was bad enough.

"Are you Tereck Strand?" she asked.

"Yes." He folded his arms, pretending he didn't feel at a disadvantage lying in bed while a pretty stranger paid him a visit.

"I'm Shandara Tem," she said. "Master Adrun said I might want to talk to you about my project."

"What project?" Her name was familiar, though he couldn't imagine why. He had no reason to know any Bards by name. Some of the Trainees, certainly, as they shared classes, but not anyone in full Scarlets.

She gave him a quiet smile. "I'm studying the emergence of difficult Gifts. My particular interest is late-onset manifestations."

He stared at her, feeling suddenly as cold as he had when he'd plunged into the river. "That has nothing to do with me."

"Oh." She stopped smiling. "Master Adrun said you saved your friend's life by using a latent Healing Gift. Wait—" She held up her hand as he started to speak. "—just listen for a few minutes, and then I'll leave. You don't have to deny or admit to anything. All right?"

"Very well." Part of him wanted to demand she go

immediately, but another part—the part that had buzzed with wasps on the riverbank—kept him from speaking the words aloud.

Was it true that he'd saved Ro? If it was, which he could not quite believe, then that was worth acknowledging.

Worth a great deal more, really. His thoughts shied away from the implications.

"Thank you." The Bard sat gracefully on the second bed. "Gifts are funny things. They have a mind of their own sometimes—sort of like Companions, I suppose. Maybe they come from the same source. Any amount of wishing, or forcing, or rejecting can't control a Gift, no matter how much we might want it to be the case."

There was a rueful note in her voice, and Tereck suddenly recalled where he'd heard her name before.

"Aren't you the Bard who supposedly put the audience to sleep during the Midwinter Recital?"

She nodded. "I was a Trainee then, and yes I did. It was a mortifying moment, because I hadn't been planning on doing that at *all*. Sometimes Gifts manifest when we least expect it, and in embarrassing ways."

Tereck thought on that a moment. "But can't you just ignore it? I mean, you were trying to do something, achieve an effect, and it went too far. If you hadn't been playing music, it never would have happened."

"That's because it's a Bardic Gift." She gazed at him, her hazel-green eyes full of warm sympathy. "But for me, to stop playing for the rest of my life would be like cutting off a hand. I'm not whole without my music—so I had to learn how to work with my Gift and accept it for what it was. I had to get out of my own way. I imagine different Gifts react differently to various situations."

Tereck didn't like the direction the conversation was going, but he couldn't quite ask her to leave. He dropped his gaze to the brown woolen blanket covering him.

"Let's say someone had the Healer's touch," Shandara continued. "Maybe it activates whenever that person is around someone wounded or in pain. That can happen anytime, anywhere. Beyond having unintended consequences, an uncontrolled Gift can be dangerous."

Fingers knotted in the blanket, he darted a suspicious look at her. Did Shandara have the ability to cast the Truth Spell? Could Bards even do that, or just Heralds? There was so much he didn't know about the Gifts—so much he hadn't thought he'd ever need to know.

"Dangerous how?" he asked.

She tilted her head at him. "Using Gifts—especially Healing—can drain you."

Well, that explained why he'd been in worse shape than Ro. "What else?"

"You'd have to ask Master Adrun about this, but some Healing requires a very deft touch. What if an untrained Healer attempted something, and ended up killing the person they were trying to help?"

Tereck shifted uncomfortably under the covers. That was a terrible thought. "Couldn't the person just not use the Gift?"

"Is that possible?" She raised one eyebrow. "Could you be around someone in pain and simply ignore it?"

"This isn't about me."

"Perhaps it isn't, after all." She let out a sigh, then stood and smoothed the red silk of her tunic. "I'll leave you to your rest then, Tereck Strand. Thank you for listening to me."

He felt as though he'd disappointed her. And maybe himself. But for him to have the Gift of Healing simply wasn't an option.

"I appreciate your visit," he said, though truly he hadn't.

"I wish you well," she said, moving to the door, then standing aside as the Trainee came in with another cinnamon bun. "Enjoy the rest of your breakfast."

"Thank you," Tereck said.

Then she was gone, and the lad handed him the pastry.

"I already ate mine," he said. "But here you are. I've got to get back to the main infirmary."

"Go ahead."

The Trainee darted away, leaving Tereck to eat his cinnamon

bun in solitude. Somehow, it didn't taste half as sweet as the first one.

During the next week, Tereck concentrated on his classes, and tried to put the events of that day out of his mind. Whatever Shandara Tem had said, he was determined to ignore any future manifestation of his Healing Gift. If that was even what had happened.

That determination began to erode one morning in his history class.

At first, Tereck thought his inability to concentrate was due to tiredness, but soon he realized it was something more.

A girl in the front row, Trainee Elwen, winced as she leaned over to pick up her fallen book. The disorienting blur slipped over Tereck's eyes, and he saw a lavender light pulsing from just below her stomach. The wasps buzzed annoyingly in his head.

Clenching his jaw, he forced himself to ignore the tickling sensation until the end of class. Whatever was wrong with the girl, it didn't seem serious.

Then, at lunch, he was besieged by an awareness of a multitude of low-level ailments. The boy two tables over seemed to have a toothache, and one of the girls seated nearby had a bright flare of pink on her hand. Blinking, Tereck saw with his normal vision that her palm was bandaged. At least she'd seen the Healers already.

"Are you all right?" Ro asked, clearly noticing Tereck's distraction.

"Well enough," Tereck said. "Just not hungry. Excuse me."

He stood, and almost lost his balance as his vision doubled again. Despite Ro's murmur of concern, Tereck snatched up his plate and cup and hurried off. He needed to get away from everyone, as fast as he could.

Going back to his room would mean passing fellow students in the hallways, and he couldn't bear it. The wasps in his head buzzed so loudly he could barely concentrate as he deposited his dishes in the tubs and then headed for the outside.

It was quieter in the courtyard, and he was beyond grateful for it. Without thinking, he turned right, away from the buildings of the Collegium. Head down, he paced over the stones. When they ended, he stepped into the grasses and kept going. It didn't matter where, as long as it was away.

Some minutes later, he fetched up at a fence. Startled, he glanced up to see that he'd arrived at Companion's Field. The buzzing in his brain had thankfully died down. He took a deep breath of grass-scented air and rested his forearms on the smooth, weathered wood. Farther down the green Field, a handful of Companions raced back and forth, the wind making banners of their brilliant white manes and tails.

He'd never wanted this. Never dreamed of being a Herald or wished for any kind of mystical ability. Ever since he was a child he'd been practical. Focused on the future, on his role as heir.

Hadn't he?

Something flickered through his thoughts, a niggling memory. Tereck closed his eyes, feeling the spring sunshine on his face, and tried to recall what it was.

A book! There had been a book once, with gold lettering and bright illustrations, filled with fanciful tales he'd begged his older sister to read him. She almost never did, and only late at night, by the light of a single candle.

One day he'd found the book tucked under her mattress and pulled it out. He'd taken it to the Hall and sat by the fire, happily leafing through the colorful pages. Pictures of Gryphons and Mages, Kings and Adventurers filled his mind. Until his father had snatched the book from his hands.

"What's this?" Lord Strand had demanded, closing the cover and reading the title. "*Tales of the Past?* More like Tales of Rubbish. Where did you get this?"

Wide-eyed, Tereck had stared up at his father's stern features and said nothing. The cold edge to Lord Strand's voice meant trouble, and Tereck had already learned it was better to keep quiet when faced with that icy tone.

"Nothing to say?" Lord Strand had turned and tossed the book into the fire. "Listen up, my boy. These things don't exist, and believing in such nonsense makes a man soft. You don't want to be soft, do you?"

Mutely, Tereck had shaken his head. Behind Lord Strand,

the flames were devouring the book. As Tereck watched, a bright illustration of a regal Gryphon blackened and curled.

"Good. No heir of mine should give any credence to claims of magic and such. Provided he wants to remain heir. Now, off with you, and no more fancies, you hear?"

"Yes, milord," Tereck had said, then scampered back to his room, holding back tears at the thought of that beautiful book burned all to ashes.

A quiet nicker returned him to the present. He opened his eyes to see a Companion standing a mere yard away. It regarded him from one deep blue eye, its coat shining silver in the midday light.

Tereck swallowed, tasting the memory of his boyhood tears. After that day, he'd heeded his father, and turned his mind only to practicalities. Lord Strand's expectations were like iron, a cage that Tereck had stepped into and then forgotten the bars were even there.

Until now.

Throat tight with pent-up emotion, he stared at the Companion. It was starlight and glimmer, hope and sorrow.

It was magic.

It was not for him, but that didn't matter. His father might have thrown all Tereck's young dreams into the fire, but, unlike the book, they had not burned away. Been covered over with ashes and shadows, maybe, but his yearning for a magical future was there, waiting for him to finally let himself remember.

The Companion bobbed its head, then pivoted on light feet and cantered away, a silver breeze over the green grass. Tereck took a shaky breath, then another. Slowly, he turned to face the Collegium.

His path had changed inexorably the moment he'd rescued Ro from the river. Much as he'd tried to deny it, he had a Gift—and nobody, not his father, not the Masters of the Collegium, not even the Queen herself could change that fact.

Gifts were meant to be used. For certain, his own would drive him mad if he didn't learn how to train it, to control it.

There was no denying there would be struggles ahead—not the least of them with his family.

Although . . . Tereck remembered his mother singing him ballads of valor and adventure, and how strongly she'd advocated he come to the Collegium, even against his father's wishes. Perhaps she'd suspected. Perhaps she'd buried a Gift of her own, had let Lord Strand smother it with the weight of disapproval and expectation.

But that wouldn't happen to Tereck. Breathing easier than he had in years, he strode out, headed for the Healer's Collegium. He had some apologies and explanations to make—to Master Adrun, to Shandara Tem, to Ro—and a new set of studies to begin.

Maybe he couldn't be both a Lord and a Healer.

But he was willing to try.

Dawn of a New Age
Dylan Birtolo

"Aren't you worried?"

Bassyl turned sideways and stepped ahead of Gan as they navigated the crowded market streets. The foot traffic slowed to a standstill as the bodies pressed together so tightly that Bassyl felt people on all sides. He stretched his neck, taking advantage of his height to see over the crowd.

Ahead, a priest of Vkandis strolled down the center of the road with an escort of two soldiers flanking him. The common people shoved each other to the edges in an attempt to get out of the way and give the priest a wide berth.

As the priest passed, Bassyl met the holy man's eyes for a moment before dropping his gaze. Fear crawled up his spine, chilling him despite the warm sun beating down on his neck and making him sweat. Bassyl resisted the urge to reach up and mop his head, not wanting to do anything to draw attention. The priest continued walking without a hitch in his step, letting Bassyl release his breath. As soon as he and his escort left the vicinity, traffic began flowing again.

He shrugged and looked back at Gan. "Sometimes I am, but I can't change it. I spent years trying to fight it, but that's a pointless battle."

Gan stepped close and grabbed Bassyl's arm, hard enough to pull him to a stop. Lifting up on his toes, he leaned forward so that he could whisper and still be heard over the din of business. "Don't you know what they'd do if they knew you're *shaych*?"

Bassyl ripped his arm free and walked away, threading his way through the crowd in a rush. He didn't so much as glance over his shoulder as he headed to the nearest side street that offered some shelter from the crowd.

Behind him, the larger Gan knocked a prospective buyer into one of the tables, causing stacks of decorative bowls to rattle and wobble precariously.

Once Bassyl was a few feet past the opening, he whirled around to face Gan. "You shouldn't bring it up in the middle of a crowded street!"

"I thought you said you weren't worried."

"Not all the time, no. But that doesn't mean I talk about it in the open. You're right, you know. If the wrong people did find out, I could lose everything. I've lost sleep in the middle of the night because I heard a strange sound outside my door and thought it was the Temple Guard coming to arrest me. So yes, I do worry. Why do you think I took so long to tell you?"

Gan looked down and clasped his callused hands together in front of his body, rolling them over one another. He glanced over his shoulder to the entrance of the alley before he looked back up at Bassyl. "Sorry. I didn't think about it. I was curious."

Bassyl smiled and reached out, resting his hand on Gan's shoulder. "It's okay to ask questions. I don't mind talking about it. Just, maybe save it for behind closed doors?" After a nod from the smaller man, Bassyl continued. "I need to get back to the shop. I've been gone long enough as it is. The crowds came earlier than I anticipated."

The two men entered the large press of people and navigated the path back to Bassyl's shop. Calling it a shop was a generous description. It was little more than a stall, just like most of the establishments on the street, but the location was reserved for the entire year after paying an exorbitant fee to the Temple for the rights to that tiny plot of space. Bassyl had spent three years petitioning for this specific area of street real estate. Its primary advantage was being located directly in front of his house, enabling him to resupply his wares in the middle of a shopping day without a costly trip across half of Ebervergen during the middle of shopping hours.

Once they arrived, Gan bid farewell and went about his business as Bassyl got everything ready to do open. As he put his wares on display, he felt a prickling sensation at the base of his neck, as though he were being watched. He looked around, but he didn't see anyone paying him any particular attention. The shopkeepers on either side were engrossed in their own sales and barely managed more than a passing glance at him.

Shrugging off the sensation as best as he could, Bassyl went about his business. He made sure the necklaces were displayed at the perfect angle to catch the light and separated enough to provide a potential customer with a view of as many as possible. He laid out the bracelets across the front edge of the table with practiced motions, unstacking them into two long rows ready for people to peruse. He kept everything toward the center of his stall, leaving the ends empty and less of a target for pickpockets and other unsavory characters.

Then began the process of attracting customers to his establishment. Bassyl called out to passersby to let them know how valuable his wares were, and how they were truly representative of the magnificent jewels and workmanship of Karse as a whole. The practiced words tumbled off his lips with barely a thought, even his cadence remaining the same, as well as the sing-song tone used to capture people's attention. He told the same jokes and paid the same compliments regardless of how many people stopped at his stall, only stopping to swallow some water in an attempt to soothe the itching sensation creeping up from the base of his neck.

As the edge of the sun kissed the top of the buildings to his left, the crowds thinned. What was once a continuous press of people became a scattering of three or four distinct groups wandering from one stall to another with specific purpose. Several of his neighbors had already begun packing up their wares and preparing for the trip home.

During this lull, Bassyl took stock of his wares. The day had been less lucrative than usual, enough so that it was a disappointment. He thought the number of people stopping at his stall was unusually low, but he hadn't realized that his business was less than half of what he expected. His eyebrows scrunched together as he sat down and replayed the events of the day in his mind, trying to determine what the problem was. The customers were plentiful, but fewer people seem willing to buy. He reached out and picked up one of the bracelets, turning it over in his hand and examining it. It was the same type of gear he was used to selling, but apparently it had less appeal. Perhaps the market for this quality of jewelry was tapped out and he would need to reinvest.

His mind made up, Bassyl closed up his shop a little earlier than normal. He usually ran until the Temple-mandated shut down, but he wanted to see Niana before the business day concluded. She would be able to sell him some higher quality pieces, provided she had still them in stock.

He rushed into the house, tucking the box of jewelry around the corner and grabbing the sack of coins stashed in the hidden drawer of his desk. Then he sprinted out and turned to the edge of town, heading to Niana's warehouse.

Unlike this morning, Bassyl had no trouble navigating the path through the city. Only once did he slow down to weave around a small family loading their supplies into a wagon as they closed up shop.

As he turned the last corner, he saw Niana in the front door of her warehouse, standing in front of the trading table and negotiating a deal with another merchant Bassyl didn't recognize. He slowed his pace, taking a few moments to catch his breath. He kept a respectful distance but got close enough to hear the tail end of the conversation.

"Agreed. I can get you four crates by tomorrow morning as soon as the market opens. A pleasure doing business with you."

The stranger nodded and turned to leave. When he saw Bassyl standing there, he paused, looking the other merchant over from head to toe before his nose wrinkled and he continued on his way. Bassyl watched him go, trying to recall if he knew the man, but eventually he conceded he did not. He turned back to Niana, surprised to see her stacking her logbooks without her usual care. She slammed one closed with a bent page, creasing it in her rush.

"I was hoping to do some business."

Niana shook her head as she continued closing up her business. She kept her eyes down as she sorted her supplies, making sure that everything was accounted for. "Sorry, we're closed. Temple rules and all."

"Temple law dictates that we have until the sun touches the horizon. It is still a whole hand's width above that. You never close early."

"I don't want to risk the wrath of the priests. They've been on the warpath. All the Mage burning has them worked up. Better safe than sorry."

Bassyl stepped forward and put his hands on the table, leaning forward and invading her space. She tried to reach around him and grab one of the books still resting there, so Bassyl put his hand on it, pressing down so she would have to rip it out from underneath him. That got her to raise her gaze to meet his.

"What's going on?"

"I've heard things." When Bassyl didn't respond or move, Niana shifted her weight from one foot to the other before taking a deep breath and continuing in a whisper. "I've heard rumors, and I can't risk doing business with one of you."

"What do you mean, one of me? I'm no Mage."

"I know that. If you were, I wouldn't even speak to you. I've just heard that you were . . ." Niana gestured with her hand, making vague circles in the air. She chewed on her bottom lip, looking up at him.

"Ah. Well, I wouldn't want you to be put in an uncomfortable position. I appreciate your business. When this rumor is put to rest, maybe we can continue our arrangement."

"I'd like nothing more."

Bassyl lifted his hand and stuck it out in a gesture of friendship toward his former business associate. She grasped it and shook several times. Bassyl had no delusions surrounding the release of tension in her features. It was clear that their partnership had reached an end. It was a shame, considering how lucrative it had been. Still, he would be able to find another partner, someone willing to bring goods to Karse for him to sell, minus a small handler's fee.

His steps were slow as he headed back home. His brain danced around the possibilities of who might serve as an appropriate replacement for Niana. It was a shame she'd heard something that made her uncomfortable, but he couldn't allow his trade to fail because of one failed arrangement.

Walking down his street, he froze as soon as his stall came into view. Someone had scrawled "*SHAYCH*" in crude letters along the canvas wall that helped to separate it from its neighbors.

Bassyl rushed forward and pulled the wall down, ripping it in the process. The sound was so loud and sudden, he felt it must have caught the attention of everyone in the area. He whipped his head around, looking up and down the street in both directions, but it was mostly deserted. Only a few stragglers remained, and they didn't glace in his direction. Nonetheless, Bassyl felt a familiar chill creep across his skin and sink into his bones, making him tremble for a moment. He rushed into the house and slammed the door, leaning against it with the tattered canvas still in his arms.

It took several breaths before he could calm himself enough to breathe easily and open his eyes. The sun had set, plunging the interior into darkness except for a couple of small pools near the windows. He needed to think.

Apparently, it was more than just an idle rumor. Someone had heard of his preferences and was deliberately targeting him. Who could it be? He had been so careful, always making sure to keep his activities discreet. The threat of death served as a wonderful motivator. Bassyl shook his head. It didn't matter how the word had gotten out. All that mattered was that someone, or multiple people, had heard and were taking action. It was only a matter of time before word reached the Temple. When that happened, nothing could save him.

There was no point in worrying about it now. Bassyl took the canvas and dropped it into his work area. He'd need to scrub the writing off the side, or paint over it. That could wait until morning. For now, he needed to rest. There was no point in eating, however. His stomach felt too tight to keep food down, plus he wasn't hungry after the adventures of the evening. Instead, he shuffled to his bed and collapsed on it, closing his eyes and trying to sleep before images of the Temple soldiers invaded his dreams.

Bassyl woke several hours later. He wasn't sure what caused him to wake, but he bolted upright, looking around to see if anything was amiss. He didn't see anything, so he cocked his head to listen. In the distance, he heard the distinct rattle of soldiers wearing heavy armor. The sound was faint, coming from a fair distance, and sounding like they were attempting to be stealthy.

Bassyl jumped to his feet and stood there, legs tense and knees bent as he glanced around. The guards were probably coming for him, just as he dreamed they would. This wasn't another dream, was it? Grabbing the webbing of his right hand, he pinched hard enough to make himself wince, but he didn't wake up.

He rushed over and grabbed a sack, shoving some clothes and food into it, whatever was within easy reach. Throughout it all, the sound grew louder as the guards came closer.

Thankfully, his house had a back exit. Stepping into the small street that paralleled the market road, Bassyl was struck by how much the temperature had dropped. He pulled his cloak tightly around him as he looked up and down the street, not sure which way to go. While he was debating, he saw a flash of color off to his left. It looked like a small cream-colored cat with an orange-tipped tail. It was only a glimpse, and then the animal was gone. Curious, Bassyl headed after it.

As he got to the corner where the animal disappeared, he saw the tip of the tail as the cat continued walking away from him. Bassyl found himself following the cat, not even sure of why he was doing it. One thing was sure—the animal was leading him on a path through the city, always staying behind long enough just to be seen before disappearing around a corner. While he chased the animal, Bassyl forgot about the sound of marching soldiers.

After several twists and turns, the cat jumped up to sit on a barrel across from a small house on the edge of the city. It looked sleek and regal as it sat with its head held high and its eyes riveted on the building across the way. Bassyl crept up, not wanting to disturb the animal. He was filled with a sense of awe and had a brief moment of hope. Would the animal speak to him? But surely that would mean it was a dream. Firecats were the stuff of legend, gone for generations.

When he was even with the barrel, the cat turned to look at him, and Bassyl's breath caught as he made eye contact. There was an intelligence there far beyond anything he had seen before, and a sense of serenity he hadn't experienced in years. He couldn't say how long he stood there, hypnotized by the cat's gaze. He only knew he wished it didn't have to end.

A fierce pounding shook him out of his reverie and back to the real world. Several of the Temple Guard pounded on the front door of the home, hard enough that the wood cracked under their assault. Several of the guards had torches, and the universal sneer on their faces made their intent all too clear.

:Save her.:

The voice in his head caught him by surprise. Bassyl found himself answering before he even realized what he was doing. "I can't save anyone. Not even myself."

:She needs you. The window at the back. She will be there. Tell her she will be safe.:

Bassyl opened his mouth to respond, but the guards at the front of the house began charging at the door, impacting it with their armored shoulders. The wood splintered and groaned, clearly about to give way. Cursing under his breath, Bassyl rushed forward, ducking over in the hopes that it would make him less visible as he approached the back of the house. Just as he reached it, he heard the front door crash and a scream from inside the building.

Now that he was here, he didn't hesitate. Bassyl reached up and stuck his arms through the window, reaching into the dimly lit room. Light danced on the other side of a curtain as a woman and man argued with the Temple guards. A young girl, almost half Bassyl's size, huddled in the corner, staring at him with wide eyes as he reached in. Her hands were knotted in her long dark hair and she froze as soon as she saw the intruder.

"Come with me. I'll make sure you're safe."

The child didn't move, and Bassyl was worried she wouldn't listen to his pleas. There was no way he could fit through the window; it was too narrow. A solid impact sounded from the front room, followed by the heavy *thud* of a body striking the ground. A sharp scream pierced the humid air, abruptly cut short with a sickening, wet sound. The girl whipped her head around to look at the curtain, pushing with her feet as if she could hide herself in the wall.

"Please."

Bassyl's voice caught her attention. She rushed forward, running into his hands. She was light, lighter than he expected. He lifted her up and pulled her through the window just as the curtain was brushed aside. Bassyl tucked the child against his hip, wrapping his cloak around her as he turned and ran, ignoring the soldier shouting behind him. He felt the sudden heat of a rush of flames as the entire roof blazed into an inferno, like a spark striking a hayfield in the middle of a drought. Bassyl didn't have time to thank Vkandis for the luck. He just ran.

Up ahead, the cat appeared again, dropping down from a rooftop to land in the middle of the alley. It ran off, once again taking the lead. Bassyl followed, hoping it knew where it was going as it led them on a labyrinthine trail around the buildings. He heard the city start to wake up as the predawn light made the horizon glow purple.

The entire time, he clutched the child to his side. She wrapped her arms around his chest and her legs around his waist, holding on as Bassyl ran, following an animal of legend that he swore had spoken to him. It was almost too much to accept, so Bassyl focused on just putting one foot in front of the other, drowning out the other details. He was only vaguely aware as they finally reached the far side of Ebervergen and headed toward the mountains, the feline now in plain view as it scampered across the open ground.

It must have been hours before they finally stopped, and Bassyl collapsed to the ground in front of a small cave at the base of the mountains. After they had left the city, the cat had slowed its pace, but it refused to let him rest. Bassyl was more than willing to agree, wanting to put as much distance between him and the city as possible. Even if he could make the *shaych* accusation disappear, which was not guaranteed, he was pretty sure that abducting a child—especially one wanted by the Temple Guard—would result in his execution. They did not take kindly to those who broke their laws.

The child crawled out from underneath his cloak and approached the cat, who sat still, watching the two humans. Her face was streaked with tears and worn with tiredness, but the muscles in her face and neck relaxed as she sat in front of the cat. Bassyl watched the two of them for a few seconds before the inevitable call of darkness claimed his consciousness.

When he woke, he found himself propped up against the cave wall, his cloak removed and laid over him like a blanket. The child squatted in front of him, using a stick to draw marks on the stones. The cat was nowhere to be seen. Bassyl noticed the girl was not quite as young as he had thought when he rescued her—she was just small for her age. She was still just a girl, probably only in her tenth year.

"What's your name?"

The girl sat up and dropped her stick when he spoke. She turned around so she could face Bassyl and crossed her legs in front of her. "Jocelyn."

"Are you okay? Last night was . . ." He let the words trail off, not sure how he would describe the events of the previous evening even to himself. "Your parents . . ."

"They weren't my parents. I don't know who my parents are. But they were taking care of me."

"I know this seems crazy. I don't even know how to explain it."

"Hansa told me everything. She told me that it will all be okay. Vkandis will help people like us."

"What do you mean, people like us?"

Jocelyn shrugged and chewed on her bottom lip. Bassyl pushed himself back so he could rest more comfortably, with his back pressed against the stone wall. He was about to ask another question when the cat entered the cave.

:She means people who are persecuted by the charlatans who abuse their position.:

Bassyl's face scrunched as he tried to understand what he had been told. True, he was *shaych*, but there was no way that moniker could apply to Jocelyn.

:The child is Mage-Gifted. While not the same, you two suffer the same oppressions, something that Vkandis has seen for too long.:

"What can Vkandis do? What would he do? It's been years of praying, and nothing changes. Two people can't change the world."

:One can.: Hansa turned around, her tail swishing through the air as she walked out of the cave. *:Come. We must reach Sunhame.:*

Bassyl jumped to his feet, the discarded cloak scattering to the ground in front of him. The sudden motion made Jocelyn let out a startled yelp, and she fell back away from him.

"That's insane. We can't go to the capital! You won't even tell us why or what you have planned. They'll kill us."

The voice in his head rang with laughter, but it was not unkind. It felt like the laughter of a caring parent watching a child.

:You must have faith. Or curiosity. Either one will suffice.:

Bassyl looked at Jocelyn, who was already on her feet and following Hansa out of the cave. He stepped forward, looking back at his home for the last five years, barely visible on the horizon.

In the opposite direction, Hansa and Jocelyn walked toward Sunhame, the bright spires visible through the haze in the distance. Bassyl wasn't sure about his faith, but he knew he would follow the firecat to the ends of the earth if she asked it of him.

Bassyl stood in a large press of people, trying to look inconspicuous and yet remain aware of everything around him. Jocelyn stood in front of him and held his hand, her grip loose and relaxed compared to his tight and flexed fingers. Hansa sat next to him, staring ahead at the main square as if the press of bodies did little to impede her vision.

They were near the center of the capital, where all the roads converged like rays of the sun to a central point. A statue of Vkandis stood in the center of that point, standing tall and imposing, easily visible above the heads of the throng. Temple Guards were scattered throughout the crowd. Bassyl knew there would be no way for them to recognize him, but he kept his distance nonetheless.

:I must leave you now. Have faith for just a little while longer. A new age is coming. You will be safe.:

Bassyl looked down to ask Hansa more questions, but she was already gone. He spun around, trying to catch a glimpse of the orange-tipped tail and see where the animal went. Everywhere he turned, he only saw more people.

A sudden gasp fell over the crowd, echoed by thousands of voices. Bassyl turned back to the center, and his mouth hung open in shock as the statue of Vkandis came alive and bent forward. It was a miracle. He stood up on his toes, struggling in vain to see over the crowd and determine what was happening. A low rumble permeated the crowd as people reacted to the spectacle.

Bassyl turned his attention down as Jocelyn yanked on his hand several times.

"Hansa says it's the dawning of a new age. Solaris will protect us now."

BloodLines
Phaedra Weldon

"No Karsite blood will rule Bell's Valley!"

That was the first coherent sentence Herald Ryvik heard as he and his Companion Myriil rode into town.

They had been sent by the Queen to settle a dispute over the election of a mayor for the mountain town. It seemed such a trivial thing to Ryvik. Why not handle this themselves? Do what other towns and cities did—have an election. Use the system of voting. But instead, one of the founding families of Bell's Valley had petitioned to have the acting mayor removed. Ryvik hadn't been told why, but that opening statement gave him a pretty good clue.

A blood dispute. Not a simple thing. And having just completed a full circuit for the Crown, Ryvik's attitude about being diverted from his journey back to Haven was less than friendly. He'd been looking forward to sleeping in his own bed, eating three square meals a day, cooked in the fine Collegium kitchens, as well as having time to repair his lutes and possibly compose a new set of songs. Even Myriil had talked of longing to run in the fields with her kith and catch up on the local gossip.

Yet the Queen's missive had explained why he had been selected, instead of some newly commissioned Herald. The acting mayor of the town was a childhood friend of Ryvik's, Sves Harshard. They'd spent much of their younger days together before Ryvik was Chosen and taken to Haven. Through the years they had kept in touch with one another through correspondence, and the Queen thought it best he be the one to settle the dispute.

Ryvik didn't have the heart to tell her that he and Sves hadn't communicated in several years. With his lessons and circuits as a Herald, there simply hadn't been time. In fact, he'd been surprised that Sves was living in Bell's Valley. Ryvik had thought he still lived in Bakerston.

The prospect of reconnecting with his old friend lightened Ryvik's mood as he approached the town, but it darkened upon hearing the blood feud declaration. People ran past him, some stumbling back when they beheld him in his dress Whites and spotted the brilliant white Companion beneath him. To others, Myriil would seem like an exotic horse. But Companions were nothing of the sort.

But to Ryvik, Myriil was someone he couldn't live without from the day she Chose him. She would always be a part of him.

Ryvik jumped down before his Companion came to a stop and reached out for a young man as he hesitated in his run past. "Good sir, what is happening?"

"It's the new mayor, sir. He's trying to calm the people and reassure them, but it seems the protestors aren't going to back down." With that, he bowed and continued on.

:I have a bad feeling about this.: His Companion's voice spoke in his mind.

"So do I," he replied as he pulled his lute from the saddle. "Stay here."

:What are you going to do?:

"What I was sent here to do." With a wink at her, he ran with the crowd to the center of town.

:Maybe you shouldn't interfere?:

"Too late!" he called back as he slung the lute over his shoulder. He spotted a raised dais in the center of the town's square. Standing upon it were several people dressed in official looking robes, and between them was Sves.

The years hadn't changed him much. He was taller and maybe a bit more weathered. But, then, so was Ryvik. Sves still wore his blond hair long and pulled back from his face. He wasn't dressed as fancy as the others, and Ryvik couldn't imagine his old friend dressed like them at all. He was pretty sure time and experience had molded them into two different people these days. Would Sves even recognize him?

"Close your mouth!" said a voice in the crowd. "There's no proof of yer accusations!"

"I have all the proof I need," yelled a tall, dark-haired man with a scar that ran down the right side of his neck. He was close to the stage . . . closer than Ryvik was comfortable with. He could feel waves of anger and resentment flowing off him. Whatever this man believed, he did so with absolute certainty. Unwavering conviction.

Always a bad combination.

Ryvik threaded his way through the crowd, his Whites clearing a path as he heard whispers.

"A Herald has come!"

"Let the Queen's Herald through!"

Ryvik made it to the podium just as someone screamed, "Don't do it!"

Unsure what the warning was for, he dove at Sves, his friend's eyes widening in recognition just as something very hard and very unrelenting struck the back of Ryvik's head.

Pain exploded behind his eyes as he tackled Sves out of the way. He landed on top of his old friend, then lacked the strength and coordination to move himself off as his vision darkened and he heard Myriil scream.

:Ryvik!:

Myriil was the first to greet him when he woke. *:Don't you ever terrify me like that again!:*

"Och . . . not so loud, luv," he said, putting a hand to his forehead before opening his eyes.

:You scared us all!:

"I'll live. It is the Queen's command." Ryvik tried to push himself up onto his elbows, but hands pushed him down as he cracked his eyes open.

Sves leaned over him with that all too familiar worried look Ryvik remembered from their childhood. "You scared me half to death."

"Only half?" Ryvik pushed his old friend back to give

himself air, almost smiling at the way Sves's declaration echoed Myriil's.

"The town came together when they realized someone had nearly killed one of the Queen's Heralds."

"I doubt that rock was intended for me."

"You would be right." Sves shook his head as his gaze roamed over Ryvik. "You haven't changed. Though I think your hair's more silver now. Old age already?"

"I am younger than you, remember?" Ryvik put his hand to his shoulder-length silver tresses. His mother's hair had also been this color, something she said had always been rare in her family, and the thing that her own people had used as a sign that she was magic and must be burned. So her only son had bore the mark as well, but only after their escape from Karse to Valdemar. His hair seemed washed out in contrast to Sves's yellow blond. "And I'm fine—just a headache."

"That rock split your head open—and don't mess with those bandages." He slapped at Ryvik's hand. "The Healer will have my head." He sat back. "It's been a long time, Ryvik."

"I know. And I'm sorry. But I've been on circuit ever since I was able. As of yesterday, I had been looking forward to a nice, long rest at Haven," he arched a brow at Sves. "Yet for some reason, the Queen thought it best I come here and mediate some dispute . . ."

"Oh, Ryvik," his old friend looked sad as he sat in a chair by the bed. The window behind him was open to the cool mountain breeze, and Myriil stuck her head in to gaze at Ryvik with her large, purple eyes. "I had no idea they'd send you . . . were you off circuit?"

"Aye. Bakerston was my last assignment, and I was on my way home when I received the missive in Tindale. So," he scratched at his bandaged head. "What's going on? That mob? The shouts of Karsite blood? When did that become a problem out here?"

"Oh, it's been a problem for a long time," Sves said, his voice was low and his attention on the open window. "Can she keep an eye out for us?"

Ryvik looked at his Companion. *:Can you make sure no one's listening?:*

:Of course. I can do that just standing here. Continue. And don't argue with me. I'm not letting you out of my sight!:

Frowning and smiling, he looked back to Sves. "Believe me, she's watching out for us."

"I've always been a little jealous of that." Sves's eyes hadn't left Myriil. "Your being able to talk to her. Having such a fine horse."

:You really should correct him—:

"Myriil's not a horse," Ryvik said. "As I've told you before."

"Yes, you have." He turned his gaze back to Ryvik. "The campaign to make Bell's Valley a place for the pure blooded started a few years ago, just after Lord Doreen was killed."

"Killed?"

"By Karsite soldiers. He'd learned about some poaching going on between our border and the Comb. He said he sent word for the Queen's aid, but when no response came, he took a small group of local militia there to see." Sves lowered his head. "They were ambushed and killed. I'm afraid Lord Doreen's only son, Taven, didn't take the news well. He'd left Bell's Valley to join the Queen's army, but when word of his father's death reached him, he asked to be discharged and returned to take over his father's holdings. The Doreen family is the larger of the founders here."

"So . . . I'm guessing he blames the Karsite people for his father's death."

"Yes. And anyone with Karsite blood. The truth is, he wants the job of mayor." Sves shrugged. "It's rumored he's building a small army of soldiers, assassins really, to infiltrate the closest Karsite town and seek his revenge."

"The Queen would never allow that," Ryvik hissed.

"I know. But how can she stop what she doesn't know about? Mayor Foreland was able to keep Taven's opinions to a dull roar, but after his death last month, Taven started making noises about becoming ayor. About how only those with the purest of Valdemaran blood should rule the Valley." He gave a long and haggard sigh.

"So how is it you're the acting mayor?"

"Because I was picked to be, by Foreland. He was a good friend, though not as literate as he should be. I helped him fashion letters, direct commerce . . . I practically ran everything. And those working with him knew this. So as the town's electoral staff, they put me in this position until we could settle on a vote for the new mayor."

"And you think Taven's going to win." Ryvik watched Sves's hands as he clutched at the sheet covering Ryviik's knees.

"I think Taven is going to cheat. And then he's going to take the land of everyone he believes has Karsite blood, and you can bet those are going to be the ones who don't support him."

"Wait . . . a mayor can't just usurp a landowner's rights," Ryviik's attention focused on Sves's face. "He'd have to be granted sovereignty by the Queen."

"True, but a dictator can. Ryvik, he's already convinced over half the town that Foreland's death was the first in a small-scale invasion by the Karse to seek revenge on every deserter that came across that border and escaped the Sunpriests."

"But . . . that's ridiculous." Ryvik leaned back onto the bed and felt a *twang* behind his eyes.

:You need to rest.:

:I need to do my job and stop whatever nonsense this is before this Taven causes a war where there shouldn't be one.:

"I know that," Sves said.

Ryvik pulled at his lower lip. "How is he convincing the townspeople to side with him?"

"He swears he has access to the town's ledger. The birth records? And he's been saying that once he's mayor, he can take their land and give it to the more deserving."

Oho. Ryvik arched a brow. Taven was bribing his supporters. Believing he could have the power to take the land of one and give it to someone else for their support. Ingenious, in an evil way. But easily thwarted. "Does he have access?"

"I think he does. When I first heard he was doing this, I went into the records room and found it'd been looted. Everything is gone."

"And he has it."

"Ryvik," Sves stood in frustration and started pacing. "Those records were kept as a means of showing the town how far they'd come. They were not meant to be used to spread hatred and deception."

"It's also illegal to use those records for personal gain." Ryvik was pretty sure Taven intended to keep a lot of the Holder's lands for his own use, especially any settlements close to the border where his father died. "Is it possible to have a town meeting tonight? Bring everyone together so I can speak on behalf of the Queen? I was sent here to mediate, and that's what I'm going to do."

"Well," Sves said. "We can try, but I'm more than sure Taven and his people will try to stop you." Sves' eyes narrowed as Ryvik noticed his friend's hands become tight fists. "He was the one that threw the rock."

"You're sure of this?"

"Yes. Several of those who don't support him saw him do it. His own wife warned him not to."

Was the wife the one whose voice Ryvik heard before he was struck? It was possible. "You can't bring him up on charges, can you?"

"I tried. We were waiting to see if you lived. You've been unconscious over a day, Ryvik."

Ryvik blinked and leaned back in the bed. "A day?"

:I told you! You scared us half to death!:

"Taven hasn't been seen since, and though the local law has been to his house, he's not there. We were waiting to see if he would have be brought up on charges of murder."

"Because then the Queen would get involved," Ryvik said slowly. "Sorry to disappoint, Sves, but I'm very much alive."

"I didn't want you dead!" Sves looked as if he were about to cry.

Ryvik grabbed the sheet Sves had been been clutching. His hand locked on the thick weave as his Fartouching gift instantly gave him images of things . . . events that might be experienced by Sves . . . and very recent ones. Ryvik assumed he was looking through Sves' eyes at a tall, angry young man with close-cropped dark hair. Ryvik had seen him in the crowd. Imposing. Overbearing. A soldier with rank. And power. He couldn't hear the words spoken, but he could infer the context. Sves stood in a corner of the room, and this man was slamming his hand on a desk strewn with paper. Mayor's office? This man's home? Then he saw a book, one he recognized as crafted by the publishers in Haven. He knew the workmanship . . .

And it was new. It contained a stack of pages inside, easily set in and gathered through an ingenious series of interlocking hinges threaded together by a removable shaft the diameter of a hairpin.

Abruptly the book slammed down and the Gift released him. Ryvik was on the floor on all fours, and Sves was at his side, picking him up and helping him back in the bed.

"What did you see, Ryvik?" Sves was talking to him. "I didn't know you still had that Gift. What did you see?"

It wasn't the head wound that had him now but the exhaustion from his Gift. He wasn't the weakest Herald with Fartouch, but he wasn't the strongest. He never knew for sure whose eyes he looked through, nor could he hear in his visions. But he could *see*.

And what he saw . . . made no sense. And then he was deep asleep again with Myriil's soothing voice in his mind. *:Rest, my love. I will watch over you as I think of what you saw.:*

"I . . ." Ryvik said aloud softly, speaking to his Companion. "I don't know what it means."

:No . . . but it is our duty to discover that meaning. I have faith in you, Ryvik. And I am here, no matter what the answer may be.:

Sves had a thick stew ready when he awoke, with vegetables, potatoes, and a soft meat. The fresh-baked bread was perfect, and the sweet butter was whipped to perfection.

Once he was finished, Sves set out to call the town meeting for that night so the Herald could speak for the Queen. After all, he was called in an as mediator, so . . . best to just get it started.

He watched Sves leave the kitchen and sat at the table, sipping his tea.

:We're not staying here, I hope.:

"You are." He pushed his chair back and rinsed his cup out in the sink. "I'm going to have a look at this library."

:You saw it?:

"Yes I did."

Ryvik moved back to his room and rummaged through his pack, noticing someone else had already done the same. He wasn't missing anything, but it was still disheartening. "There weren't enough records in that ledger to account for the age of this town."

:So you think there are more records there? What if this Taven already has them?:

"Then I won't find any. But if what I saw in that vision was true . . ."

Ryvik grabbed the sink and steadied himself. He still felt weak, and now a bit nauseated. He'd been struck on the head before and survived much more easily. Though he'd never been unconscious that long before.

:You're not getting better.:

"No . . . but I can't stay in bed all day. I'll be fine."

Ryvik didn't have much in the way of an assortment of clothing. Something to sleep in, a change of clothing for those nights he wanted to play music, and two sets of dress Whites. He donned the music clothing just so he wouldn't stand out so much. Dark pants, boots, a dark shirt and blue jerkin.

Without the Whites he was less recognizable, and once he removed the bandages, carefully, he blended in with everyone else. He found the library easily enough with some help and walked through the front. The door had been taken off its hinges and propped to the side. Apparently after Taven's people raided the inside, no one bothered to make the repairs.

The inside smelled of dust and time, with a hint of mold here and there. Not a good sign for a repository of paper. It looked more like a library than a hall as he walked around the edges. Shelves faced each other in a sort of fan pattern on either side. The books were still intact, as were a few doors leading into various reading rooms. It seemed like an odd design, so markedly different from the rest of the town.

In fact, it reminded him of one of the temples he'd visited in Hardorn during an undercover job to help another Herald, who'd been captured.

One of the Priests of the Sun. But . . . how was this possible? Was this, or had this been, an actual temple? And the town had converted it into a library? Ryvik looked closer at the center table. Moving the piles of books around, he uncovered the table's surface. And sure enough, there it was. The symbols of the Priests of the Sun in the center.

His vision blurred, and he braced himself against the table. A roar dulled his ears, and he thought for a moment he was going to collapse.

"And what exactly are you doing in here?" The voice echoed inside the cavernous building.

Ryvik looked at the doorway, forcing his head to clear. The figure was little more than a silhouette in the light of the sun filtering inside behind him.

"Heyla . . . can I help you?"

"That's what I was about to ask you."

The man stepped inside, and Ryvik was able to get a better look at him. He recognized him from the vision he'd seen when he touched the sheets. Tall, broad, with short hair and a soldier's carry.

"You would be Taven Doreen?" Ryvikk asked as he moved around the center table, putting it between them.

"And you would be Ryvik Sersein. Oldest son of Bose and Carolyn Sersein . . . and related by blood to the Sersein family in Rethwellan."

"Aye," Ryvik said. "I've no shame in my blood line. My father escaped persecution in Karse for his Mage Gifts. He settled in Valdemar with the Queen's blessing."

Taven narrowed his eyes. "You look ill. Have you eaten since you woke?"

That seemed an odd question. "Yes. I have eaten. Who ever threw the rock at me didn't manage to kill me. So you can tell Sves' attacker that he failed. And also . . . tell him that grief can cleanse, but it can also drive us mad."

Taven took a few steps to the table. Ryvik held his ground. He wasn't frightened of the man's size. He knew he could outrun him, and he knew the ins and outs of a Sunpriest temple. He just wasn't sure if those ins and outs were still working, given this building's advanced age and neglect.

"What do you know about grief, boy?"

"More than you're willing to concede. But bringing more violence to the people who killed your father isn't the answer."

"Oh? You think that's what this is about?" Taven shook his head. "Well that's fine. You can die believing your friend is innocent in all this."

My friend?

:Ryvik . . . :

:I'm okay.: He thought about the vision he'd seen when he touched the sheets. The angry look on Taven's face and the ledger. "What brings you to this place?" he asked, keeping his voice low, even.

"Waiting for you."

:Get away from him.:

:I don't feel . . . so good. Maybe if I use one of these doors they build in for fast escapes . . . :

Ryvik placed his hand along the outside of the table. If he remembered correctly, these center daises were equipped with what he called escapes. In truth, they were props used by the Sunpriests when they needed to make a quick escape and wanted to make it seem as if they'd vanished into thin air. He'd only triggered one once by accident while in Rethwellan, and the fall afterward had been a painful one. As long as he wasn't standing on the trap door . . .

Ryvik moved to the right, his gaze on the ground. It was hard to read the floor patterns with all the books strewn on it—

And there it was. A diamond shape carved among the circles. The *only* diamond. And Taven stood on top of it. His hand found the trigger. Now he just had to make the decision to use it or not, and that would depend on Taven's actions.

"What exactly do you think he's not telling you? Because I'm still not clear on a lot of things. For instance, where are the rest of the records?"

Taven's expression wavered. He shook his head. "I don't know what you mean."

"The birth records you stole from here were bound in a new ledger. One of the nicer ones made in Haven. A *single* ledger. This town dates back decades, Lord Doreen. Not all of those births could fit in a single book. So what you're looking for is the complete set. The bigger question is: Why? Because you believe knowing everyone's lineage is your key to getting through the gates to hold the mayor's position?"

"Mayor's position?" Taven snorted. "I have no ambitions for that title here. Nor any of the other titles. Not in Bell's Valley. But enough of that. Come with me before you pass out." The bigger man stepped forward, putting half of his weight on the trap door. That was enough for Ryvik, so he depressed the mark under the dais.

Too late he realized he'd been wrong about the door when the floor gave way beneath him. He looked down in time to see a diamond under his own feet.

Taven moved fast, his arm outstretched as he grabbed Ryviik's wrist, preventing him from falling through the hole into darkness. His position was still precarious, as he was into the hole from his thighs down, being held only by his wrist.

:Ryvik!:

Ryvik used Taven's hold as a ballast as he strained his shoulders and bent his knees to bring his feet up and braced them against the edges of the hole. To his surprise, Taven used his other hand to finish pulling him clear and then dragged him to the desk's side.

Ryvik started to panic when the larger man didn't let go of him immediately. "Let go of me."

"Not even a thank you?" Taven's expression darkened. "So typical of a Herald."

He reached behind him with his free hand, his other still gripping Ryviik's wrist. If the man squeezed any harder, he was pretty sure he wouldn't be able to play his lute for some time. Ryvik wasn't going to let on how much this was hurting his head or how nauseated he was feeling. He assumed Taven was going for a weapon to finish him off. The sounds of Myriil's hooves banging against the door echoed throughout the cavernous room.

"Tell your horse to stop."

Taven pulled his free hand out from behind his back. It held a vial of something yellow.

"She's not a horse."

"Then tell your Companion to stop, or she's going to get the town's attention, and that's not what I want."

"Oh, so you don't want them to see you kill me?"

The expression on Taven's face confused Ryvik. He didn't look angry or menacing anymore, but concerned. "You think I want to kill you?"

Ryviik's gaze shifted to the vial of what he assumed was poison. Taven looked at it, closed his eyes and then sighed. "I see why you'd think that."

"And you're breaking my wrist."

"Better a broken wrist than dead, Herald."

Taven pulled Ryvik into him, turning him so that he used Ryvik's own arm to restrain him. Pulling the stopper out of the vial with his teeth, Taven forced the open end between Ryvik's lips. He sputtered and gagged as the thick liquid filled his mouth, then Taven's hand covered his mouth and nose. "Swallow it if you want to live."

:Myriil!:

:Drink it!: His Companion stopped kicking at the door.

Confused, but ever trusting of his Companion, Ryvik swallowed it. A few seconds later he started to heave, and to his surprise, Taven walked him to the hole and bent him forward so he could vomit into it. After his stomach finished wretching, he shook as Taven helped him sit in one of the chairs by the desk. The tall soldier knelt down in front of him and forced his eyes open one at a time, then nodded. "You'll survive, now."

"What . . ." Ryvik's throat felt raw and abused. Almost as if he'd swallowed leather polish. "I thought you—"

"Wanted to kill you? No. I wanted to make sure you weren't."

Ryvik slowly blinked at Taven, and after a few minutes, the nausea that'd been plaguing him vanished. "What . . . was it?"

"Antidote. Luckily I'm good at studying my enemy. And Harshard isn't as well supported as he believes."

Harshard? "Sves? Are you trying to tell me *he* poisoned me?"

"When you didn't die from the rock, yes. It would have been in something you ate."

The stew?

Taven held the empty vial up. "What would the Queen do if one of her Heralds was killed on her errand?"

Ryvik pursed his lip. "Any number of things."

"One possibility—and I'm sure they thought of every contingency—would be to transfer sovereign rights to the acting mayor until her envoy could arrive. She would be placing him in charge to maintain order without prejudice." He set the vial on the desk. "Your death would have precipitated a coup to take over this town, take our lands, and take our rights so that Sves Harshard could hand it all over to his Karsite brothers."

Ryvik blinked. He didn't say anything at first as he processed Taven's take on events. He didn't believe him. "Sves would never do that. He's loyal to the Queen."

"Not when it comes to his buddies. Sves isn't the same man I think you once knew. He has a vendetta against my family."

"Against you? He says you have one against him."

"My father killed his mother, Minoa. It was an accident, in the town square in Bakerston. A runaway horse. But Sves never forgave him for it. A few years later my father was ambushed along the border by Karsites. I learned about the death while serving the Queen, and she gave me leave to return home. It's taken me nearly a year to piece everything together, including infiltrating the Karse border myself to find out exactly who those men were." He narrowed his eyes at Ryvik. "They're his childhood friends, fleeing Karse and the Sunpriests. He made a deal with them to kill my father, and he would give them land and holdings here in Valdemar. Several of them have families with children showing signs of the Mage Gift."

"But the Queen would have granted them asylum," Ryvik said. "There's no need to do this."

"If Sves were a sane, thinking man, he would believe you

were right," Taven rubbed at his chin. "But he's consumed by grief. Grief for his mother and her family still in Karse. The prejudices against Karse blood are real. Old wounds, lost family, resentments toward their parents' homelands. I wasn't the one who incited the protests, but he was able to attach my name to them. Every name he's used is in that book he stole from the previous Mayor."

Ryvik remembered the argument Taven had with someone . . . holding the ledger. "Did you fight with Sves about a half-filled book of records?"

Taven's brows arched. "Yes, I did. I discovered what he'd done, how he'd set you up, and how he planned on taking down every one of the landholders whose names were in that book. All with Karsite blood in their veins. I confronted him, and he showed me the book and told me there was nothing I could do about it. That I would pay for the sins of my father." His mouth pulled to the side. "And then you lived . . . thwarting their plans. Which is why I was following you. You're not safe here, and he's invested too much time in arranging the aftermath of your death." He paused. "I will say that he didn't know the Queen would send you. He was surprised and sad when you appeared to save him."

That might account for the odd, wide-eyed look he'd given Ryvik before the rock struck him. "I'm not leaving. Not until I do what I came here to do."

Ryvik looked around the center desk and again at the hole. The book Sves had wasn't complete, so where were the original documents? He asked Taven as much.

"That's why this place is sacked," he gestured to the room. "Sves was in here for weeks looking for the originals."

"Documents like that should be public record, so if they're hidden, there has to be a reason. I would assume Foreland is the one who hid them, so they would have to be easily accessible." Feeling much better, Ryvik hummed a tune he'd had rolling around in his head as he put his hand on every surface he could find. His Gift tickled now and then, telling him the memory hidden there was too soft, not enough strength behind it.

Until he knelt under the table and put his hand on a piece of parchment. He saw elderly hands place a six-inch thick bound book on the center desk, the entire area being a much cleaner place. He then moved his hand under the desk, on the opposite side of where he'd triggered the door earlier.

The center of the table lifted, revealing a square, hollow tower of some kind built inside. It was filled with other stacks of similar books. The old man replaced the book he'd set on the table, and the vision vanished.

"You okay?"

"Yeah," Ryvik shook his head and blinked several times as the Gift released him. "I just . . ." He stood carefully as he walked around Taven to where he could see what Foreland saw from where he stood. He knew he'd been in the former mayor's memory. Feeling along the edge, Ryvik found the depression and pressed.

There was a *hiss* of air just before the shelf he'd seen in the vision rose in the center of this table as well. Stacked where he'd seen them were six other books.

Taven took the top one, opening it to a random page. "Garrison Locke, birthplace Rethwellan. Son of Joset and Tas Barrows, blacksmiths. Left on the doorstep of Brahms and Ket Locke as a child. Showed signs of magic at a young age, saved from the Sunpriests . . ." He flipped a few pages and then set the book back in the shelf. "This is it."

Ryvik gave Taven a wicked smile. "And these are exactly what I want to use in my mediation tonight."

"I don't know if I can protect you from Sves' supporters."

"You won't have to." Ryvik picked up a book and went to the index. "There is safety in truth."

The entire town poured into the meeting hall across from the Hall of Records. Taven had accompanied Ryvik to the building via a back entrance and then left him there to retrieve Ryvik's things at Sves' home. Now dressed in his Whites and feeling more like himself, Ryvik walked out onto the platform. He caught the "ohhs" and "ahhs" from the crowd as they beheld what the students called their "shoot me now" uniform.

A young boy walked beside him, carrying the town's records; he placed them on the table Ryvik had asked for.

Sves came from the wings, nearly running to the books, and was stopped by the boy. "Where did you find those?"

"At the Hall of Records," Ryvik said, barely able to look at his old friend. "They're public information. Please take your seat." He waited for Sves to leave the stage and sit on a single chair in the center.

Everyone's eyes were on Ryvik. "Ladies and gentlemen of Bell's Valley, good evening. I am Herald Ryvik. My Companion is Myriil, whom I'm sure you've all seen outside. I hold this distinction, this honor, because my parents made it possible. If they had not run for their lives into the lands of Valdemar, I would not have survived past perhaps . . . my twelfth birthday. Or maybe even my sixth ."

"Your blood's not pure!" Someone shouted. Same voices as before.

"You're a Karsite!"

"Yes, I am," Ryvik said. "Ryvik Sersein. Oldest son of Bose and Carolyn Sersein, of the Sersein nobles of Rethwellan. Nobility. And yet my parents settled in Bakerston and led a normal life for me."

He put his hand on the stack of books. "These are the entirety of the birth records of everyone ever recorded in Bell Valley's history. I've not read all of them, but out of the three hundred or so I looked at this afternoon, *all* . . ." He paused. "All. Of. Them. Carried Karsite bloodlines. That means that all of your ancestors, your grandmothers and cousins, your grandfathers and great-grandmothers gave up what they might have had to come to Valdemar to make a better life. To survive."

He swept every person there with his gaze. "This is a town of survivors. Strong, mighty people, made of both bloods. The fighting tenacity of Karse and the peaceful, freedom-loving blood of Valdemar. This town has a uniqueness to it, a spirit that can't be conquered. So when I see citizens fighting citizens for bearing the same stigma inherent in all of you . . . it saddens me. And it saddens the Throne."

Ryvik moved to the edge of the platform. "For centuries, this town has governed itself in peace and elected the one best fitted to lead such a diverse group into the future. If you allow this kind of bigotry to destroy you, then what was it your families fought for? What would they say if they saw the violence . . . and the hatred I've seen since arriving?"

Taven came from the wings just then and faced the crowd. Some people hissed and booed, but they grew quiet when he bowed to them. "I am Taven Doreen, heir to the Doreen lands. My name is in that book, as are my ancestors. My grandfather smuggled his wife and his two children out of Karse and into Valdemar after being told he was to submit his children for Mage testing. He'd already lost one child to the fire, and he chose not to lose another. The children he saved were my mother and my uncle. My mother married into the Doreen family, and together their blood made me." Taven thumped his chest. "Second-rank soldier to the Queen of Valdemar and forever her protector. I am not here to avenge my father's murder. I am here to support my people, my town, and my family from those who would tear us apart." He bowed to them. "It is now that I would like to volunteer myself as your mayor, as one of your bloodline."

Silence deafened Ryvik when Taven stopped talking. Then a second wave of noise took all of his hearing away as the crowd stood up and clapped for Taven, shouting his name and cheering. He looked at Taven, and Taven smiled back. Ryvik knew his work was done.

After slipping off stage, Ryvik grabbed his pack by the door and his lute. Myriil was ready for their first stop back in Bakerston, and then the long journey back to Haven.

A shadow appeared at the back door, and he recognized Sves. "It's done, Sves. Let it go."

"You would support him?"

Ryvik slipped his lute over his shoulder. "Taven didn't try to have me killed, Sves. Twice. And for what? For stealing land that could be given freely? Let go of your mother's death. I think when you do, you'll find you can be at peace."

"Ryvik—"

"It's done. This was the easiest way. The town will support Taven, and he'll leave you alone. He's promised. You can choose to live here in anonymity, or you can be on your way. No one will know you tried to kill me for self gain, old friend. Not even the Queen."

"But you can't let this happen!" Sves grabbed at Ryvik's Whites.

Ryvik spun and as he did, he put all of his weight into the punch he slammed into Sves's jaw. His knuckles screamed in pain, but it was nothing compared to the satisfied feeling he got as he watched Sves crumple to the ground.

Once outside in the cool mountain night, he wrung his hand out, bending his fingers. He'd broken skin. Great.

:That wasn't very Heraldlike of you.:

"Nope," he replied as he settled his pack on her saddle, then mounted into place and took the reins. "That was the Karsite blood in me."

In Name Only
Kristin Schwengel

"I'll ssshow them. I'll ssshow them all." Sheski's words were low and hissed, vibrating with determination. Her crest feathers flattened in fury as her mind replayed the overheard words.

"Sheski? She's barely a Silver at all. She was only approved because the ranks are so thin." The voice had sounded like Cloudfeather—and the words did as well. He'd never bothered to hide his scorn for her, the smallest gryphon among the guards and protectors of White Gryphon.

"The grrreat Ssskandrrranon's mate Zhaneel was sssmall, the firrrst of the grrryfalconsss," she muttered, her claws tearing deep furrows of frustration in the leaf-littered soil. "If *ssshe* could ssserve White Grrryphon, why not I?"

"Why not, indeed?"

Sheski's head snapped around at the invasion of *her* secret hiding spot, then she relaxed as she recognized the intruder. "Sssneaky Haighlei," she replied, her beak gaping in what passed among gryphons as a smile.

Deavann, her partner in the Silvers, grinned back. "Clever beats brawn any day, and one day Cloudfeather will learn that." She shrugged, a dark cascade of narrow braids rippling over her shoulder. "If he's lucky, it won't be a painful lesson. Or fatal." Dea's voice was deceptively mild, concealing her own anger. Unlike Sheski, Deavann had heard the rest of the tirade, and Cloudfeather's disdain for the too-small gryphon extended to her human partner, still considered an outsider by some Kaled'a'in. She may have been adopted as ClanSib, but to those who thought like Cloudfeather she would only be Haighlei, and not worthy of the name of a Silver Gryphon.

Shaking free of her dark thoughts, Dea reached up to scratch the gryphon's golden-brown crest feathers, soothing her without words. "At least we're finally going to get out of White Gryphon on an assignment."

"Guarrrd duty isss sssooo *borrring*." Sheski dragged out the words to emphasize the tedium of stability. White Gryphon had stood now for generations, the cliff face and town above well-established, its alliance with the Haighlei kings strong.

"King Obaseki is determined to have the treaty with the Khyrsmi renewed well ahead of the Great Eclipse, so that it can be confirmed at the Ceremony. I'm still not sure why he thinks it important enough to send one of his own sons to negotiate it."

"It isss a newer alliance," Sheski pointed out, her diction clearing as her anger eased. "Perhapss there are Haighlei who do not look at the Khyrssmi fondly, and the King wishess to make his sstand clear?"

Dea thought for a moment, nodding slowly. "The first treaty was barely agreed upon before the last Ceremony, so there must be some who do not believe it a proper alliance." She shrugged again. "It may be a small, simple assignment, traveling with a full contingent of Haighlei warriors and Priest-Mages and several other Silver pairs, but it is *something*."

As the diplomatic expedition traveled, one of the honor guard was clearly smitten with Deavann, and the Prince often invited the two Silvers to join his elite men at the front of the column, ahead of the other Silvers and the rest of the Haighlei. Sheski found it amusing, especially when she realized that Dea did not share Ewalen's interest. Cloudfeather and his gryphon partner Harfryth were furious, as it meant that they were not the first of the Silvers—but because it was by the Prince's invitation, they could say nothing.

Despite the pouring rain that grounded the gryphons and

turned the paths to sticky mud, they made good time to the great black-rock chasm dividing the lands of the Haighlei from the unclaimed lands between Haighlei and Khyrsmi. The meeting place was in this neutral territory, not quite a day's journey from the chasm, and the Prince hoped to arrive first.

The chasm was steep and slick, sharp rock walls dug out by ages of flow from the rushing river far below. In the downpour, the river itself was obscured in swirling mist. The winds that had tossed about those gryphons who dared try to launch were fiercer here, alternately flattening and mantling both feathers and clothing. A single wood and rope bridge was all that spanned the distance, and the heavier gryphons eyed it distrustfully.

Prince Egharevba, however, barely paused before gesturing to the scouts of his honor guard, who stepped onto the bridge, hands clinging to the ropes as the winds surged around them. When those two had crossed and waved to indicate that the far cliff edge was safe, the rest of the honor guard started forward, the Prince among them. Ewalen was with the last pair of Haighlei, and Dea and Sheski followed him, beginning their crossing when the Prince was about halfway over.

When Sheski and Dea were nearly to the far side, Cloudfeather gave the command to the rest of the Silvers, and Harfryth stepped forward.

The moment Harfryth's heavier weight settled on the bridge, Sheski felt a strange ripple through the wood beneath her claws, although it did not move.

"Hurrrry!" she shouted, Sending a warning to Frostmoon, the oldest of the Silvers, and the one with whom she could most easily Mindspeak. The winds tore the word from her beak, but Dea and the last of the honor guard heard her and lunged for the end of the bridge. Harfryth took another step, and the bridge shuddered and collapsed as though it had split in its center. Two paces from the far side, Dea leaped as the wooden slats fell away from her feet, her arm snaking through the end of the rope lattice that remained secured to the rock. She had just enough time to brace her feet in front of her to prevent her momentum from slamming her into the solid rock. The other guards reached for the rope, pulling her up the cliff wall.

Sheski's wing muscles ached as she strained against the swirling winds, barely managing the half-dozen wingbeats that carried her to safety. Looking back, she could see Harfryth had done the same and now stood, as bedraggled as she, on the far side.

:Are you well? And Deavann?:

:Well enough,: Sheski replied to Frostmoon. *:It must have been magic, set to trigger when something of a certain weight came onto the bridge.:*

:And the Mage Weather made sure all the gryphons were afoot.:

:For once, it's a good thing that I am small.: Sheski allowed a wry note to enter her mind-voice. *:If they were targeting gryphons, whoever did this will be disappointed that I made it across.:*

The Prince and the captain of his honor guard spoke rapidly in low tones. From Captain Onabu's sour expression, Sheski guessed he was losing the argument, and this was confirmed when the Prince addressed the small group.

"We must get to the truce field first, so we cannot wait for the bridge to be repaired. Among us, we have sufficient gear to manage, so if you—" He waved his fingers at Sheski and Dea. "—have what you need, we must move on."

Dea nodded. "Sheski and I are accustomed to carrying our essential equipment with us at all times."

Sheski relayed the Prince's orders to Frostmoon, bracing herself for his outraged denial.

:We cannot allow the Prince of the Haighlei to travel so unprotected, even though the Khyrsmi are already allies. Surely it will take no more than a day or two to rebuild enough of a bridge to at least allow the humans to cross. The Prince must not travel on alone, without the rest of his men and the Silvers.:

:We are *Silvers.:* Sheski's mind-voice was flat with her own anger. *:The Prince is right. When we camp tonight, I shall use the teleson, for we will soon be beyond my range.:*

With that, she closed her mind, blocking out Frostmoon for the first time in her life.

Dea watched her closely, reading the language of her flattened crest feathers and nodding when Sheski bowed her head to the Prince, who had watched the silent exchange with visible unease.

"Let usss go forrrth," Sheski said, and the small group moved into the thickening trees and pounding rain.

The winds and rain began to ease when they had traveled barely a candlemark from the chasm and stopped entirely before they had finished another mark. The dense forest brightened, and cheery birdsong rippled around them. At the next clearing, Captain Onabu called a rest, and all began spreading out soaked gear to dry.

Sheski shook herself, then launched to the air.

:What in the hells *do you think you are doing? Your feathers are still wind-damaged, and we don't know what might be watching the skies. You're not even wearing any of your protective gear.:* Dea's mind-voice was furious, the depth of her concern revealed by the fact that she used Mindspeech. Generations of alliance with the Kaled'a'in and gradual change among the Haighlei had still not made it possible for most of them to accept its casual use. Even among those like Dea, who had become ClanSib Kaled'a'in, it went against their centuries-old horror of the Gift and was only used when absolutely necessary.

The gryphon glanced down at her partner, but her wing-beats never slackened. Dea's face was impassive as she watched the takeoff. Sheski gryph-grinned—the Haighlei would not be able to read *her* expressions, but Dea had to preserve the image of the two Silvers.

:I'm only going just above the canopy to orient myself.: *And to look at the weather*, she thought silently. A few more wingbeats, and she burst through the top of the trees and began a low circle to look behind them.

As she suspected, the dark clouds were very isolated. Frostmoon and Priest-Mage Aisosa knew the weather was Mage-driven, but she didn't think they realized that the rains

surrounded the traveling party so closely. Her own Mage Gift
was minimal, so she hadn't even attempted it, but those who
looked while they journeyed had failed to track the source of
the weather.

Banking around in her slow loop, she turned her eyes
from where they had come from to where they were going.
With the gryphon patrols grounded, they relied upon rough
maps and knowledge of the land from the few Haighlei who
had journeyed this far into these wilds. Now, she could
clearly see the line to the south where the land climbed
higher and thick forest thinned to the grassland the Khyrsmi
tribes traveled, with the rise of great mountains beyond.
Among the pale grasses, she identified movement, the darker
shape of the Khyrsmi negotiating party. Much nearer to the
Haighlei, though, she saw what could only be the truce field,
a broad, flat plateau between forest and grassland, cleared
and devoid of any vegetation or rock-forms that might be
used for an ambush. Having seen what she was looking for,
she folded in her wings and descended through the treetops
to where the rest awaited her news.

"I saw what may be the Khyrsmi in the far distance on the
grassland, Highness," she reported after her landing. "We are
nearer to the truce field than they, but not by much. With
haste, we should arrive and be able to set camp before dusk."
She did not relate what she had observed about the weather
clouds.

"It is good, then, that we did not wait," Captain Onabu
admitted. "We must press on and keep the advantage of arriving first and receiving them."

Protocol and appearances, Sheski thought with a hidden
smile. *But are the Kaled'a'in that much different?*

The Prince nodded briskly. "We can dry out later. For
now, we move, at pace."

The Captain barked out a few commands, and the Haighlei sprang into action, gathering up the oiled capes and canvas that draped over every nearby branch. In minutes, the
group packed up and began a rapid march through the trees.

Sheski and Dea, as usual, kept the rear guard in silence.

:?: Sheski Mindsent inquiry to Dea, always respectful of

her partner's Haighlei horror of Mindspeech. But Mindspeech was the only way to be certain no one overheard them.

:Fool of a gryphon. You're lucky you didn't damage any major feathers with that flight.: While Sheski made her report, Dea had been her *trondi'irn*, carefully checking her flight feathers for harm.

:I didn't look only for the truce field and the Khyrsmi,: Sheski replied, ignoring Dea's worry. *:The clouds of the Mage Weather are very local to where we were, a tight knot around the gorge.:*

Dea frowned. *:Can a Mage control the weather for that long, and over distance?:*

:He—or she—would need to be a great Adept indeed to control clouds so tightly from a long range. I know little about the Khyrsmi, but the Haighlei do not act as though they have great Mages. Certainly not like the Kaled'a'in. Could there have been a traitor and a Mage among the Haighlei contingent?:

:Never.: Dea's mind-voice was emphatic. *:Not a Mage, at any rate. A traitor, perhaps, but no Mage could have been among them that Priest-Mage Aisosa would not have found.:*

Sheski pondered what she knew. Unless the Khyrsmi had far greater Mages than the Haighlei suspected, or Priest-Mage Aisosa was far less skillful than Dea believed, there must be some other explanation, a third group or individual that had an interest in breaking up the alliance.

:When we camp and set up the tent, I shall use the teleson.:

Dea nodded. None of the Haighlei Priest-Mages were among the honor guard, so Sheski's Mindspeech was the only way for the small group to stay in contact with the others. "Even Prince Egharevba would not object, although I am sure he would prefer not to *observe* the sacrilege," she murmured with a small smile.

:It is the only explanation that makes sense,: Sheski repeated, hoping her mind-voice didn't reveal all her frustration to Frostmoon. Had Cloudfeather somehow convinced the elder Silver that her brain was inadequate as well as her size?

:I would look among the Haighlei for one who might be carrying something unusual. Just because the Kaled'a'in are far too respectful of the natural balance to create a portable device to affect weather doesn't mean no one else has considered it. The pool of magic is certainly powerful enough in these lands to create something that strong, and perhaps even to hide it, as the Mage of Silence could.: She paused, but there was no reply from Frostmoon.

:We expect the Khyrsmi to arrive tomorrow,: Sheski continued. *:Dea and I will be observers only to the negotiations, unless absolutely necessary.:*

In fact, she and her partner had decided between them that the gryphon would not even be in the negotiating tent, leaving Dea to represent the Kaled'a'in. Sheski herself would stand outside, playing the role of trained guard-beast. If the Khyrsmi didn't know much about gryphons, she might overhear something helpful.

:Agreed, Silvers,: was Frostmoon's only response, before Sheski deactivated the teleson. She wondered briefly if Frostmoon had been sharing his mind with others of the Silvers, as she had been with Dea, and if his final words were a pointed reminder to them.

The next day dawned bright and clear, weather that was more typical for the region. A dry wind blew toward them from the plains, which explained to Sheski why the trees of the forest so rapidly dwindled and disappeared into scrub. The higher elevation of the grasslands meant rainwater drained toward the rich forests, and the uninterrupted winds of the plains increased the dryness. Only grasses and low brush could survive such conditions.

Standing near the small cluster of white tents the Haighlei had set up on the northern side of the truce field, Sheski didn't even need to take to the air to see the approaching tribesmen. A cloud of yellow dust rose from their horses' hooves to give a clear track of their course. When they neared, her critical eye studied their mounts, comparing them to the magically altered Kaled'a'in steeds.

Small, barely larger than pony size, the animals were bred

for endurance and survival with minimal resources. Sheski kept herself from nodding in approbation and giving away her own intelligence. From the way the Khyrsmi handled them, the compact horses were well-trained, but not exceptional.

The riders dismounted in an impressively coordinated movement, and a few of the tribesmen—and women, Sheski could now see—gathered reins together to create several strings of beasts they led to one side of the field and staked out to graze. Again, Sheski resisted a nod as the riders tended to the needs of their mounts before all else. She turned her attention to the leaders of the Khyrsmi, who strode toward the waiting Haighlei.

Their skin tones were light, though not as pale as the northern Kaled'a'in, and their faces were round, with narrow, wide-set eyes that accentuated that roundness. Most of them had dark hair, which some wore loose and others braided back. Their garb was mostly grays and browns, accented with fur trim, a necessity among those whose homelands included the snow-peaked mountains. Each one, however, wore at least one brightly colored accent in his or her costume, either natural gemstones or dyed fabrics or feathers.

One carried an impressive hooded hawk on her shoulder, and the russet-feathered bird shifted its weight restlessly, catching Sheski's scent and recognizing it as *large raptor*. Only now did the approaching Khyrsmi see Sheski, and she noted their ill-concealed starts with amusement. She was seated in an upright "guard" posture to one side of the tent flap, with one of the Haighlei's most elaborately outfitted warriors opposite her, both of them shaded by a broad fabric awning concocted from a spare tent. She wore the protective breastplate and neck guard of her Silver Gryphon battle gear but not her fighting claws, and she knew she presented an imposing sight. *They have no way of knowing I am only a small gryphon,* she thought wryly.

Prince Egharevba and his Guard Captain also stood in front of the opening, with Dea on one side, in a place of prominence. The whole array was constructed to present a subtle image of *superior receiving tribute* instead of *greeting between noble equals*.

One of the three Khyrsmi in the front, an older man, narrowed his eyes, and Sheski guessed that he had read the wordless Haighlei message.

Carefully, she thinned her shields. She had no intention of reading any of the Khyrsmi, which would be a violation of every bit of her training in the use of her Gifts, not to mention the terms of the Kaled'a'in alliance with the Haighlei. But she was open enough that, if any of them projected strong, unguarded thoughts or emotions, she would pick up the flavor of those thoughts with her small empathic Gift. It wasn't much, but it might help them figure out who was involved in the sabotage of the bridge and the strange Mage Weather.

From the older Khyrsmi, she received only an impression of affronted dignity, and her focus turned to the next of the leaders, a lean-muscled, attractive woman of middle age, with a scar along her right cheek. Her posture proclaimed her a fighter, and as such her emotions were calm and controlled—Sheski would get little from her. It was she who bore the large red hawk on a carefully constructed shoulder-pad. The last of the three was also the youngest, and Sheski guessed from the shape of his face and eyes that he was either son or nephew to the older man.

"Honored Ones, we are pleased to greet you in the name of King Obaseki," Captain Onabu said in the Haighlei trade tongue, sweeping a precisely not-too-low bow to the three Khyrsmi.

"Through me, Chieftain Naranbaatar returns your greeting," the oldest of the three replied in the same language, his own respectfully shallow bow directed to Prince Egharevba. Sheski almost grinned, for with that bow the elder showed his perfect understanding of Haighlei protocol and revealed that he could play the game but preferred not to. Fortunately for the alliance, the Prince himself cared little for stilted formalities, so she guessed the negotiations would be smooth. *Except for the sabotage of the bridge, this would be fun*, she thought sourly. *The Kaled'a'in have much in common with these people, with their hawks and horses.* A sudden burst of anger from the larger group of Khyrsmi caught her attention, and she kept one ear on the diplomats while studying the rest of the tribesfolk.

The anger was quickly stifled, too soon for her to even guess from whom it had arisen, but her keen eyesight picked out other details. They were clearly expert horsemen, and all carried small bows, ideal for mounted combat or close quarters, strung opposite the natural curve of the wood for greater power. Their swords, too, were small, with a slight curve at the tip that she guessed was less likely to stick in a target in a moving battle.

Most of them were strong, fighting men in their prime, with a few women like the one who bore the large hawk. There was only one other older man, although not as old as the chief diplomat. Her Mage Sight read traces of magic around him; it felt like shaman's magic, but not as strong as Kaled'a'in Adepts. He wasn't likely to be the source of the Mage Weather.

Movement caught her eye, bringing her focus to another Khyrsmi, a much younger man. His hand caught the edge of his cloak, and he nervously fingered the clasp holding it over his shoulders while he studied the waiting Haighlei. That clasp had an unusually bright blue stone at its center, a blue like the lagoon at White Gryphon on a calm, sunny day, when one could see the sands at the bottom. His eyes scanned the Haighlei in turn, with what seemed more than idle curiosity. *Although if any of them could "read" a gryphon's body language, they might think the same about my attentiveness,* she thought. *And considering his youth, some anxiety is to be expected—he's probably had less training for this sort of thing than Dea and I.*

"You come with a small group, Prince Egharevba," the older man said, his gesture encompassing the honor guard, drawing Sheski's attention back to the diplomatic greetings. His voice and inflections gave the trade tongue a musical sound.

"To bring an army would be an insult to you and to the peace between us," the Prince replied smoothly, and Sheski's crest feathers lifted in amusement. *Of course, he chooses to forget that a good-sized battle contingent stands on the other side of the black-rock gorge.*

"Come, let us step into the tent for its shade and comfort," the Prince continued. "My noble mother would be horrified that I have kept you standing and talking in the sun!"

"The sun, we are accustomed to," the older man replied with a smile that creased the weather-worn skin around his eyes, "but a comfortable cushion for a seat would be a pleasure."

When the six diplomats—Prince Egharevba, Captain Onabu, Deavann, and the three Khyrsmi—entered the tent, Sheski and the other Haighlei guard relaxed their stances. The rest of the Haighlei stationed themselves along the forested edge of the truce field, while the Khyrsmi did the same on the plains side.

:?: Deavann nudged her mind.

:We've settled in to wait, the Khyrsmi on their side, the Haighlei on ours.:

:You can listen through me. Simpler than repeating everything to you later.:

Sheski blinked at Dea's openness, then carefully aligned her mind to her partner's so that she could hear the conversation. She did not use Dea's eyes to see as well, imagining instead the placement of the six inside the makeshift meeting tent. It was not as formal as the Haighlei would have liked, for the most elaborate gear had been carried by the servants still on the far side of the chasm.

Protocol dictated that the Haighlei, as nominal hosts of the meeting, introduce themselves first, and Captain Onabu was just speaking of Dea herself.

"—Last is Deavann of White Gryphon, representing our Kaled'a'in allies."

"We are honored to meet one of the Kaled'a'in, although she does not have the appearance of a northerner." It was still the oldest Khyrsmi who spoke, and Sheski could hear notes of humor and question in his voice.

Dea chuckled. "Indeed, noble sir, my late honored parents were of King Obaseki's kingdom, but as an orphaned child I was adopted into the Clan of White Gryphon. I am pleased to act for both the people of my birth and the people of my heart."

The Khyrsmi nodded approval at her words, then began

his own introductions. He, Ganbaatar, was brother to Chieftain Naranbaatar, and the younger man was the Chieftain's heir, Chuluun. As Sheski had guessed, the young man was also Ganbaatar's son. She wondered idly if the Chieftain did not have children of his own, that his nephew was his heir, or if the tribesmen chose their heirs from among all the possible candidates. The woman, Sarnai, was referred to as "the Chieftain's Hawk," which Sheski supposed to be similar to the captain of the guard or a chief bodyguard.

:I don't quite trust her, this Sarnai,: Dea Mindspoke suddenly. *:She's so controlled in response to all of us, but her eyes tighten when she looks at the younger one.:*

:Maybe it's not about us and the treaty at all,: Sheski replied, an idea dawning in her mind. *:Maybe it's an internal power struggle, and the treaty with the Haighlei is an opportune time for someone to act against the Chieftain.:* She considered for a moment. *:I'd almost rather it were just about the Haighlei. It would be much easier to accuse them of sabotaging the treaty.:*

:Now there I disagree with you. If it's internal, we only need to point it out and let them deal with their own.:

:Unless someone decides to drop another bridge while we're on it. Or try assassination.: She paused again. *:I don't think that would be their style, but one never knows. The Haighlei would find it appalling enough to reject the treaty entirely.:*

:And a rejection at the Eclipse Ceremony would be doubly damning. There might be no coming back to alliance after that.:

Sheski was silent for a long time, listening to the back-and-forth of the diplomats through Dea's ears while she pondered what they knew—and didn't know. If there was a traitor among the Haighlei, he or she must be one who disliked the alliance with the Khyrsmi. *But still willing to work with one or more of them for a time, in order to disrupt the treaty. Is the Haighlei traitor working with Sarnai, the Chieftain's Hawk? If she is displeased with the heir, is she planning to start battle with the Haighlei? And perhaps arrange that the young man doesn't survive the encounter? Our full party would have been too large for a score of Khyrsmi to consider taking on, but the smaller honor guard is an even match.*

She fanned out some of her feathers to catch the tiny breeze that snaked under the tent awning. It all made sense in her head, but she had nothing she could point to for proof. With a whisper of power, she shifted her attention to the musical voices of the Khyrsmi on the other side of the field, using a hint of magic to help her understand their speech. She needed every bit of information she could get in order to protect the Prince and preserve the alliance. If the negotiations went well, it would only be a few days for any plots to play out.

:We have crossed the bridge and are coming with the fewest warriors possible. Harfryth and Cloudfeather, of course, Priest-Mage Aisosa, Truthsayer Itohan, myself, and a bare half-dozen Haighlei guards. The rains make it slow going, though we should still arrive before midday.:

Sheski frowned at Frostmoon's words, which meant the unknown traitor must still be present among the small guard group. *:The treaty negotiations have gone smoothly these past two days. All will be ready for Priest-Mage Aisosa and Truthsayer Itohan to confirm when you arrive. If Dea and I are right, one of those with you is the one responsible for the Mage Weather. Be cautious and travel well.:* She didn't add their other speculations, but released the link with the teleson and turned to her partner.

"I suppose we should tell the Prince and Captain Onabu to expect rain in the next few marks," Dea said with a small smile.

Sheski nodded, reading her own worries in the tightness around Dea's lips. They were both certain that *something* was going to happen, but neither had any idea what it would be. Silvers might be prepared to handle the unexpected, but they always preferred to know what was coming.

"Should we tell Captain Onabu and the Prince our suspicions?" Dea had suggested it several times, but Sheski shook her head, her golden crest feathers dancing.

"We can point to nothing. From your observation of the negotiations, Sarnai has been utterly professional, except for the darkness in her eyes when she looks at Chuluun, and sometimes Ganbaatar. On guard outside the tent, I have heard enough to pick up a little of their language, and her own son, Turgen, travels with them. He's the youngest one, full of first-time nerves, with the bright blue cloak pin." Dea nodded that she recognized the description. "I think Chieftain Naranbaatar is actually his father."

"Which explains Sarnai's resentment of Chuluun. But why would the Chieftain's nephew be his heir, and not his own son?"

Sheski shrugged. "We don't know enough of the Khyrsmi to say. And even if we put all these circumstances together, and if we believe there is a traitor among the Haighlei who is allied with Sarnai, we still cannot say *why* they are trying to harm the alliance. And without any proof, we sound like speculative, fear-mongering grannies."

"Nothing else to be done, then, but make what plans we can." Dea opened the tent flap, and the two Silvers crossed the Haighlei camp to the Prince's larger tent.

The Prince was already prepared for the day's negotiations, his loose trousers mostly covered by a knee-length crimson robe embroidered with golden thread. The glittering sun's rays beaded around the split neckline were far less elaborate than what Sheski had often seen among the Haighlei, but this was the most decorated garb that had made it across the gorge. It was still impressive, the fabric stiff from the combined weight of gold thread and gemstone beads. He looked up as they entered. "What word from the others?"

"They have crossed the chasm, and the Mage Weather continues." The Prince frowned. "They have split the contingent," Sheski continued, "to leave most of the warriors at the gorge to guard the backtrail and prevent further sabotage."

Prince Egharevba raised his brows. "Why should they not all travel with Aisosa and Itohan?"

"Did not Ganbaatar comment on the small size of your company when the Khyrsmi arrived?" The Prince and Captain Onabu nodded. "And did you not say that it would be an insult to have brought a larger group?" Another nod. "Then how could we explain a small army?"

Onabu's eyes widened, the whites stark against his dark skin. "By all the Gods," he whispered. "We would have been shamed. It is good that you remembered and warned the others."

"If we need to explain the late arrival, perhaps we can hint that Priest-Mage Aisosa's advanced age required slower travel."

"If you value your knuckles, I would only suggest that well out of the Priest-Mage's hearing," Dea said drily, and they all grinned. Aisosa might be the oldest traveler among the diplomatic group, but he was as fit as any of the Prince's elite guardsmen and would surely take offense at any implication of weakness. "It would seem that whoever wished to disrupt the confirmation of this alliance is still intent on doing so," Dea continued. "I suggest that Captain Onabu take extra precautions—without *appearing* to take extra precautions, of course." Her expression was perfectly bland.

The Prince chuckled. "Of course," he replied, his voice equally bland.

Captain Onabu informed the Khyrsmi that the Priest-Mage and Truthsayer would arrive in the late morning and that the final confirmation of the treaty would take place then. The Khyrsmi, in turn, spent the morning gathering their gear, obviously intending to return to the high grasslands as soon as the diplomacy was complete.

From her station near the tent, Sheski listened to their musical chatter with carefully concealed interest. Most were excited to plan their departure, with a sense of relief that their obligations had been met. Only from Turgen did she read a vague sense of unease, an elevation of his nerves. There was anticipation around him, as well, but it was not the happy sense of the others. As the skies clouded and the first spatters of rain struck them, his unease peaked, and she closed her shields to prevent her own stomach from roiling in response.

Several of the Khyrsmi pointed at the skies and exclaimed their astonishment at the strange weather, and a frown creased the shaman's face. He had not been involved in the previous days' negotiations, but she often saw Ganbaatar deep in conversation with him. He half-closed his eyes, and she was certain he used his own magic to "look" at the weather patterns. His frown deepened, and as soon as he emerged from his partial trance, he went to Ganbaatar.

On their side of the field, the Haighlei sighed with resignation and retrieved their oil-capes from the tents. Over the next candlemark, the rain intensified and the winds shifted to come from the forest instead of their usual track from the high mountains.

In the drenching rain, the small party's emergence from the forest path was far less impressive than any of the Haighlei would have wished. Even Harfryth was a diminished and bedraggled gryphon, looking far less impressive than the preened and dry Sheski, despite her larger size.

Alert to every movement, Sheski studied the approaching Haighlei, searching for any unusual behavior. What caught her eye was a flash of color: One of the fighters wore a pendant, prominently displayed, with a brilliant blue stone at its center. A piece of the puzzle fell into place in her mind.

:I think—: she began to Dea, but her thought was interrupted as the man reached into his belt pouch, and movement among the Khyrsmi flickered at the edge of her vision. Without hesitation, she leaped forward, brushing past the Haighlei guards who flanked her. *:Get Turgen!:*

The Haighlei and Khyrsmi stood in frozen astonishment as she lunged into the midst of the newcomers, pushing Aisosa and Itohan aside to reach the one who turned as if to flee. He had no chance against her speed and strength, and she flattened him beneath her, her talons folded to make bruising fists of her forefeet rather than raking his flesh. His head struck the ground hard as he fell, and his body went limp.

Even as Sheski rushed through the Haighlei, Deavann ran toward the Khyrsmi. As she bore down upon them, a single arrow flew from their midst, a wild shot that ripped through the loose fabric of Chuluun's tunic. Before another could join the first, Dea seized Turgen, one arm trapping the young man against her, knocking his bow to the ground, while the other brandished one of her paired swords.

"What is the meaning of this?" Prince Egharevba's voice boomed out and silenced all chatter and protests. Even Ganbaatar blinked, for this was not the friendly negotiator he had worked with for two days, but the regal Son of the King.

"Examine this one's belt pouch and possessions," Sheski said, speaking slowly to make sure her diction in the trade tongue was as clear and crisp as possible. She didn't move from the fallen Haighlei, not knowing how long the man might be stunned. "I think you will find among them the artifact that has been affecting the weather." She almost chuckled aloud at the voluble response among the Khyrsmi to her words.

:You must be a better actor than you think,: Dea's mind-voice was calm, even amused. *:That, and none of them know anything about gryphons.:*

Priest-Mage Aisosa hurried forward, as did the Khyrsmi shaman, while Frostmoon upended the unconscious man's belt pouch over an oiled cape that he hastily smoothed out on the ground. Among the usual personal items were a tiny folded piece of paper and a smooth, oblong stone that glistened silver-black as the raindrops struck it. Frostmoon seized the paper, tucking it in his own pouch to keep it from getting wet, while Aisosa reached for the stone.

"Stop!" cried the shaman, his words freezing Aisosa's hand in midair. "Let us study it before we touch it." He gave the Priest-Mage an apologetic half-smile, but what he might have said next was drowned out by Ganbaatar.

"Deavann of White Gryphon, why do you threaten my nephew?"

So, he is the Chieftain's son, Sheski thought, lifting her head from the man she held trapped and turning to the Khyrsmi.

"Look to the arrow that lies at your son's feet," Dea replied, her swordarm never lowering.

Ganbaatar paused, then turned to examine the ground behind him, where the forgotten arrow lay. Stooping, he picked it up, then came forward to join the Prince and Captain Onabu. "It is a strange arrow," he said, holding it out to them.

"It's fletched to look like a Kaled'a'in arrow, although too short to be used in our bows," Sheski said, drawing the startled attention of the Khyrsmi back to her.

Dark eyes slightly widened in trepidation, Ganbaatar walked to stand in front of her. "So, you are clearly another of the delegation, but we have not been introduced."

"I am Sheski Fellskae," she replied. "Deavann and I are Silver Gryphons, as are Harfryth, Cloudfeather, and Frostmoon." She tilted her head toward the other three. "We are the guards and scouts and protectors of the people of White Gryphon and our Haighlei allies."

"And why do you pin down this one, while your partner holds my nephew?"

"We believe that they have been acting together, along with some others, to disrupt the alliance between the Khyrsmi and the Haighlei, and possibly to harm your son."

Ganbaatar narrowed his eyes and opened his mouth to speak.

"You would believe the word of this talking animal?" Sarnai erupted in fury. "I might as well ask the advice of the hawk on my shoulder!"

The elder Khyrsmi drew himself to his full height and turned back to her. "I will believe the evidence of my own eyes and wits, Chieftain's Hawk," he replied, and Sarnai closed her mouth with an almost audible *snap*.

Priest-Mage Aisosa, Frostmoon, and the Khyrsmi shaman had been having a hasty conversation, and now the shaman bent and drew a circle in the mud around the cloak that held the strange stone. Both he and Frostmoon paced around the circle, and Sheski's Mage Sight identified a series of shields being built around the stone, one from each of the three men. As the first shield closed, the wind ceased, and with the second layer the rain lessened, until with the third shield it stopped entirely. The Haighlei who had come with the storms heaved sighs of relief, shaking out sodden hair and clothing and eyeing the clouds above distrustfully.

The man beneath Sheski stirred, and she focused her attention back upon him. Before she could say anything, Captain Onabu and two of his guards were beside her, binding the dazed man hand and foot and dragging him to kneel before the Prince and await his commands.

With one of the possible conspirators secured, and the Mage Weather temporarily neutralized, all eyes turned to Dea, who had not slackened her grip on the young Khyrsmi. He had not struggled much against her and now looked more like the frightened child he was.

:He's younger than I believed him,: Sheski Mindspoke Dea. *:No more than twelve summers, if that.:*

:Old enough to attempt murder, even if it was someone else's instruction,: Dea replied shortly.

"Deavann, release my nephew," Ganbaatar said, his voice calm but firm.

Dea loosened her hold, allowing the boy to stand away from her but keeping her sword ready.

"Turgen, come here," Sarnai said, but Ganbaatar spoke before the boy could take more than a step.

"Hold, nephew." The boy paused, his eyes flickering back and forth between his mother and his uncle.

"An arrow flew from among the Tribe," Ganbaatar said, and the boy nodded reluctantly, eyes widening in fear. "This arrow was aimed at another of the Tribe," he continued, his voice dropping into an almost ritual cadence. Another terrified nod. "This arrow was designed to start a battle, in which more than one of the Tribe might have been wounded or killed." A shiver rippled through the boy, but still he stood. "What honor could this action have brought to the Tribe?"

"None, Uncle," came the whispered reply.

"And what is done to those who dishonor the Tribe?"

The boy's face went white, and he could not speak.

"Ganbaatar, this is ridiculous. You cannot banish the Chieftain's son." But there was a note of uncertainty beneath the stridence of Sarnai's words.

"I can, however, banish the one who attempts to murder the Chieftain's heir." Ganbaatar's eyes never left his nephew's. "Odgerel Sarnai, surrender your sword, your bow, and your hawk to Shaman Oktai. You are no longer of the Tribe."

It was Sarnai's turn to go white as the shaman moved to stand in front of her, his hands held out. In the stunned silence, she handed over her weapons, then carefully shifted the hawk's carry-pad off of her shoulder and onto the shaman's. As she walked past the Khyrsmi, each of them turned away from her, except Ganbaatar and Turgen, who faced only each other.

Sarnai slowly walked to the pony lines, unfastening the smallest and shabbiest of the animals. With one hand grasping his withers, she vaulted up and rode off bareback, not looking behind.

:Well, that was unexpected,: Dea Mindspoke drily.

When Sarnai had reached the dry plains, disappearing in a cloud of dust, Ganbaatar opened his arms, and his nephew flung himself into them with a burst of hot tears. The older man soothed him, while Dea sheathed her sword and returned to stand by Sheski and the other Silvers. The Haighlei and the Khyrsmi looked uncertainly at one another, all rules of etiquette failing them.

"Truthsayer Itohan, I request your services, both to confirm the new terms of our alliance with the Khyrsmi and to unravel the truth of what Sheski and Deavann have prevented." The Prince spoke with all the formal gravity he could muster, attempting to restore the dignity of protocol amid the bewilderment that surrounded them.

As the dance of diplomacy reasserted itself, Frostmoon leaned forward between Sheski and Deavann, pitching his voice so that only the five Kaled'a'in could hear him.

"*Well* done, Silvers."

Ripples and Cracks

Larry Dixon and
Mercedes Lackey

The Hawkbrothers' k'Valdemar Vale, meant to be a common point for the nation of Valdemar and the Tayledras to understand and work with each other, has had a few rough times. The Wingleader of their gryphon population, Kelvren Skothkar, took it upon himself to scout rumored Valdemaran internal conflicts. South of Deedun, he rushed into a rescue, was shot up, hacked up, and grounded fighting off a formidable mercenary unit. Lost to the Tayledras, and monstrous to the Valdemarans who retrieved him, Kelvren gained respect from the military and locals by using the last of his energy to heal a dying soldier.

Mistreated by the nearest town's mayor, though, Kelvren gathered his strength, used his talent for theatricality, and rallied the camp's troops into favoring him. Word reached Haven, and famed gryphon Adept and explorer Treyvan dashed north to help the stricken gryphon. A desperate gamble with the new nature of magic was Kelvren's only hope against a slow death, but it would most likely result in his incineration. A small chance was still a chance, and to him, a bold attempt beat certain failure.

Hundreds gathered to watch the attempt: to create an energy node directly under—and through—Kelvren, within a Change Circle left over by the Storms. Treyvan's arcane abilities did much more than rejuvenate Kelvren. Unexpectedly, Kelvren arose and blazed like a sun, then flew into the night, leaving a lingering trail of bright light on the road he flew over, toward the keep of the rogue city's commanders.

By the time Valdemaran troops took the criminals into custody, Kelvren was long gone, yet he'd left his mark on Valdemar, and in the memory of thousands of people. He could fly again, and, intending to be seen as a good omen and inspiration, he flew over Ghost Cat and the other Clan settlements—Errold's Grove, Kelmskeep—and finally headed toward k'Valdemar at daybreak . . .

What a sight I must be! What an amazing sight! Kelvren thought as he approached k'Valdemar Vale. Two gryphons surged up through the Veil when he was leagues away and now banked in behind him, level, one on each side in an escort formation. Gleefully, he called to them, feeling as if he were in a scene from a story—a *legendary* story—returning triumphant, blazing with magic, magnificent and battle-proven and handsome, with an honor guard!

Kelvren led the pair in a wide circle over the Vale, where he could see humans, *hertasi*, *tervardi*, even *dyheli* looking up at the spectacle. The Veil around the Vale distorted with the flyover, creating a rainbowed halo of light on its surface that followed him toward the Vale entrance. *Excellent!* he thought. *I didn't even plan that part. It must have looked great! I hope the artists were paying attention. And the songwriters.*

Kelvren's escorts followed his lead, falling back farther so the glide to the entry road would be unobstructed for the lead gryphon. Kelvren slowed and backwinged, creating dazzling flashes and shadows against the trees and decorations, despite the brightening sky. The hundreds of rods surrounding the Vale, used here as posts for a burgeoning vineyard rather than buried or disguised, glowed when he coasted down to lightly touch the stonework. His flight was so effortless that he simply stepped down to the paving. The Vale's rods gave off the illusion of a glow, bending toward him through the twining of grapevines.

That doesn't seem natural, but then again, neither am I right now. I am something new! Maybe they're bowing to me. Maybe someone's making them look like they're bowing, as some welcome-home gesture! That is adorable.

His escorts landed more firmly, carrying their momentum

into a distance-closing stride. Kelvren didn't recognize either of them, but then again, he had been gone a long time and must have missed new gryphons' arrivals.

"We will escort you farther," the nearer of the two gryphons said as she approached. She was a breastplated and badged Silver Gryphon, umber and white with a narrow black crest. "The *trondi'irns* want to see you immediately, and the senior Mages, too." She sounded anxious—no, she was edgy. "I've been Wingleader in your absence. You should know that you can't resume command until you're cleared by them." She flicked her wings twice and raised her head, as if ready for an angry challenge. She added, "You've gone strange."

Kelvren looked at her and at the other gryphon. They both had their fighting claws strapped on, and Kelvren's glow glinted back at him from their razor curves, from the two gryphons' eyes, and from their badges. "I am still a senior Silver Gryphon. I am only different in my appearance," Kelvren replied suspiciously. "I am still Kelvren Skothkar."

"They'll determine who and what you are now," the new Wingleader said flatly. "We will walk you in, or you can attempt to flee. If you try, the archers will drop you, and we'll finish you." For emphasis, she repositioned her forelegs a little wider apart, making the fighting claws more obvious. She had absolutely *no* warmth in her voice. "Don't make this a sad day."

Kelvren opened his beak to reply and tried to speak to her with Mindspeech, but he found her utterly walled off. He then darted his gaze around, seeking other minds to speak to, but he found no one talkative. His vision was disrupted by the glare from his own body, but even so he had no doubt that unseen Tayledras scouts were ready to fell him should he try to take flight. No opponent saw Tayledras scouts until they chose to reveal themselves, and a target knew a scout was nearby only when they saw an arrow-shaft sticking out of their gut. "I can't imagine what you'd think I could be—" he began, and was cut short.

"Neither can we," the new Wingleader snapped. "There are things we can't imagine, so when a flyer who appears to be our missing Wingleader arrives ablaze like a new sun, we want to know more before we trust anything. In you go."

Kelvren agreed with the logic of it, sure, but that didn't stop him from sulking. Huffily, he refolded his wings a few times and stalked toward the Vale's main entry and the intricately laid red stones marking the Veil's boundary. The tall arch's usual complement of guards and greeters were gone— no festive celebration? He'd been heroic, and returned to . . . this? It wasn't fair. It wasn't *right*.

Wait, he thought, *Wait. This* isn't *right. There's no cheering crowd for me to be modest in front of. Did something happen to the Vale? Is this the real Vale? And this new "Wingleader?" I don't even know her, rank badges or not! I'd better be on my guard. . . .*

The Vale smelled the way it should: flowers and aromatic oils, flavorful smoke, scents of cooking, healthy gardens, and generally full of life. Yet, apart from Bondbirds and the colorful flash of messenger birds, Kelvren saw nobody except for the two gryphons behind him after he passed through the Vale entry.

His ears twitched in aggravation; he could hear voices aplenty, but aside from his surly escort, he saw no one of any intelligent species around no matter where he looked. He paused to rise up on his hind legs and then a single foot, part-perching in the air as gryphons could, and saw some humans and gryphons thirty-some wingspans away behind cover of archways and hedges.

His movement only agitated his well-armed escort. The Wingleader snapped a sharp "Down!" at him, and Kel complied with a grumpy hiss back at her. Another pair of Silver Gryphons flew over, banked, and landed on the wide main path ahead of a four-way branch of paths. These two he knew well from before he'd left; in fact, he'd trained them in high-altitude search patterns. *Or did I?* he wondered. *They look the same, but if this is some kind of illusion or mental attack, or if the Vale has been replaced somehow . . . they might* only look *the same. They don't act happy to see me, and yet, they*

*would surely have been part of the searchers for me, when I
went missing.* It wasn't hard to spot that they bore the fighting
claws and armored equipage of someone expecting a
deadly fight, too—definitely not daily wear in a Vale and not
for a polished honor guard to receive their heroic leader.
Even gryphons had a dozen outfits, thanks to the *hertasi*. No,
these four were herding him as if he were some high-
ranking—or high-powered—prisoner.

A mere three wingspans from the second pair of gryphons, Kelvren asked them, "What has happened here? Why
aren't there throngs of people here happy to see me?"

Kurrundas, the gold-crested female on the left, answered
guilelessly, "Because no one is happy to see you."

"That hurts," Kelvren replied equally honestly. He stopped
midway between the escorts. "And it doesn't make sense.
Why wouldn't everyone be happy to see me? I am Kelvren!
The Brave! Hero of the North, Finder of the Lost, and Ally
of Valdemar! Best friend of the Owl Knight!" He shot a very
pointed look backward. "Wingleader of k'Valdemar!"

"Don't try me," the new Wingleader growled.

"Control your jealousy," Kelvren retorted, then looked
back to Kurrundas. "Seriously, Kurry, what is going on? I've
never been disliked here, especially by the gryphons."

Kurrundas shifted her weight from foot to foot and ground
her beak, and finally replied, "I have been ordered to not talk
with you." It was in a tone that actually said, '*I want to tell
you so much that we'd be here for a candlemark, but I don't
dare.*' Just the same, she did add, "Just go where we're guid-
ing you, and they'll explain it."

Kelvren overdramatically flicked and swished his tail at
them all as he turned onto the rightmost sidepath. If there had
been branches to "accidentally" snap back at his "New Wingleader," he would have, purely to spite her. Kelvren knew
k'Valdemar's layout to the smallest walkway, the highest tree,
and the deepest pool, and before long he stepped into a council circle as expected, which was anything *but* unpopulated.

Kelvren's senses had only a moment to register the two
dozen or more humans, gryphons, and *hertasi* before he was
assaulted from multiple directions, by binding spells, mind

readings, paralysis, and things he couldn't even identify. Rings and tendrils of colored Mage energy whipped around him and rebounded wildly, licking at some of the attendees, who dove for cover. Short thundercracks and sizzling sounds erupted from below him.

Kelvren threw his body upward as if to escape, but found himself with a single foot firmly frozen in place on the paving, his wings up half-spread and his back arched in, immobile but for his harsh breathing and a single strangled cry.

He threw a side glance from a tear-pooling eye at Tyrsell, the kingstag of the *dyheli*, and Kel understood the paralysis at least. No creature yet known could resist his body- and mind-control. Tyrsell's control over Kelvren was so complete that the kingstag utilized the gryphon's internal lift to support him in a pose suited to a statue, without even tipping sideways. He felt his wings being spread fully, only they weren't being yanked at; his wings "wanted" to be wide open. Little wonder that when Tyrsell was not around, the Tayledras said he was probably the most powerful being alive. Sure, he could be attacked with a spell, but what good was that when Tyrsell could just make the Mage's body impale itself on his horns while he kept calmly eating leaves?

Millions of motes of entoptic light swirled and pulsed with Kelvren's speeding heartbeat, obscuring his vision further. His head pounded and his hearing was disrupted, but he could hear voices, some in his mind.

:*He thinks he is Kelvren.*:

"*Whoever he is, he's a mess inside. His pain's blocked almost completely. I mean, wide open, it's amazing he can even breathe the way he's pumped up. His intake's like nothing I've ever heard of.*"

:*How did his bones not splinter with that kind of swelling?*:

:*They have, in three places I've found so far, and who knows how many fractures besides. This is too dangerous.*:

"*I can't recommend him staying in the Vale. In fact, I put forth that we exile him immediately, for everyone's safety. We can chain him someplace neutral and keep the rest of us out of danger from him.*"

"Are you just stupid? This is Kelvren, we owe him."

:Are we agreed it's Kelvren, now? Not some other monster?:

:Watch it.:

:You know what I mean.:

"This is Kelvren's home, regardless of what he did and what happened to him. It is also the most stable and guarded place we could put him."

"So you want him to go unstable here in the center of our home, where things are the most controlled? Won't that, logically, do the most possible damage to everything?"

"We can shield him and stabilize him, and the best healing Mages are here. We can watch the Veil to see his effects on it, like during that flyover."

:Again, are we all in agreement now that it really is Kelvren?:

:If it isn't, it's the most convincing copy ever made. I'll say yes.:

"Yes."

:Yes, I agree.:

"I can't win the argument that he be kept far away from your parlor, apparently. So, he'll roast the lot of you. Fine. I still want him under constant monitoring, and I mean by Mages and more. And he still has to answer for what happened at Deedun."

"The Shin'a'in proverb states, "The hero who will kill you should be admired from a safe distance." Just because we love him doesn't mean he can't unintentionally destroy us."

"I'll take care of that as best I can. Just make him better."

:This is Kelvren and he is a friend to the herd. Kelvren is to have the best treatment from all of you or I will be displeased.: Oh, that was surely Tyrsell.

"Agreed that this is genuinely Kelvren. Tyrsell, let him down, with limited movement, would you? That's safer for everyone."

Kelvren's dizziness ebbed, and he found himself able to move, albeit as if weighted down and navigating a mud bog. His vision cleared somewhat, and he tested his jaw movement before shrieking, "What is *wrong* with you all?"

Just two body lengths away, his dearest friend, Darian k'Valdemar, stood with his hands folded in front of him, brightly lit both by Kelvren and by the seething field of his magical shields, normally invisible but now lit in thousands of short silvery tendrils pointed at the glowing gryphon. His hair was cut back more harshly than usual for a Vale resident, and he wore a lightweight pair of silver symbolic pauldrons. "I know this is a shock, Kel. The reports we got, and what we could learn as you came home, and now—how you look— it's surprised us."

"*You* feel surprised? Guess how I feel! I thought I'd return to a hero's welcome. Instead I was brought in by my *replacement* and ground-bound, by my *friends*!" Kelvren growled, well past a reasonable tone.

"We *are* your friends," Darian offered. "That's why we're gathered. We wouldn't allow anyone to hurt you, and *as* your friends, we need you to calm down, so we can work on your internal injuries."

I'm convinced this is the real k'Valdemar, whatever is going on. I don't have the imagination to hallucinate in this kind of detail. If I was hallucinating, I'd have hallucinated twenty weeks of feasts, adoration, and exhausting sex, not this kick under the tail.

Nightwind, Kelvren's longtime friend and his *trondi'irn*, stepped up beside Darian. Her heavy gloves were folded through her smock's belt, her sleeves were rolled up, and she was sweating profusely. Her husband, Snowfire, in light scout leathers, stayed within a few arm lengths of her, and her sister, Nightbird, stood in a wing position to them both. Nightbird wore a silver-piped shield-styled woven breast-plate with her Silver Gryphon badge in the center. Night-bird's badge was the same size as her sister's but was in a more prominent position; Nightwind considered herself more caregiver than enforcer and just kept her badge pinned out of the way on her sleeve.

Nightwind wiped her brow, and confirmed what Darian said. "My first look inside you tells me that you can't feel pain right now, and that means you will injure yourself worse without knowing it, and starve yourself, too." She opened her arms and slowly, deliberately closed them until she held the gryphon's head in her palms, causing Kelvren's vision to constantly adjust to her. "We have to work deep on you, Kel, and so I'm ordering you to surrender," she spoke clearly. "Keep your eyes on me, Kel, and let your defenses down. Concentrate on me, believe in me, surrender to me, and we will save you."

Kelvren let the throng on the council circle fade far away in his perception and drop out of focus, until the kind, concerned face of his *trondi'irn* thumb-brushing his cheek-feathers was the last thing he was aware of.

Kelvren lost awareness of time, of place, and of his body. There were periods of unknown duration when he perceived a bewildering separation of his consciousness from his body, as if they'd been very precisely cut away from each other and set aside in the sun to bake. He honestly did not know that k'Valdemar had gathered so many *trondi'irn* until he'd undergone the most invasive examinations of his life. Tyrsell was present for many of the procedures and tests that Kelvren underwent, occasionally walking past Kel's field of view before shutting off his consciousness as easily as flicking away a fly. Firesong was there a few times, in his Adept finery and mask one moment, and an eye blink later it would be night, and Firesong would just be standing up in a basic, single-layer garment while *hertasi* washed his hands for him and helped him back into his robes.

Each time, Kelvren awoke without any grogginess. He wasn't ever really drugged, he was simply being shut off and on. Sometimes he'd notice he felt well fed, another time he felt upside-down, and another time he was aware of standing fully on his hind legs. On occasion he would see piles of bloodied bandages and instruments, obviously from *trondi'irn* work, but he felt no pain. He couldn't remember speaking to anyone, nor anyone talking to him.

This time when he awoke, he spotted Tyrsell, Nightwind, the rump of another *dyheli*, two *hertasi* with a stack of scrolls with his name on them, a few unknown Hawkbrothers, and a *kyree*. They and a few *trondi'irn* he knew were tidying up the glade they were in now, and as they left, he saw that two humans under a vine-wrapped awning were Nightwind and Darian. It was late afternoon, but of what day, he couldn't tell.

Nightwind, her eyes as gray as stormclouds and her knee-length hair dyed as black as a new moon night, shrugged on a fresh set of *trondi'irn* working clothes: belt, scarf, and apron. Wearily, she approached where Kelvren lay perfectly symmetrically on a grassy spot among clover. The *dyheli* kingstag, Tyrsell, simply turned and walked away out of sight, sending :*Good fortune to you, friend of the herd, gentle slopes and tasty feeding.*: accompanied by faint mental images of exactly that, but they were full-sensory ones. It was a strange feeling indeed to have the subtleties of berries, grasses, and leaves on your tongue, and register the tastes, when you weren't even the same species as the one who had put them there. Tyrsell was accompanied by another *dyheli* Kelvren had known since youth, Snowfire's usual mount, Sifyra, and they walked through a curtain of vines under a stone arch, where a coiled pair of plump, brightly colored snakes dozed.

Kelvren flexed each pair of appendages in turn. Everything felt better than it had in months, and his full-body glow had lessened significantly. He asked the obligatory first question, the one that everybody asked when they regained awareness, regardless of their era, situation, or species.

"How long was I out?"

"Six days, and maybe ten candlemarks," Nightwind answered. "I know you've been hurt before, Kel, but this time, you were in a bad way like *nothing* we'd seen before. We learned a lot from you. A lot *about* you. You've had almost a hundred people looking you over or consulted by teleson, and there's nothing quite like this in any records. *Kyree* historians all the way back to White Gryphon were asked about it, and *trondi'irn* from two Vales were brought in. Everyone from Adept to handwaver in the Vale's been talking about you. We think this is unprecedented."

"I drew a crowd, at least," Kelvren commented, immediately sorting out the part that was important to a gryphon, while standing up and fanning his wings. They tingled when he did, and the tingle flowed into his chest and spine heartbeats later. "I remember arriving, being insulted, being assaulted, then surrendering to you. Some *sketi*-sack even said I should be exiled!"

"We aren't proud of that," Darian conceded. "They only saw the surface problems. You know as well as any of us how tricky magical biology can be."

Kelvren returned to his self-absorption. "It was Treyvan that did this to me, did you know that? Treyvan himself! Whatever it was, he made it work, and he did it for me. This was done by the *best*."

"We know; we investigated you very deeply. We went into memories past what you think you know. Firesong said it was a brilliant solution, 'for a generalist like Treyvan.' What Treyvan did was very risky. He turned a known ruin into a new *kind* of ruin." Nightwind sighed and shook her head.

Darian took up the thread of conversation, "You survived long enough to make it here, but you're not just *in* trouble, you *are* trouble. In a few more ways than usual. We *think* you will live, but it may not be long, and it won't be the life you had before all of this."

Kelvren huffed at Nightwind and Darian, and walked in a wide circle around them. "Hurrh! I thought I taught you, Dar'ian, none of us live long, and every new moment means the life we had is gone. So give me the details, what is such a ruin now? I feel good. Hungry, but good." He said the last part loudly enough that any *hertasi* nearby would get the hint.

Nightwind took up the answer, "Without getting too technical, we rebroke your bones, set them, accelerated their healing, and repaired a significant amount of internal damage. Your *virtusgan*—the larger-bone linings—normally draw in magic energy at a steady rate and refuse the rest, but yours were dying off when Treyvan got to you. That meant your *virtutem* organ was essentially going dry, and your spleen tried to compensate. Your *indusvenarum* system had nothing to distribute, so it was shutting down. When Treyvan's gamble actually worked, the *virtusgan* feasted. In fact, it gorged and didn't self-limit. It became dangerously swollen, the *virtutem* had too much to handle, and you had *virtusgan* ruptures all through your body. You were so overwhelmed that what should have been agony from it was just washed away. You didn't have a clue how hurt you were. Just the opposite, in fact. You were euphoric."

"Of course I felt euphoric! Look what I had done!" Kelvren proclaimed. "I rallied a Valdemaran army! I lit their path to victory!"

"You—did do some impressive things," Darian said, tactfully.

Nightwind said, "And you came back. Your feathers were as dry as any I've ever seen. Without *trondi'irn* care, you went unoiled too long. You could have gone up like breezecotton if a campfire had popped a spark near you."

Kelvren turned his head to look himself over. "I think I knew that somehow. When I felt that new energy surge up into me, I was scared. I thought I'd turn to ash, But then I thought, *to dump away the heat from too much magic power, use it for something.* The fastest, simplest thing I knew was Lightcasting. You should have seen it!"

"During your interrogations, I didn't just see it, I *felt* it," Nightwind replied. She was, after all, an accomplished Empath, which was a significant part of why she was a successful *trondi'irn*. Even when she did not know a creature's anatomy intimately, she could at least understand what they felt, and that informed her healing abilities. "Tyrsell and the stronger Mindspeakers linked us all. Believe me, now they know *far more* about gryphons and their needs than they likely *ever* wanted to."

Darian joked, "I think Greywinter wants a gryphon costume now. Much of what you like appeals to his tastes. He is newly, ah, invigorated."

Nightwind chuckled, but she returned to solemnity soon enough and rubbed one of the gryphon's ears. "You went through so much, Kel. I have lost gryphons before. You were close to being my third. I have never worked on *anyone* like you. I am so sorry, you were pushed too far when you were interrogated—"

"When I was *what*? Who was responsible for that?"

"We all were," she lied. Kelvren could usually tell when a human was lying, and he had known Nightwind so long it was very obvious she was covering something up. "We needed to know what you knew, so the search went deep into your mind. Too deep. Too far *back* into you, and it made you—well, it hurt you. In your mind. There were some arguments about what to do, and what was done made your breathing and your heart stop, and—the important thing is, we brought you back."

It's not difficult to imagine whose horns that "mistake" lay upon. Tyrsell was never spoken of as being gentle, and the kingstag had all the subtlety of a horizon-wide thunderstorm over a wildfire. *It also explains the mental tone of that farewell. It was solemn and apologetic. What she's trying so hard to hide is probably that Tyrsell found me to be too much of a threat to the Vale and killed me, and the others beat away at reviving me.*

"Firesong and I fixed the trouble," Nightwind continued. "Together, and with help from k'Vala, we put things into a . . . kind of working order. It took a while."

"It is a wonder you are making any noise at all, since you're putting so much work into not *saying* anything," Kel grumbled.

Darian spread his hands. "It is just that we don't know what memory of the past few days you actually have, Kel. We're afraid that if we say the wrong thing, you might get angry."

Kelvren's building displeasure peaked. His eyes flashed then pinned at them both before he abruptly stood up and stalked out toward his home. "Angrier."

They deserve better than that from me, but right now, I just don't want to be near them, he thought. *I hate the idea of that damned dyheli laying every secret I've ever had out bare as a book page. We keep secrets for good reasons, but dyheli don't. They only know indifference, neutrality, invasiveness, and more invasiveness as their degrees of "secrecy." Now they all know who and what I actually am, not what I want them to know. It is infuriating!*

Crows and ravens chased two falcons through the distant branches, disturbing a roosting vulture who loped through the air for someplace more peaceful. Kelvren shouldered through the arch's thick wall of trimmed vines to find the *hertasi* Ayshen and his mate Drusi, the *dyheli* stag Sifyra, and the human *kestra'chern* Silverfox there.

Oh, here's a coincidence, the same dyheli stag Tyrsell was with. I'll lay odds he's Tyrsell's prize pupil. Probably here to paralyze me if he feels like it, or share my deepest thoughts if he feels bored. "Bring me a bowl of berries and I'll tell you Kelvren's deepest fears!" Won't that be fun? Just hilarious, you hoof-holes.

Sifyra twitched both ears forward and stared at Kelvren.

Silverfox did not exactly show age ungracefully, but although his hair matched Nightwind's in length, by now a full third of it was streaked in stripes of light gray. The two *hertasi* wore long, customized tool-vests and tailcuffs with long fringe to match the vests and each other. They stood in a semicircle on the far side of the pathway junction, and Ayshen was showing Silverfox some decorative chains when Kel stepped right into the middle of them. The four of them weren't blocking Kelvren's way, but it was clear they'd been waiting there to be an escort.

:*Greetings, Sky Warrior,*: Sifyra Mindspoke to the group. :*We are here to assist.*:

"Assist who, exactly? Me, or those who near-killed me after I was treated as an invader, and my mind was cut up like a feast of ribs?" Kelvren snapped.

Ayshen and Drusi both just went a bit wide-eyed. Ayshen dropped his chains, then swiftly picked them up and pocketed them.

Silverfox rocked back a little, then commented, "Ho. Ah. That punches the air out of our happy welcome-back." He raised his arms from his sides. "I think I understand why you're upset. Don't rage at us, Kel, we're your friends. You're no enemy of ours." He spread his hands wide and palms up, in a k'Leshyan display that translated to "I have no weapons, I bare no claws toward you." Silverfox then gestured down the path toward Kelvren's cliffside home, and the *ekeles* near there, far from the Heartstone. "We're here to walk with you. Firesong wants to see you."

Ayshen chimed in, "And that's where your meal awaits, with sweetbread and the honeywater mix you like." Drusi added, "Baked just for you. We have missed you so much. You're the talk of the halls."

Kelvren was placated by this, and let his hackles drop somewhat. He became aware that he was illuminating the four as much as any of the magelights dotted around the walkway. He raised his head and looked around over the others' heads and noticed something odd about the lights. The lights looked as if they pointed toward him. In fact, every magelight in sight was flaring toward him, as if they were candles, and a breeze blew their flames in Kelvren's direction. Something here was very strange.

Silverfox had apparently noticed the phenomenon, too, and ventured, "Kel, there are some situations that are different now, and you have some changes ahead. No small number of things have happened that relate to you, and we need to explain what they are."

Without acknowledging Silverfox at all, Kelvren suddenly snapped his gaze to Sifyra and loudly said, "You called me *Sky Warrior*, not *Wingleader*. Ever since I have been Wingleader of k'Valdemar, you have called me by my rank."

:*I call you as you are, with the respect due to you.*:

Silverfox ushered Kelvren along, although the gryphon was reluctant to break his stare at the *dyheli*. "That is part of what we need to explain to you. We just don't want to do it out *here*. Let's get to the receiving room at our *ekele*, shall we?" Ayshen and Drusi vanished in a burst of *hertasi* speed, presumably going on ahead. Nightwind and Darian followed the irate gryphon through the vine-fall, and Darian said, soothingly, "You're probably just famished, Kel. You know how you get when you're hungry."

Grrr. I am not a gryphlet!

The *dyheli* stayed several body lengths back, but always within sight.

Kelvren grumbled, "It isn't hunger that has me angry. It's the feeling that I am being handled because I'm as dangerous as a leaking oil bomb. I feel like I always have eyes upon me, and not in the way the *hertasi* are always watching. It feels like I have scouts ready to slay me with bowshot and Mages ready to vaporize me at any moment. It is like I can hear the whispers of their thoughts with Mindspeech, and the whispers are all about how to be rid of me."

To his shock, Silverfox replied with disarming frankness, "That is fairly accurate."

Darian started, "Some of the—" and was cut short by an explosion.

The walkway magelight nearest to Kelvren at that moment disintegrated with a loud crack, sending hot shards of glass all around, and a whip-crack of light the width of a human thumb lanced from the explosion into Kelvren's wing feathers. Everyone flinched, and when Kelvren recoiled from the explosion, the magelight on the other side of the path did the same thing when he leaped near it. The magelights, made to last for decades of steady light, hadn't faded—they'd detonated.

Quite literally, the glowing gryphon's eyes blazed.

"Maybe you should stay toward the center of the path," Darian suggested.

Everyone agreed, and they all edged away from Kelvren.

The *ekele* of Firesong and Silverfox had expanded constantly since their arrival from Haven. Broad walkways now led to new levels, where decks large enough to host a half-dozen gryphons or thirty humans served as the roofs of tall gathering rooms beneath.

Silverfox led Kelvren into the largest of these rooms, laid out as a much more comfortable version of an enclosed council circle. The center of focus was a huge pile of lounge cushions with a graduated, curving stone perch nearby. Serving shelves and various amenities were placed artistically in every direction, mostly formed of sinuously curved blonde wood. Two heavy tables were laden with slabs of beef and swine, one side cooked, the other raw. Heavy glass carafes of beer and honeywater were chilling off to the side, and a *hertasi*-sized bounty of baked goods completed the layout. The floor was hard-tiled in sandy colors, but when Kelvren stepped in, he could feel that he stepped not only onto hard stone but also through several layers of shields. He noticed one other thing immediately after seeing the meal laid out: Aside from the carafes, the room had been cleared of anything easily breakable.

Firesong leaned by the only other exit, his arms folded, and commented, "You do know how to light up a room, don't you?"

Silverfox almost soundlessly joined Firesong, and guided him by one elbow to the nest of cushions. Darian and Nightwind followed Kelvren through the shields and inside, and the *dyheli* stayed outside. Kel was fine with that, and centered his gaze on the food he'd been promised.

Firesong gingerly removed the day's mask, and with it the six long falls of braided hair and feathers that obscured his scarred ears. Kelvren knew Firesong's appearance startled most people, Tayledras or not, but after years, most people had come to think of the masks as Firesong's actual face. Only in private, with close friends like Kelvren or Silverfox, would he let himself be seen unmasked, because neither of them cared what he looked like—for very different reasons, of course. For Silverfox, it was love. For Kelvren, it was indifference. The gryphon didn't care about what a horror Firesong's face was—he only cared about someone's "need to be hurt." If someone was beautiful but tyrannical, they needed to be hurt. If someone was ugly but kind, they didn't need to be hurt. Firesong was ugly to the nearly exposed bone by human standards. Much of his face had been burned away by molten metal, but Kelvren only cared about his quality of character. Because of that, Firesong didn't "need to be hurt."

"I am here for two reasons, Firesong," Kelvren growled. "Food and courtesy."

"Food first," Firesong wisely replied. Kel needed no further invitation to dig into the meal—very literally. He immediately sat down on his haunches and grasped a great chunk of meat with his talons and hooked his beak in, pulling away deep bites.

Firesong leaned into his mate's touch. Once his overmask was set aside, the thin, perforated leather undermask that matched his skin color was peeled away by Silverfox's gentle fingers. After Silverfox laid both masks across the perch, he retrieved cold water for both of them. Darian and Nightwind each sunk back into heavily padded chairs.

"I want to talk to you about power," Firesong finally said.

"Still eating," Kelvren replied. Firesong sighed and waited. Darian cleaned out an ear with a finger. Nightwind took a boot off and emptied it of grit. Kel packed his gullet well, downing a carafe of beer to follow the first helpings of meats. The sounds were enough to make any prey animal flee.

"Are you ready to—" Firesong began.

"No," Kel replied.

Darian worked on the other ear now, and Nightwind rubbed at her foot. Firesong picked and scratched reflexively at some of the burn scars on his forehead and scalp, though they had been unchanged for years now. His expectedly dramatic presentation could not overcome the focus of a hungry and perturbed gryphon.

Silverfox lit some incense and waited Kelvren out. Finally sated, for the present, Kel lay down to face Firesong.

"I want to talk to you about power," Firesong began again.

"I want *you* to tell me what isss happening in k'Valdemar. What madnesss has overtaken everyone? And what did all of you *do* to me?" Kelvren growled, despite his packed throat and crop.

"It isn't madness. It's all completely logical," Firesong replied.

"Most madnesssses are *completely* logical, to thossse who are mad. I am *outsssside* this madnessss."

"You may judge the supposed amount of madness for yourself, but we'll explain things as they are," Silverfox replied, seating himself on some of Firesong's cushions.

Firesong took a deep breath, and started in.

"We need you to look at our history, Kel. Of White Gryphon, of the Far Flights, of k'Vala and k'Valdemar and the Storms. Think of what we have lived through and what we have seen. Remember how many strange things, and awful things, we have experienced. Think of what you have experienced. You were trapped by a cold-drake once, yes? And you know how *dyheli* can control minds and bodies and that some Adepts and Masters can do the same, yes?"

Kel nodded, thinking he knew where this was going. "Of late, I know that *very* well, and I don't like it. At all. *I don't like it*. But go on."

"There are creatures from *beyond*—that is the only way to describe it simply—and demons, and there are even shapechangers that are a part of our world. Now consider what has happened, from where we could understand it. You, k'Valdemar's Wingleader, vanished in a conflict inside Valdemar, in an area riddled with Change Circles. Your teleson went silent. We searched for you, using probes of magic above and below our world, and could not find you. We despaired, and took risks of our own, and could not find you. We nearly risked invoking Kal'enal for you."

This mollified Kelvren just a little. *Calling upon Kal'enal always means a heavy price, if the call is answered at all. Velgarthian deities only help those who are out of other options or chances, and the further from hopeless someone is, the more it costs them. That they even seriously considered it for me means a lot.*

"Suddenly, there was a faint, far-away detection of a Gate, and not long after, a flare, of a new node. And then, after a pause we narrowed down to Deedun, something fast aimed directly for us and closed in," Silverfox added, while Firesong had a drink.

Firesong resumed the explanation. "In Oversight, you looked like nothing less than a fireball headed our way, or a major demon. Then the—whatever it was—you, it turned out, making a show of it, which I understand—scouted over all of our allies. You actually left a wake behind you that disturbed the Lines at the time. You never knew this. Treyvan saved you by creating a node under you, and then, before he had any chance to calm you—or the node's energy—down, you left. You made your now-famous Flight and then aimed yourself for home. Only, to everyone at home, you looked like a possible attacker coming from the heart of Valdemar—again, a place full of Change Circles, and no stranger to demon infiltration." He paused to let that sink in.

Darian leaned back, and hooked his elbows over the chair's back. "While you were in flight, the Companions relayed a short form of what happened, though they knew very few details. It was only in the last candlemark before you landed that we recognized it was actually, possibly, you."

"Ssso you asssumed I was a *thrrreat*, not your Wingleader rrreturning," Kelvren added up.

Darian just gestured in a way that conveyed "obviously." "Worse than that, there was a reasonable possibility that you were another creature trying to *look* like our missing Wingleader. We *wanted* it to be you, Kel, but wanting something against facts leads to ruin. Remember k'Sheyna. And if it was some creature using you, or the appearance of you, it probably knew all of our secrets and relationships. We had to be sure it was really you."

That explains why the new "Wingleader," as she claimed, was so caustic to me. If I was an impostor, she wanted me to know they were aware of the possibility and that they'd kill me before I even crossed the red line. She even goaded me to try something.

Kelvren mulled that over for around twenty seconds before deciding he had room for more beer. "Then I want to know this," he demanded between gulps, "You knew who I was quickly. So. Why have I not been greeted as a hero, and why are so few people coming near me?"

Firesong frowned, and answered, "Two main reasons. They treat you like you're diseased because you came back changed in a way that threatens all of us, Kel. I had to fight for you to stay in the Vale at all, and you aren't allowed anywhere closer to the Heartstone than this. Here is the ugly truth, Kel." Firesong leaned forward, with as deadly serious an expression as Kelvren had ever seen on him. "Every time you move, you draw in more energy. Ambient, anchored, focused, it is all affected, and you draw it toward you. It strains your body intensely, so you have to discard it. You used Lightcasting before, but at the same time, you were flying, which only drew in more energy. If you discard the energy in your sleep, it could be in a wild form, in any amount, in any direction. Gryphons gather the energy needed to live by movement—you learned that as a gryphlet; that's what gryphon wingbeats are for, as much as maneuvering. If you move, you gain energy. If you fly, you gain even more energy, which in turn keeps you flying. But now, if you move at all, you gain *too much* energy. And, if you stop moving, you starve your new *need* for energy. And if you don't use that energy, you burn."

Kelvren looked very alarmed. *I know from my magecraft training how to ground and center, but that requires, well, ground. Is he saying I could fly and just erupt into flame because I couldn't ground? Or that I'd only fly if I were continually casting? This is awful . . .*

"And, if you move in areas with heavily structured spellwork, like k'Valdemar, you draw their energy toward you and disrupt the structure."

Skies above, it gets more awful.

"That explains why the magelights exploded," Nightwind offered.

Firesong glanced at the others. "Magelights exploded?"

Darian replied, "Ho, yes. From the stone core through the glass. Blazing hot, too. Their stored energy arced straight into him."

Firesong went deep into thought. "That bears out what we learned when we tried so much of, one could say, the usual things while Healing. You weren't there for all of that, Darian. It wasn't that the spells didn't work, it was that they lost cohesion." Firesong had done so much teaching over the past several years that he'd developed a habit of explaining things, even if it wasn't needed. It was a significant difference from his purposely enigmatic, brash flair of twenty years ago. "The manner wasn't just disruptive, it was disjunctive. Disruption would be like a loud noise drowning out a chant so it couldn't be heard. Disjunction would be breaking the chant into random, very loud noise."

Darian finished, "Which is what the Cataclysm was, eleven hundred some years ago. Two massive, radiating, cascading disjunctions. I remember my lessons, Firesong. So, again, you are proven right by insisting we keep Kel on isolated, evacuated paths. You can gloat about being right again."

"I've never stopped," Firesong absently replied, and pointed two fingers at Kelvren. "But it emphasizes that we can't allow you to fly, and we must keep you away from crafting circles and the like, because you could catastrophically harm even established spellwork just by being too near to it." Firesong sat back, cracking his spine and shoulders, adjusting to his new position. "Our Heartstone is robust, but we feed it by careful alignment of the Lines we draw to it. Imagine what would happen if you got near the Heartstone during its daily tuning. You would be like dropping a boulder into a clear, steady stream."

"*Sketi.*"

"Yes. *Sketi.*"

"I can't stay here!" Kelvren blurted, and jumped to his feet. "Why would you tell me this *here*, in the *Vale*? I should be far away from here!"

"You're safe enough for the moment, inside the protections in this room, Kel. So stay calm, and digest a while. No one is exploding just yet," Firesong reassured.

"Yet," he says. Yet! I would be afraid enough if it was only I who could burn up, but this means I threaten everyone by even existing!

Silverfox said, "We may have thought of some things that can be done."

Kelvren looked up and around, twitching his ears in agitation, and paced in figure-eights. "You may have ideas, but you aren't the only clever ones. I remember Nightwind said I was *held*—" he nearly spat the word, "—for over six days. What happened at Deedun?"

"Ah. That is another situation." Firesong looked to Silverfox, and it was clear that the next part would be bad news. They both look to Darian, who got up to stand squarely before Kelvren.

He spoke slowly and steadily, clearly trying to be as calming as he could be. "Kelvren, you—as we understand it all, and from what we learned in your mind—we know you did the right things. We know you were gryphon fierce, and brave, noble, and heroic."

"As it should be," Kel replied.

"But—Valdemar is not doing well at the moment. The border wars, the attacks in Haven and on the Traderoads, and the Storms, plus lesser-known troubles, have resulted in the Heralds, Guard, and no small amount of the Valdemaran population supporting them being far away from the center of the country. The Crown could only assist so much with the bad times deep inside their borders and could spare only so many Heralds. In short, the small keeps, holders, barons, trade leaders, and so on have fallen back upon their own troops and tightened their local control. They are infighting, in the absence of the system that stabilized Valdemar before. It isn't just Deedun that is troublemaking. The trouble is all over."

Kel blinked blankly at Darian.

"This means that ambitious, greedy, or scared people are using rumors as weapons, to gather influence, and so, over-whelmingly, your noble actions on Valdemar's behalf, has been interpreted by many as, ah . . . as the Crown bringing in monsters from the Pelagirs and using the might of the terri-fying Hawkbrothers against the small folk of Valdemar."

Kelvren screamed in rage, and by the way the others winced and fell back, it actually hurt them. "*That is untrue!* Untrue! *Wrong!* It is not how it is! I did what was right for an ally!"

Firesong yelled back, "We know! We know! But our truth is not what they see!"

Kelvren continued to rage. "Then they are liars, and they twist what happened! I defended the Crown and its troops! *I was a good ally!*"

Again, Firesong shouted. "*We know!* But that's bad too! Some of us argue that by acting as a full combatant and not a scout, you pulled us into Valdemar's internal struggles, and we can't afford that! K'Valdemar's current position is precar-ious enough as it is!"

Kelvren fumed, beak shut, but his sides heaved in fast, deep breaths. His nares whistled with each inhalation.

"Which ultimately means *what*, exactly?" he snapped at the four.

"Which means," Darian gasped as he rubbed at his temple, "diplomatically . . . it is a difficult dance, Kel, and we're doing the best we can with a new dance floor and new steps. What we came up with is, your actions have been claimed by Lord Breon and disavowed as an action of the Tayledras. He has claimed officially that you were under his orders to act on your own best judgment."

"But—I *wasn't*! I scouted for all of us, and we shared the information with Kelmskeep as a favor—"

"—but in the mess Valdemar is in, Breon's story is better," Darian countered.

"For who? For Breon, for Valdemar, for the Vale, for the Tayledras? No, I *hate* it! As Wingleader, I hate it! It makes us gryphons sound—uncontrollable! It makes me sound impulsive and undisciplined!"

Firesong and Silverfox instantly met eyes with each other and held their breaths. Both shook their heads and exhaled a moment later.

"Silver Gryphon Chief Redhawk put forth the suggestion that until you are reliable, physically and mentally, you should not be Wingleader. Your responsibilities are, as the final say put it, suspended," Darian explained. "And that allows us to honestly say that your rank was taken from you if Valdemaran leaders take issue against Breon."

Kelvren slit his eyes, and his crest and hackles went up.

"Kel," Nightwind pleaded, "we don't know whether your condition will make you insane, or simply fall out of the sky suddenly. We don't know if you'll unknowingly walk past a Working in progress and suddenly incinerate yourself and half of the Vale. A Silver Gryphon has to be relied upon to execute justice, and a Wingleader must be sound enough to take gryphons into danger without question. As an *absolute*. Right now, Kel, you are one big, glowing question. You are still beloved, and still respected, but you can't actually be trusted to be Wingleader because of what you underwent in that Change Circle. Hate it if you must, but you know it is reasonable."

"I *do* hate it! Diplomatsss, lordsss, and power-grabbersss turned my virtue, then my pain, into a reassson for my punisssshment?" Kelvren clawed at the tile, vaguely aware that he was drawing his talons side to side, sharpening them.

Darian drew his hands to his sides for fear that Kel would snap at them. "It was my solution. Valdemaran culture is different from ours, Kel, they—they prefer to have someone to blame. They don't just act upon a circumstance like we do. They prefer to fill a target with arrows first and then check if it was the cause of the problem. Breon's taking the arrows for you, so we have the time to fix your body if we can. We can fix your reputation later."

"I hate it," Kelvren growled, but he gave the situation its due thought. *I sacrificed myself to save a Valdemaran, and so Breon is making a sacrifice to save me. I can't disrespect that, but I don't have to like something to respect it. A gryphon's life is worth the story the gryphon leaves behind, and this is not where I wanted my story to go. I haven't even had gryphlets yet! Wait—how am I ever going to have any young? I could burst into flames on someone's back! I do not want to be remembered that way either!*

Darian said softly, "Rukayas is new to k'Valdemar, from k'Leshya by way of k'Vala, but she is the oldest gryphon here now, and Redhawk appointed her as the new Wing-leader."

"Rukayasss. Her name is Rrrukayasss. Hurrrh."

"And you're glowing brighter," Firesong added. "I'll draw you down. Just open up a bit, Kel, let me take some of that energy from you."

"Oh," Kelvren grumbled, "*now* you *ask* before taking something from me."

"Food and *courtesy*," Firesong chided, quoting the gryphon.

"I hate you *so much* right now," Kelvren growled back.

"Neither for the first nor last time will you hate me," Firesong said while the room dimmed in response to his gestures. "You could only survive this in two ways that we know of. Three, really, but you wouldn't like that one."

"Oh? What is that one?"

"Leave forever so you aren't a problem to us."

"Like Skandranon's last flight."

"So some stories say."

Kelvren shook his head. "I do not want to be like him *that* way. And his acts of heroism brought him nothing like these lies and intrigues and hate from others."

Silverfox's composure vanished. He covered his face with both hands, laughing. "Sorry, it's just—sorry. Please. Go ahead."

"What?" Kelvren demanded.

"Just that *kestra'chern* have stories from Amberdrake's side of history."

"To continue," Firesong picked up smoothly, "the other two ways I have considered work together. One, we can train you to be a Mage much, much better at handling magic power and more sensitive to feeling it around you. Two would be—" he hesitated.

Firesong opened his mouth to speak a couple of times, but it was half a minute before he finally continued. "Two would be to create a Heartstone for you. A very, very small one. Heavy, but not too heavy. Portable. This has been tried in the past and the concept is sound, but there were no—longlasting successes. I am curious; in your Flight, did it ever occur to you to tap a Line or a node to Lightcast? Or did you only use your own power?"

"I did as felt right. I used what I had inside me, what I collected as I flew."

"Ah. Interesting. That deserves some further thought. You've partly answered an old theory about whether a living thing can be a node, with that. And a node can feed a Heartstone."

"*Sketi!*" Kelvren exclaimed, sitting down abruptly.

"Yes. Very big *sketi* if we can make it work. It is your life, Kelvren. I mean that sincerely, it is your life—you live or die by this. Right now, nobody wants to come near you because they think you're as likely to explode as talk to them, and you're politically toxic. That can change over time, but meanwhile, we just have to keep you alive."

"I hate this. This is not right," Kelvren repeated.

"It isn't right, but it is the way it is," Firesong answered.

Darian rested his hands on Kelvren's right *alula*. "I know this is a terrible situation, Kel, and I know you want someone to slash and bite. I say, don't even bother to blame anyone, because you have more important things to work on. Your survival must be ensured. It is like k'Sheyna. It is true that their Adepts did not think of what happened as being an attack from Falconsbane, or anyone. They just dealt with the situation, and yes, that caused them much sorrow. But had they gone looking for enemies to blame at the time, instead of calming the disruptions, their situation would have been far worse. I say, don't fall prey to cursing others and complaining about what you deserve and don't deserve. These people in Valdemar are much different from everyone you knew far West, and you are going to have to adapt yourself to them, because they are more numerous than our kind."

Darian smoothed Kelvren's feathers along the leading edge of his wing, and it did soothe him. Firesong and the others exchanged a pointed look, and they began slipping away, Firesong leaving first. Kel didn't really care—he was well fed now, they weren't contributing anything to the conversation anyway, and, more importantly, they certainly weren't giving him cozy feather-scratches. Besides, he was still especially irritated with Firesong, so, begone with them.

"Hurrrrr," he grumbled, lying down again. "I do not like it, and it is not fair, but the world does not move by what I like, and it has never been fair. But listen to yourself, Dar'ian of Errold's Grove, referring to yourself as Tayledras, not Valdemaran!"

Darian sat down on the floor in front of him, cross-legged, and worked a hand into Kel's neck feathers, scratching soothingly. "I've had to learn all this myself. You were there for it. And technically, yes, I was born in Valdemar."

"Dar'ian, my parents taught me, wherever you land is your home. But I feel that k'Valdemar is *most truly* my home. It is what I think of as *your* home. Your parents raised to you to be a child, Errold's Grove raised you to be a boy, we raised you to be a man, and then you made yourself an adult. And alongside you, I went from someone to be cared *for* to someone who is cared *about*. I do not want to leave our home, Dar'ian. Or be chased away because of what happened. I was *good,* Dar'ian."

"Yes. Yes you were," Darian murmured into Kelvren's brow feathers. "You did the right things. You were there for me, you fought for me, and then you went out and did it again for people you didn't even know. You don't deserve all of this, but there's that world-isn't-fair thing, again, isn't it? But you know that I will always be thankful for you, and you'll always be with me somehow."

"For you I would be shot and slashed a hundred times," Kelvren rumbled, then added after a few moments, "But not all at once."

Darian chuckled and twisted around to rest his back against Kelvren's side, as they'd done dozens of times, basking in the sunlight. This time, though, the gryphon *was* the sun. "I don't know if it helps, but not everybody in Valdemar is afraid of us, or of you."

"They *should* be afraid of me. *Everything* should be afraid of me."

"We all are, we just hide it well. What I mean is, the Crown and most of Haven think of us as strong allies, and they think of gryphons as wonders. I know right now you must think of all Valdemarans as a bunch of idiots, but try to walk in their paths for a moment. For most people in Valdemar, until the Storms, they tended crops, built roads, milled grain, and were ordinary soldiers at most. The ongoing border wars were distant. Magic was just something in old legends, not something that was in their lives every day, affecting them personally. And then came the Storms. Instead of being something *good,* something that made roads that never needed repaving or built walls so strong that nothing could knock them down—something that helped and protected them—it was something horrible that brought strange beasts and diseases, ripped their ordered lives up, and scattered the pieces. And then, the news—mostly rumors—came that the Crown's sudden allies were the Ghosts of the Deadly Forests. It would be like you flying a patrol, being blasted into the ground by twenty whirlwinds, then being helped up by people who only spoke by clapping hands, wore giant hats, and ate poisonous tree bark."

Kel thought about that for a moment. "It would be hard to relate to," he agreed. "I would not think much about why those people were that way, I would only think of my own pain and well-being and that I was knocked out of the sky."

"Yes, and now *every* demonstration of magic is looked at as something to be feared until it can be *proved* it isn't going to hurt them. And there are a thousand minds like that, versus every one Valdemaran who understands," Darian sighed. "That is part of what I am doing as a Knight of Valdemar. It's a rank and title they all know and understand. I don't have to be highborn to hold it. In fact, at least half of the Knights are as much mongrels as I am. So ordinary people consider me one of them. But it *is* a title and a rank, and high enough that the highborn grudgingly allow that I belong with *them*, too."

"And so you cut your hair back, and wear your armor. You have to appear more Valdemaran to them," Kelvren replied as he twisted his head nearly upside down so his friend could reach deep inside the feather layers.

Darian sighed, "I even keep Kuari far away when I go into Valdemar now. And I ride a horse. Being a Knight is not the same as being a diplomat or envoy. I can deliver messages of peace, sure, but they're delivered in an armored fist. It's understood in Valdemaran culture that Heralds and Knights have our diplomacy backed up by pikemen and archers. So here I am Dar'ian k'Valdemar, and there I am Knight Darian Firkin."

"You are a gryphon now," Kel pointed out, feeling very proud he had thought of the analogy. "Not a bird and not a beast! Something better!"

Darian laughed ruefully. "Yes, I guess I am. But if I'm a gryphon, Kel, I am going to ask you to trust me with something more important to you than your life. I am going to ask you to trust me with your *reputation*."

"Mrrrph," Kel replied dubiously, and beak-nudged at Darian's shoulder and chest harder than was necessary.

"Kel, we have been friends for a very, very long time now," Darian pointed out earnestly, pushing back. "It's not going to be quick—and it probably won't be everything you want *or* deserve. But I'm going to stake *my* reputation as the Owl Knight alongside yours, because you are that important to me. You must leave your story to me for a while."

Kelvren huffed, "Becaussse if I went to them, I would just be a magical war beassst raging about injustice while brandissshing my claws, yes? So you must speak about me and for me. Hurrrh. As much as it amuses me to frighten others, maybe it is best that I don't display myself for a time. It is the way of a Wingleader. We train in formations and combined attacks to multiply our force and to defend each other should one of us become defenseless. We have to trust in our flight companions. There are some battles I cannot fight myself . . . so I suppose you will fight them for me."

Kelvren laid his head down flat on the floor, his beak-hook tucked between the edges of two tiles. He heaved a loud sigh, and the lighting shimmered around them.

Darian blinked rapidly, as if his eyes were stinging him, but he smiled. "And in the years to come, if I find myself in a battle in which claws and beaks are all that can save me, I shall depend upon you."

At that, Kel raised his head high. "My talons are at your service, now and evermore, Dar'ian Owlknight."

"Well, right now, I'd like you to trust us, and sleep," Darian told him. "Or your *trondi'irn* will probably skin me."

"I would not like you to be skinned, friend Dar'ian," Kel replied gravely. "You would be most uncomfortable without your skin. Perhaps she could settle for stripping your clothes off instead?"

Darian choked on a laugh and stood up. "I'll see you again, Kel," he replied, but then he sighed while dusting himself off. "I have to ride overnight and leave from Kelmskeep at dawn. Val and I are taking thirty of Breon's loyal soldiers to garrison Millbridge, and then we're off with an envoy and a strongbox to make sure the Weavers stay allied. I wish I could stay here, but I know you would want me to go. Our friendships must often fall second to our duties, but a true friend knows that duty is part of what makes someone their friend." He stopped at the doorway and added, "I'm going to make what you did in Valdemar—*for* Valdemar—mean even more."

They both said nothing for a minute, as if trying to memorize each others' appearance and expressions.

"You are my hero, Kel," Darian finally said.

"You are my hero, Dar'ian," Kelvren replied.

Then the Owl Knight turned away, and departed into the dusk.

Kelvren had stuffed himself at breakfast, and sleep and food had gone a long way toward soothing his temper. So he was also ready to listen as Firesong spoke or, more properly, lectured.

"An Adept is well-learned, but primarily an Adept is a durable, fast-thinking problem solver. This is one of the great truths of being a Tayledras Adept. It is not the high magic that makes an Adept, it is the clarity of mind to solve the problem of the moment. That moment could be all the time there is to act in, and the Adept must let in other concerns only when things are safe. Time taken to think about hate, love, blame, or justice could be an Adept's last thoughts. Adepts find dangers and traps all the time, but they are taken as the way of all life, and the world, not as something done *to* them."

"We discussed this already," Kel growled. "None of you want me to think about blame and the wrong I am being done."

Firesong instantly replied, "It is so important, we repeat it. You are an emotional soul, Kelvren Skothkar, and while passion has served you well in life, it can be your death now. We are going to try to teach you Adept ways so you can control the ruin inside you. Let that sink into your feathered skull a while."

Kelvren did. *I doubt they expect me to become an actual Adept, but he did talk about a small Heartstone. A Heartstone is like a rain-barrel that draws in and stores power to be drawn out as needed. But . . .*

"We should not do any of that here," he declared. "Not in the Vale. Not even *near* the Vale. I won't allow it. If my training strayed, I could tap the Heartstone of the Vale or affect the flow into it. We need to be far away if we're going to attempt this. And not in Valdemar, nor near the Clans. If I fail, I don't want anyone to see it . . . and I know that you can shield anybody nearby if I did."

Despite today's mask, Firesong looked both impressed and smug. "So you want to travel again, so soon?"

"I want to keep k'Valdemar and our allies safe. Here is not the place."

Firesong nodded. "An expedition it will be, then. Because you're right. I was going to lead up to it, but you suggested it yourself." He did a little bow, and Aya sparked in a shower of light-dust on the stone perch. "Smart gryphon. A Healing Adept's way involves not only fast thinking but also how to prevent harm in every direction and every level of repercussion while you're doing it."

Firesong interlaced his fingers and leaned forward. "Magic at Adept-level is something you can barely ever escape. It hums in your head, it constantly brushes at you like a breeze or a scent. Magic can have surges, and crackle, and go awry. It can have flavors, and it can drop away when you need it, only to reappear stronger an instant later. The larger swells appear in your mind like waves of life and lightning, as tall and wide as you can comprehend, but it may have a single flaw among its millions of threads that you must smooth away, or it will twist something leagues from you into something hideous and deadly. Some power drops from the Over, right through ours, and into the Under. Out there, in the Pelagirs, an Adept with their senses wide open could feel changes like that with every step."

Firesong stepped back then, having Kelvren's full attention. "So, when all that you can perceive has a potential for disaster, an Adept must live by *how do I turn what I encounter into an advantage*? That is why I think you can save your own life, because it is how you already think, Kelvren. Believe me, I know. I was in your head. What you did in Valdemar was Adept-style thinking."

Kel considered this and decided he was flattered. "Ssso. Let us look at this. How can my being a pariah become an advantage?"

"Ah. Because your admiration for Treyvan and Hydona

and Skandranon can make you like them, if what I have in
mind can be done," Firesong answered with a sly look.

"How?"

"Because not being needed as Wingleader here means you
can leave here as you choose. Being claimed by Breon's
statement means you do not have to be tried for justice in
Valdemar," Firesong answered. "In short, because of what
has happened you are uniquely—*free.*"

*If these words came from anyone else but Firesong, I'd
drop them in a lake. But—yes, he is right. Being Wingleader
meant I was bound here to lead others. Now I am not only
replaced, I am redundant. Dangerous, even, to have around.
And that is their loss, too. And I can't go deep into Valdemar
again because I'm the best known, brightest target, so . . .*

Firesong stood up, whirling in an obviously practiced the-
atrical turn so his robes billowed out before draping, and concentrated for twenty heartbeats. He gestured in two circles and
then a rectangle with his slender, tightly gloved hands and
called up an image in midair of a very well-known map. It
distorted at first, pulled at by Kelvren's affliction, but Firesong
used his palm to pull the map image back into proportion.

"The Storms were caused by disruptive waves of harm-
fully structured magic power peaking and trenching in ripples between the Over and Under realms. With the help of
several wise and lucky people, we determined that these were
the results of the 'antispell' blast from the detonation of Urtho's Tower and Ma'ar's Stronghold, traveling all the way
around our world and returning to their places of origin all
these years later."

Kel nodded. He had heard this before. "As you have explained, a cascading disjuncture."

"Yes." Firesong nodded. "As they got closer, the waves
became more concentrated and frequent. All indications were
that we could expect a new Cataclysm unless we did something about it." The map showed these waves in motion like
ripples from a stone, only flowing in toward the stone instead
of away. "During the Storms, we stopped one of the returning
Cataclysm loci from expanding back outward from the remains of Urtho's Tower by giving it a place to go, channeled

away from our world. But the question remains: What happened to the other locus, from the point of Ma'ar's ancient stronghold?"

Kelvren listened intently. This was a good question, and it sounded as if Firesong had been considering it for some time now. And if *Firesong* was concentrating on something for a good long while, it was probably worth thinking about. The fact that Firesong was talking about it now meant it somehow involved him.

"The waves should have concentrated, violently exploded outward, and while it would technically have caused less devastation than the original Cataclysm, it should still have leveled hills and forests and killed untold numbers. Exhausted as we were—we who were left alive, anyway—we braced for it." The glitter in Firesong's eyes reminded Kel that the Adept had very much put his own life at risk back then.

Firesong's map image increased in size until the shape of a well-known body of water with the sketches of a few very faint, craggy islands near its shores filled Kelvren's vision. "The waves, with all their power, poured in to the second location, as expected. And then they vanished. No mountain-powdering explosion, no disintegrating, rock-melting firestorms. Because of the haze caused by the Storms, no one has ever found out why. No one can Farsee or scry there, nor can any creature's vision penetrate the haze. Prayers and spirit realm queries go unanswered. The waters and weather are too treacherous for a ship exploration."

What is Firesong getting at? Kelvren wondered. *If no one can See there, and no one can go there, how is anyone supposed to find out what was there that had absorbed all that power? And what does all that have to do with me, for that matter?*

"If you can learn what I can teach you, if we can create this new Heartstone, if you can control your ruin, and if a few dozen other factors fall into place as I have in mind," Firesong teased, "I ask you this, Kelvren the Bright." He let the map image stay in place and faced the gryphon.

"Would you dare to explore what is at the center of Lake Evendim?"

About the Authors

Nancy Asire is the author of four novels: *Twilight's Kingdoms*, *Tears of Time*, *To Fall Like Stars* and *Wizard Spawn*. *Wizard Spawn* was edited by C. J. Cherryh and became part of the Sword of Knowledge series. She also has written short stories for the series anthologies *Heroes in Hell*, edited by Janet Morris, and *Merovingen Nights*, edited by C. J. Cherryh. Other short stories of hers have appeared in Mercedes Lackey's anthology *Flights of Fantasy*, as well as in the Valdemar anthologies. She has lived in Africa and traveled the world but now resides in Missouri with her cats and two vintage Corvairs.

Dylan Birtolo resides in the Pacific Northwest, where he spends his time as a writer, a gamer, and a professional sword-swinger. His thoughts are filled with shapeshifters, mythological demons, and epic battles. He's published a few fantasy novels and several short stories. He trains in Systema and with the Seattle Knights, an acting troop that focuses on stage combat. He jousts, and, yes, the armor is real—it weighs over 100 pounds. You can read more about him and his works at www.dylanbirtolo.com or follow him on Twitter at @DylanBirtolo.

Jennifer Brozek is a Hugo Award-nominated editor and a Bram Stoker-nominated author. Winner of the Scribe, Origins, and ENnie awards, she has been writing role-playing games and professionally publishing fiction since 2004. With the number of edited anthologies, fiction sales, RPG books, and nonfiction books under her belt, Jennifer is often considered a Renaissance woman, but she prefers to be known as a wordslinger and optimist. Read more about her at www.jen-niferbrozek.com or follow her on Twitter at @JenniferBrozek.

Brigid Collins is a fantasy and science fiction writer living in Michigan. Her short stories have appeared in *Fiction River*, *The Young Explorer's Adventure Guide*, and *The MCB Quarterly*. Books 1 through 3 of her fantasy series, *Songbird River Chronicles*, are available in print and electronic versions on Amazon and Kobo. You can sign up for her newsletter at tinyletter.com/HarmonicStories or follow her on Twitter @purellian.

Ron Collins is an Amazon best-selling dark fantasy author who writes across the spectrum of speculative fiction. He has contributed a hundred or so short stories to professional publications such as *Analog Science Fiction & Fact*, *Asimov's Science Fiction*, and several other magazines and anthologies. His fantasy series *Saga of the God-Touched Mage* reached #1 on Amazon's Dark Fantasy list in the UK (#2 in the US). His short fiction has received a Writers of the Future prize and a CompuServe HOMer Award, and his short story "The White Game" was nominated for the Short Mystery Fiction Society's 2016 Derringer Award.

Brenda Cooper writes science fiction and fantasy novels and short stories. Her most recent novel is *Spear of Light*, and her most recent story collection is *Cracking the Sky*. Brenda has been nominated for the Phillip K. Dick and Canopus awards and won an Endeavor Award. Her nonfiction has appeared at *Slate* and *Crosscut*, and her short fiction has appeared in *Nature* Magazine, among other venues. She lives in the Pacific Northwest where she gardens, bikes, writes fiction, nonfiction, and poetry, and she loves sunrises.

Dayle A. Dermatis has been called "one of the best writers working today" by *USA Today* bestselling author Dean Wesley Smith. Under various pseudonyms (and sometimes with coauthors), she's sold several novels and more than a hundred short stories in multiple genres. She is also a founding member of the Uncollected Anthology project. A recent transplant to the wild greenscapes of the Pacific Northwest, in her spare time she follows Styx around the country and travels the world, all of which inspires her writing. She loves music, cats, Wales, old houses, magic, laughter, and defying expectations. For more information and to sign up for her newsletter (and get free fiction!), go to dayledermatis.com.

Larry Dixon is the husband of Mercedes Lackey, and a successful artist as well as science fiction writer. He and Mercedes live in Oklahoma.

Rosemary Edghill can truthfully state that she once killed vampires for a living. She has worked as an editor, a book designer, an illustrator, and a professional book reviewer. She is also an established ghostwriter. Her hobbies include dogs, bad television shows, and the Oxford comma. Her next project under her own name is an urban fantasy for Baen Books.

Rebecca Fox always wanted to be John Carter of Mars when she grew up, because of the giant birds. Since it didn't look as though that career path was going to pan out anytime soon, she got her Ph.D. in Animal Behavior instead. She makes her home in Lexington, Kentucky, where she shares her life with three parrots, a Jack Russell terrier named Izzy, and the world's most opinionated chestnut mare. When she isn't writing, Rebecca teaches college biology and spends a lot of time outdoors doing research on bird behavior.

Michele Lang writes fantasy, science fiction, crime, and romance, as well as nonfiction. Her *Lady Lazarus* WWII historical fantasy series was published by Tor Books, and a new urban fantasy series is releasing soon. Michele is a recovering lawyer who has practiced the unholy craft of litigation in both New York and Connecticut. She lives in a small town outside of New York City with her husband, her sons, and a rotating menagerie of cats, hermit crabs, and butterflies.

Fiona Patton lives in rural Ontario where she can practice bagpipes without bothering the neighbors. Her partner, Tanya

Huff, and their two dogs and many cats have taken some time to get used to them but no longer run when she gets the pipes out. She has written seven fantasy novels for DAW books as well as over forty short stories. "Haver Hearthstone" is her ninth Valdemar story, the seventh involving the Dann family.

Angela Penrose lives in Seattle with her husband, five computers, and some unknown number of books, which occupy most of the house. She writes in several genres, but SF/F is her first love. She majored in history at college but racked up hundreds of units taking whatever classes sounded interesting. This delayed graduation to a ridiculous degree but (along with obsessive reading) gave her a broad store of weirdly diverse information that comes in wonderfully handy to a writer.

Stephanie Shaver lives in Southern California with her family, a couple of cranky cats, and a garden in various states of disarray depending on what's due next. When she isn't working, cooking, camping, or writing, she's probably assisting a toddler snail hunt. She can be found online at www.sdshaver.com.

Jessica Schlenker is a professional geek and biologist with a master's degree in IT security and a background in trumpet. **Michael Z. Williamson** is an immigrant, veteran, bladesmith, and SF and fantasy author best known for the "Freehold" universe. He plays several instruments, but prefers not to inflict them on people. Instead, he shares his writing.

Kristin Schwengel lives near Milwaukee, Wisconsin, with her husband, the obligatory writer's cat (named Gandalf, of course), a Darwinian garden in which only the strong survive, and a growing collection of knitting and spinning supplies. Her writing has appeared in several previous Valdemar anthologies, and she has wanted to write a story involving gryphons for a while. This is the first piece she has ever written in which the writing actually started with the very first line.

D. Shull is pleased to have the time again to write after completing both a BA and an MA in Communication, and is still looking for a cool job that makes use of both those degrees—after having been a proofreader, editor, and a teacher of public speaking. Though they enjoy reading for fun, they can't shake the habit of reading academic work either. They were born, raised, and still live in California, with very good reasons for staying there, thank you very much.

Born on an Indian reservation in northern California, **Louisa Swann** spent too much time in a papoose carrier. Determined not to remain a basket case forever, she escaped the splintered confines, finally settling down on a ranch where she spins tales to humor herself. Her writerly eccentricities have resulted in numerous short story publications in various anthologies, including Mercedes Lackey's *Elementary Magic* and *Valdemar* anthologies (which she's thrilled to participate in!); Esther Friesner's *Chicks and Balances* (Chicks in Chainmail); the Fiction River anthologies, including *Alchemy & Steam*, *Valor*, and the upcoming *Visions of the Apocalypse*. Find out more at www.louisaswann.com.

Growing up on fairy tales and computer games, *USA Today*-bestselling author of urban fantasy **Anthea Sharp** melded the two in her award-winning Feyland series. She now makes her home in the Pacific Northwest, where she writes, hangs out in virtual worlds, plays the fiddle with her Celtic band Fiddlehead, and spends time with her small-but-good family. Anthea also writes award-winning Victorian historical romances as Anthea Lawson Visit her website at antheasharp. com and join her mailing list, tinyletter.com/AntheaSharp, for a free story, reader perks, and news of upcoming releases!

Elizabeth A. Vaughan is a *USA Today*-bestselling author who writes fantasy romance. Her first novel, *Warprize*, was rereleased in April 2011. You can learn more about her books at www.writeandrepeat.com.

Elisabeth Waters sold her first short story in 1980 to Marion Zimmer Bradley for *The Keeper's Price*, the first of the Darkover anthologies. She then went on to sell stories to a variety of anthologies. Her first novel, a fantasy called *Changing Fate*, was awarded the 1989 Gryphon Award. Its sequel, *Mending Fate*, was published in 2016. She also writes short stories and edits anthologies. She would like to thank the Sisters of St. Mary and their award-winning cashmere goats (St. Mary's on-the-Hill Cashmere) for their help with this story. She also worked as a supernumerary with the San Francisco Opera, where she appeared in *La Gioconda*, *Manon Lescaut*, *Madama Butterfly*, *Khovanschina*, *Das Rheingold*, *Werther*, and *Idomeneo*.

Phaedra Weldon grew up in the thick, atmospheric land of South Georgia. Most nights, especially those in October, were spent on the back of pickup trucks in the center of corn-fields, telling ghost stories, or in friends' homes playing RPG. She got her start writing in Shared Worlds (*Eureka!*, *Star Trek*, *Battletech*, *Shadowrun*), selling original stories to DAW anthologies, and sold her first urban fantasy series to traditional publishing. Currently she writes three series (The Eldritch Files, the Grimoire Chronicles, and the Zoe Martinique novels) as well as busting out the occasional *Shadowrun* novel (her most recent one is *Identity Crisis*) as well.

Through her combined career as a professional author and her background as a cover artist, **Janny Wurts** has immersed herself in a lifelong ambition: to explore imaginative realms beyond the world we know. She has written eighteen novels, a collection of short stories, and thirty contributions to fantasy and science fiction anthologies. Novels and stories have been translated into fifteen languages worldwide. Best known for the *War of Light and Shadow* series, her other titles include stand-alones *To Ride Hell's Chasm*, *Master of Whitestorm*, and *Sorcerer's Legacy*; the *Cycle of Fire* trilogy; and the *Empire* trilogy, written in collaboration with Raymond E. Feist. Her paintings and cover art have appeared in exhibitions of imaginative artwork, including, NASA's 25th Anniversary exhibit, Delaware Art Museum, Canton Art Museum, Hayden Planetarium in New York, and have been recognized by two Chesley Awards and three Best of Show awards at the World Fantasy Convention.

About the Editor

Mercedes Lackey is a full-time writer and has published numerous novels and works of short fiction, including the bestselling *Heralds of Valdemar* series. She is also a professional lyricist and a licensed wild bird rehabilitator. She lives in Oklahoma with her husband and collaborator, artist Larry Dixon, and their flock of parrots.